Hatchett and Lycett

Hatchett and Lycett

NIGEL WILLIAMS

VIKING
an imprint of
PENGUIN BOOKS

VIKING

Published by the Penguin Group
Penguin Books Ltd, 80 Strand, London WC2R ORL, England
Penguin Putnam Inc., 375 Hudson Street, New York, New York 10014, USA
Penguin Books Australia Ltd, 250 Camberwell Road, Camberwell, Victoria 3124, Australia
Penguin Books Canada Ltd, 10 Alcorn Avenue, Toronto, Ontario, Canada M4V 3B2
Penguin Books India (P) Ltd, 11 Community Centre,
Panchsheel Park, New Delhi – 110 017, India
Penguin Books (NZ) Ltd, Cnr Rosedale and Airborne Roads,
Albany, Auckland, New Zealand
Penguin Books (South Africa) (Pty) Ltd, 24 Sturdee Avenue,
Rosebank 2196, South Africa

Penguin Books Ltd, Registered Offices: 80 Strand, London WC2R ORL, England

www.penguin.com

First published 2002
1

Copyright © Nigel Williams, 2002

The moral right of the author has been asserted

Set in 12/14.75pt Monotype Dante
Typeset by Rowland Phototypesetting Ltd, Bury St Edmunds, Suffolk
Printed in Great Britain by Clays Ltd, St Ives plc

A CIP catalogue record for this book is available from the British Library

ISBN 0-670-91255-7

Once again

for Suzan

Attaquons dans ses eaux
La Perfide Albion!

Augustin, Marquis de Ximenez,
*Poésies révolutionnaires et
contre-révolutionnaires*
(Paris, 1821)

PART ONE

Prologue

20 August 1921

"Come on!"

Alec could run faster than him. And here, in the woods behind Albion House, it was important to run fast. Even on a day like today there was something frightening about the way the trees whispered to each other. People in Crotchett Green said it was haunted. "If people have died unhappily or violently," Lucius had said, with his usual confidence, "their ghosts never leave the place where their bodies have been laid until they have been revenged. And someone was murdered in those woods."

Lucius was only eight but he knew an awful lot of things, thought Hatchett, as he wheezed along behind his friend. Alec was running, as he always did, easily and lightly; he looked as if he could keep this up for days and days and days, if he had to, like one of those Indian scouts in the book they had read at school last week. The distance between the two of them was getting greater. At any moment Hatchett was going to be in the middle of the dangerous place and Alec would be miles out of sight; the ghosts would come and get him and drag him, screaming, to the ground.

He had had nightmares ever since his father disappeared. He had been the cleverest boy in the class until his father disappeared. Now he had to work and work and work to make the smallest kind of progress.

Some people said that Hatchett Senior had run off with another woman, for he was reckoned to be the most handsome vicar of St Mary and All Angels in living memory. Others had whispered that he had gone mad and, one afternoon, while tutoring a boy from Kirkby in extra Latin, the Reverend Arthur Hatchett had removed his trousers and underpants and run out into the rain,

3

cackling to himself. A few months after he had disappeared, when people had given up looking, Hatchett could have sworn he saw him walking down the high street. He was on the point of running up to him so that his father would pick him up and swing him round in a circle – one of their favourite games – when he realized he would have been leaping into the arms of Mr Caulby, the ironmonger from Hanover Street. Grown-ups looked so similar.

His glasses seemed to be falling off the end of his nose, as usual. His socks were coming down as well. Soon, he knew, his trousers would start to come loose. Ahead of him Alec had cleared the trees and was standing out in the sunlight looking towards Albion House.

"Come on, Hatchett! Slowcoach! Come on!"

It was as well Lucius wasn't here or he would be doing his best to make sure Hatchett never got through the dangerous patch of ground. He would be laughing at him, sneering at him, trying to trip him up. As he skirted a pile of brambles, Hatchett lowered his head and started to count to himself. Not long before I'm in the sunshine. Ten – nine – eight – seven – six – "Come on!" – five – four – three – two – one . . .

To his surprise and relief, Hatchett found he was already there. He was standing in the open field. Alec was grinning at him. "There," he said, "that wasn't so bad, was it?"

"It was terrible," said Hatchett, "it was really frightening."

The two of them started across the field towards Alec's back garden, which was a world in itself. Albion House was a magical place, a warren of playrooms and dining rooms and nurseries and oil paintings in old frames like they had in the art gallery in Croydon. Hatchett and his mother lived in three rooms in a shabby street just behind the gallery. "Ever since your father went off," he could hear her saying, in that grim Lancashire accent of hers, "every penny counts, Dennis. Every penny counts."

In Alec's house money didn't matter. There was roast beef on Sundays and, once, he had been allowed a sip of cider – something his mother would never have permitted. There was a hammock in the trees over by the tennis courts and there was croquet and huge flower-beds crammed with plants that had magical names –

snapdragon, heartsease, lily-of-the-valley. Hatchett, who was already a lover of words, rolled these round his tongue the way Mr Lycett tasted the red wine at Sunday lunch, an open smile on his big, handsome face.

Alec looked worried about something.

"What's the matter?" said Hatchett.

"Nothing," said Lycett. Then . . .

"Lucius is going to have to go away!" he said.

Hatchett stopped, an almost unbearable pleasure stealing over him – the kind of pleasure you got when they cancelled double maths or said you didn't have to do games. "But that's amazing!" he said. "That's fantastic! That's wonderful, isn't it?"

Alec didn't answer this. But he didn't seem as pleased as Hatchett would have thought he would be. They were almost at the back gate that led from the open field into their garden. He looked up at the back of Albion House, its brickwork warm in the summer sun. "You think our family is all nice and wonderful," he said. "Well, it isn't."

"It's better than mine," said Hatchett, who could not think of anything more glamorous or wonderful than belonging to Lycett's family.

"They're going to send him," said Alec thoughtfully, "to a special school."

Lucius, thought Hatchett, was the kind of person who needed a special school. Preferably one with bars on the windows, a diet of bread and water and ten lashes with the cat o' nine tails if you were late with your homework.

"A strict school," went on Alec, "a very, very strict school. A bit like a prison."

This was better and better. "Is it," said Hatchett, pushing his glasses back up his slippery nose, "a long way away?"

"It is," said Alec solemnly, "a very, very long way away. Apparently it is in Devon."

"Gosh!" said Hatchett, "Is it on a minor road?"

"A really minor road," said Alec, "and so far away he won't be able to come home in the holidays apparently. Apparently it is over a hundred miles to where he is going!"

Devon was a long way away. There was, Hatchett liked to think, a wall round it. You had to knock at the gates before they let you in or they poured boiling oil over you. It was just the place for Lucius.

They walked slowly up the lawn towards the french windows, at the right of the house. The sun sparkled on all the glass. On the lawn a single magpie hopped sideways and studied them cautiously.

"I think," said Alec eventually, "we all might be going away in time. I mean, we might be moving, selling the house."

Hatchett pushed his glasses back up his nose. This was devastating news. "Why?" he said. "Will you be moving away from Crotchett Green?"

"I don't know," said Alec. "Mummy and Daddy argue all the time. And I heard him say the other night that if they could get away from this cursed place, they might be all right."

"Is there a real curse on this place?" said Hatchett, in wondering tones. It seemed impossible to believe.

"Daddy said it was cursed!" said Alec darkly. "I heard him!"

He looked very serious. He had a pale, slightly freckled face and high cheekbones. He always looked serious, but today he was looking extra serious. "Lucius put a curse on it, Daddy said. He did something and put a curse on it! That's why he's being sent away."

"What did he do?" said Hatchett, quickly, casually, as if he didn't much care about the answer.

"He killed someone!" said Alec, in a low whisper. "But it's a secret and you're not to tell anyone."

"I won't tell anyone," said Hatchett. "It's a complete secret. How awful, though! How absolutely awful! He killed someone."

Alec was nodding seriously.

"Who was it?" said Hatchett. "Was it anyone we know?" Alec's mouth had closed in a prim line. But Hatchett couldn't help asking more. "Was it a teacher?" he said. "Was it old Loosebottom?"

Alec started to giggle helplessly. He often laughed at things Hatchett said but it was understood between them that calling Mr Lewis Loosebottom was one of his happiest inspirations. The word "Loosebottom" would start them off wherever they were and whatever they were doing. Hatchett, as usual, felt the urge to go on. When you said things that made people laugh they were like puppets and you were pulling the strings. Only – this was what made it particularly nice – you were a puppet too, jerking and twitching just like them, not really knowing why you were doing it or how long it was going to last. Alec was making this up. Lucius couldn't really have killed someone. He was, everyone said, very advanced for his age. But he was only eight.

Alec was laughing hard. He was really quite red in the face.

"He hit him on the bottom with a hammer, which is why it's a loose bottom, and his head fell off!" said Hatchett.

But Alec had stopped laughing. "You're the only person I will ever tell," he said. "I'm telling you because you are my best friend and you have a right to know. But it is a terrible secret and you must never tell anyone or I will never, ever speak to you again. It is true. He killed someone."

Hatchett, who still wanted to believe that this was one of Alec's rare flights of fancy, nodded with the seriousness that Alec's voice seemed to require. "God will find him," Alec continued, "and he will be punished."

This was comforting. It was time Lucius received some punishment. Only last week he had twisted Hatchett's ear until he screamed aloud in pain. In many ways, thought Hatchett, stringing him up on a gallows – which was what they did to murderers – was a pretty good idea. For now, as well as bullying and teasing and publicly shaming Hatchett, he had forced his whole family out of this beautiful place. Hatchett was filled with intolerable gloom at the thought that he might never be able to come to Albion House again. He had come to think of it as his. And Alec's father seemed so pleased with him always, and asked him questions and laughed when he said something funny, which he usually tried to do. Although, to his surprise, people seemed most amused by him when he was trying to say something serious. Lucius, once again, had managed to spoil things.

"If I get a scholarship," said Hatchett, as they got closer to the house, "I shall go to Kirkby."

"When I'm grown up," said Alec, "I'll come there as a teacher and be in the cricket team and I'll pick you."

"I won't be there," said Hatchett. "I'll be too old to be at school then."

"Maybe you'll come back," said Alec. "Maybe you'll be a teacher there too."

"Maybe I will!" said Hatchett, cheered by this thought. He didn't like things to change. And he very much did not want to lose his friend.

They were about fifty yards from the french windows. Alec suddenly grabbed his arm and pulled him into the bushes. "He's over there!" he hissed. "Lucius is over there! With Daddy!" And indeed, on the terrace under the ivy-covered wall, were Lucius and Alec's daddy. They both looked very serious indeed. Lucius stood, ramrod straight, like David facing Goliath in Hatchett's *Children's Bible*. Everything about him – from the set of his neck and shoulders to his uplifted chin, blazing defiance at the giant in front of him – suggested the sin of pride. Lucius, like Lucifer, was conceited and now he was to be thrown out of this beautiful garden.

He was a bully and he deserved it. He probably did kill someone too, thought Hatchett, as he watched Alec's brother from the safety of the shrubbery. He jolly well looked like a murderer.

Alec's daddy was saying very angry things to Lucius now. As Hatchett watched, Alec's mummy, who was always so beautiful, and wore jewellery, even in the mornings, came out from the house with one of the maids. The maid (it was Bella) was dragging what looked like a large suitcase. So it really really really really was true! Lucius was going away!

Alec's daddy was saying what looked like more angry things to Lucius. But Lucius, instead of looking at the ground, which was what you were supposed to do, was answering back. Grown-ups did not like you to answer back. You nearly always lost your temper when you answered back. In fact, sometimes you could lose your temper just thinking about the things you would say if you ever got the chance to answer back – without grown-ups interrupting you because you had lost your temper.

Lucius was still answering back. Alec's daddy put his hands on Lucius's shoulders. Lucius started to scream and stamp his feet. Both parents picked him up, then, and carried him inside. They quite often did that with Lucius. Alec had told Hatchett that when people came round he was locked in his room, as if they didn't want anyone in the village to know he existed.

Then, round the corner of the house, came old Loosebottom and his daughter. They must have been expecting him. That was why they had taken Lucius inside. Loosebottom looked serious. His wife had some disease. As usual, his daughter (what was her name?) did not look like a girl. Although she was wearing a dress, and a stupid frilly one at that, she scuffed her feet at the ground like a boy. She did not, like other girls, look up, carefully or eagerly, into grown-ups' faces. She looked, thought Hatchett, who had seen her, though not talked to her, in both street and playground, like the sort of girl who would tuck her dress into her knickers and do handstands. Fun.

What was old Loosebottom doing here?

It wouldn't be about Lucius because nobody really knew about Lucius. Lucius had been sent to a school for children where you paid because he was too naughty for their school. Unless someone had told about him. Perhaps word had got out about Lucius and his habit of killing people. He had almost certainly, thought Hatchett, with a small thrill, killed more than one. All three adults were now talking, seriously. The girl started to look at the ground – the safest place to look.

Alec was dragging him further back into the bushes. "Loose-bottom," he whispered, "has come round to talk about me. And my Latin. He says it isn't up to scratch. That's his daughter, isn't it? Do you know her? What's her name?"

"I've never really seen her before," said Hatchett, "but she looks all right, doesn't she?"

Loosebottom's daughter was gazing over in their direction. She looked, Hatchett thought, like the kind of girl who liked to play with boys. She looked nice. It can't have been much fun to be Loosebottom's daughter. They probably conjugated verbs over tea;

you probably still had to call him "sir" even though you were his own daughter.

Hatchett and Alec crept further and further into the rhododendron bushes. Some of the branches scratched, and once or twice a fly – or was it a wasp? – buzzed horribly close to Hatchett's face; but it was cool and private at last and you felt no one could get you. They still whispered, though – just in case.

"He really did kill someone, didn't he?" said Hatchett.

"Of course he did," said Alec. "Did you think I was making it up?"

"Of course I didn't!" said Hatchett hurriedly. There was an awkward silence. Then Hatchett added, "Who did he kill?"

His friend paused. Two spots of crimson appeared in his cheeks, as if he was wrestling with something inside himself. His mouth wrinkled like a prune and he glanced back, briefly, in the direction of the wood from which they had just come. "It was only an old tramp," he said, "an old tramp with straw in his hair and smelly socks with holes in them. An old tramp who was asleep in the woods and who no one would miss, you see. Lucius poured petrol on him and set light to it." He paused fractionally, and added, in the kind of voice he used when leading the prayers at Sunday school, "Tramps are still people. You can't just set light to tramps whenever you feel like it. You start with tramps and . . . you end up with . . . people like us!"

Hatchett looked back at him in the gloom of the shrubbery. "You must never tell anyone this," Alec went on, "and it must always be a secret between us. I've never told anyone else this and I never will."

"I promise!" said Hatchett. Then he peered through the bushes towards the big, welcoming house where, in the kitchen, away from the heat of the sun, there was lemonade. The girl appeared to have gone, along with her father. That was as well, really. Girls were nothing but trouble when you wanted to play with your friends. Norma. That was her name, thought Hatchett, pleased that he had remembered it. Norma. Norma Lewis – the Daughter of Loosebottom.

I

3 August 1939

"Come along!" called Norma. "Come along! In a line! Come along!" Eighteen, nineteen, twenty, twenty-one . . . no, she'd already counted Mabel Hughes. She should never have taken so many girls. Adding them up was getting harder and harder. They were a slippery bunch, even in Croydon, but since they had been in France, keeping track of them was like itemizing sand. Why was this?

"Le train," she went on, sounding even more English with each new vowel, *"va parteer! Eel faut vérifier les nombres!"*

But they had already started to trickle into the boat train. Perhaps she had given those last three words a bit too much *éclat* or brouhaha, or whatever the French word for "oomph" was. Nothing to be done. She had counted them just before they stopped for coffee. Unless the Misfits – out of sheer spite – had just tiptoed away into the *sixième* or the *quinzième* or wherever they were, they were pretty well certain to be all here.

None of them, thought Norma, as she gripped the handle of the door to their coach, liked France enough to stay in it any longer than was absolutely necessary. They didn't like the smell. They didn't like the food. They had been violently affronted by the lavatories and they were still, after two weeks, completely baffled by the language, the currency and the traffic. Every time they passed anyone who looked vaguely English, romantic, dreamy Jacqueline Rissett would look as if she was about to ask them for asylum.

Norma herself was now considerably less keen on France than on Croydon. She had thought, before she got there, it might be rather romantic. She had always enjoyed talking French, although now, she realized, she only really liked using the language in front of English people who didn't speak it. She and the dom-sci mistress, Jennifer Doran, had had some fun with Maurice Chevalier (not the performer but a French *assistant* who had come over to Saltdene School two years ago). He had driven a red Alvis at great speed along the country lanes near Crotchett Green, a few miles south of South Croydon. He had had a rather romantic moustache.

But any expectations she might have held about Frenchmen had been lowered by seeing them in their natural habitat. Frenchmen were different in France. You couldn't blame them for striding around as if they owned the place – since they obviously did. But you could take exception to the way they looked at your legs and your behind and that part of the anatomy that, in lessons with the girls, she always referred to as "la poitrine".

"*Non*, Jacqueline!" she heard herself say, as a bespectacled Jacqueline Rissett peered out of the door in front of her, "*dedans le train*, if you please!" She couldn't see a conductor anywhere and, as so often when boarding a train, she found herself unable to believe that it was the one she was supposed to catch. The swarthy little man on the *quai*, whom she had asked earlier, had said, "*Oui! Oui! Train de bateau!* Calais! Douvres!" but Norma still felt she needed a second opinion. Preferably an English one.

There was one immediately to hand. Waddling towards her down the drab platform came a figure she thought she might be able to trust. A woman in tweeds, of about fifty or sixty, with a small suitcase and, under her left arm, a copy of *The Times*. For a moment, Norma felt like running down the Gare du Nord and flinging her arms round the stranger.

The woman seemed quite pleased to see Norma. Perhaps she, too, had had enough of the French.

"Is this the boat train? For England?"

The woman stopped and put her suitcase down on the platform. "Oh," she said, "I thought it was. But now you ask me I am not so sure." The two of them stood in the sombre light of the Gare du Nord – above them black iron and dirty glass, and in the air the acrid smell of engines. "Perhaps," said the woman in tweeds, "we should ask someone. Do you speak French?"

"I teach it," said Norma, "but I'm not sure that I speak it."

The woman in tweeds laughed in a way that Norma found comforting. It was curious. Now she was talking to someone, in English, about whether this was, or was not, the boat train for England, she felt increasingly confident that it was. And even if it wasn't, she said to herself, at least there would be plump, friendly women like this on board. "I'm sure it is!" she said, with new-found strength.

There seemed to be more and more English people to hand. Outside, in the impersonal, cobbled streets around the station, they were swallowed by the city. They started to shrug, to look shifty, to become, well, French.

But now – that chap in the black hat and the patent leather shoes, that lanky boy in the blue blazer, they were as English as her pupils, and she could read their faces as clearly. Why did they all look so anxious? Was it simply that they were not surrounded by familiar things? Or was there some fundamental fear at the heart of every English person that only another English person could spot? And if there was, what was it?

It wasn't as simple as the fear that war was on its way – although that was part of it. It was the fear of fear itself, the feeling that when it finally arrived you might not behave as well as you thought you would. "War," her father was always saying, "sorts out the men from the boys!" and Norma supposed it sorted out the girls from the women too.

"Are you all right, Jacqueline?" she said, as the plump woman wandered off down the platform, looking slightly woebegone, as if all Norma's fears about the journey had, somehow, passed on to her like a disease.

"I'm fine, Miss Lewis!" Jacqueline Rissett replied.

Where was her second hat? She usually clutched it tightly in the delicate fingers of her left hand.

Jacqueline Rissett's mother had made her daughter a full-time job. She had provided her absent-minded only child with almost every optional extra in the Saltdene School shop, and was so concerned that the girl might lose her scarf, her socks, her pencil case, her gloves or her hat that she usually made her go out with two of everything in her possession. Jacqueline often bulged like an anaconda after a particularly large meal. Today she seemed reasonably slim. And one hat down. Although she might have been better without any headgear at all. All the girls customized their hats to a certain extent, but Jacqueline looked as if she had been jumping up and down on hers for hours. It gave her – she was really quite a pretty, fine-featured girl – the air of a farm labourer or a comedian.

"Are you sure you're all right?" said Norma.

"Oh, yes, Miss Lewis! Yes, I am!" And then, just as distressed as she had seemed when she emerged from the train, Jacqueline Rissett went back into it. The girl was shaking like a leaf. What was up with her?

Norma decided to get on to the train. What did it matter if it was going to Brussels or Amsterdam or Lille? The crunch – as her father kept saying – was coming, and in a month or two there might not be any Brussels or Amsterdam or Lille or, for that matter, any Dover either. The thought of a world without Dover made Norma Lewis, in spite of herself, gasp quietly. But there was no reason why the bombs, when they came, should spare Dover. They would rain down from the skies – her father said – and whole streets and cities would be ablaze in a matter of minutes. There would be – her father was sure – terrible problems with the sewage.

Sighing, she put one hand on the door of the carriage once again. She was just about to pull herself up on to the footplate, when, out of the corner of her eye, she caught sight of a black and red blazer. She didn't see the boy wearing it at first – although she knew it was someone from Kirkby, the nearby boys' school that had accompanied them on the trip. But as soon as she saw that it was Peckerley she found she was scanning the platform for signs of Dennis Hatchett.

He was right next to him, of course, mooching along the platform. He didn't look so much older than the sixth-former. His raincoat was too big for him, and if his trilby was designed to give him a worldly air it only made him look more like an overgrown chorister. He kept his hands deep in his pockets, his trilby at a more than usually aggressive angle, but his clothes didn't seem to belong to him. They made Norma think of a schoolboy who had raided his parents' dressing-up box. And the moustache! His toothbrush moustache seemed, today, even more obviously pointless than usual. Why didn't he shave it off? She must have told him to do this twice a week, ever since the cursed thing first appeared, around the time of the Munich crisis. Norma was invaded, once again, by a profound sense of helplessness. Her life was bound up with Hatchett in ways she did not even want it to be.

Well, not only with Hatchett. With Lycett, of course, as well. Hatchett and Lycett were like peaches and cream or love and marriage or fish and chips or sausages and mash. There was something inevitable about the fact that if she saw Hatchett then she expected Lycett to be there. Which he wasn't, of course. He was safely back on the playing-fields of Croydon. But it felt as if he ought to be just round the corner.

She supposed she must have seen Hatchett and Lycett around the village when she was a child, but her first conscious memory of them was at that awful dance, years ago. They must have been about fourteen. Then, all three were pupils, rather than teachers, at local schools. They had walked home, a little way behind her, but if it was a pursuit it had been of a chaste, unthreatening kind.

"There goes Norma Lew-is! She is lo-o-ovely!"

It had been Hatchett who had shouted that from the other side of the road. He had always been the more forward of the two.

It was funny how first encounters dictated the course of relationships. Their three-cornered friendship had never really moved on from the night of the school dance. They had always been Hatchett and Lycett rather than Alec and Dennis – although, if one of them was promoted to first-name terms, it was probably more likely to be Alec. They had gone on to huddle in the corner at joint school events. Later, when Hatchett and Lycett were at Cambridge and Norma was at Manchester, they went to concerts and dances together. Sometimes, in the long vacation, the three of them would bicycle up on to the Downs behind Croydon and lie in the long grass, looking up at the summer sky. They talked of the things they were going to do. Lycett was going to join the Army and see the world. Hatchett was going to write poetry. He already did write poetry although the poetry he was going to write was of the kind people would publish. It might also, thought Norma, although she would never have dreamed of saying this to him, be comprehensible.

Norma was going to help people.

In fact all three of them had ended up as teachers at their old schools. Alec enjoyed himself on the games-field. Norma became passionately fond of her girls, and Hatchett inspired the sixth form. "He is a marvellous teacher!" was what people said about him, even those who disliked his brusque way with people he considered stupid or his open flirtation with the Communist Party.

Peckerley was not Hatchett's only companion. He was, as usual, part of a crowd of sixth-formers who all seemed to be enjoying themselves hugely. Now that there were no other adults around, a few were calling him by his first name. Peckerley was the most conspicuously enthusiastic of them all. He was a good six inches taller than the junior modern-languages master of Kirkby Grammar School, Crotchett Green, Croydon – but Dennis Hatchett did not seem at all embarrassed by this fact. He looked up keenly at his favourite pupil as if he were a friend. He pulled at his Gitane in a characteristically show-off fashion and, for an awful moment, Norma thought he was going to offer it to Peckerley. Then he saw Norma. Hatchett staggered slightly and, pantomiming astonishment, put his right hand to his breast as if about to swoon.

"*Mais alors! C'est* Norma Lewis! *C'est la belle cruelle! Évidemment! Ah, ça alors! C'est formidable, mes braves!*"

Hatchett was always saying things like this. During the whole trip he had showed himself to be particularly good at shrugging, eye-rolling and meaningless exclamation; on balance, Norma thought, he seemed even more French than the average Frenchman. But now – perhaps because they were about to leave all this behind – he had added a new range of gestures. He tucked his right hand into his hip and flared out his fingers in a positively effeminate manner, then crabbed his head left, exhaled sharply and raised both eyebrows twice. After this, to Norma's horror, as Peckerley grinned foolishly in her direction, Hatchett craned his neck backwards over his right shoulder and spat on the platform. *"Alors quoi?"* he said. *"On va voir des choses, n'est-ce pas, petite fille?"*

This, presumably, was addressed to Norma. His attitude had changed towards her. Alec still seemed the same – courteous, amused, slightly distant, a bit like an older brother – but ever since the joint production of *The Tempest*, she had had a horrible feeling that Hatchett was starting to get seriously interested in something more than friendship. It wasn't simply the way that he stared – he stared at everyone – but a number of incidents, none remarkable in itself, which, when taken as a whole, added up to the beginnings of serious assault. He had offered to get her coffee – twice. He had never got anybody coffee in all the years she had known him. It was not out of place for him to have sat next to her on the coach trip to Stratford-upon-Avon, especially since the only other person with a vacant seat next to them was Lawrence Bolt, the Boy with the Peculiar Ears. But his manner during the journey had been odd. He looked flushed, hectic. He had talked about the poetry of Ronsard in a distinctly suggestive manner. And then there had been the Question of the Tomato Sandwich.

Before the matinée, the two schools had shared a picnic lunch by the river. The staff sandwiches had been kept in a large cardboard box by Jennifer Doran. "I teach swimming and domestic science," she had giggled as she opened the box, "so don't complain if the bread is damp!"

Quite a few of the male members of staff laughed at this – as they often did at things Jennifer said – and Norma, speaking in a crosser voice than she had intended, had cut in with, "Somebody will have to share."

"In fact," said Ludwig Groenig, who had reached the impossibly distant age of forty and was known as the Viennese Physics Master Who Knew Two Nobel Prizewinners, "two people will have to share. It is not feasible for one person to share!" Here he had snickered in an unpleasantly foreign way. The awkward silence that so often followed one of his remarks was broken by Hatchett saying, "Norma and I will share the tomato sandwich. It will bring us closer together."

Then he had got to his feet and, putting his head to one side and shuffling to and fro like Maurice Chevalier (the performer not the French *assistant*), he began to croon to a melody unfamiliar to Norma, "Closer together! A tomato sandwich brought them clooser togee-ther!" Ludwig Groenig seemed to find this funny. So did several of the boys.

Norma pictured him now, dancing sideways across the neat English grass, as she hesitated before what seemed to her the most significant step in the long journey home. He looked, she decided, a lot less ridiculous in the Gare du Nord. She found herself intrigued by his delicately cherubic face and funny, piercing, cold-blue eyes. There was still a lot of the schoolboy about him but he was growing up. For the first time in the years she had known him, she found herself noticing his wrists. They were thick and matted with dark hair. He was probably physically rather strong.

Before he could start going on about Ronsard or the Rive Gauche or any of the other things he usually went on about, Norma hoisted herself up into the train, trying to keep her expression bright, but not too bright, interested but not too interested. "If by '*des choses*' you mean the war, I suppose we are going to see some things," she said, with a brief glance in Peckerley's direction, "but I'm not sure it's necessary to worry the boys with them."

Peckerley flushed scarlet. "I'm eighteen, Miss Lewis!" he said. "I'm not that much younger than Mr Hatchett. I'm old enough to fight for my country!"

Was this something he had heard somebody else say? He said it with the unnecessary clarity with which her father pronounced the Lord's Prayer – as if trying to convince himself of the truth of it. Suddenly, looking at him, gawky, coltish with a thatch of blond hair, so utterly English on this most alien of railway stations, Norma felt ridiculously close to tears. To her horror – as if he had somehow divined this rush of emotion in her – Hatchett came closer to the train and, in full view of his favourite pupil, was whispering something urgently in her ear. At first she didn't understand it – even though he was speaking English and not using any words of more than two syllables.

"Marry me!" Hatchett was saying, right there on the platform, under the watchful eyes of Mabel Hughes, who was peering out at them from the window of a nearby compartment. "There's going to be a war. It's all going to end. We might as well get married. And I'm in love with you. I've always been in love with you. I tried to tell myself I wasn't but it didn't work. You're the girl for me. I'll always be in love with you. That's one thing that is never going to change."

Norma looked up and down the platform. "I'm sorry?" she heard herself say, in a high, squeaky voice. "I didn't quite catch that!" If only he would go away! Didn't he have boys to look after? If she said, "No," to him right there on the Gare du Nord, with Mabel Hughes (who had now been joined by Jacqueline Rissett and poor little Mayhew, all openly staring), would he be even more French than usual? Would he, perhaps, spit? And this time in her direction? Or would he shake his fist and curse? Would he (the thought was too awful even to contemplate) cry?

Foreign men did sometimes cry, and Hatchett abroad was quite clearly capable of any of their worst excesses. Even in England he was capable of embarrassing displays of public emotion – like the time he had got up on his chair after Windlesham played the Elgar cello concerto and shouted, "Huzza!" as the last note died away. But there was a look about him – an unsubdued, foxy expression just visible behind his tortoiseshell glasses – that suggested that even if she told him he was a repulsive little worm, he would not necessarily be put off his stroke. She didn't think, of course, that he was a repulsive little worm. She would have said – if anyone asked her – that he, along with Lycett, was her closest male friend. She liked his cleverness, his cheek, his peculiar mixture of crudeness and delicacy, his respect for authority and his natural insubordination. But liking someone wasn't the same thing as agreeing to marry them, for God's sake! All she needed to do was to find some phrase that would enable her to climb up into the train and put an end to this conversation without suggesting that something serious had happened.

"I think," she said, realizing, with a jolt, that perhaps nothing serious had happened since his manner, as usual, was humorously theatrical, "that I said I would marry you when your first volume of poems was published. But we would both have to ask Alec's permission."

This was perfectly true. Three years ago, in a tea-shop in the next village down from Crotchett Green, Hatchett had announced to her and Lycett that one day he was going to marry her. Lycett had said, on the edge of a sports-field at around the same time, that one day he and Norma were going to elope and live in a hut in the Black Forest. They were always saying things like this. They didn't mean anything. Why, then, had she decided, almost as soon as he started to speak, that this time Hatchett was serious? And why was her first reaction one of panic?

Was she interested in him? Was that it?

It was very hard to tell whether you were interested in men. On the whole you were supposed not to be interested in them – or at least to look as if you weren't – in case of being thought forward. But if you were actually friends with them, it was impossible, sometimes, not to behave as if you were interested in them, because of course you were. The trouble was, she decided, as she stood there, one foot on the platform and the other on the train, with Hatchett studying her foxily, that you never knew when *that* was going to creep into a friendship with a person of the opposite sex.

Could men and women never be just friends? Was that it?

Hatchett's expression suggested that Norma's first impression of what his proposal meant had been wide of the mark. There was something both reassuring and depressing about this. She hoisted herself up on to the train. At least she was now looking down on him.

"Of course we shall have to ask Alec's permission," he was

saying. "I will have to go on my knees to him to ask for your hand. It will be the talk of the town. And he will give up all pretensions to you for the sake of preserving our friendship. We are both Englishmen. Besides, he never knows what to do with women whereas I do."

Norma laughed. "Oh," she said, "you're an expert on women, are you, Hatchett?"

"I am," said Hatchett. "I seduce them in foreign hotels. I whisper French poetry to them under the stars and then they are mine. All Lycett does is try to persuade them to watch him kick or throw or strike balls of various sizes and descriptions."

"In that case," said Norma, uncomfortably aware that this was exactly what Lycett was always trying to get her to do, "you will have no difficulty in finding someone to marry you, will you? You don't need me at all, do you?"

Hatchett's face broke into a smile. When he smiled, his face changed completely. He looked, she thought, like a naughty but likeable small boy. "Ah, but I do!" he said. "You are as necessary to me as salt is to meat! When the time comes I will cast aside Lycett like an old shoe!"

It was odd that Hatchett and Lycett were friends, really. She had always thought it had something to do with Hatchett not having a father, while Lycett Senior was always very present in his son's life. The Reverend Arthur Hatchett had disappeared when his son was quite young and people in the village still said he had run off with another woman – since he was considered the most avant-garde vicar St Mary and All Angels had ever seen.

"I think," said Norma, "we had better get on this train before it leaves us behind."

Hatchett bowed low. "*Und so*, my dear," he said, pinching his Adam's apple between the thumb and index finger of his right hand and vibrating it tenderly, "may I be allowed to hop?"

"You may hop and hope all you wish," replied Norma, in her Jane Austen voice," but you know in your heart of hearts, do you not, Mr Hatchett, that I am promised to Mr Lycett body and soul. I have said compromising things to him at a cricket tea and he has certain letters of mine in which I refer, with more frankness than is considered mannerly in a lady, to his legs!"

Hatchett staggered a few paces back and drummed the upper end of a right fist on his breastbone. "Letters!" he cried. "Letters! Then I am doomed! You have mortgaged your soul to one who is little better than an animal! A brute being whose appetites and desires and shameful habits are the talk of Croydon! What shall I do now?"

"Get on the train, if I were you," said Norma, not unaffectionately, "before they lock you up."

"I shall dance!" said Hatchett. "I shall dance! Since there is nothing else left for me I shall dance!"

She sneaked a glance back at him as she dived into the first compartment and, to her horror, saw that he did actually appear to be dancing along the Gare du Nord. He had taken off his trilby and was waggling it to and fro at the end of a left arm thrust out yearningly to one side, like a performer in a concert party, while his right hand, still clutching the Gitane, blew imaginary kisses at her. His footwork, she noticed, was surprisingly nimble. He had attracted a small crowd. As well as Peckerley and Lowestoft, the president of the Language Society, one or two French porters had stopped to look. One seemed to be applauding.

In spite of herself, Norma found she was smiling.

Stricken by the thought that she might be encouraging him she occupied herself with the inhabitants of her compartment. There was Alice Everett, who taught Spanish, and four of her pupils. They had originally intended going to Barcelona. Everett had some thought of trying to get the girls to meet General Franco, of whom she was a keen admirer. Paris was a compromise forced on them for economic reasons. They had spent most of the fortnight trying out their rudimentary Castilian on French waiters and museum attendants. Alice herself, a mannish, horsy woman in her forties with a fondness for garish clothes, seemed, to Norma, unusually subdued.

"Hatchett's playing the fool again, young Lewis," said Everett, yawning slightly as she spoke.

"Yes!" said Norma. Everett looked at her sharply. There was something different about her this afternoon, thought Norma. Usually she was sharp in conversation, especially on political subjects. Norma hoped she was not going to start going on about the wonderful things Hitler was doing for German roads and trains. But she showed no sign of doing so. In fact, for the last hour or so, she had been almost soporifically cheerful.

"Do you find that young man attractive?" she said. "Is he the sort that gels go for these days?" This was such an untypical question from Everett that Norma did not even attempt to answer it. She was a mystery, really, was Everett. Before they had gone away together Norma had thought she was a fairly typical spinster schoolmarm. She certainly never discussed men. Now, after sharing a room with her for two weeks, she wasn't so sure. Some of her underwear was positively shocking. And one evening she had gone off with Mr Breeze to a night-club – which had provoked a great deal of comment.

Everett was looking at her narrowly. "Desire," she said, "leads us into the strangest places! From which sometimes it is very difficult to return! I am always telling the gels to be careful! Their beauty is so precious and so innocent! The world tramples on loveliness, don't you think?" Norma did not know how to reply to this. But Everett continued: "You know that cup of coffee we had earlier," she said, "in that café? It tasted funny. I wouldn't be surprised if some Frog Johnnie hadn't slipped something into it!"

For a language teacher Miss Everett was more than usually chauvinistic.

"'Leafy' Green," she went on, "told me that some man in Deauville put something into her aperitif. In order to stimulate her sexually."

A lost cause, thought Norma, in Miss Green's case, since her favourite garment was a tweed suit and her first love the girls in her Spanish class. "Do you think that that is what has happened to you?" she said, watching Everett for signs of ungovernable lust.

"Do not be ridiculous, young lady!" said Miss Everett sharply. "I hardly think a French café proprietor would attempt to use aphrodisiacs on the passing trade." Her voice lowered dramatically. "But there are people in our party," she went on, "who would stoop to such things."

Who on earth could she be talking about? The idea of anyone using drugs to stimulate Everett sexually was too awful to contemplate. Alan Breeze, perhaps?

Alan Breeze was the Kirkby chemistry master at Saltdene, a small, neat man in his late thirties with a beaky face, a thatch of blond hair and an overdeveloped dress sense. From what Norma had heard, he needed no chemical aids to get what he wanted out of women in the Croydon area. She shuddered, as she often did, at the thought of Mr Breeze's private life. He had quite a nice wife and two small children all of whom he ordered about as if they were members of his own private army. What had Breeze and Everett been doing going off to a night-club?

The train had started to move out of the station.

"I am a little tired!" said Everett. "Perhaps you would be kind enough to billet my Spanish girls next door for a wee while! And while you are at it, perhaps you could make sure we have a full complement!"

She was always ordering Norma about. Obediently, in spite of a mounting sense of frustration with the older woman, Norma ordered the Spanish girls out into the corridor. Four of them. There were twenty-nine girls in all. Including her and Everett that made thirty-one. There were four Spanish girls so there should be twenty-seven girls in the rest of the coach. No. Twenty-five. She hadn't counted her and Everett. It was twenty-nine plus two. Twenty-five. Not twenty-seven. Norma had never been any good at mathematics. Sighing, she opened the door of the compartment next to hers and shepherded the Spanish girls into it.

This was Misfits' Corner. All in neat uniforms (hats included), perhaps because they couldn't afford smart clothes. Girls who hung around teachers. They had been hanging around her and Everett and Mr Hatchett and Mr Breeze when they stopped for coffee earlier.

Jacqueline Rissett was certainly one of them but she, for some reason, did not appear to be here. Skulking somewhere. She had been doing rather a lot of skulking recently. Although she was a warm, almost motherly girl, she was capable of erratic behaviour. Perhaps she had bought some unsuitable novel and was proposing to smuggle it back to England. Or – Norma was invaded by panic once again – even more unsuitable underwear.

"Miss Lewis," said thin, snobbish Janet Frosser, as the Spanish girls squeezed into the spaces available, "how fast will the train go?"

"We do not know, Janet," said Norma.

Her friend, Elinor Wreays ("friend" wasn't quite the word – totally devoted slave was more like it), touched Janet on the wrist. "I expect it will go very, very quickly, Janet," said Elinor, "and we will be home before we know it." Neither of them, thought Norma, had got anything whatsoever out of the trip.

"Trains in France," said Mabel Hughes, ghoulishly, "are often late. They sometimes stop for no reason. In the middle of the countryside. For hours."

Where had Mabel got this information? And how had she managed to give it that threatening, sinister quality she managed to impart to the most mundane remark? Mabel was tall and straight, with a pale face and large black eyes. She had the air, thought Norma, of a sinister governess or a more than usually threatening housekeeper. She was not popular with some girls but among the Misfits was seen as something of a leader. She was, as far as Norma could make out, Jacqueline Rissett's confidante and a devoted disciple of Everett.

"French trains," said Norma sharply – it was always good to let Mabel know who was in charge, "are very reliable indeed!"

Where was Rissett? Before she could even think about looking for her, Norma felt a small hand tug at her sleeve and looked down to see Ruth Mayhew, the girl on a scholarship, who was too young. "Miss – are we in England yet?" She looked as if she had been crying. She had been crying for most of the trip.

"We will be in England very soon!" said Norma brightly.

Mayhew looked out of the window suspiciously. "It doesn't look like England, miss . . ." she said.

It didn't. They were coming out of Paris. The landscape – vaguely unfinished as so much of northern France seemed to be – went on and on to the horizon in a tiring manner. The farmhouses still had that naked look, as if they had abandoned all claims to permanence, while the dark clouds moving in from the west gave the whole thing a decidedly Gothic aspect. "We have to cross the sea to get to England," said Norma.

This seemed to surprise Mayhew. She was pulling at Norma's sleeve again. "Miss," she was saying, "when you was having coffee before we come to the station . . ." Behind her, Norma could see the rest of the Misfits glaring at the little girl. There was an odd atmosphere in the compartment.

"What, Mayhew?" said Janet Frosser, in the languid tone she always used for cutting remarks. "What about when we had coffee? Did you have one of your premonitions? Or one of your 'feelings'? Is the train going to crash?"

Mayhew stopped suddenly. Whatever it was she had thought of saying, she clearly decided it was not, for the moment, for public consumption. Mayhew was a great one for Gothic moments, intimations of disaster, terrible secrets that usually turned out to be the fact that she had lost her glasses or forgotten her homework. None of the other girls really liked her.

"People think I'm stupid, miss," she said darkly, "but I'm not as stupid as I look."

"Of course you're not, Mayhew!" said Norma, and then, aware that this was rather a rude thing to say, felt impelled to add, "You're on a scholarship! So you can't be stupid, can you?" She turned her back on Mayhew and went out to count the next compartment, then realized she had forgotten how many there were in the first, went back to count them, realized she hadn't added on herself, Everett and the Spanish girls, added them on and found she had eighteen people in the first two compartments. That couldn't be right.

Everett never even bothered to count. She really was an infuriating woman. Norma decided to go and have words with her.

"Miss," said Mayhew, who had sidled out into the corridor

after her, "I think I've started!" Norma froze. Had she heard this correctly? She looked down at the dwarfish little girl, her pale hair plastered across her forehead, her uniform somehow even more institutional than a school uniform ought to be, giving her the air of a long-term patient in a lunatic asylum. Mayhew appeared to be gesturing, dramatically, towards her groin. "Down here, miss!" she hissed. "I've started!"

"I am sure you haven't, Mayhew!" said Norma briskly. "Are you bleeding?"

A look of sheer horror passed across Mayhew's face. "No, miss!" she said. "Should I be?" Still pointing at herself in a most unattractive manner, the little girl shambled towards Norma – but her French teacher stepped neatly to one side, slipped into her compartment and pulled down the blind behind her. Everett was lying back against the leather seat, her mouth hideously open and an apple, out of which she had taken one huge bite, still in her left hand.

"Listen," began Norma, hardly able to look at the woman, "may I say how tired I am getting of having everything heaped on my shoulders? While you have been off swanning around Paris, taking in the night-life with Mr Breeze, I have been making travel arrangements and reading to the girls and dealing with the people in the *pension*, and you sit there . . . eating apples!"

Miss Everett did not have the decency to wake up to listen to this tirade. She continued to lean back against the cushions, head to one side, mouth still ajar and, as Norma watched with horrible fascination, the apple slipped from her grasp and rolled on to the filthy floor of the carriage. Norma was about to shake her into wakefulness so that she could shout at her even more, but as soon as she got a little closer, she lost all urge to criticize. She looked up at the blind to make sure that no one could see in and was highly relieved to discover she was the only witness to Miss Everett's condition. She felt cold, though, suddenly, and found herself groping for something charitable to say or think about the woman. For Alice Everett, quite clearly, was dead.

2

Norma had never seen a dead person before although, according to her father, if Hitler had his way, there were soon going to be quite a few in the Croydon area. According to Mr Lewis, as soon as Goering got going, Purley would be a raging inferno, Selsdon a hole in the ground and Sanderstead and Godstone piled high with the charred remains of their citizens. You would be tripping over corpses on your way to work.

She had imagined somehow that they would look more obviously dead. In fact, although she felt the vein in Everett's neck several times, she still feared the woman might leap up at any moment. She looked so in the middle of things.

The first thing that Norma did was try to tidy her up a bit. She never liked people who sat there gawping; and Everett looked as if she had passed over to the other side in the middle of the kind of mouth-stretching one usually only lays on for the benefit of a dentist. You could almost, thought Norma grimly, as she tried to jam the poor creature's lower jaw back into place, see her breakfast. It would not stay shut. In the end she got down Everett's cardigan from her luggage, folded it into an improvised cushion and leaned her fellow teacher's head against it at an artistic angle.

Then, when she had tidied away the apple into her bag, Norma arranged her colleague's hands in her lap.

Everett was on the edge of being a graceful corpse, when the train banked sharply to the left and braked. She shot out of her seat and on to the floor. With some difficulty, Norma got her back into position – this time dumping her own overnight bag between Miss Everett's knees to act as ballast. Then she reached into the pockets of her coat for her French dictionary. *"Est-ce qu'il y a un morticien dans le train?"* Was *"morticien"* the French for undertaker?

Perhaps she would be made to stay behind with the corpse. The girls would be sent on and she would be left alone in some French hotel. *"Je reste ici pendant quelques semaines à cause de ma collégue qui est mort soudainement dans le boat train!"* *Morte*, not *mort*, because Everett, in spite of her gigantic nose and square shoulders, was feminine.

It was as she was struggling with the grammar necessary to convey her predicament to others that Norma first realized she could not face it alone. And, when she came to think of who might help her, it was not small, handsome, cadaverous Mr Breeze who came to mind. She needed someone of her own age, and Hatchett, after all, was one of her oldest friends. It was entirely her fault that she had decided to take his joke proposal seriously.

It had been a joke proposal. Hadn't it?

Of course it had. She and Hatchett and Lycett were friends. Annoyed with herself for ever questioning Hatchett's limitless capacity for facetiousness, Norma got up, smartened her face in the mirror opposite and decided to look for the modern-languages master. She had learned a lot of new things about him on this journey and one was that he clearly had a rapport with French railway officials.

Very slowly and carefully, Norma let herself out of the compartment, trying not to think about the fact that someone might ask Everett for her ticket while she was gone. She put her head into the next compartment. "Miss Everett," she said, "is having a little nap. You are on no account to disturb her." The Spanish girls, one of whom seemed to be sitting on Mayhew's lap, nodded solemnly. They were in awe of Miss Everett.

To add to Norma's difficulties, the engine driver seemed intent on showing off. As he moved the train faster and faster across the featureless fields that led to Amiens, the corridor played tricks with each footstep, until she felt she was on some fairground ride, designed to take your breath away and leave you dizzy. And, once she had got past the coach that was full of her girls, the passengers who stared out at her from behind the grimy glass of their compartments had a definitely sinister aspect. That man with a moustache, hands folded primly in front of him, looked like one of the murderers in the Chamber of Horrors at Madame Tussaud's. And didn't the woman opposite him, the one with the shopping, and the wart on the end of her nose, look like the Madame who had dismembered her second husband and served him up to her third as a kind of *hors d'oeuvre*?

The passengers she encountered as she went deeper and deeper into the bucking centre of the train seemed to push against her deliberately (one young man in a jersey nearly sent her flying) and, when she finally caught sight of a familiar black and red blazer, she could have cried for joy. It was Peckerley.

"Are you all right, Miss Lewis?"

"I'm fine, Peckerley!" she said. Just a little matter of a dead Spanish teacher to sort out and I'll be right as rain. "Do you know where Mr Hatchett is?"

Peckerley grinned and mimed raising a glass with his left hand. "He and Mr Breeze went for . . . er . . . refreshments," he said. Norma peered anxiously past him down the corridor, which, as she looked, swerved like a mechanical snake to reveal the harsh light of yet more coaches behind it.

Mr Hatchett and Mr Breeze, who was carrying a large bottle of *vin ordinaire*, clattered into view. Hatchett was still wearing his trilby. As she watched he took the bottle from Mr Breeze and, after a deep draught, brushed the back of his hand along his moustache. He might have the look of a schoolboy about him, she thought, with something like relief, but if he was a boy, he was a tough one.

"Could I have a private word, Mr Hatchett?" she said. Although she caught a glance between Peckerley and Breeze, there was no suspicion of a snigger about it.

She and Hatchett moved a little way away from them. Norma looked, speculatively, back at Breeze. There was something rather furtive about his manner today, she decided. Breeze, who taught chemistry in rather too intense a manner to the girls of Saltdene School, was occasionally "lent" by the headmistress to Kirkby Grammar. Miss Leach said she felt it was good for him to be among men. Having seen the way he looked at some of the girls Norma could not help but agree.

Norma whispered, "It's Everett – something terrible has happened to Everett!"

Hatchett looked at her over his glasses. "Has she exposed her naked breasts to strangers?" he said. "Or has she finally turned the corner into madness?"

"She's dead!" hissed Norma, before Hatchett could heap any more insults on the fresh corpse of her colleague. Judging by the movement of the train the poor woman was by now probably lying on the floor of the compartment with her behind in the air and her face in Norma's overnight bag.

"Dead?" said Hatchett.

"Dead!" said Norma.

"Dead?" said Hatchett.

"Dead!" said Norma, who was beginning to feel like a character in an Italian operatic duet.

Hatchett moved closer to her. To her consternation, he smelt strongly of garlic. "How did this happen?" he said, in conspiratorial tones.

"She just died!" said Norma. "I looked away for a moment and there she was with her mouth open, as dead as a doornail."

"Are you sure?" said Hatchett. "Have you examined her thoroughly?"

"I know when someone's dead!" snapped Norma. "She'll be as stiff as a board if we don't do something pretty sharpish."

Hatchett looked grim. "The French are pretty strict about this sort of thing," he said, in the tones of a man used to people popping their clogs on the other side of the Channel. "There's a thing called a *juge d'instruction* . . ." he went on, shrugging in a convincingly foreign manner. "*Et alors il y a la police judiciaire . . . Ici en France, ma chérie, y a pas la présomption d'innocence.* We are all guilty in the eyes of French law, and English people particularly so!"

He seemed to have abandoned francophilia rather quickly, thought Norma. He redeemed himself in her eyes, however, by bracing his shoulders and marching off down the train in the direction from which she had just come. Obediently, she followed him.

When he got to their compartment, Hatchett's expression was grave. "Perhaps," he said to her, "you ought not to see this."

"But I already have," said Norma.

Hatchett's eyes narrowed. "Perhaps," he said, "you ought not to see it again."

Norma felt somewhat confused by this. She did not wish to seem ghoulish, but she found she was surprisingly keen on getting another look at Everett. She was morbidly curious to find out whether she had stayed in the same position.

"I think," she said slowly, "I would rather be in there than out here – knowing she's in there with you." She wished she had not said this. It seemed to imply that Hatchett was the kind of man who was liable to get up to unspeakable things if left alone with a cadaver. Even if he had sailed fairly close to the wind in his talk to the French Society entitled "Corruption and the Symbolist Poets" he wasn't a dangerous man. Or was he? There was a sort of suppressed wildness about him. Why did she make herself sound so foolish when in his company? It was, she thought, as she followed him through the shuttered door, another very good reason for not considering him as a marriage prospect.

"Marriage prospect." Why was she even thinking about such things?

Everett had moved quite a bit while Norma had been away. For a moment, Norma thought she might have come, briefly, back to life and attempted to stage a gymnastic display in order to prove herself match fit. The contents of Norma's bag were strewn all over the floor in a way that suggested someone had tipped them out, and Everett had managed to get even more closely involved with her cardigan. It was now wrapped around her head as if she had been trying to towel dry her hair.

"Oh, my God!" said Norma. "I left her all neat and tidy!"

Hatchett did not answer this. He seized Everett under both arms and propped her up on the seat that faced the one on which she had been sitting. Brusquely (had he done this kind of thing before?) he set her legs neatly together and, as Norma had done, arranged her hands in her lap. Why was it that people felt the need to get

corpses to behave as if they were in one of Miss Sullivan's deport-
ment classes? But Everett was still clearly not disposed to go along
with what Miss Sullivan always described as Quiet Sitting. Her jaw
kept dropping open, like a goldfish's when prospecting for food.
Eventually Hatchett picked up one of the Spanish girls' hats,
jammed it on to her unruly mop of hair and wedged the elastic
under her chin.

Norma only realized that this was not simply another case of
death bringing out the undertaker in all of us when Hatchett, giving
the corpse a shrewd glance, said, "We shall have to get her through
French Customs . . ."

"How do you mean?" said Norma.

"I don't think," went on Hatchett, "that we should declare her
until we get to Dover." He seemed remarkably unmoved by
Everett's death. But then, dead or alive, Everett was one of those
people who provoke nothing but mild irritation. "I don't think,"
he went on, speaking for both of them, "that we can leave her in
France. If you want my opinion Hitler will go through the French
like a knife through butter."

"No," said Norma, "we can't let the Germans get their hands
on her!"

This was, she saw immediately, an even more stupid thing to
say than the last stupid thing she had said. Why on earth should
the Nazis be interested in a dead forty-year-old schoolmistress? She
had been panicked, of course, by what Hatchett had said about the
country whose language he taught with such dedication. He had
the air, as usual, of being right about things.

"I will obtain a wheelchair," he said and, like the Scarlet Pimper-
nel, vanished into the train.

Once again, Norma was alone with her colleague. It was suddenly
rather frightening to be alone with a dead person. How long would
Hatchett be away? Where did he imagine he was going to get a
wheelchair? He had seemed terribly confident about it. Perhaps
French trains always had them.

It was no good. However hard she tried to think about other
things, Everett always seemed to be looking at her. Norma tried

33

sitting on her side of the compartment. That was worse. Every time she stole a peek at her (the temptation was impossible to resist) she had the distinct impression that the dead woman was squinting sideways at her. Eventually, as yet more blank fields and blanker minutes passed, she decided to sit bang opposite and outstare her.

Finally Norma could bear it no longer. She reached out in the direction of the face, and then, with the tips of the index and third fingers of both hands, drew Everett's eyelids down. They were, she thought, surprisingly vivid to the touch. Nothing cold or clammy about them. Of course, Everett's hair was still growing, her stomach still getting on with the job of digesting that apple and –

Digesting.

What was it the woman had said just as they boarded the train? There had been something funny-tasting about the coffee they had drunk in that café, just before they reached the station. For a moment Norma experienced a flicker of distress. She, too, had had coffee. Was she going to keel over, or – almost more painful to contemplate – develop some frightful illness and end up in a hospital in Soissons, gesturing helplessly at her midriff?

No. She was all right. But Everett, quite definitely, wasn't.

Why, though? A heart-attack?

As she was thinking about this, the compartment door slid back and there was Hatchett, complete with moustache, trilby, owlish glasses and coat that was three sizes too big for him. "There is," he said, in that testy, decisive voice of his, "a shortage of wheelchairs on this train. I am making enquiries about a stretcher."

"What," said Norma, wildly, "is the French for stretcher?"

Hatchett's mouth crinkled in a small smile. "I have had to resort to mime," he said. He cast a quick look over at Everett. "Is she behaving herself?" he said.

"Really, Mr Hatchett," said Norma, deciding to talk to him as if they were in the presence of a pupil, "I do not think that that is a proper manner in which to speak of the dead."

"There is no proper manner in which to speak of the dead," said Hatchett, as he retreated once more into the corridor, "although the past tense is usually appropriate."

He really was an infuriating chap, thought Norma. He was . . . peculiar. One day last year, she and Hatchett and Lycett had gone to Brighton for the day. They had been passing a woman holding out birdseed, in her cupped hand, for the benefit of the seagulls. Without warning, as he passed her, Hatchett had swooped his neck down and gobbled some of the seed out of her hand. She should have asked for help from someone older. From Mr Breeze. Then, as she thought about Mr Breeze, his strong smell of cologne, his unctuous manner, his unreal thatch of blond hair (was it, perhaps, a wig?), she realized he would have been an even worse proposition. Anyway, judging from the way he and Everett had been carrying on during the trip, he might well have allowed passion to cloud his judgement, thereby guaranteeing they all had to sit in a shed at Calais for the rest of the night.

She became aware that the door was not quite fully closed and that Ruth Mayhew was peering in at her through the crack. Instinctively, Norma moved forward on her seat to block the girl's view of Everett.

"Miss," said Mayhew, "can you get pregnant from a toilet seat?"

"No!" said Norma, emphatically. There was a silence. She could see just enough of Mayhew's pinched nose and mournful eyes to remember just how unattractive the rest of her was. She had the impression, somehow, that Mayhew (brilliant at maths, unable to spell, scarcely able to read and write) was here because she knew something about what had happened. She was about to get up and slam the door on her nose when behind the thin slice of Mayhew appeared a slightly broader tranche of Rissett. Without appearing to notice, Mayhew tugged back the door a little further. "Is Miss Everett all right?" she asked.

"She has fallen asleep," said Norma.

That was the kind of phrase they wrote on gravestones, wasn't it? So it wasn't quite a lie, said Norma to herself, for she worried about that kind of thing. "You may retire to your compartment now," she said. Reluctantly, Rissett obeyed. Mayhew followed her. Norma was alone with the corpse once more.

It was not until well north of Amiens, after Hatchett had sallied forth to try any receptacle capable of accommodating the body of an English schoolmistress in early middle age, that they decided to walk the deceased Spanish teacher on to the boat. "We will have to involve Peckerley," said Hatchett, lowering his voice.

"And I suppose," said Norma, "we ought to tell Mr Breeze." Neither of them seemed very happy about this. Eventually Hatchett said he would have to tell Breeze and Peckerley together. He came back with only Peckerley for company. When Norma asked him how Mr Breeze had taken the news, Hatchett and Peckerley looked at each other in a most peculiar manner.

"It was curious," said Hatchett, eventually. "The man seemed almost relieved. At least he won't have to squire her to night-clubs. Not that there are many of those in Croydon."

Norma did not know what to say to this. She had rather hoped that she was the only one who had suspected that Everett had switched her affections from the fifth form to a married man. She had spent more time alone with him than was proper.

"They had a fearful row the other night," said Peckerley. "I heard them. Don't know what it was about but it was a fearful row."

"I thought they were going about together rather a lot . . ." said Norma.

"They went off together to argue," said Peckerley. "She had probably found out he was up to no good with one of her girls. Everett was a terrible snooper. It's an awful thing to say but it's true. They weren't friends or anything. He was trying to suck up to Everett about something anyway."

As often before, Norma was dazzled not only by the range of Peckerley's knowledge about the staffroom but also about his worldliness in interpreting it. "Up to no good with one of her girls" indeed. If there was anything like that going on she would have noticed it.

For the rest of the journey, she and Hatchett and Peckerley sat with the dead woman. At first they made some attempt to discuss her better qualities, but after a few minutes it became clear that she did not really have any. "She was a first-class musician," said

Hatchett, folding his arms and looking at her beadily. Everett's head lolled forward on to her chest in an ungainly fashion.

It was after Hatchett had sent his star pupil out for bread and wine that he said, "These letters – referring to Lycett's legs. Presumably if I got hold of them I would be able to use them to . . ." here he gave an instant leer and crouched in his Richard III position on the seat ". . . force my attentions on you. In the manner of Count Fosco."

They were back on familiar territory now and Norma, with what might have been a mild pang of regret that his earlier proposal had not been much different from the time he had asked her to name their first child Eulalie even if it was a boy, said, "I was foolish, I know, to refer to Lycett's legs in print. Or even handwriting. I was carried away. But I know he will not use his legs against me. And should the letters – there are seventy-three of them – fall into your possession I trust you will behave like a gentleman. Some of them make mention of his ears!"

Hatchett allowed the left side of his mouth to droop and, to improve the effect, he dribbled briefly. "I am not a gentleman," he said, doing the leer again.

It was strange. Even when they were confined to a French railway compartment with the fresh corpse of one of their colleagues they were carrying on as they had always carried on, since they were all in the fourth form. If either of them ever wanted to break out of that pre-ordained pattern of behaviour, it would be almost impossible for them to do so. Once again Norma chided herself for reading too much into what were, after all, still adolescent habits of mild flirtation. And once again she found herself asking whether she was suffering from some undiagnosed passion of her own.

Aware, perhaps, of her slight frustration with the familiar routines, Hatchett's tone became serious. In a friendly, open kind of way, he said, "You do find Lycett attractive. He is a very attractive chap."

"You are both," said Norma, aware of how important it was to be even-handed with the two of them, "attractive chaps."

"I mean," continued Hatchett, in his very, very reasonable voice, "you might, you know . . . I mean you might . . . even though the three of us are . . . well, you know . . . you might consider him as a . . . as a marriage prospect."

"I don't consider people as 'prospects'," said Norma, hotly. "You make me sound like an investor in the stock market." Then, fearing she had spoken with too much passion, she returned to the slightly arch humour that was their usual way. "I am a Modern Young Woman, Mr Hatchett," she went on, adding a touch of Scottish governess to the voice. "I have read D. H. Lawrence. I use the words 'birth' and 'control'. Sometimes together. Sometimes in public!"

Perhaps, she thought, with a touch of sadness, she would never really find out what Hatchett thought about anything. Almost desperate now to try to find a way of responding to the seriousness of his last remark, she found herself watching this conversation as if she was a powerless spectator rather than a participant.

Hatchett, meanwhile, needed no invitation to be utterly and completely silly, even when a fellow member of staff was in the early stages of rigor mortis only three feet away from him. "All women approach all men as marriage prospects," he said, making his Oscar Wilde face and waving an imaginary cigarette in the air. "That is their tragedy. No man does. That is his. And by the same token, the term Modern Young Woman is simply a euphemism for a girl who is old enough to know better."

"I went to a university where women were allowed to join the Union," said Norma, surprised by the heat in her tone – Hatchett was always capable of getting her to rise to intellectual argument, "so I must be a bit modern. Daddy always said that girls should have the same chances as boys."

This silenced Hatchett. He furrowed his brow and made a brave attempt to look as if he was thinking about the Rights of Women. He was probably, thought Norma, considering the fact that, although she was not supposed to know this, he and Lycett had once referred to her father as Loosebottom. Maybe they still did.

After a while he became almost serious again. "If you did, though

. . . I mean if you ever did, you know, start to feel . . . you know . . . like that . . . about Lycett . . . I mean, I assume you don't but it is possible, of course, it is always possible . . ." although he said this as if it was about as possible as Hitler taking up English country dancing ". . . and if you did, I mean, you would . . . you know . . . tell me. Wouldn't you?"

"Of course I would, Dennis," said Norma, the use of his first name signalling one of their few moments of direct intimacy. "Of course I would. You know how fond I am of you two boys. And I am sure you tell each other everything, so it would be impossible to keep it from you."

Hatchett took some time to think about this. "I suppose that's true," he said eventually. "I mean, he tells me things he wouldn't tell to anybody else."

"What things?" said Norma, quickly.

Hatchett threw back his head and laughed. "Women!" he said. "Restless unsatisfied women!"

"Even if that is a quotation from the Ancient Greek," said Norma, "it is still pointless and offensive."

"All I mean is," said Hatchett, serious again, "that he and I go back a long way. Our parents knew each other. I knew his . . ."

"Knew his what?"

"His family," concluded Hatchett, lamely.

There was something about Lycett's family, although Norma wasn't sure she knew what it was. Everyone knew the Lycetts, of course. They were important people in the neighbourhood. But there was something odd in their history. Her father had mentioned something of the sort – but in the manner he did when anything painful or scandalous was under discussion, a manner that let you know, very clearly, that you were not supposed to ask questions. Alec never, ever talked about his family, except to say how much he cared for and respected Mr Lycett Senior.

She had been to their place once, when she was small. One afternoon. With her father. She remembered hardly anything about it. Had Alec been there? Maybe even Hatchett as well? She really couldn't recall. In those days Albion House had seemed a big and imposing place. It had frightened her a little. People still said about Alec's parents that it was a bad marriage. So perhaps she had picked up some . . . atmosphere. He was rich, of course, was Alec's father. Shipping or something. He had not, like Hatchett's father, been stupid enough to join the Anglican Church or to enlist in the Great War.

"I think," said Norma, "that we will always go on like this. The three of us. Just like this. Best friends. And then one day we will meet different people and get married and have children and still know each other and our children will still be friends."

"Yes," said Hatchett, slightly wistfully, "that is what I would like to happen. So perhaps it will."

He didn't sound sure about it, though. Neither, if she was honest, was she. Even if, at some level, that was her wish for all of them, things were already too complicated for it ever to come true. Norma had sometimes wondered whether they were a late local manifestation of those bright young people of the twenties who didn't want to think about anything but pleasure. What she had thought they were avoiding was the war that everyone knew was coming. But perhaps that wasn't it at all. Perhaps they had been avoiding each other even while they played at friendship, only now, as in other, more public matters, the reckoning was coming.

Peckerley came back in carrying a baguette, some cheese and another bottle of wine. "Is it all right to eat in the same room as a dead person, sir?" he said.

"In some countries, Peckerley," said Mr Hatchett, "it is mandatory."

Peckerley and Hatchett started talking about the Maginot Line. People – men especially – were always going on about the Maginot Line. Norma imagined it as something like the Great Wall of China, and underneath it a vast network of tunnels containing millions of Frenchmen in *képis* and baggy trousers. Not that she could relate these Frenchmen to the ones she had seen lounging around the Champs-Élysées, taking two hours to finish a cup of coffee. She had gained the impression that the first thing these types would do was to offer the invading army the menu *du jour*.

"The Poles will offer him a run for his money, sir!" said Peckerley, with almost pathetic eagerness.

Hatchett nodded sagely, as if he and the sixth-former were part of some Army Group Command. "You have to remember," he said, as if he had only recently discovered this, "that Poland is an extremely flat country."

Norma wasn't really listening to them. She was trying to think of what had been so different about Everett's behaviour when she got on to the train. And considering, once again, the curious nature of her closeness with Mr Breeze. What was it she had said about the coffee? There was something not quite right about Miss Everett's death.

"Look, sir!" said Peckerley, breaking off a high-level discussion about the state of the Polish Army. "Calais! We're already in Calais!"

Norma looked out at the ghostly darkness of the summer evening. They seemed to be clanking past trains, shrouded in quiet sidings, and through the open window came the unmistakable smell of fish. Long before the train jostled its way into the lighted island of the platform Norma heard, from way ahead, a lonely voice cry, "Calais Marine! Calais Marine!" Then there was a huge illuminated clock telling her it was eight fifteen. She looked sideways at Everett sitting bolt upright, a Saltdene School hat still fixed on her untidy hair. She looked, thought Norma, about as dead as a person could get.

How on earth were they going to get her past Customs?

3

Hatchett sent Peckerley off to tell Mr Breeze that he and Peckerley would be carrying Miss Everett on to the boat. Norma was just getting up to count her charges again when Hatchett put his hand on her arm. "I do apologize," he said, "for carrying on like that at the Gare du Nord. I had had too much to drink at lunchtime."

"I assumed," said Norma, "that it was another one of your jokes."

"There is always a serious element to any joke," said Hatchett.

"So you really were asking me to marry you?" Why did she feel so offended by the obvious truth that he had been doing nothing of the kind?

"Well," said Hatchett, "you know . . . sometimes I say things as a joke and then I realize I mean them. And sometimes I mean them and they sound as if I'm joking."

"I think, Mr Hatchett," said Norma, in her Scottish governess voice, "you had better make up your mind when you are being serious fairly quickly. Or some lady will end up suing you for breach of contract."

This was more or less an open invitation to Hatchett to do his Hamish the Notary voice. Somewhat to her relief he didn't.

He was pouting thoughtfully. He looked as if he was assessing the fifth form in oral French or wondering where to go for his dinner. Then, rather disconcertingly, he smiled. His smile was electric. It transformed his face, made him come boyishly alive. He nodded at the slumped figure in the corner. "It would be easier just to leave her here to be shunted off into some siding . . ." he said. Norma gaped at him. "If we're going to take her with us," he continued, "we need to get her looking a bit livelier."

For a moment Norma thought he might be serious. Perhaps he was suggesting placing his hand up the back of her dress and working her like a ventriloquist's dummy.

"I suppose she'll have to come, though," he went on. "The Froggies may attempt to make off with her if we leave her unattended. The corpse of an English maiden lady can change hands for a small fortune on the Continent."

Norma flushed with irritation. A little of this sort of thing was fine. He was welcome to make a joke of their friendship, since the whole relationship depended on neither of them ever being serious for too long. But this was a different matter. The woman in front of them might have been a difficult travelling companion and a third-rate teacher but she was dead. That ought to count for something.

Fortunately, before she was required to respond to Hatchett's remark, Peckerley slipped into the compartment. He looked, thought Norma, conspiratorial and eager. "You take the left side, Peckerley," said Hatchett, "and I will take the right." He bowed, briefly, in Norma's direction. "Per'aps," he said, in an almost perfect imitation of Maurice Chevalier (it didn't really matter which one because they both sounded exactly the same), "Meess Leweess would be so good as to take 'er luggage?"

"Girls!" called Norma, as she preceded them into the corridor. "Miss Everett is feeling poorly."

"She looks terrible," said Jacqueline Rissett, who sounded genuinely concerned.

There was a terrific noise of metal sliding against metal and the coaches shuffled crazily into each other like soldiers drilling themselves into a line at a speed inspired by panic. Peckerley and Hatchett temporarily lost their footing and for a moment Norma thought Five A's form mistress might end up on the floor. At the last minute, however, master and boy retained control and the three of them skeetered off down the corridor as if Miss Everett was taking part in some complicated parents' race.

It was cooler here. There was a breeze. She could smell the sea.

"Miss, did she eat something?"

"Miss, did she have a tummy upset?"

"Miss, is she drunk?" (Laughter.)

"Miss, did she have an ulcer because my daddy has an ulcer?"

"Miss, did something fall on her from the luggage rack?" (Laughter.)

"Miss, was it a case?" (More laughter.)

"Miss, will she be all right?"

"Miss, is it her time of the month?"

This last was from Mayhew. She really must have a serious talk with Mayhew. Any moment now she would be telling them all about her latest dream or suggesting they were being followed by a criminal gang. To Norma's relief, Mabel was glaring at her. Mabel was the sort of girl who would have made a good wardress, and she was usually able to keep Mayhew in order. The Misfits, as usual, stayed close to the teachers but, meanwhile, the rest of the girls were streaming down the platform, following the crowd. Norma took longer and longer strides, until she was almost running to keep up with the out-of-control crocodile. They were now in the middle of a long, low shed full of sinister-looking men in blue overalls. In the distance Alice Everett was flat on her back on what looked like a small trailer. Peckerley and Hatchett were leaning forward at an angle, straining like drayhorses, as the body of the head of Spanish rattled past the last few Frenchies before the English Channel. Gitanes fixed to lower lips, sleeves rolled up in a self-conscious fashion, they stared at her with the general air of insolence Norma associated with working men who spoke no English.

Someone had been stopped in the far corner and two men were going through her bags. As Norma watched, a big fat man with particularly dirty dungarees was pointing and laughing at Everett. To her horror Hatchett seemed to be pointing at her as well. Everett, even from this distance, still looked spectacularly dead. Norma had never seen anyone so obviously dead in her whole life. What was Hatchett saying to the man? As Norma rounded up the girls and tried, unsuccessfully, to get them to stand in twos, she watched, out of the corner of her eye, the last policeman who stood between them and the quay where the huge muffled shape of the English packet waited for them. *The Pride of Britain*, the ship was called.

"Now," said Norma, "shall we show them what polite and nice and well-behaved young girls we are?"

"Shall we, Elinor?" said Janet Frosser.

"Yes, Janet," said Elinor Wreays. "Let's!" And, arm in arm, the two girls marched into the ship. Mabel glared at two of the Spanish girls, who were giggling together. She looked, thought Norma, even more like Mrs Danvers than usual. All she needed was a bunch of keys at her waist to complete the picture.

Norma walked up the gangway. "Straight upstairs into the fresh air!" she called. "We don't want any of us feeling queasy, do we?"

Mayhew had been sick nine times on the way over, once over Everett's shoes. Janet Frosser had turned bright green. As she had suspected, the memory of the outward journey quietened them. Although Mayhew did manage to simulate a retching movement, which sent Janet Frosser and Elinor Wreays off into fits of giggles. "Now," said Norma, in control again, turning back at the head of the gangway and freezing those two with a look, "walk on!"

And walk on they did. Past the assembled mass of idle foreigners, out into the sweet, cool blackness of the summer night came twenty-nine (please, God!) English schoolgirls, ambassadors for their country in a world that needed a little civilized behaviour. One, two! One, two! Don't look at that man scratching his belly in public and, whatever you do, do not allow your eyes to stray in the direction of the cranes and warehouses over to your left where a man appears to be urinating against a wall in public. One, two! One, two! Two at a time up the gangplank!

"Now we're not in France any more, are we, miss?" said Mayhew to Norma. She had pressed herself close to her favourite teacher and her pathetically small hand had found its way into Norma's. From time to time she cast anxious glances over towards the other Misfits, and Norma thought she might be on the verge of another confidence.

"No," said Norma, briskly, looking down at a gigantic metal stump decorated with rope, and a featureless stretch of concrete, "that's the last bit of France we'll see." She felt sorry for the girl again. "Are you homesick?" she said to her.

"I am a bit, miss," said Mayhew, in a small voice. Norma put her arms round her and gave her a squeeze.

Nations, thought Norma, as English congealed on the tongues of those around her, were all to do with language and its tricky secrets. Here, in the belly of the ship, safe from abroad at last, her fellow countrymen revealed themselves to her and to each other like pigs at the trough of their mother tongue. Big ugly vowels bumped into each other. Consonants clashed like badly chosen wallpaper. She led the girls past an elderly man shouting at his wife, and a family with two screaming toddlers, up on to the deck. There, about half-way down the ship's length, were Hatchett and Peckerley, tucking up Miss Everett in what looked like a wheelchair.

Norma arranged her girls on a row of white seats a little way off from the dead teacher and, in a deliberately jaunty manner, approached her deceased travelling companion. Mabel Hughes, she became aware, was staring at her. So was Mayhew. "How are you feeling, Miss Everett?" said Norma, in an extra loud voice.

"Much the same," said Hatchett, and added in a whisper, out of the corner of his mouth, "i.e. dead."

"You got a wheelchair," said Norma brightly.

"Yes," said Peckerley. "Mr Hatchett was brilliant. We went to the purser's office and –"

Ah! There was Jacqueline Rissett. Where had she been hiding? She seemed to be deep in conversation with Mabel Hughes. Mabel looked as if she was the recipient of some amazingly important schoolgirl secret. Then the two girls moved closer to them. Really, they were behaving even more oddly than usual today.

"Jacqueline and Mabel, return to your places, please," said Norma.

"I want to ask Miss Everett something," said Mabel Hughes.

She looked, thought Norma, rather strained and unhappy. Weren't the parents rather peculiar? Cranky in some way? Vegetarians? Communists? Fascists? "You may ask it later," said Norma, firmly.

"Possibly," added Hatchett, under his breath, "with the use of a ouija board."

46

Norma interposed her body between Mabel Hughes, Jacqueline Rissett and the wheelchair. "Go back!" she said. "Now!" Like dogs foiled of their prey the two girls backed a little way off and circled warily.

Mabel Hughes was still looking at her. "How is your niece, Miss Lewis?" she said, in an oddly reverent tone.

Norma assumed, as was usually the case with Mabel Hughes, that this was some kind of trick question, designed to show her off as the most serious, the best, the goodest girl in the class. Mabel loved teachers – especially Everett. So Norma did not answer it directly. "I don't think we have time to talk about her now," was all she said. What on earth was Mabel Hughes asking her about her niece for? As far as Norma knew, she was still in India. Jacqueline Rissett, as she usually did, looked as if she was waiting for a man on a horse to ride up and take her away.

"Sit!" said Norma. Mabel Hughes sat.

"We must tell someone responsible," Norma whispered to Hatchett. Miss Everett's head rolled forward on to her chest. "When are we going to tell someone?"

Hatchett looked down at Miss Everett. "I think," he said, eventually, "that we should get her as far as we possibly can."

He was clearly beginning to see Everett as some kind of challenge to his ingenuity. She had begun to resemble a baton in a relay race or a parcel in some complicated party game played by children. Before he could get all excited about getting her to, say, Stornaway by tomorrow night, Norma said, "I suppose we could wait till Dover."

"Victoria," said Hatchett, who clearly didn't think Dover would stretch them enough, "we should get her to Victoria. We could say we didn't notice she was dead until southern Kent."

"I think," said Peckerley, with great solemnity, "we should get her back to Croydon. It's what she would have wanted."

Norma was beginning to think they were both mad. And that her girls were following suit. What was all this about her niece?

Norma had always tried to tell the truth. She was a very bad liar. She should have had the courage to insist they told the truth earlier.

47

But, even now, she found herself unable to do so. Was that why she had not told Hatchett about that business with Everett and the coffee? "Why didn't we notice she was dead?" Peckerley was saying, worried about his motivation. "Were we just unobservant? Could anyone be that unobservant?"

"She was feeling poorly," said Hatchett, pacing in the way he did when rehearsing the school play, "and we got her into the wheelchair and she seemed to be asleep and the next time we checked, which was Victoria –"

The siren of the ship wailed, loud and long. The girls rose and fluttered to the starboard railings like birds thrown against the sky in the evening. The boat lumbered out into the calm waters of the port. And Norma, counting her charges mechanically now – six, eight, twelve – totting them up in one swift glance, the way one might read the upturned faces on a row of dice, made them come to thirty. She counted them again. This time there was no doubt about it. Somewhere along the way she had gained, not lost, a child.

Deciding, in the moment that she had come to this conclusion, that it was final and absolute proof that the events of the afternoon – Hatchett's proposal, Everett's death, the business with the coffee – had driven her completely and utterly potty, Norma felt her way to one of the vacant seats, lowered herself into it and, on the verge of tears, sank her face into her hands.

"What's the matter?" Hatchett was saying, as he stood over her.

"Nothing!" said Norma. "Go away! Please go away!"

Hatchett moved a little further off but kept his eyes on her face. He clearly thought she was about to throw herself over the side. Ridiculous youth! Norma decided she would not even attempt to count the girls again until they got back to Saltdene, then shook out her hair, sat up straight and summoned them back from the side of the ship. "Now," she said, "I think we should tell a story, don't you? To pass the time?"

Mayhew's eyes widened. "A murder story, please!" she said.

"Yes," said Jacqueline Rissett. "An Agatha Christie story! I know all the Agatha Christie stories!" Elinor Wreays, Mabel Hughes and

Janet Frosser were all looking at her with more than usual interest. Although none of the others really liked Agatha Christie, the Misfits seemed to have an insatiable passion for her, and Jacqueline Rissett was the acknowledged expert in the field. It was Mr Breeze, thought Norma, irritably, who had fuelled this interest of theirs by insisting on their reading *The Murder of Roger Ackroyd*. Norma did not like detective stories.

"I got a murder story by Agatha Christie," said Mayhew, in a bloodcurdling whisper, "that I made up myself."

"Oh," said Norma. "How nice!"

"It's a true story," went on Mayhew, "what is based on fact as well as my imagination." Norma smiled encouragingly. Then, out of the corner of her eye, she saw one or two of the Misfits glaring at her stunted, hard-working scholarship girl. There was suddenly, although Norma could not understand why, a definite air of tension about the proceedings.

"There was a person," continued Mayhew, in thrilling tones, "who had done something very bad. Very wrong. Very evil. Very, very wicked indeed." All the girls shifted uncomfortably on their benches. "This was a person that went around poisoning people for no reason in cold blood. She gave them things such as arsenic and strychnine for no reason whatsoever. Purely for the pleasure of watching them die in agony!"

"I suppose, Mayhew," said Norma, "that is a reason. Although not a very good one, I grant you."

They were out of the harbour now. On the open sea the wind smacked into the ship with surprising force. More and more of the girls, alerted by the excitement Mayhew's story had generated almost ahead of its opening paragraph, were drifting back from the rail at the edge of the deck.

"Oh, yes, miss," said Mayhew, raking her audience with her eyes, "that is what she gave her victims. Poison. And plenty of it. With the result that they all of them died horribly, groaning and choking and being sick with green stuff all coming out of them like slime."

This seemed generally approved of by the other girls. Norma

stole another glance down the deck. The boat, edging out into the Channel, was now rocking from side to side. Everett's wheelchair spun backwards into a lifeboat and, as the steamer pitched over on to its side, it slid off down the deck in the direction of the Channel. It moved with surprising speed. If Peckerley – always the star rugby player – had not thrown himself at the runaway machine, Miss Everett might well have been granted a low-key version of burial at sea. As it was she only lolled forward once more, a bit like a guy responding to a successful bonfire. Peckerley pushed her smartly down on to her seat, and patted her shoulders. "There there, Miss Everett," he said. "Easy does it!"

Who would have thought that the boy was such an accomplished actor? He and Hatchett, who had joined his pupil in the task of arranging the blanket round Everett's knees, were being far more pleasant to her than they had ever been when she was alive. "I'll wheel her along the deck," said Hatchett breezily. "Give her a bit of air. That'll perk her up." The two marched off towards the prow of the ship.

The boat had slowed now to a regular rhythm, and the shore lights of France were only just visible through the darkness. Once more Norma felt glad that England was an island. If Hitler wanted to reach it, he would have to cross these miles of heaving, unpredictable water. She drew her coat closer to her.

There was now only one girl left looking at the sea. Hatchett, Peckerley and Everett had disappeared. Norma looked round at her party. How could she have acquired an extra pupil?

"Poison," went on Mayhew, "is a woman's weapon. Or, in this case, a girl's weapon, which causes horrible agony!"

Norma looked over towards the rail again. Really, Mr Breeze should never have encouraged her girls to read this Agatha Christie rubbish. It was the sort of thing her fool of a stepmother read. And what was that ghastly play to which the school had been taken? *Black Coffee*. That was it. An improbable series of coincidences and a smattering of pharmacology.

Would the girl by the railing never come over to join them? Was this the mysterious newcomer?

"Anyway," continued Mayhew, her tiny pale blue eyes searching the faces of her audience, "there was another girl that knew the girl which had done this deed. And that gave her power over this girl, who was a wicked, evil-minded and powerful person. A witch, in fact."

As she said this, the girl standing over by the rail, looking out at the dark sea, started to move away towards the prow of the ship. Norma got to her feet. The girl seemed to be moving away rather fast, but she did not want to draw attention to the fact that she was following her. "Carry on with your story, Mayhew," she said, "but try to make it realistic. After you Jacqueline Rissett can tell one."

Who was this girl?

When she got to the prow of the ship there was no sign of anyone. On the port side was a staircase leading down to a lower deck, still in the open air. Norma took it. No one on the lower deck either. She wandered back towards the middle of the boat. The rail here ran right down to the other end of the vessel and, about fifty yards away, she caught sight of a familiar blue hat and a familiar blue mackintosh, disappearing through a pair of doors. This time she ran.

When she got to the doors the blue hat and coat were disappearing down another staircase, crowded with people, that led further down into the bowels of the ship. Norma pushed her way through a group of men in suits, laughing loudly at some incomprehensible joke, and saw her pupil disappear through a pair of double doors into the bar. She followed the girl in and saw immediately that this was a highly unsuitable place for a young girl to be. The place was crowded and smoke-laden, and her quarry seemed to have vanished into the thickening air among faces, reddened with alcohol, that reminded her of puppets' masks, leering and swaying before her as the ship rolled steadily forward through the Channel.

It did not take her long to realize that there was no exit apart from the door by which she had entered, and she was sure the girl had not taken that route. Over by the bar she caught sight of Mr Breeze, who did not see her. He was drinking alone – a glass of something that looked like whisky – and scanning the bar in a highly furtive manner. She wondered, again, exactly what had been going on between the chemistry master and the Spanish mistress.

She decided not to speak to him, and struggled on through the drinkers. The smoke burned her eyes and the voices hurt her ears. To her left, a fat man slapped the man next to him on the shoulder and turned towards her with an empty grin. "Hullo, darling." She ignored him and pushed on forward. It was only when she got to the far end of the bar that she realized the girl seemed to have vanished.

Had she slipped out of the far door when Norma wasn't looking? It was extraordinary, really, that she had managed to join the rest of the group without being noticed. And how, while we were about it, had she managed to find herself a Saltdene School uniform? It was then that she remembered Jacqueline Rissett, who always carried two of everything and had, suddenly and inexplicably, appeared without her second hat. She remembered the way the girl had stared at her on the platform, just as they were about to leave.

It was only then that she saw the small door marked *Ladies*, set in the bulkhead to her left. The mysterious newcomer must have gone in there.

Why would Jacqueline Rissett dress up someone in a blue coat and hat so that they could attach themselves to the party? Norma's first thought was that there must be some sinister motive behind the thing. Her second thought was that it was somehow connected with the murder of Miss Everett.

That, she realized afterwards, was the moment when she became convinced that Miss Everett had been murdered. She had absolutely no logical reason for supposing this might be the case, apart from that odd business about the coffee, and no case whatsoever for connecting the strange addition to their party to the death of the Spanish teacher. But she did. Indeed, long after they had got back to England she continued to connect the two events. Which perhaps explained why, as she opened the door to the ladies', she did so slowly and cautiously, as if the strange figure might turn out not to be a girl at all but some hideous hag, who would leap out at her from one of the cubicles, a wicked knife raised high in one gnarled fist.

"Hullo?" said Norma, looking around carefully. The lavatory was empty. There were two cubicle doors. One was ajar. The other was firmly closed. "Hullo?" she said again, swinging the first door open and finding, to her relief, that the cubicle was empty. There was total silence in the overlit room. With a feeling that this was somehow improper Norma lowered her eyes to the gap between door and deck – wider than in the lavatories found on *terra firma*. She saw a pair of shoes that didn't look like Saltdene shoes, but a length of sock that was undoubtedly uniform issue. "Whoever you are," said Norma, "I must ask you to declare yourself! I must ask you to step out of that cubicle!" There was no answer. Norma went up to the door and tried the handle.

"I am going to count to ten," she continued, "and if you have not come out at the end of that time I am going to the captain of this ship and I am going to report you for . . ." For what? Impersonating a schoolgirl? Stealing a uniform? ". . . for attaching yourself to a group of girls without asking permission!" went on Norma, feeling that this didn't really sound serious enough to warrant her tone of voice.

"One – two – three – four – five – six . . ." Norma paused. "Are you a friend of Jacqueline's?" she said, eventually. "Is that it? Is this some little joke the two of you have cooked up?" If she was a friend of Jacqueline's the girl on the other side of the door chose not to reveal the fact. Then the door opened slowly.

In front of her was someone she had never seen before in her life: a pale girl of about fifteen, with strong features, full red lips, shining black hair and huge, intelligent eyes. It was, Norma thought, one of the most impressive faces she had ever seen. Not exactly beautiful, the nose and the chin were too prominent for that, but the high forehead, the almost masculine confidence of the features made her think that the owner of this face was a person of extraordinary power. There was something unusually adult about it, too, but behind the maturity of the expression lay haunting traces of a childhood lacking the privileges that should be accorded to the young. Those big eyes were fixed on Norma's face and Norma saw in them a terrible fear.

"Please," said the stranger, in a curious, precise, foreign voice, "you must help me. You must help me, please. You must help me get to England. It is most important that I get to England."

Dennis Hatchett's Diary

4 August 1939

8 a.m.

I don't think we would have managed to smuggle a fifteen-year-old girl through Customs if we hadn't, at the same time, declared the corpse of a forty-year-old lady teacher. I have always been a great believer in giving the Men of the Excise a little sop to distract them – to make a great show of the extra bottle of wine while all the time priceless carpets and Chinese opium rest snugly in the concealed compartment of one's briefcase.

And Everett, a woman I never liked when she was alive, in death played her role of conjuror's stooge to perfection. It was I, however, Hatchett of the School Play (my Malvolio is still spoken of in hushed whispers in Croydon), Hatchett of the Marlowe Society (where I gave the fullest and most intense reading ever of the Second Gravedigger in *Hamlet*), Hatchett the Ham, who had the brilliant idea of acting out the discovery that the old trout had popped her clogs, under the watching eyes of the homebound crowd. As we were wheeling her into the shed, muffled up like some granny on a winter stroll through the park, I stopped suddenly, ran round in front of the chair and, with a low cry, went into a performance of the kind usually given by a Shakespearian character who has just spotted that there is a large and hostile army in the vicinity. "Hi ho!" "Do mine eyes deceive me?" or "Can such things be?" might not have been what I actually said but they give you some idea of the tone.

By the time the men in uniform had gathered round me I was fully primed. I gave them my opening line, "I think Miss Everett may be dead!", with such intense seriousness of purpose that the local *Volkspolizei* positively reeled. I think if I had added that we had a large consignment of illegal Jews destined for the Croydon area they would not have batted an eyelid. As it was, I had the pleasure of watching Norma sweep off our poor little blighter into the boat train along with all her other charges.

I suppose she is a Jew.

We have no way of knowing. She could, for all I know, be a German spy. A branch of the Youth Division of the German Secret Service, sent to glean a few nuggets of information about the English secondary-school system. If this were to be the case I am sure that the Führer would be convinced that England is about to fall. One glimpse of Breeze's teaching methods, for example, or his habit of ogling the Saltdene fifth and sixth forms would prove that we have no moral fibre whatsoever.

What an absolutely loathsome bunch the Nazis are! I know this is not a very controversial thing to say but I feel the need to set it down. If only because Hitler has so many supporters in the staff-room of Saltdene School for Girls, Croydon. What is it about single, middle-aged lady teachers that makes them such suckers for the *Übermensch*, the Will to Power and the Eradication of World Jewry?

She is a Jew, though, is our Rachel. She is one of those people I had only read about before, forced to wear a yellow star stitched to their clothes. And I believe the few fragments of her story she has chosen to reveal to us. I don't know why I believe them. I just do.

"Mr Hatchett," Norma said to me, using, as she always does, my full name when there are pupils in the vicinity (we were being closely observed by Mesdemoiselles Hughes, Rissett, Mayhew, Wreays and Frosser), "may I have a word?"

And I knew something serious was up.

We were in mid-Channel when that happened. The two of us wandered down the moonlit deck towards what I always think of as the poop although it is probably known as the stern or the gunwales or, for all I know, the bilges. We were being watched by schoolgirl eyes for any traces of sexual abandon and, as we disappeared behind a lifeboat, there was audible giggling.

There, cowering like some eighteenth-century stowaway, was a striking-looking girl with ringlets of black hair, large blue eyes and the general air of a fawn who has wandered into the path of the local hunt. She was in Saltdene School uniform, although I could not remember ever having seen her before.

"This," said Norma, in a violent whisper, "is Rachel."

"Hullo, Rachel," I said, polite to the last.

"Rachel," said Norma, "is originally from Vienna but has been living in Berlin. She is Jewish."

I tried to look as if it was normally the case in England to give racial or religious affiliations when making introductions. "I am Hatchett," I said. "I am a lapsed member of the Church of England."

"Her father," said Norma, in that pained way she affects when I am being humorous, "is in a camp. So is her mother. She has got to get to England. If she stays in Germany she will be imprisoned. She has no papers. But there is someone in England who will help her. Although she won't say who it is."

I have always admired Norma's ability to process information. But I thought this was one of her best efforts yet – comparable to her summary of Bowes and Lyle on the Uses of the Subjunctive. I took Norma aside and asked her how a girl from Berlin happened to be in Saltdene School uniform.

"She approached Jacqueline Rissett on the Champs-Élysées! This morning," said Norma, with what sounded like maternal pride, "and Jacqueline lent her her spare uniform. She told the other girls that she was my niece. When they asked why she had a German accent she told them Rachel had been brought up by Swiss nuns in Calcutta."

I stepped back a pace. Norma talks about her pupils all the time – as most teachers do – and I had got the impression that Jacqueline Rissett was a dreamy, impractical girl. It appears I had underestimated her. Her talent for improvisation alone ought to secure her a university place.

"I do have a niece in Calcutta, as it happens," said Norma, "and I have mentioned her to some of the girls. But she has never had anything to do with nuns. When I last saw her she had blonde hair. But that was twelve years ago. She was three."

57

This conversation was becoming increasingly surreal. Remember, at the other end of the ship, my French-scholarship hope was standing guard over a deceased colleague. I peered round the end of the lifeboat at our party and Norma tapped me on the shoulder, imperiously. "What are we going to do with her?"

She was very agitated. Norma's apparent calm has always concealed a quite febrile spirit. Her sudden gusts of emotion – very often to do with some wrong, real or imagined, practised on others – are one of the things I love most about her. Or, rather, one of the things I like most about her. If I start using the word "love" then we three are all finished.

Of course, I did use it on the station platform. And I could see that she thought, for one brief moment, which frightened both of us into orderly retreat, that I meant it. Maybe for one brief moment I did mean it. No matter that I was slightly drunk. Love, as all the poets keep reminding us, nearly always surprises those whom it decides to grip. And love that comes out of friendship, the delicate blend of compromise, self-interest and shared enthusiasm that seems to offer some shelter from the violence that sexual encounters engender, could be the most frightening and surprising of all.

There is too much at risk for me to go falling in love with Norma. It would create the most ghastly problems with Lycett. And she is far too bossy for someone like me. I find myself thinking about her and Lycett, sometimes, and wondering what he feels about her. It's not something he and I have ever really discussed. But recently, when she talks to him, I have noticed that she looks straight into his eyes, whereas with me she still looks over my left shoulder, as if to emphasize the fact that she is slightly taller than I am. At the last Old Boys' Match, when Lycett was kicked in the groin by an ex-pupil, Norma uttered a low cry and leaped from her seat.

Has she always carried on like that? Is their relationship changing? Was that, perhaps, why I behaved so disgracefully at the Gare du Nord?

Now, of course, Norma and I are accomplices.

"You have no papers? You have no sponsors?" I said to the girl in German.

She shrugged with a weariness I have often seen on the faces of refugees in newsreels. She looked as if she had lost that most precious gift given to the young – the ability to be constantly surprised by life. "There wasn't time for papers," she said. "Anyway, I don't think my papers do me much good in Europe just now."

"Were people after you?" I said. "Were the police after you?"

She didn't answer that. I think she had decided we weren't going to help her. She sat, disconsolately, on a coil of rope while Norma and I moved a little bit away from her.

"We don't really know anything about her . . ." I said.

"No," said Norma.

"She could be anybody."

"Yes," said Norma.

"You know I'm a Jew!" said the girl.

"Do I?" I said, in English.

"Yes," said the girl.

"Maybe I do," I said. Then I went over to her and put my hand on her shoulder. "Look," I said, "we won't let them turn you back. England is a civilized country. If we can find this person who is going to help you then . . ." I stopped. I simply couldn't bear the steady focus of her eyes upon me. That ageless look of suffering.

"Please don't make me any promises," she said. "The only person to have kept his promises to the Jews is Hitler."

I looked at Norma. Norma looked at me.

"We smuggle her in," I said. "You'd better work on Rissett. I think this cover story is going to need a little bit of work."

In fact la Rissett seems to have done an absolutely first-class job, right down to explaining why Norma had so pointedly ignored her "niece" until half-way across the Channel (something about fear of favouritism, I seem to remember). The girl should be in MI5. Somehow or other, anyway, we have done it and Rachel is now installed in Norma's flat. The only other person in the know is the man I must stop referring to as Loosebottom, and, as Norma's brother is somewhere up-country and out of contact in India, there are moments when I think we shall actually get away with this crazy scheme of ours.

I now have to write an article for the school magazine about our trip. "The fifth form had a thoroughly enjoyable trip to Paris, in spite of the mysterious death of Miss Everett (see page twenty for obituary) and the arrival of an illegal immigrant from Berlin who is now living in Albion House with Miss Lewis and posing as her niece!"

It's weird Norma living in Alec's childhood home. I don't like it somehow. I know it makes him nervous – although I suspect I am one of the very few people in the world who knows why it makes him so nervous.

21 August 1939

11.30 a.m.

War looking increasingly likely. Uncle Joe signed a non-aggression pact with Hitler today, thereby knocking on the head any slight vestiges of enthusiasm for the Communist Party in the breast of D. Hatchett. The man down the lane has started digging an enormous hole in his back garden. I think I heard someone say he is building an Anderson shelter. All anyone talks about is guarantees to Poland. I am not quite sure what we will guarantee them. That we will be jolly cross with Herr Hitler if his boys in grey mince into another European capital. That should scare the shit out of him.

The average English Tommy has the air of one of Peter Pan's Lost Boys. And their officers – even Lieutenant Lycett, it has to be said – have the air of men more concerned with *placement* than plans of attack.

Off now to Norma's for another council of war about Rachel. Mother, who is in the other room, has asked me why I want to go out. An unanswerable question. "To get away from you, Mother!" Not precisely. But she and I are as distant now as we were when I grew up in that lonely, fatherless house. I think I was always a little in awe of her misery. Even now, when she has acquired the complexion of a walnut and the posture of a witch in full cauldron crouch, I remain slightly frightened of her. "If he hadn't gone," she used to say of the Reverend Arthur Hatchett, "I expect I might have done." I never felt, when she said this, that she was boasting of her ability to live without my father. I thought she was boasting about her ability to do without ME. The first lesson of my life – a useful one – was that I was utterly and completely dispensable.

2.30 p.m.
"Well, then!" I said, brightly, as I put my head round the door. "I am off!"

Mother broke wind in a spectacular fashion. It was such a loud noise that I really thought there must be some conversational intent to it. At the very least, I felt, I was supposed to make some acknowledgement that it had happened. Perhaps even a compliment of some kind. It must have lasted about forty-five seconds, and had the percussive qualities of a motorcycle engine or a small machine-gun.

She does this all the time. I don't mind the noise. What I do mind is that neither of us is equipped to discuss it. I don't mean by this that I want either of us to engage in an intense conversation about the issue; but an occasional chuckle about it might be a start. Or even a few well-chosen words of criticism from me. Or apology, even, from her. What we get, as in so many other important areas of human experience, is silence between us.

"Where to?" she said.

"To Norma's," I replied.

"Oh . . ." said Mother, very, very cautiously, as if some great catastrophe that she had dreaded for a long time and been unable to prevent was now actually going to come about ". . . oh . . . Norma. The girl with that funny black hair. Mr Lewis's daughter. You're still friendly with her, are you?"

I didn't rise to this. I brought Norma home once. Not on her own, of course. With Lycett. She was always very comfortable with Lycett. She thought that, unlike Farmer, whose father kept a pub, he was a Nice Boy. It was 1931 and I had just heard I had got a scholarship to Cambridge – although the Nice Boy didn't get one. Mother made us cucumber sandwiches and eyed Norma carefully from the other end of the table. After tea, when we took our bikes out to cycle down into Croydon, she addressed her only remark to her. "That," she said, "looks like a very expensive dress." I never brought Norma home again.

I don't, as it happens, make a habit of visiting Norma on her own but, on the few occasions when I have done so, I certainly didn't tell my mother that that was where I was going. Why did I do it today? A belated attempt to introduce the two of them. I don't think Mother ever really had a conversation with Norma's dad, even though I was his star pupil for many years. Maybe she consciously avoided him. Loosebottom was suspected of leftist leanings during the General Strike and, like a lot of timid people, Mother has amazingly reactionary views.

I don't really like going to Albion House, of course, any more than does Lycett, which may be one reason why the three of us always seem to meet on neutral territory. After they moved out, not long after Lucius was sent away, the place was broken up into flats and the garden, once so beautifully cared for, is now overgrown, and vaguely sinister. That was where I found Rachel and Norma, sitting out in what used to be the vegetable garden and is now a tangle of bushes and long grass, in the middle of which is a sundial and a broken garden seat. Rachel was reading from a phrasebook that looked as if it dated from before the last war. "'How is your father?'" she was saying, as I crossed the remains of the lawn towards them. "'Is he indisposed?'"

"'He is well'," replied Norma, peering over her shoulder, "'although he has had rheumatism.'"

"'Has he jaundice?'" said Rachel. Norma did not seem able to answer this question. Rachel continued, "'Should we call the doctor?'" Norma did not answer this question either. "'I think,'" went on Rachel, "'he has a yellow complexion. I think we must take his temperature.'" Norma did not comment on this. There was quite a long pause and then Rachel said, "'He has a temperature of ninety-five. He has a temperature of a hundred and two. He has a temperature of a hundred and five. He is delirious. He has lost consciousness. I am alarmed. Please call a doctor. The doctor is not available.'"

She looked up at Norma. "You think this is bad?" said Rachel. "Wait until you get to the railway station!" She turned over the page and, very quickly, read the following: "'Where is the railway station? Is there a possibility you could call a porter? Porter, porter, why do you not answer me? My train leaves in five minutes. Are you being insolent? This is my luggage! Please secure my luggage! That is not my luggage, this is my luggage! Please hurry! This man is bothering me! Where may I find a policeman?'"

"It was my father's," said Norma, slightly sheepishly. "Actually, her English is frightfully good. I have been giving her lessons on my brother and his wife. Just in case anyone should ask."

"Daddy," said Rachel, "obtained a first-class degree in history at the University of Oxford. I was taken to India at a very young age. It is very hot." She smiled, showing a curiously large gap in her front teeth. "I don't think," she said, "that Miss Lewis's brother will be here to question me. I think it will be war." Then she stopped smiling and her eyes crept back to her book. Thinking about her parents, I suppose. Poor kid.

I jerked my head at Norma and we moved a little way away, looking down the garden towards those grim woods where Alec and I used to play all those years ago. When we were at a safe distance I looked back at Rachel. She was wearing an old grey cardigan of Norma's and a dress I thought I remembered her wearing the year she went up to Manchester. After only a few weeks, she was already starting to look English. "Has she said any more about herself?" I said.

"Not much," said Norma. "Her father seems to have been some kind of scientist. And involved in politics of some kind. The friend she has over here – a friend of her father's – is also some kind of scientist. But she seems nervous of contacting him. She won't tell me who he is."

"Maybe he has no papers," I said, "and if he's a German citizen and it's war . . . What do we do with her?"

"We send her to school, I suppose," said Norma. "We can't hide her under the floorboards." She straightened her shoulders and went into her Victorian-heroine impression. "We shall have to take her into society, Hatchett," she went on. "I will ask Miss Leach if she can come to Saltdene. I think she will fit in fine."

Staring straight ahead of her, in a strongly flavoured Viennese accent, Rachel said, "'How much is this variety of cheese? This is too much for a cheese. Bring me the other type of cheese. Why have you given me Roquefort? I detest Roquefort. I demand to see the manager. Show me more examples of your produce. Please do not be impertinent.'"

"Well," I said, "I suppose we might get away with it. But I wish you wouldn't keep calling me Hatchett. It makes me feel I am still at school."

"You are! You'll always be at school, Hatchett!" said Norma, with the sweetest of smiles. And she leaned over and gave me a peck on the cheek. It was, I have to say, a little more than a peck. It was a kind of quasi-nibble. And she stayed in the general area of my nose long enough for me to get a very satisfying whiff of her – lily-of-the-valley and clean linen.

"Have you seen Alec?" I said, as casually as I could manage.

She gave me a look, as if to say, "Why don't you ask him?" and then said, "He's always on parade. Or doing Army things any-way. If the Territorials get called up I suppose we won't see him for ages. I went down to the nets to watch him play cricket the other day. I took Rachel. I suppose she is going to have to learn about cricket."

"Cricket," said Rachel, "is a very interesting game. England are 321 for four." She grinned. "Europe is going up in flames and that is what is in the headlines. England are 321 for four. It is a very interesting game with very complicated rules and metaphorical implications."

"Did you read that in that book?" I said, somewhat dazzled by this verbal display.

"No, no!" said Rachel. "This book does not refer to cricket. It assumes, I suspect, that foreigners will fail to understand it. There is some force in this argument."

I smiled. "How did you like Mr Lycett?" I said.

"I think he is very good," said Rachel. "He has a hard ball, which he has thrown at a boy who holds a rectangular piece of wood, which is called the bat. This boy wears leg armour. He is called, I think, Peckerley. He was on the boat. But I do not understand why Mr Lycett has thrown the ball in the way he has done, waving his arms like so. It is very amusing."

"He is trying to hit the stumps!" I said.

"What are the stumps?" said Rachel. "And why does he want to hit them?"

"Because," I said, "then Peckerley will be out."

"Why?" said Rachel.

She still has a lot to learn about England.

We had tea after that and talked of other things. In the middle of tea, Jennifer Doran, the domestic-science mistress, arrived. She has red hair and is, I suspect, pert. Otherwise there is nothing remarkable about her. She and Norma talked, with some enthusiasm, about varieties of sponge cake. In so far as she was aware of Rachel at all, she seemed to accept that this raven-haired creature with a nose prominent enough for *Die Stürmer* was Norma's brother's child. The power of propaganda! I stood Doran for as long as I could, but when she announced that "Britain should be neutral – like Switzerland!" and asked me to tell her where exactly Czechoslovakia was, I decided it was time to go.

Norma said she would walk me to the door. Before this Rachel business, I don't think she would have been quite so assiduous. On the rare occasions when I visited her at Albion House I was allowed to drift in and out like a member of the family. I must say that I enjoy this new and unusual sense of a conspiracy between us. As I was leaving I looked across at Rachel and said, "If you're writing to your father, do remember me to him!" I saw her eyes express, briefly, surprise, then panic, then unhappiness and finally well-simulated good manners.

"I will!" she said – or, rather, "I vill!" And then, obviously worrying whether this was unacceptably German in tone, added, "He has had jaundice! A temperature of one hundred and five! He was, at times, delirious!"

"Oh!" I said, before she could get on to the subject of his

rheumatism. "I had heard something of the kind from Norma. But I understand the doctors say he will be fine."

"Oh, yes," said Rachel calmly. "Soon he will be eating Roquefort. His favourite cheese."

Unabashed by the nature of this conversation, she flashed a smile at Doran and, as Norma and I moved off back towards the house, I thought I heard the two of them discussing varieties of French cheese.

"We are never going to get away with this," I said.

"Oh, yes, we are!" said Norma.

"Did Alec ask you to watch him and Peckerley play?" I said, as we stepped through into the gloomy hall. "You haven't said anything to him about Rachel, have you?" I hadn't intended to say this. Nor did I want it to have a petulant, jealous ring. But it did.

Norma laughed easily and resumed her bantering tone. "Really, Mr Hatchett," she said, "your mind is dwelling too much on the compliments I have paid to Mr Lycett's legs." Then she turned to me and, taking my right hand between both of hers, addressed me with complete seriousness. "I love both you boys so much," she said, "and I feel terribly guilty we haven't told Alec about Rachel. We always said we would have no secrets from each other."

I couldn't actually remember any of us ever saying this. And to get the three of us to sign up to it would have involved committee discussion as lengthy and hard fought as that practised in the League of Nations. "I fear," I said, "that this is a secret that must be shared with as few people as possible. Four is far too many as it is. Especially when one of them is a fifteen-year-old schoolgirl whose idea of the world seems to have been gathered from the cheaper types of women's romance stories."

"You're such a snob about books," said Norma. "Cheap fiction can be very potent. And extremely worthwhile, provided its morality is satisfactory."

But she has always been attracted to Lycett. Ever since she has known him. Even if this attraction, up to now, has been entirely concealed from both of them it will not always be like that. Things are changing. The world we knew is fading away in front of our eyes. I think –

3 p.m.
Broke off from writing this to take a look at Mother. She is sitting, bolt upright, on the sofa, staring at the wall. I did not let her know I was taking a look – as I had my eye glued to a crack in the door.

3.30 p.m.
Where was I?

Standing by Norma's front door.

"Well," she said, "now you have someone on whom you can practise your German."

"Indeed," I said, "although if events in Europe continue to follow the course they have taken so far we may have to take up residence in a soundproof box in order to have this conversation."

"She is so frightened . . ." said Norma.

"Yes," I said.

It was only when I had stepped out into the brilliant afternoon and we were standing in the lane outside Albion House, looking down at Croydon, silver in the distance, that Norma said, "Oh. By the way. They did an autopsy on Alice Everett. And it appears that she was full of something called hyoscine hydrobromide."

"Oh!" I said. "And what is that when it is at home?"

"You are not recommended to sprinkle it on your breakfast cereal," said Norma. "It's a registered poison."

With which she went back into the house, leaving me to look down at a still unbelievably peaceful slice of the English countryside.

5 p.m.
Just been in to see Mother. This time I made the mistake of talking to her. She has started to talk about my father again. There is, now, no trace of regret about the fact that he walked out on us. Instead, she chooses to dwell on his virtues. "Your father," she said this afternoon, "was a very handsome man." Then she farted, loudly, for about a minute and a half.

PART TWO

4

3 September 1939

When he was thirteen, Alec Lycett had actually got down on his knees, in the presence of other people, and prayed to Jesus. He had talked, with apparent confidence and familiarity, to a completely invisible person. He had said appallingly intimate things, things like "I am afraid I am not a very good person, Lord!" and "Please help me to be better, Lord!" and asked completely unanswerable questions ("What is the meaning of suffering?" etc., etc.) to a deity he had never seen and never, really, if he was honest, thought he had a hope in hell of seeing. He had had the loudest amen in the fourth form and had told his father that when he grew up he wanted to go into the Church.

He hadn't prayed since leaving Cambridge. Unless you counted a brief attempt to trade a future devotion to good works, Gospel transmission and public affirmation of the Christian faith in return for avoiding what looked like a potentially fatal road accident. But he still believed in God. If you had stood Alec Lycett up against a wall, pointed a gun at him and asked him to give a truthful answer to the question of whether there is or is not a Divine Being he would probably have said, without a trace of sheepishness, that he thought there was Someone up there. Who He was or what He was doing or why He (or indeed he) was doing it were a different matter, but he (as opposed to He) would have said, ". . . It stands to reason . . ." although secretly he knew that reason didn't come into it ". . . it stands to reason that there is someone . . ."

Well, thought Alec, as he pulled his uniform out of the cupboard, if there is a Someone, He is not talking to me. And I am not talking to Him.

The trouble with God, of course, was that Alec had been brought up to believe that He was on his side. God had been good to the Lycett family. He had given them good health, a steady income and a large house in what was, without argument, the centre of the civilized world, i.e. Croydon. And for years, Alec suspected, the Lycetts had prayed to God very much as one might address a favourite head waiter. But, since meeting Hatchett, he had started to think that it was somehow wrong to lounge up to God and ask him for things. Especially for things you wanted, like beer or women or extra runs.

He had met Hatchett when they were both seven, for God's sake. Hatchett was just part of his life. Like Lucius. He didn't want to think about Lucius. Nor, while we were at it, did he really want to think about Hatchett. This wasn't, for God's sake, anything to do with Hatchett. Was it? This was to do with Hatchett's father – the Reverend Arthur Hatchett, who spent every Sunday morning telling you you were damned to hell and then did what he did, the lecherous bastard, thus proving that he was damned to hell as well, the hypocrite.

Hatchett Junior had complicated Alec's dialogue with the Almighty, though. So in a way it was to do with him.

The way he talked to Him now (and it wasn't really Him to whom Alec talked but him – it was just like a dialogue with an old and not quite trusted friend) was very matter-of-fact. As Alec laid out his uniform on the bed and started to dress for church, his voice, booming out in the narrow bedroom, was solid, reasonable – the kind of voice his father had used when explaining things to him and to Lucius.

"Look, Alec," Alec said to himself. "Look! Norma is an attractive girl. All that has happened is that you have started to notice that fact!"

He was, he realized, as he laid out the jacket and the trousers on the narrow bed in the room his father had bought for him (room? it was a whole house! for a chap who was only just twenty-six!) using God's voice to tell him things he (and He) already knew.

"Look, Alec," said Alec, "Norma is an attractive girl. All that has happened is that you have started to notice that fact. For years you went around treating her as if she were a chap. On the evening of the first day the three of you started at your respective schools, you all went out to the pub to get drunk. Even if Norma only drank two halves of bitter she joined in a rousing chorus of the Kirkby School song as you all rolled home. She has always been an honorary man. And now, for some reason, it is very, very hard to think of her in that way. No one is to blame for this. Probably nothing will come of it. But at some stage, my friend, you are going to have to DECIDE WHAT TO DO ABOUT IT!"

This, of course, was a lot harder than it sounded.

Alec pulled the trousers off the bed and started to struggle into them. They were dark blue with a thin red line down each side and, even for a uniform, they were, Alec thought, pretty classy stuff. The 4th Croydon Light Infantry were not a particularly distinguished regiment. In the Boer War they had made a famous three-hundred-mile forced march – in the wrong direction. In the Great War they had had the tidiest and best cared-for section of trench in the whole of the front line – and, perhaps for this very reason, they seemed very reluctant to leave it. But their uniform was generally considered fantastic. Their ceremonial outfit, into which Alec was climbing now, was a figure-hugging number that gave them the look of assistant bullfighters. The jacket was mainly in white, with epaulettes the size of soup plates, although it was worn only in private by those above the rank of colonel. And to show that they meant business, they had no fewer than three combat uniforms, desert khaki, jungle green and tundra grey.

The ceremonial, however, was perfect for church. And it gave his rear end a dramatic sweep that Norma would not be able to ignore. As Alec got into the jacket – a lot of gold braid and a waist high enough to make you want to prance around snapping your fingers and shouting, "Olé!" – he found himself wondering, yet again, whether he was misinterpreting the way she was looking at him. It was very hard to tell with women. There had been a girl at Cambridge who he was sure was looking at him like that. It turned out she had gastroenteritis. But Norma, he was fairly sure, was showing welcoming signs: she was so keen to preserve eye-contact with him, these days, that only the other week she had nearly walked into a lamp-post while trying to do so. And she –

He stopped to get the full effect of himself in the mirror. Not bad. Not at all bad. He was generally reckoned to be a good-looking chap. He wasn't, of course, as bright as old Hatchett, but neither was he stupid. In fact, "not stupid" was the sort of thing people said about Alec Lycett, thereby suggesting he had the kind of ratio of decency to low cunning in his character that was completely acceptable in middle-class society. A man who could play rugby but hadn't got into Cambridge just because he could. A man who could do a sharp deal in, say, the shipping business and who had gone into teaching not out of some vague ideal about nurturing young minds but because the holidays were good and you got to play all the sport you wanted. A man who was almost as sharp as his father.

But in fact, thought Alec, as he fiddled with the crowning glory of his uniform, known even in the Territorial branch of the regiment as a "half-beret", he didn't really have the cynical edge that had helped Lycett Senior hang on to the family fortune. If he wore, sometimes, an air of muffled rage, a hangdog look almost, that said THIS MAN COULD BE DANGEROUS, it was probably not a frustrated urge to do the other chap down but a deep-seated frustration that he wasn't the kind of person who could do that. Alec Lycett was stuck with the fact that, for most of the time anyway, he was really quite a good person. And though he knew that, really, he was an impostor in the field of virtue, he was hopelessly stuck with the role of decent chap.

He wasn't good. He knew that. But he was committed to pretending to be so. And that seemed to involve just as many responsibilities.

If he had really been able to live up to the bad side of his nature, he thought, as he tilted the beret slightly forward over one eye, he might have ended up coming first rather than second. Alec Lycett had been captain of the second eleven and second in almost every subject apart from mathematics, in which he had been third. He had been assistant head of school, a vice-prefect, a regular runner-up in the long jump, the hurdles and the hundred-yard sprint and – this was, in a way, the cruellest thing of all – he was known as one of the best losers in the Croydon area. Alec Lycett lost in the English manner, with head held high, right hand extended and a positive gleam of pleasure in his eye. You would have thought, as he stepped up to the net and clapped Victor Smith on the back (the odious, the conceited, the vulgar, the brainless Victor Smith), that he was genuinely pleased that the Lycett service game had gone to pieces. When he just missed a scholarship and Hatchett got one, Alec didn't mutter some ill-judged half-compliment and stare at the floor, he threw himself at his friend with the enthusiasm of a man who has just been told by the woman he loves that she is about to have his baby.

But in spite of all this, Alec knew himself, deep down, to be a bad person. Oh, he knew that all right. Something in him, even as he was being decent, was full of an inexpressible hatred that was largely directed at himself. He shuddered now as he recalled one of Hatchett's father's sermons on this very subject – not living up to the ideals you had set yourself, being less than you should be – and said aloud to his reflection in the mirror, "Second rate, Alec! Second rate!"

This coming-in-second thing was at the heart of his problem with Norma. A foreigner, or a Jew, for example (and there were many fine Jews, there was quite a lot of the Jew, he often thought, about Hatchett), would have had no scruples whatsoever about simply snaffling the girl. Hatchett, if he had had half a chance, would have snaffled her the way he snaffled tea-cakes from the table or dug into his roast beef without waiting for anyone else's to arrive. Lycett's auntie had once referred to Hatchett as "that boy with the hard eyes and the terrible table manners". When it came to Norma, when it finally got round to one of them making a play for her, Alec suspected that his oldest friend would have no qualms whatsoever about coming first.

Did Hatchett want Norma, though?

It was pretty hard to work out what old Hatchett wanted. He

did give out signals, but unless, like Alec, you were a bit of a Hatchett expert, decoding them was no easy matter. If he rubbed his stomach in a certain way, for example, it was pretty likely that he fancied going out for a walk. Pulling his right earlobe meant he was about to start a political argument. When he fancied girls he usually made a point of looking in the opposite direction whenever they were around, and of disagreeing with everything they said.

Norma, however, wasn't just any girl. She was Norma. She was Loosebottom's daughter, for God's sake. And Hatchett and she had not just one but twenty different ways of behaving to each other. With Alec, she was more or less like any girl with any boy, but she and Hatchett seemed to be in some twenty or thirty plays of their own devising, all running concurrently. Sometimes he would make her half-bows, open doors for her and call her "my dear Miss Lewis", as if they were both in some eighteenth-century novel. At other times they were in some Victorian melodrama, and Hatchett, sweeping his academic gown about him, would croak things like "Your father's fortune will accrue to me!" before vanishing off down some school corridor.

For years Alec had assumed this was harmless fun. The sort of thing that people in the Dramatic Society did all the time. But, just lately, he had begun to wonder whether some of it was no more than a ruse on Hatchett's part. The satirical impression of a sentimental friendship, for example, might be a way of softening her up for a real *grande passion*. If this was about anything else, of course, all Alec would have had to do was ask him. There was almost no subject under the sun about which the two friends did not share opinions. Alec knew exactly what his pal thought of Debussy, the Communist Party, even the merits of the available Crotchett Green women. They both knew, for example, that Jennifer Doran was the sort of girl you would like to . . . well . . . get close to in the . . . er . . . physical sense. But they also both knew that neither of them wanted to get too close to the domestic-science mistress.

But about Norma they never talked. Any more, thought Alec, as he went to the window to see if his father's car had arrived, than they talked about Lucius. He shook himself like a dog coming out of water and shivered slightly. He didn't want to think about Lucius. And he shouldn't really be thinking about Norma like this. Norma was just there, like the A23 or the Conservative Party. She was their missing sister, their other third, their partner in innocence. Would things between the three of them ever change? Who could know? They were all in their mid-twenties, when no one knows anything about the future apart from what they do not want it to be.

It would be like incest, anyway, thought Alec, as he looked into the brilliant sunshine of the street for signs of his father's Rolls-Royce. Neither of them could ever be interested in Norma like that.

Except he was. He had to face that fact. Som thing had given him the idea.

It might, of course, have been her. Hatchett took the view that women decided everything about relationships and there was simply nothing you could do about it except wait until they picked you out of the line. This was probably why he had never been seriously involved with anyone, unless you counted that girl with the spectacles from Girton. But how on earth would Norma let him know she was interested in him? "A look in the eyes", according to Hatchett (one of the greatest theoretical experts on women in the south-east of England), was all it took. But what kind of look? Did touching you on the arm count? She did a lot of that. But, then, she had been doing that fairly regularly since 1931.

There was a blast on the horn from outside.

Alec's father was a master of the one emphatic gesture followed by the carefully prepared silence. When summoned to his study (a grim room on the first floor of Albion House, where he never did any studying) all it would take was a "Well?" from Alec Senior for Alec Junior to feel completely in his power. Being loved by his father, he decided, was part of this business of coming second. His father was in his path, immovable, still, after twenty-six years, the most powerful thing in his world. If he hadn't seen, with his own eyes, all those years ago in the woods behind Albion House, his father crying like a baby, his face distorted, ugly with tears, Alec would never have believed it possible.

He shivered just thinking about that business in the woods. He gave himself a final once-over in the mirror and went out on to the landing. Outside, there was another imperious note on the horn from the Rolls.

Perhaps, here was a frightening thought, Alec's interest in Norma was a response to the fact that, since coming back from the French trip, she and Hatchett had quite definitely changed. Death, of course, brought you closer together. And murder – as he and Hatchett knew all too well from the Lucius business – had a way of binding you secretly, irrevocably to anyone who shared your knowledge of the guilty truth of the affair. Well, some of your knowledge anyway. There was no proof, of course, that Everett had been murdered, but quite a lot of people in the staffroom were already assuming that that was what had happened.

There was also the question of Norma's niece.

Alec was in the front garden now, smelling the roses and the summer air, and waiting for the third blast from his father's car. It came, as it always did, just when he was expecting it. He didn't rush out into the road but dawdled by the hedge, thinking about Norma's niece. Her name, for a start. You could call your child anything you liked, although most people didn't, but he simply could not believe that Norma's brother, even though he had never actually met the chap, would call a child of his Rachel. Had he married one of the Tribe of Israel? Surely Norma would have said something about it if he had. Because the people Alec knew simply didn't marry Jews. He himself had absolutely nothing against Jews – apart of course from the handwringing, the moneygrubbing, the failure to make proper eye-contact, the bad losing, the inability to mix, the low quality of sportsmanship and the excessively loud demonstrations of laughter, tears, etc. – but he couldn't imagine one of them becoming part of his family. And if that had happened to Norma he was fairly sure she would have mentioned it.

Or would she?

One of the confusing things about what he was starting to feel for Norma was that he had suddenly understood that he had no idea, really, what she would choose to mention or not to mention to him. She was, he had started to perceive, part of that sophisticated cosmopolitan world to which he had never quite belonged. Hatchett, somehow or other, had joined it. He had nipped out for a few minutes, somewhere in the middle of his second year at Cambridge, and come back sophisticated. One minute he had not had a moustache. The next minute there it was. He had shaved it off at the end of the third year and allowed it to grow again a year after he had graduated.

Norma's niece was a bit like that. There was an element of conjuror's apparition about the girl; and the way that Hatchett and Norma looked at her seemed to emphasize the fact that she was a secret that only the two of them shared.

Alec went out slowly into the street and looked along it to where his father's open-topped car was parked. His mother was sitting next to his father, neither of them speaking, staring ahead the way they did. It was probably, thought Alec, quite good fun to be Jewish. It certainly couldn't be worse than being a Lycett.

"Well!" said Lycett Senior, as Lycett Junior drew level with him. "Well well well! Alec, as I live and breathe!"

"Alec also!" said Alec, indicating his father with a gesture that was, he realized, even as he made it, cribbed from Hatchett.

Lycett Senior was highly amused at this unusual demonstration of wit from Lycett Junior. "Alec also!" he said, chuckling in the general direction of his unresponsive wife. "I like that! Alec also!"

Why had he given them the same name? Was it simply to confuse things? If that was the idea it had succeeded superbly. Because, to the horror of all who knew them, the Lycetts had more or less done away with the conventional forms of family address – at least since Alec was about eight years old. "We are equals!" Alec's father had said to him, when he still was Alec's daddy, at around the time Lucius was sent away. "The fact that I am your father should not matter a row of beans. What does it matter that I knew you when you were unable to speak, stand, dress yourself or control your bowel movements? The fact that I knew you when you were twenty-one inches long should make no difference whatsoever to our relations as adults. Between us it should be Alec and Alec. We're the same. We're equals."

Breakfast was particularly difficult.

"Pass the toast, Alec. No, not you, Alec, Alec!"

"Alec!" Two heads turn in the direction of Mrs Lycett, who looks mournfully away, defeated as usual by her family.

"Which Alec do you want?"

"I can't remember now."

Oh, yes, they were the same. They were one and the bloody same, all right. So when Mrs Lycett screamed up the stairs that she hated Alec and everything he stood for, that to her Alec was a weak and pathetic creature and she only stayed with him because of the house and the money, that Alec was a coward who had not fought for his country like some other people, including poor little Dennis's father – then she was talking about him. He was only eight years old but he had never fought for his country. He would never have held his tongue while the fox gnawed away at his vitals like in the story Loosebottom told them. He would have screamed and screamed and screamed just the way his father had in the woods because he, Alec Junior, was a great big coward and his mother did not love him, no, not one little bit.

"Look at him, Mrs Lycett!" said Alec Senior, who never stopped trying to interest his wife in his remarks. "Look at our boy! Doesn't he look . . . dangerous?"

Alec's mother's face, as usual, betrayed nothing. As far as she was concerned, her expression seemed to say, both Alecs could go and jump in the nearest lake whenever they felt the urge. And, perhaps responding to this signal from his almost always silent, unreachable mother, Alec himself was not able to respond to the adoring compliment. He could not, anyway, think of anyone anywhere in the world who was less dangerous. He was punctual, reasonably God-fearing, conventional, patriotic and almost always polite. He never got drunk, disagreed with people older than himself in public, and the worst word he had ever said in front of his mother and father was "belly button". If Alec Senior thought he was going to turn his son into a hard man by saying that he was, he had another think coming. Because he knew, thought Alec, he knew what a bloody little creep his son was. He had turned him into one, for God's sake.

"I imagine Norma will be there, will she?" said Alec Senior, as Alec Junior climbed into the car.

Alec didn't know how to respond to this. He knew his father didn't like Norma. He didn't like her father and he didn't like her. But he pretended to like her. Because he had some stupid idea that she would be a "conquest" of Alec's. "She will be swooning at the sight of you, dear boy," his father was saying.

Alec wanted to say, "She won't. And if you want to know the truth, Father, I am a lot more scared of the average English girl than the average German soldier. That poor drowned owl of a schoolfriend of mine – Dennis Hatchett, the Reverend Arthur Hatchett's son, that boy you always patronized so energetically – has more of a chance with her than I will ever have."

But he didn't say that. It might not, of course, be true. Like a dutiful Englishman, Alec got into the Rolls with his parents and allowed himself to be driven to church. It wasn't so bad. By the end of the day they would be at war and none of this would ever matter. Not the girl, not his father, not the uniform. Not any of his sad history. Very soon there would be no more chocolate soldiers. The real thing was starting now. Alec snapped his fingers as he stared out at the green fields that sloped up away from the aerodrome towards the Downs beyond. The real thing. Now. Now. Now.

"I thought," said the Reverend "Mary" Anstruther, the vicar of St Mary and All Angels, Crotchett Green, "that I would take twenty minutes out of morning service today."

Hatchett looked up at the façade of what had once been his father's church. Mary, a tall thin man in his mid-fifties with a large, bulbous nose usually decorated with a dewdrop, had taken up the position shortly after the Reverend Arthur Hatchett disappeared and, for about five years after Hatchett's father was presumed dead, he made a point of asking after him with every appearance of sincerity. The church was not an impressive building. It had a Victorian spire, an Elizabethan rood screen and a medieval back wall, but even though bits of it were of proven antiquity, *le tout ensemble* resembled a Victorian public lavatory.

There were already quite a few people out on the grass in front of the church. Over by one of the gravestones was Mr Breeze, accompanied, as he always was on these occasions, by Mrs Breeze the Chemistry Master's Wife, Master Breeze the Chemistry Master's Son and Miss Breeze the Chemistry Master's Daughter. In spite of the fact that all of them, apart from Mr Breeze, were holding each other's hands, they did not look a Happy Family.

Hatchett tried to move away from the vicar. Any moment now Norma, probably with her father and almost certainly with Rachel, would walk down the narrow lane and in through the lych-gate.

Crotchett Green, although it was so close to Croydon, was still an English country village, its two grammar schools dating from the fifteenth and nineteenth centuries respectively and one of its quaint, half-timbered houses earning a place in an architectural guide. Even its wholly timbered pub, the Queen Victoria, dating from 1922, was a place where people still knew each other. Knew each other too damn well, thought Hatchett, as Mary picked his way through the churchyard grass to make up the distance between them. Just because he had known Hatchett's father, the man seemed to think he had the right to treat Hatchett, a convinced agnostic since the age of twelve, as if he was some kind of religious insider.

"Quite a good turnout!" said Mary, with a broad wink at his predecessor's son. "But the Prime Minister is due to talk to the nation at eleven fifteen. They will want to be out by ten forty-five."

Over by the Lycett family tomb – a small marble shed topped with an angel that looked as if it was practising the first position in ballet – "Leafy" Green, the other Spanish mistress, still in full mourning for her friend Everett, was engaged in intense conversation with Jacqueline Rissett's mother. Jacqueline Rissett's father, as usual, was conspicuous by his absence. Jacqueline's eyes, Hatchett noticed, were, like his, constantly drawn to the lane that led to the church. For whom was she waiting?

"The problem really," said Mary, in a man-to-man, we-know-there-is-not-much-to-this-religion-lark fashion, "is knowing what not to cut. It's all pretty dull stuff, is the *Book of Common Prayer*. There isn't much going on in the Church calendar on the fifteenth Sunday after Pentecost. Let's face it, Dennis, all anyone will want to think about today is how far Adolf has got on the road to Warsaw. The Bible is rather less relevant than the old Atlas of Eastern Europe. Think you not?"

He inclined his head even closer to Hatchett's. He smelt strongly of some kind of cologne (or was it alcohol?). His surplice, clean, white and billowing out behind him in the breeze, had, as always, a sort of learner-driver aspect to it. Even after all those years in the job, Mary still did not look as if he expected anyone to believe he was really the vicar. And, while we were at it, did he have to wear quite such a large ring?

"All the psalms," went on Mary cheerily, "can go. I've never much cared for the psalms. The Opening Sentences of Scripture I have cut to the bone. And I had a devil of a job – if you will excuse the expression – in finding a bit of the Bible that seemed . . . well . . . right for today, if you know what I mean."

Jacqueline had seen something. She craned her head forward. Had she seen what she was looking for?

"The shortest quote on offer," said Mary, "is 'Repent ye: for the Kingdom of Heaven is at hand!' Matthew three verse two. But that makes it sound as if the entire body of the Luftwaffe is going to be converging on Croydon in the next half an hour."

"I suppose," said Hatchett, "it may be doing just that."

Mary shot him a swift, nervous glance. "I thought," he went on, "of going for 'Rend your hearts and not your garments!' because I have never run that particular quote up the . . . er . . . flagpole before. But there are liable to be some pretty hysterical women in the congregation this morning. It is important not to encourage them." Here he gave a significant nod in the direction of Leafy Green, Jacqueline Rissett's mother and the headmistress of Saltdene, Helena Bonham Leach, who had just joined them. Hatchett, meanwhile, had seen what he was looking for. There in the distance, coming round the corner of the lane, were Norma, Rachel and Loosebottom, a kindly man in his sixties with a shock of white hair and a profile that suggested a bird of prey contemplating its next meal.

Rachel's first ever ringside seat at the Christian rite, thought Hatchett. So long as she knelt when everybody else did she should be fine. She didn't look like the kind of girl to have religious scruples and, when they had discussed the subject last week (nearly all conversations with her were theoretical rather than personal), she had said, "Just because I am a Jew doesn't mean I believe in God." The one thing Hatchett was sure of as far as she was concerned was that she was one of the most intelligent people he had ever met in his life.

"I had originally had something from Isaiah in place for the first lesson," Mary, one of the least intelligent people Hatchett had ever met, was saying, "but almost all of Isaiah is pretty threatening stuff. In the end I've gone for this amazingly vague bit from Nehemiah. Something about putting guards on the temple. God knows what it means but it does sound remarkably soothing. The guards could be the RAF sort of thing."

Jacqueline Rissett had seen what she was looking for. Coming from the same direction as Norma, Rachel and her father were the Hughes family. Mr and Mrs Hughes were, as usual, dressed with the solemn precision of undertakers. And their daughter Mabel, severe black dress, hair scraped back from her pale forehead and a face that was a unique blend of the gaunt and the pudgy, advanced on her local place of worship with the solemnity of a girl stepping out to her own execution. She and Jacqueline were close, Hatchett remembered. And yet the look on Jacqueline's face wasn't exactly schoolgirl ecstasy. It was more like fear.

"The other thing," Mary went on, "is that I really must not mention this business of Miss Everett's death. It is a hot potato. A very hot potato indeed."

"It is," said Hatchett, gravely. "It is also, as far as I can see, a nice kettle of fish."

Mary gave him a sideways look. Mabel and her family had joined

Leafy Green, Jacqueline Rissett, her mother and Miss Leach the headmistress; after a brief chat to Peckerley, and Vera Dummell, the Most Difficult Parent in the Third Form, Norma and her father joined them. Rachel stayed close to the adults. Mabel and Jacqueline whispered together, a little apart from the rest. There was something decidedly conspiratorial about them, thought Hatchett. Every so often they would look over at the Breeze family and start to whisper even more urgently.

"You were there," said Mary, "when she actually passed over."

"I can't say when that was," said Hatchett, feeling, as usual, the urge to get his story straight about the facts of Everett's death. "I just happened to notice she was no longer with us as we came into the Customs shed."

Mary's nose twitched. He looked, Hatchett thought, as if he was prepared to see the funny side of Miss Everett's departure from this life.

"Some people are saying," the vicar whispered, his reedy falsetto vibrating with the thrill of it all, "that it was murder. It is not, therefore, something to which I am going to allude in my sermon. It would not be in good taste."

Mr and Mrs Frosser, Mr and Mrs Wreays and Janet and Elinor, who had their arms round each other and were each, for some reason, carrying a small posy of wild flowers, had arrived and were deep in conversation with Mr and Mrs Hughes. A man Hatchett had never seen before was in company with the Hugheses – a sallow-faced fellow in a blue suit who looked as if they had been keeping him in a box underground for the last few years. Who was he? A relative? A policeman? There had been a rumour that Croydon CID were going to send someone down to the school to interrogate all those who had been on the French trip.

Hatchett tried to imagine some lynx-eyed man in a shabby mackintosh asking him awkward questions about his whereabouts during the last hours of Alice Everett.

Then, last as usual, in a motor-car, in an open-topped, expensive motor-car, came Mr Alec Lycett, Mrs Alec Lycett and Master Alec Lycett, who was got up as if he belonged to a Tyrolean brass band.

He saw Hatchett and grinned. Suddenly, Hatchett was in the school production of *The Tempest*, in which he and Lycett, aged ten, had been cast as nymphs. Hatchett had not been allowed to wear his glasses and had walked into a tree, designed and built by Mr Bowles the woodwork master, at the dress rehearsal. Lycett was jabbing his finger in the direction of Norma's father, who seemed to be deep in conversation with Rachel. "Loosebottom!" Lycett was mouthing. Some jokes – especially very old and very bad ones – never seemed to lose their power over you. With that lightening of the heart he always felt when he saw his oldest friend, Hatchett started away from the vicar and towards the car.

It was then that he saw Alec look at Norma.

Of course, he had been expecting to see that expression. That was why he saw it. But that didn't mean it wasn't there. He had seen Alec look at her thousands and thousands of times over the years and there was much in his friend's face that Hatchett would have expected to see. There was that puppyish desire to please, the slight but acceptable degree of narcissism that you would expect from a chap as handsome as Lycett, and there was that familiar air of wholesome, enthusiastic innocence, suggesting that he and Norma were about to set off on some E. Nesbit adventure or were figures from some character-building school story. But this time there was something else in the look. Hatchett knew what it was although, for the moment, he could not find words to describe it.

It was only afterwards that he realized that Lycett was looking at her as if she was a saint, someone who could absolve him from some terrible sin that was known only to him and God. He expected something from her smile and when it came he gathered it in to himself as if he were afraid someone else would catch hold of it. Oh, my God, thought Hatchett, as the congregation began to file into the church, he's fallen in love with her. Where on earth does that leave me?

Alec nearly always sat with his mother and father in the first pew in the right-hand aisle. This wasn't anything as formal as the "Lycett family pew". In fact, Alec Lycett Senior was often at pains to say, as he moved into it every Sunday, "This is not, repeat not, the Lycett family pew. It is just where we happen to sit." No one else had ever tried to sit there but, then, almost everyone in the village knew how much Alec Lycett Senior had given to the repairs of the roof.

So when Alec, instead of sitting between his mother and father, crossed the aisle, nodded nervously in the direction of the altar and moved into the pew where Norma, her father and Rachel were sitting, Hatchett felt he was right to read a good deal into the gesture. Lycett Senior had an expression of self-congratulatory amusement on his big, weak, handsome face. "Look at my son!" he seemed to be saying. "There's no stopping him!"

Hatchett was almost sure that Alec's father disliked Norma. He disliked any sign of independence in women, which was one of the reasons he had always got on so well with Hatchett's mother. Women, in Lycett Senior's world, were there to be told what to do or to tell servants how to do it. He was always calling them things like "the fair sex" or, occasionally, "the weaker people". Perhaps he thought his son was going to ravish Norma then abandon her like some Victorian squire.

Mr Hughes was whispering something to Mr Frosser. Mrs Wreays was saying something to Mrs Hughes. Hatchett sidled into the Lewis pew, and found, with some dismay, that he was sitting next to Loosebottom. Norma was on the other side of his old Latin master. Rachel was on the other side of Norma. And Alec was on the other side of Rachel. What was she saying? How would the girl cope? He caught Norma looking anxiously at her as well.

"How is the brilliant Hatchett?" said Loosebottom, who still talked of his favourite pupil's way with *Oratio Obliqua*.

"Very well, sir!" said Hatchett, feeling, as he always did when talking to Loosebottom, as if he was wearing short trousers and a peaked cap.

"How is your father?" Alec was saying to Rachel. Hatchett and Norma tensed their shoulders in unison.

"He is well," said Rachel, "but he has had jaundice. Also rheumatism."

"I am sorry to hear that . . ." said Alec, about to turn his attention to Norma, but Rachel continued to do her duty.

"Soon," she said, "he will no longer have a temperature and will be eating his favourite cheese."

"Now, Rachel," said Norma, in a brisk and sensible voice, "they probably sing different hymns in India. So you just follow me."

She looked, thought Hatchett, as if she was afraid the girl was about to start banging her head on the pew in front of her and moaning bits of the Torah. Rachel looked at him and managed to suggest a wink without actually moving her eyes. Norma addressed herself to Alec. Hatchett was almost sure that this was to head off any further overtures in the direction of Rachel. But he found himself, although he didn't want to, wondering whether she had noticed the way Alec had been looking at her.

At the moment he seemed to be staring at the ground and grunting awkwardly, which was how he quite often talked to women. Hatchett had once, when they were at Cambridge, offered to provide him with a list of things women liked to talk about. Once he had written a letter, on Lycett's behalf, to a woman called Alison Bourne with whom (he had said) he was madly in love. The letter began, "My darling Alison, I am burning with love and desire for your body . . ." and got worse. It kept them amused for two weeks but they never sent it.

Hatchett looked at his friend. People, he was thinking, do not change. Alec, he felt sure, was still the sort of boy who folded his trousers carefully before he went to bed. Hatchett dropped his, in a puddle, wherever he happened to be standing, ideally as close as possible to his mattress; then he stepped out of them into the comforting embrace of his blankets.

Why did Alec so want to be good? Why did he always look as if he thought he wasn't? Perhaps he had somehow caught the Puritan disease that had made Hatchett's father preach those fiery sermons Sunday after Sunday. His appetite for virtue became even greater after Lucius was sent away. He told the truth all the time. And, by "telling the truth" he didn't mean what Hatchett meant by the words – that is to say, not lying. What Lycett attempted was the near impossible task of accurate description, even in the most trivial answer. "Why were you late for school?", for example, would be answered with, "I didn't walk fast enough." This answer, as soon as it had been given, would be rejected as slovenly, self-seeking, inaccurate. "What I really mean to say, sir," Alec would add, with an intensity so acute it almost removed all traces of priggishness, "is that I dawdled. I mean, I went deliberately slowly, really, because I was worried about the maths I hadn't done." Then, in case his superiors might lose interest or even – perish the thought – forgive him, "I mean, really, sir, I was late because I wanted to be late."

These days, though, Alec wore his perfection with a pained air. Hatchett had thought his friend might be in the grip of some spiritual crisis: as undergraduates, they had wasted hours and hours discussing such imponderables as the existence of God. But now he knew differently. He knew in the way Alec had sometimes known what Lucius was feeling. He was crazy for Norma, thought Hatchett, mad about the girl, head over heels or, to use one of Norma's phrases, "potty for her".

Alec was trembling violently, a sure sign that he was about to say something. After about a minute he jerked his head to the right and delivered his opening line. "Er . . . how's your father?"

Norma looked at him with some surprise. "He's here!" she said, in what was almost a squeak. "Right beside me!"

"I see that," said Alec, "but . . . er . . . is he OK?"

"How does he seem to you?" said Norma.

Alec peered over her shoulder. "He seems in pretty good shape," he said, "but of course it's impossible to tell on such a brief inspection. I mean . . . you've probably had the chance to . . . er . . . have a really good look at him. And so you might . . . er . . . be able to tell me rather than the . . . er . . . other way round."

Norma looked at him, and then, to Alec's obvious consternation, she put her hand up to her mouth and laughed – a noise that reminded Hatchett of a tuning fork coming into casual contact with a chunk of Waterford glass. "Oh, Alec!" she said. "You are funny!"

This could be good for Lycett. Funny was good. Although she made conscientious attempts to suppress it, Norma had a sense of humour. It was one of the things Hatchett liked most about her. He glanced sideways at his friend, who was still blushing scarlet, and found it impossible to resent his attempts to charm the girl. It was curious: jealousy wasn't an emotion you could feel in regard to someone you genuinely liked.

Then he thought, But suppose she is in love with him. I mean, really in love.

Suppose she wants to marry him, live with him, have his children!

Suppose they move away somewhere and I never see either of them again! A feeling of utter isolation came over him. It was something he recognized from childhood but much, much worse than the familiar feeling of being an only child.

"I could be funnier," Alec said to Norma, "if that is what you would like."

To Hatchett's relief, Mary appeared, as if by magic, in the pulpit. He made a habit of popping up out of it when least expected; there were those who swore he had a secret tunnel to help make his entrances so astonishingly theatrical. As usual he was wearing a suspiciously large number of robes (there were rumours that he inclined towards Rome) and he had swapped his offensively large gold ring for an even larger one.

Alec and Norma fixed their eyes upon him. No, thought Hatchett, he had been wrong about the look in Lycett's eyes. If he was starting to feel that way about Norma, he would have told me. What I am responding to is the imminent collapse of the world I have always known. Lycett and Hatchett and Norma are going to stay the way they have always been.

"I am so glad," Mary began, "to see so many of you here today and, in view of the great events that are unfolding before us even as I speak, I would like to let you know that I shall be giving a slightly shortened version of the service this morning."

"Thank Christ for that!" muttered Hatchett, rather more loudly than he intended.

"As you know," went on Mary, "Mr Chamberlain is due to appear on the wireless very shortly and so, instead of the normal order of prayer, I am simply going to give an address. I don't like the word 'sermon', although I suppose you could call what I am going to deliver a sermon. And although I want us to pray together we will not pray in the usual manner."

Members of the congregation were looking at each other nervously. What did this mean? Were they supposed to squat instead of getting on to their knees? Did the world situation call for them to get on to the floor and roll around dribbling like some American fundamentalist sect?

"We are not going to pray for peace," said Mary, in tremendously serious tones, "because it is too late for that. We are going to ask God for peace because God, and only God, is capable of giving us peace, instead of what we are going to get which is, well, let's face it, war, but He will give us peace when He thinks it is appropriate and not before. And so we are not going to ask Him for it this morning. We are going to ask Him for deliverance. For deliverance from . . . whatever is in store for us. He will, or rather He may, decide to 'let us off lightly' but on the other hand he may not."

He paused here, as if aware that he had suddenly accorded the Almighty a lower-case initial letter. For one delirious moment Hatchett thought he might be about to start the sentence again, but in the end he decided to push on, to follow to their logical end the confusions engendered in his brain by thirty years as an ordained priest of the Church of England.

"Well," said Mary, his fluting, reedy voice rising even higher than usual, "what does God have in store for us on this morning of September the third 1939? I would like, dearly beloved brethren, to try to offer us a few words of comfort on this subject. I am not going to talk about the thing which is on all our minds and I do not propose to dwell on the enormous conflict now brewing in Poland, which threatens to wipe out the things we hold most dear – our homes, our little children, our aged relatives who are too weak and infirm to dodge the huge bombs and the gas that will soon start falling or drifting across the Channel or whatever it does, poisoning the crops and wrecking our gardens in a matter of days about which we can do nothing at all except to choke to death or be blown to smithereens or whatever . . ."

Ruth Mayhew and her mother, who since her daughter's entry into the grammar school had made a point of going to church so that her daughter could be in the company of what she termed "nice people", chose this moment to enter the building.

It was, thought Hatchett, a welcome diversion from Mary's sermon, which was having a definitely adverse effect on the congregation. Leafy Green was clutching the side of the nearest pillar. Delicate little Jacqueline Rissett had drawn her head into her neck like a tortoise and her huge bushbaby's eyes looked out at the world as from a deep cave. Her lower lip did not look particularly secure. Mabel Hughes sat bolt upright as always, looking a little like a formal family portrait from the nineteenth century – Mabel Hughes, Spinster of Le Havre.

"Jesus Christ," went on Mary, clearly attempting to steer his sermon into safer waters, "died for our sins. But He did not – and this is the interesting thing – really die at all, which is the message I am giving you this morning, and neither will we. Even if, as I say, enormous howitzers are trained on this very church, for example, which has stood in this spot undamaged, apart from the Reformation, which I am personally not too proud of, for at least six hundred years. Even if, as I say, these howitzers or whatever they are should succeed in shattering, for example, the roof, and masonry should fall down through the air squashing the worshippers, whose screams would probably be ignored by the completely heartless Nazis, who would not give twopence whether we lived or died, we would not actually die. We would die, of course, in the technical sense of that word but we would be reborn almost immediately in Christ, which is why I have chosen the text I have chosen this morning, which is . . ."

At this point Mary lowered his eyes to the text he had chosen for the day. "The text! What text?" his panic-stricken features seemed to say. In his desperate desire to take a few hundred words out of the Collect and slash the Psalms to pieces, thought Hatchett, he had probably forgotten what text he had chosen. Had he even chosen one?

"Repent," said Mary, "for the Day of Judgement is at hand. Rend your hearts and not your garments but soon, very soon, your garments may be rended for you. Over in Europe a ghastly man with a moustache is walking roughshod over all we hold sacred. Although I have personally never been to Czechoslovakia I am told it is a delightful country, whose people are full of a kind of wily charm that friends of mine have found irresistible. But we do well to remember today that the Lord – for He is King – hath told us that such things, like the death for example of Alice Everett, a member of this congregation, whom many of us hold, or rather held, dear, such things do not happen by accident. By which I do not mean that the death of Miss Everett, whom we mourn today, was, in any sense, murder, although there are suspicious circumstances surrounding it, but it seems fairly likely that, exactly as in the case of Czechoslovakia, it is something that could have been avoided if strong action had been taken earlier."

Mary took a deep breath and wagged his finger ominously at his congregation. He seemed to have forgotten any qualms he might have had about putting the fear of God into his audience. This, thought Hatchett, was now a good description of his mission.

"Oh, yes," he went on. "We are going to see a terrible and hideous cataclysm. Over in Europe terrifying and ugly things are happening. And in England also. Here, in Crotchett Green or, to be more precise, Dover, or possibly France, a harmless middle-aged lady dies horribly. The two are not unrelated. I am not saying that Hitler is actually responsible for the death of Alice Everett, although he has done worse things. Hitler, of course, has other things on his mind. The dismemberment of Poland, for example, which, later this morning, may well lead to a conflagration in which you and I and everybody in this church will be consumed or rather peppered or perhaps, shall we say?, torn apart by shrapnel assuming he wins, which he may well as he has, as I have said, a large and well-equipped army. But the murder of Alice Everett is exactly the kind of trick up to which Hitler could have got. One of the reasons we come together to worship God is to remind ourselves that our solemn duty as Christians is to resist evil wherever we find it. To struggle against hatred and ugliness and beastliness and those things which, as Jesus tells us, are the work of the Devil himself."

There was more movement in the congregation. Mabel Hughes, whose grim jaw was looking more and more determined, stepped out into the aisle. She thrust her arm forward with the emphasis of a conductor or an angel arriving with bad news. She was pointing at someone, although for a moment nobody in the church could make out who it might be.

"I need to say something!" she said, her flat, colourless voice nearly cracking with the strain of projection. Every head turned in her direction. Perhaps, thought Hatchett, for the first time in his period of tenure, someone was about to complain about the quality of one of Mary's sermons. "I need to say something about Miss Everett," went on Mabel.

She sounded, thought Hatchett, as if she was about to burst into tears.

"Miss Everett," Mabel continued, "was murdered. And I know who murdered her. And I am going to tell."

Who was she going to tell? Hatchett wondered. The congregation, presumably. There was a touch of the seventeenth century about this, he reflected, unable, as always, to stop his mind drifting towards the pedagogic.

There was silence in the church. But Mabel Hughes, having made her bold opening statement, seemed to have nothing to add to it. Perhaps this was simply a bid for attention. She was the kind of girl who was always trying to impress teachers. Before she had the chance to add anything, however, her mother hissed, "Mabel! Come back here at once!"

Hatchett glanced around the church. It was not the first time it had occurred to him that Everett had been murdered. But it was the first time it had occurred to him seriously. Who would have wanted to kill Alice Everett? After two weeks cooped up with her in a *pension*, probably every single pupil and member of staff on the school trip.

Mabel did look as if she was going to say something else, but before she could do so, Mary leaned forward in his pulpit and came out with the one line that was guaranteed to shut up the lot of them.

"Let us pray!" he intoned. Everyone pitched forward on to their knees. Hatchett went into a sort of half-crouch, shading his eyes with his right hand, and from this position was able to observe Mabel Hughes, who was still standing in the aisle, wondering whether to address a couple of hundred people who were almost all on their knees, staring at the floor.

The only two other people in the congregation who had not bowed their heads were, to Hatchett's surprise, Jacqueline Rissett and Ruth Mayhew, both of whom seemed to be staring, goggle-eyed, at Mabel, the Strictest Girl in the Fifth Form.

"Let us pray," said Mary. "Let us pray, as we have often prayed before for world peace. It seems, as I have said, unlikely, but, perhaps, while there is still a ghost of a chance we should try to pray for it even if those prayers are doomed to remain here below rather than fly up above where they belong. O Lord, influence, we pray you, the hearts and minds of statesmen and politicians, whether they be here in Croydon or in London or Warsaw or Paris or even, Lord, Berlin, to where a very special thought goes out today that we hope will affect the Reich Chancellor's heart in a positive way and make him see that there are other ways of furthering the cause of his country than by invading Poland. Protect us, O Lord God. Protect also the Poles, the Dutch, the Belgians and all the other people who stand in the Führer's way. And protect also the Führer himself from his greatest enemy – Himself!"

Mary looked up, his face registering a kind of dumb horror at the fact that in giving Adolf an initial capital he had now put him on the same level as the Almighty. Presumably, thought Hatchett, the average German felt the little creep was on a par with He Who Made All Things. There was a brief pause, and Mary came up with the word they were all waiting for: "Amen." This was the signal for a wild stampede for the doors of the church.

Hatchett found himself trapped behind Loosebottom as the citizens of Crotchett Green fought their way towards the sunlight. Norma, holding Rachel's hand, seemed, with the cunning women seem so often to exhibit in queues, to have almost made it to the exit. Lycett, ignoring his parents (most unlike him), was by her side. How had he managed that? They were both talking with some animation.

Sudden unwelcome jealousy returned. The way she was looking at him was different. It was a look she had never granted to Hatchett – sly and yet predatory at the same time. Oh, and happy too. Happy – she was at the church doors now and the sunlight was burning a halo at the edges of her beautiful black hair – happy in a way she would never be with him. Her happiness excluded him, hurt him. He was back, once again, at the lunch table in Albion House, Lycett's old home, and Lycett's father was leaning over him, saying, "I am afraid, young Hatchett, that your father may have simply run out on his family. I don't want to have to say this – but it may be the case." He was the outsider again, a small boy pressing his nose against a shop window, too poor to buy any of the things inside.

He started to fight his way through the congregation, aware as he was doing it that he was displaying something that, to strangers, might look like panic. There was an element of desperation in the crowd, most of whom were clearly keen to bag their place for the public relay of Chamberlain's broadcast in the Kirkby School Hall, but Hatchett did not wish to seem associated with it. He slowed his pace. Opposite him, Breeze was shielding Mrs Breeze, Master Breeze and Miss Breeze from any possibility of undignified exit, by standing at the exit of his pew and spreading his hands behind him as if he was about to launch himself from a diving board. By now Norma and Lycett would be out walking towards the lane. Hatchett stepped forward, in front of the odd-looking, sallow-faced man he had seen with the Hugheses earlier.

"Steady on!" said the man, in just the voice Hatchett would have expected him to have – a sort of petulant, nasal whine.

He was being ridiculous. If he, Hatchett, was interested in Norma why didn't he make a play for her? The reason he didn't, he suspected, was that he didn't really have deep feelings for her or for anyone else. His fear of Lycett falling in love with her or of her falling in love with Lycett was simply a fear of change.

When he got outside Norma and Lycett had disappeared. Mabel

Hughes was being hustled away by her parents before she could cause any more embarrassment. Mayhew seemed to be trying, and failing, to attract Leafy Green's attention, while Jacqueline Rissett, her face still as shocked and defensive as that of a small mammal that has been wakened too early, was about the same business with Mr Breeze. Breeze, however, a man normally keen on attending to the needs of adolescent girls, was ignoring her. He despatched Mrs, Master and Miss Breeze and, to Hatchett's irritation, headed in his direction.

With Hatchett, the older man's manner was, as always, elaborately masculine. His beaky, handsome face trembling as if on the edge of some risqué story, he once again gave the impression of a senior clubman initiating a junior into the mysteries of some masculine sanctuary.

"Well, young Hatchett, what do the young Turks of the common room make of this, then?" he said, in patronizing tones. "I am baffled! What on earth has got into that Hughes girl? Murdered, indeed! Who would want to murder Alice Everett? She simply had too much of that stuff she took for her fits."

Hatchett looked at the chemistry master. He seemed, he thought, remarkably well informed about Miss Everett's medical condition. Hatchett could not ever remember hearing anything about fits as far as Everett was concerned. The two of them came out of the churchyard and started down the lane towards the school.

"Do you think young Lycett is interested in Miss Lewis?" said Breeze. "I always thought she belonged to both of you. I must say, though, that if either of you ever landed her I assumed it would be you. If you can make them laugh you can make them do anything, I always say."

Stifling an urge to smack the man in the chops, Hatchett quickened his pace to the point at which Breeze's legs, which were modelled on the lines of a dachshund's, were whirring along with the speed of a mechanical toy.

"I expect," gasped Breeze, "Mabel was furiously jealous. She had the most frightful crush on Everett and she, like all the class, thought I was paying the old bat too much attention. I was simply trying to be nice to her to make sure she didn't spread ghastly stories about me." He paused and peered at Hatchett. "Had she been spreading nasty stories about me, young Hatchett?" he said.

He's like some fussy, self-important little bird, thought Hatchett, or a pompous official in some Ruritanian civil-service department. "What kind of nasty stories do you think she might have been spreading?" he said, by way of reply.

For a moment, it looked as if Breeze might choose to be offended by this remark. He was always very conscious of the dignity he was supposed to have acquired simply because he had been teaching for fifteen years. Then, deciding to be amiable, he opened his mouth, displaying a full shark's set of large white pearly choppers, and gave a fairly good impression of an uproarious laugh. "I have a terrible reputation," he said, waving his hand back at the congregation. "I am sure all these old biddies regularly convince themselves I am a mass murderer. I ask you! Do I look like a mass murderer?"

He preened his neat grey jacket and smoothed down his thatch of blond hair. With his heavily lined features, his slightly protruding eyes and his wide repertoire of obsessive, tidy little gestures, Hatchett thought, a mass murderer was exactly what he looked like. He gave a vaguely negative grunt and, walking even faster, moved on down the hill towards Kirkby Grammar School.

5

Kirkby Grammar School had been founded in 1565 by a man called Roger de Gomme, which is perhaps why, for as long as anyone could remember, the boys had been known locally as "the Stickies". It was founded as a refuge for "twenty poore scholares", but by the eighteenth century it had degenerated into a kind of finishing school for wealthy or titled male drunks. In 1889 – three years before Saltdene School was founded by an energetic lesbian called Howlett – Kirkby was taken over by a high-minded headmaster to whom one history of the school refers as "Croydon's answer to Matthew Arnold". He got rid of all the teachers, strictly forbade the keeping of animals on the premises and more or less barred the place to anyone who didn't know the Greek alphabet. He beat wrongdoers with a large whip, which was still kept in a cupboard behind the stage in the main hall – known, in the time Hatchett had been acquainted with the place, as Old School.

This morning, thought Hatchett, as he came into the front quad, it had an unsupervised air about it, reminiscent of its eighteenth-century past. School had not actually started yet, but some boys were still wearing the familiar black and red blazer. They stood, with their parents and siblings, wearing the sheepish, unclaimed look they usually wore on Speech Day. There was already a queue to get up the stairs and into Old School.

Hatchett joined the crowd, and found himself next to Miss Leach, a suave hawk-like creature in her early forties. Quite a lot of these people, he thought, must own wireless sets. Presumably listening to what the Prime Minister had to say in the middle of a crowd of other people offered a kind of reassurance. Norma and Alec must be in the hall by now.

"Well, now, Mr Hatchett!" said Miss Leach. "Here we are!"

"Here we are!" said Hatchett, who was always having this kind of conversation with Miss Leach.

"My girls and your boys!" went on the headmistress, in her forthright tone. She looked down at the gathering crowd in the quadrangle below them, leaning one arm on the railing of the steps, and looking, as she usually did, like an Edwardian masher scouting for eligible fillies.

"Indeed!" said Hatchett.

"In the event of war we at the girls' school are to be turned into something to do with the RAF," went on Miss Leach, in her faintly exquisite Scottish accent, "so I understand the Saltdene girls may well have to get closer to the Kirkby boys. A rumour that has caused an epidemic of sniggering in the fourth form. I understand Ruth Mayhew is going round telling people that it is possible to get pregnant from a toilet seat that has recently been used by a boy. And the swimming-pool is a similarly risky area for girls who do not feel they are ready to have children."

"I am not sharing toilet facilities with men, Miss Leach," growled Leafy Green, who had joined them on the steps. "Men!"

Hatchett bowed briefly.

Pushing their way through the crowd came Jennifer Doran and her accomplice in the domestic-science department, Mary Peel. They were carrying a large steel bucket of what looked like orange squash and an enormous wicker hamper. "We have made three hundred fish-paste rolls," said Jolly Jennifer, as she was known, and pushed back her red hair from her eyes with her right forearm. In case anyone should fail to grasp the enormity of this task, she added, "Phew!"

"Phew!" answered Miss Leach.

Jennifer offered one to Hatchett. It was the size, consistency and weight of a small cannon ball. Hatchett tried to bite into it. He failed.

"Have you seen Norma?" he said to Jennifer, who nodded up at the hall. More and more people were filing into the quad.

"I understand," said Miss Leach, as they shuffled nearer to the door, "that it will not be possible to relay the broadcast through loudspeakers. There are technical problems."

"Which are?" said Leafy, in a gruff voice.

"There are no loudspeakers," said Miss Leach.

"I understand," said Breeze, who had managed to wriggle in next to them, "that a boy in the upper fifth has volunteered to take down the Prime Minister's words in shorthand and relay them to the crowd outside with a team of runners."

"Which boy?" said Hatchett.

"Farrar, I believe," said Breeze.

"I teach Farrar," said Hatchett. "He knows as much about shorthand as I do about nuclear physics."

No one argued with this remark. Above him, on the balcony at the top of the steps, Hatchett could see Farrar, the self-styled shorthand expert, standing with a small earnest third-former called Ashby. Ashby was saying something in a high, squeaky voice. Next to them, wearing his rugby blazer, his cricket tie and his French-scholarship cap, was Peckerley.

"Ashby will relay the words to Peckerley," said Breeze, in the confident tones of an insider, "and Peckerley will read them to the waiting masses."

They were almost at the entrance. Just as they went into the hall Leafy plucked at Hatchett's sleeve. "I have been talking to young Mayhew," she said. "She seems somewhat confused but as far as I can make out she seems to be saying that there may be some substance in what dear Mabel said in church. And Mabel is a trustworthy girl who was almost as fond of dear Alice as I."

Here Leafy broke off to adjust her black hat, perched atop her not quite natural blonde hair, which gave her the air of a hanging judge about to pass sentence. She had been in energetic mourning for Everett and, although a stout woman with a broad backside, was almost down to two meals a day as a sign of respect.

"Alice Everett," she said to Hatchett, in tones that suggested he would never, could never, really appreciate or understand what she was saying, "was a marvellous human being. She brought life and love and warmth to all around her. She was devoted to young Mabel, you know. And she was working on a monograph on the life of Lope de Vega." She died just in time, really, didn't she?

thought Hatchett. As they moved forward into the hall, he looked for signs of Norma or Alec. None. "If, as Mayhew suggests," went on Leafy, "and I have to say she was not making much sense – she seemed to have thoroughly frightened herself and it may simply be one of her stories – if what poor Mabel said in the church is true, then Alice was foully murdered. I would like to get hold of the man who did it and strangle him with my bare hands."

She was capable of strangling any number of men with her bare hands, thought Hatchett, and if the way she was looking at him was any indication, he was fairly high up on the list of suspects. They had argued once or twice about the miners. Hatchett pushed past her, and found that his way down the hall was blocked. People were standing in both aisles. Children were sitting on their parents' knees and the smaller boys and girls were jostling together, two or three to a chair. Down in the third or fourth row he finally caught sight of Norma and Alec.

They were deep in conversation. Alec seemed to be doing most of the talking. This, thought Hatchett, was unusual. Worrying, even. What were they talking about? Norma was laughing now. Alec could make her laugh. The conversations they might have had in his absence began to haunt him. Hours at rugby matches, when he had assumed she was yawning with boredom. Perhaps, in fact, they had been laughing like this, sharing an intimacy to which he could never aspire, laughing at him possibly, with his drip-drip-drip of jokes and his tweed jacket with a leather patch and his childishness and his dream of being a writer and his –

Stop it, Hatchett. Stop it now.

From behind the heavy red curtain, bunched at the edge of the stage, Mr Veitch appeared. He was wearing his MA gown, trimmed with white fur, and as was his custom, he stood silently for a moment, waiting for the noise to subside. Veitch had been described as "a headmaster's headmaster" and his little tricks of oratory and staging were famous at Kirkby. Hatchett particularly relished his habit of bowing elaborately to any woman over the age of twenty, and his fondness for pointing his nose at the ceiling in order to simulate thought was legendary. But this afternoon Hatchett understood, for the first time, his grasp of headmasterly gravitas. He was a man who believed in the office, and as he came to the edge of the stage, the worthless human part of himself seemed to be leaving his body behind so that he was almost all headmaster. As he stood there, his black button eyes twitching across the assembled faces, the chattering slowly died and, when there was perfect silence, he said, in his curiously high, melodious voice, "Thank you all so much for coming."

"You would have thought," whispered Hatchett to himself, "that he was making the broadcast not Neville."

A figure had squeezed in next to him from the balcony at the head of the stairs. It was Farrar. He was clutching a pencil, and a large piece of white paper on which were written the words PRIME MINISTER'S SPEECH. Next to him was the diminutive figure of Ashby.

Behind Veitch, "Stinks" Mullery, the head of physics, crawled out from under the table on which the radio sat and started to fiddle with the knobs. A voice telling you what tactics to adopt when approaching tinned food was replaced by a noise not unlike that made by frying chips.

"We are about," said Veitch, "to listen to an historic broadcast. Which will undoubtedly change the face of the world as we know it." The crackling got louder. "I know," went on Veitch, "that we all hope and pray that, whatever our Prime Minister says to us today, we will take his message to our hearts."

"If," said Hatchett, looking at his watch, "the Prime Minister is allowed to get a word in edgeways." Farrar and Ashby sniggered. They both found Hatchett amusing. Quite a lot of other people were looking at their watches.

"We do not know what he is going to say," went on Veitch, "but we can be pretty sure that whatever it is it will be worth listening to. He is, after all, the Prime Minister." No one tried to argue with this.

Suddenly the sound of an electric organ blared out from the speakers.

"It's Sandy Macpherson," whispered Miss Leach to Leafy. Leafy affected not to hear her.

Norma was looking sideways at Alec, who was sitting bolt upright, as focused on the stage as a dog on a rabbit. At least he wasn't talking to Norma, thought Hatchett, and was immediately ashamed of the thought. Did he want his friend gone? Was that what he was thinking? They were going to send him away, of course, weren't they?

For the first time Alec's uniform seemed real. It hadn't before. In fact, although he would never have dreamed of saying so to Alec, Hatchett secretly considered it rather silly. The hat, particularly, which did not do justice to his head. And, although no one had ever suggested there was anything wrong with Alec Lycett's behind, his Croydon Light Infantry trousers somehow managed to suggest that there was. But, now, Hatchett rather missed the days when it had had a light-opera quality. There was something horribly serious even about the tunic. It seemed to suggest that, unless the people in charge of things made a very determined effort indeed, very soon people might be firing real bullets at the man inside it.

This thought brought on that lightness in the chest, the feeling of falling again. This – the broadcast, the war, him, Lycett, Norma – it was all suddenly terribly, terribly serious.

"This is the BBC," said Veitch.

A second or two later, a voice from the wireless said, "This is the BBC."

"We are now going over to the Cabinet Rooms at Downing Street," said Veitch, turning to look expectantly at the wireless.

"We are now going over to the cabinet rooms at Ten Downing Street," said the wireless.

"For a message from the Prime Minister," said Veitch.

A voice from the wireless said, "For a message from the Prime Minister."

Veitch nodded complacently.

"And now," he said, waving his arms as if he had produced the broadcast himself, "the Prime Minister! Mr Neville Chamberlain!" This was followed by an agonizing silence. For a moment, Hatchett thought the headmaster might be about to improvise a message to the nation himself. And then, out of the silence, came a reedy, desiccated voice that didn't seem to be coming over the airwaves at all. It was as if a ghost had wheedled its way into the hall and was now asking them all for sympathy for some crime it had committed.

"I am speaking to you from the Cabinet Room at Number Ten Downing Street," said the voice. "This morning the British Ambassador in Berlin . . ." at the back of the hall next to Hatchett, Farrar, who had lied about his shorthand, scribbled I AM SPEAKING TO YOU BERLIN, as the Prime Minister soldiered on ". . . unless the British Government heard from them by eleven o'clock that they were prepared at once to withdraw their troops from Poland, a state of war would exist between us."

Farrar, still a long way behind, wrote, A STATE OF WAR EXISTS BETWEEN US. "I have to tell you now," went on the Prime Minister, "that no such undertaking has been received, and that consequently this country is at war with Germany." Farrar was sweating visibly. Next to him Ashby, ears quivering with excitement, reached out for the piece of paper. Hatchett, painfully aware that a crowd of people out in the quad was waiting for news, hissed to Farrar, "Be quick about it! It's war, man! War over Poland!"

POLAND. WAR, wrote Farrar, in big, childish capitals, then tore off sections of his piece of paper, in a manner clearly modelled on journalists ripping telexes out of machines in cinema films, and thrust the message into Ashby's hands.

"Is this all?" said Ashby.

"No!" hissed Hatchett, aware that they were being stared at by people near them.

Chamberlain's voice, as dry and stuffy as the hall itself, continued, "The situation in which no word given by Germany's ruler could be trusted, and no people or country could feel itself safe, has become critical. Now we have resolved to finish it."

"Write, man!" hissed Hatchett to Farrar, who wrote, PEOPLE COUNTRY CRITICAL WE HAVE RESOLVED TO FINISH! He handed this to Ashby.

Ashby said, "Is this it?"

"It'll have to do," said Hatchett. He had lost all sense of where they were in the broadcast now. All he knew was that two or three hundred people were waiting outside and that it was important to get the news to them as quickly as possible. A strange sort of solemnity had come upon him too, and he had the urge to stand to attention or salute or something like that.

The mood had clearly affected Mr Chamberlain in the same way. "May God bless you all," said the Prime Minister.

"May God bless you all," said Veitch.

"May God bless you all," said Farrar, scribbling in capitals on another piece of paper and thrusting it at Ashby.

"May God bless them all," said Ashby. Then he turned on his heels and ran out into the daylight. Hatchett followed him.

Outside Peckerley was staring down nervously at a sea of expectant faces, as Ashby, face bright red with the importance of it all, pushed his way through the mob and proudly handed the senior boy a jumbled mass of papers. Peckerley looked at them in some confusion. For a moment Hatchett thought he was about to make a complaint about the form in which the Prime Minister's message had been handed to him. But this was a solemn occasion and Peckerley was a good boy. Eventually he managed to clear his throat and come out with the words, "This is the Prime Minister's message!" The crowd beneath him, about three hundred strong, surged forward. "He was speaking to us," said Peckerley, peering down at Farrar's jumble of notes, "from Berlin." This caused a mild sensation. Mrs Hazebrook, from South Croydon, said to her neighbour that she thought this was probably a good thing, and her neighbour agreed. They were probably sorting things out at last, she said, just like they had at Munich. "Apparently," Peckerley continued, "a state of war exists between us and . . . er . . ." He looked at his sheet. He could see the name of only one country he recognized. "A state of war," he went on, "exists between us and Poland."

This went down surprisingly well. A lot of people seemed to think that the Poles had had it coming. Mr Sargent, the butcher, who had three girls at Saltdene, said if we didn't get the Poles now they would undoubtedly be coming for us in a few years' time.

Jenny Leese, the music mistress, said she thought it was probably a clever ruse to buy us time. Declaring war on Poland, she said to Minnie Sharless, the other music mistress, who had left-wing leanings, would probably lull Hitler into a false sense of security. Peckerley, out of words, motioned to Ashby. "We have," said Ashby, in shrill tones, "resolved to finish off all people in the country who are critical."

This was less popular. Some people said it was time to get tough while others said they thought that, whatever Hitler might be trying on, this was still a democracy. Minnie Sharless said that if only Chamberlain had woken up earlier to the need for a tough line on Fascists and Saboteurs, we would not be in this mess in the first place and that she personally would have no objection to shooting Halifax and his clique in the back of the neck like the mad dogs they undoubtedly were. She added a few dark words on the subject of Alice Everett and her like. Mr Sargent said he wouldn't go as far as that but that he was totally behind the invasion of Poland and that when we had "rolled up" the Poles we might be able to make a start on Russia, Germany and France. There was widespread enthusiasm for the invasion of France, with almost everyone agreeing that the French were rude, complacent, treacherous and too close for comfort. Peckerley, who had been studying his notes closely, said, "May God bless you all! This is it! God bless all of you, every one!"

"God bless us all!" shouted Mr Sargent.

Hatchett felt it was time to reassert himself. He went to the railings and, in his best schoolmaster's voice, said, "It's war! It's war over Poland! We are at war with Germany! As of now!"

The faces of the crowd looked up at him. They still had not got the message, he decided. If things went on this way the people of South Croydon could be wandering around for months unaware that Britain and Germany were about to commence hostilities. They would be off on the boat train to the Black Forest, with their walking boots, or taking their wives, children, and buckets and spades to resorts on the Baltic Coast. They just didn't seem to get it.

"War!" said Hatchett again. "You know? Bang bang bang! Us and Hitler! W-A-R! I suggest we all go home and start digging trenches or putting sandbags up against the windows because from everything I have heard their air force is shit hot!"

There were signs, at last, that the news was filtering through. Alan Freeless, who had been having an affair with his secretary, clutched his wife for the first time in eighteen months. Benjamin Lot, the antiques dealer, shook his head, whistled silently and sucked his teeth for two minutes. Janet Frosser and Elinor Wreays burst into tears and fell into each other's arms. Jacqueline Rissett and her mother held hands. Mabel Hughes, who was standing between her parents, looked up into Hatchett's face and stared and stared and stared.

Hatchett turned back towards the hall and, on his way in, encountered Norma, Alec and Rachel. Norma had a hectic look about her, but before any words had been spoken, Hatchett knew it was not to do with anything the Prime Minister had had to say.

"Dennis," she said, "you know how fond I am of you. And – I don't know quite how to say this but . . . Alec and I need to talk to you rather seriously."

Norma, Rachel, Hatchett and Lycett were walking down the hill towards the TA Centre. Hatchett had tried to persuade them to go and have a cup of tea but Lycett said he had to be drilled at twelve o'clock and, in the light of what they had just heard on the wireless, stamping round a parade-ground might be, well, more useful than having a cup of tea. He had thrown Hatchett an unusually critical look as he said this.

Norma was rather on Alec's side in this. If they were all going to be blown to bits – and she seriously expected men in grey uniforms to be leaping out at them from the bushes at any moment – they might as well die with their boots on. Not, thought Norma, that she or Hatchett had any boots. Hatchett was not the type of man ever to have boots. Oh, God! She felt dreadful. She felt so, so guilty.

She had never expected any of this to happen. And especially not now. As if there weren't enough things going on already! When she and Alec had come out of the hall, Dennis had got that hurt, vulnerable look she knew and loved so well. He looked like a baby owl that had been taken away from its nest. It wouldn't be so bad if he hadn't been so determinedly brave about it. He must have sensed, back in the church, that something was going on. Although, of course, it had been going on for a lot longer than that. It, whatever "it" was, had started when she and Rachel had gone to watch Alec at the nets and he had come out, in his cricket whites, and met her eyes in that way he had and . . . No, if she was honest it had started a long way before that. It had started, although she didn't know so, when she had first met him, at that dance all those years ago. She hadn't known then but now she did, so it was as if she had always known.

But why today of all days? Why did it have to become official on the day when war between England and Germany acquired the same status?

It would have been a lot easier to have had this conversation without Rachel. But she wasn't yet at the stage when Norma felt she could let her out on her own. When the time came to have the serious talk, she was going to have to ask the poor girl to stand a few yards off because Norma, who valued her self-control, was afraid she might cry and, for some reason, it was important to her that Rachel felt she was tough, impervious to the weakness of tears. So for the moment the four of them walked, like some oddly balanced family, together down the narrow lane that led to the parade-ground. There were poppies and daisies and Queen Anne's lace in the hedgerow and the sun warmed Norma's back. We are at war, she said to herself, over and over again. But no matter how many times she said it, it still did not seem real.

The TA shed and the parade-ground were now in view. Like everything else about the British war effort, thought Norma, they radiated a spirit of amateurishness. Even the roof of the TA hut looked provisional. The surface of the parade-ground was pitted with holes and craters, making marching across it a seriously risky business, and the small wooden notice by the front gate – 4TH CROYDON LIGHT INFANTRY (TERRITORIAL DIVISION) – did not threaten trespassers with dire punishments or impress the casual passer-by with military style. It looked, she thought, like an obscure Nonconformist church or a not-very-well-off Scout hut. And all around was green England.

"You and Mr Hatchett must talk about serious matters," Rachel was saying to her quickly. They had walked a little ahead of the other two.

How did the girl know this? She was astonishingly observant.

"I will walk away a little. Really, if you wish I can wait at the flat. I will not disgrace you. I hope I have not said the wrong thing in the church." She paused, then grinned, showing the gap in her front teeth. "I hope this is correct, Auntie!"

Norma found she was grinning too. "I like being called Auntie," she said. It was really too ridiculous. She was only about ten years older than Rachel.

Rachel put her arm round Norma's waist, leaned into her and whispered, "Have you always loved Mr Lycett?"

Really, the girl missed nothing! Not for the first time Norma found herself marvelling at how much Rachel seemed to have gleaned about her hosts while giving away practically nothing about herself. There were times – and this was almost certainly simply a reflection of the fact that Rachel was far more occupied with her own thoughts than most girls of her age – when Norma suspected she might be the bearer of some terrible secret. But who would confide such a thing to a fifteen-year-old girl? No, it wasn't quite as crude as a "secret" – this was the war and the fear of the war talking – but that Norma thought her refugee, her stray animal, her guest without papers, knew something that she didn't. Those long silences in the flat when she stared out of the window at the sky, or the way she grabbed at certain books – usually ones concerned with science – made Norma think that both Rachel and her father, of whom she did occasionally speak, were exceptional people. People who saw things that most people could not see.

"I think," Rachel was saying, "that you love them both. But you love Mr Lycett more. And Mr Hatchett is sad. I am sad for him. He is very nice. He speaks good German. And he has read a great deal.

But you do not have lover feelings for him. That is why I have been sent on ahead when you come back from church with Mr Lycett."

"Rachel," said Norma, "in English we would probably say 'romantic feelings'."

The girl, who always seemed to know when her presence was not required, nodded slowly, as if memorizing this instruction, and walked briskly ahead.

Norma stood in the lane, waiting for the two men to catch up with her. They were laughing about something as they often did. When they came level with her, she seized them both by the waist and said, "Now! You are both to promise me you won't do anything foolish like join the Army!"

"I have already joined the Army," said Alec, indicating his uniform. "What do you think this is?"

"A theatrical costume of some kind?" said Norma. "And I suppose I'd better tell Hatchett, don't you think?"

Hatchett was looking between the two of them. "Well," he said, "I suppose I'd better hear the bad news."

Now that she had got to tell him, Norma realized she could not put what had happened this morning into words. Trying to describe what had happened on the way from the church to the school seemed to make it more, not less, ridiculous: "I was just turning into Crotchett Green Lane when I realized I was in love with Alec. Alec turned to me and gave me a sort of . . . look . . . and I knew . . . that we loved each other."

"You know how fond I am of both of you . . ." she began, finally.

"You keep saying that," said Hatchett. "I find it very disturbing. I am a very boring, pedantic kind of person, you see. I always want to know exactly how fond you are of me and exactly how fond you are of him."

"I know," said Norma, loosening her grip on both men. They walked on a few more yards. "Alec," she went on, eventually, "do you have anything to say?"

"Yes," said Alec. "Yes, I have. You see, Dennis, old man . . ."

There was a long silence.

"Yes?" said Hatchett, in acid tones.

"I think," said Norma, eventually, "that he is trying to tell you that he has just asked me if I would consent to become engaged to him."

There was another long silence.

Lycett nodded vigorously. "Yes," he said, "that is what I was trying to say. I think."

Hatchett was clearly expected to make some response to this. Norma felt she owed him something more. But it didn't seem appropriate, or fair, to start going on about Alec's eyes or his cheekbones or the way the muscles on the back of his neck tensed when he was concentrating on something. This was not the time to make a short but eloquent speech on the elegance of his shoulders or that funny thing he did with his wrists when he wanted to let you know he was amused.

She had thought that love would arrive, announcing itself like some butler letting you know that a minor European royal was at the door. But actually, she realized, it was much simpler than that. Love was what she had always felt for Alec. It was a very simple thing, as simple as hunger or thirst, and the hardest thing about it was probably putting a name to it. That was what she had been frightened to do for all these years. Now she had done so. And so had he.

He hadn't put it quite like that. What he had actually said was, "Norma, I am most frightfully in love with you and I think we should get engaged."

"And what," Hatchett was saying, in that detached way he said most things, "did you say when he asked you to become engaged to him? What were your actual words?"

For a moment, Norma thought this was just a typical piece of pedantry on his part. It was a question asked for the sake of it, so that he could have one more little item to add to the rag-bag of quotations, opinions, half-baked mathematical formulae and scraps of foreign languages that were floating around inside the Hatchett head. It had no more emotional content than, say, "Bach has one fast tune and one slow tune" (one of his favourite dicta) or "Sir Arthur Sullivan wrote pub ballads," or (one of her favourites because she was sure it was untrue but could not think of the case that proved it to be so), "There are no great novels set in Birmingham."

But then she realized that his tone, that of a prosecuting counsel, or a Socratic interviewer confidently leading his subject to intellectual doom, meant something more than that. He did not really expect her to tell him that she had answered yes. In spite of the anxiety she had seen in his eyes when she and Lycett came out of the Old School, in spite of the little-boy-lost look that had both touched and irritated her, Hatchett still assumed that it was him, and not Lycett, whom she loved.

The arrogance of this staggered her. It brought her up short.

Hatchett was an optimist. He had certainty. God alone knew where he had got it. His father was a drunken eccentric who had, in all probability, run off with another woman. His mother was a cowed, hopeless creature who couldn't let her only son go but did not really seem to want him much either. But Hatchett wanted the world to conform to his dream of it and that gave him an extraordinary strength. The strength was there in the way he stopped, and repeated the question as if for the benefit of an admiring court. "And what, Miss Lewis – think carefully before you answer this question – exactly what – there are laws against perjury – did you – this is your responsibility, my dear – say when he asked you to become engaged to him?"

Grass trembles. Cows bate their breath. Norma answers.

"I said yes, Dennis. I am in love with him. I want to marry him."

Collapse of Hatchett. Trees burst into flame. Choir effects from on high. Clouds part. Chariot lowered from heavens. Norma and Lycett step into it hand in hand. Hatchett's head droops and he falls on to his knees on the hard earth, sobbing, as his two oldest friends head for the skies, her head on his shoulder.

What happened was almost as sensational.

There was a long mechanical wail. It filled the air so effectively that it was impossible to tell from which direction it was coming. At first Norma thought it was some kind of summons, the voice of a mechanical God calling the faithful to prayer. Then she suspected it was some kind of practical joke, for there was something frankly implausible about the noise, as if a giant had sat on a whoopee cushion. It wasn't until it had died away, which seemed to take an extraordinarily long time, that Norma realized it was an air-raid siren.

"My God!" said Lycett. "They've been quick about it!"

"The Hun," said Hatchett, "is notoriously efficient."

"Perhaps," said Norma, trying to keep the hysteria out of her voice, "we should take cover." She looked down the road. "Rachel!"

Rachel, apparently quite oblivious of the noise, was examining the hedgerow.

Perhaps this sort of noise was an everyday occurrence in Hitler's Germany. "Rachel!"

Rachel turned towards them.

"We should dig in!" said Hatchett.

"Yes," said Lycett, "dig trenches."

"Isn't there," said Hatchett, who, like his friend, seemed to be on the edge of a giggling fit, "some kind of special walk you do when bombs are in the vicinity?"

"Yes!" said Lycett, who seemed relieved that the conversation had been steered away from emotional questions. "Like this, old man!" He put his hands over his ears and, taking tiny steps, did a kind of squirming run backwards and forwards across the lane.

"Or this!" said Hatchett, crouching like Quasimodo, staring up at the sky and then scuttling sideways like a crab making for the shelter of a rock.

"No, no, no, like this!" said Lycett and, uttering a loud scream, he dived for the nearest bit of hedgerow, wailing, "It'th the Narttheez! Help, help, help, it'th the Narttheez!"

Hatchett was now choking with laughter. Thrusting out his buttocks, he went splay-footed and, waggling his posterior, pushed one finger up his nose, raised his right shoe high off the ground, then rotated it in crazy circles before allowing it to come to rest.

This, thought Norma, as Lycett, too, allowed himself to be quite overcome by laughter, is probably how the English will behave when the sky actually does darken with armed parachutists in coal-scuttle helmets. "For God's sake!" she heard herself say. "It's an air-raid siren!"

They both stopped. Neither looked in the least abashed.

"It's a practice," said Lycett, "or a mistake. Bound to be."

"Bound to be," said Hatchett. "This is a free country. This is a democracy, for God's sake. We are, therefore, unprepared for war."

Rachel, who had been watching all this stony-faced, did not seem at all concerned. "Is it a fire alarm?" she said.

"Maybe," said Norma, in what she hoped was a soothing voice, "it is."

Down on the TA parade-ground, Major Gooderson had emerged from the TA shed followed by a few of the unlikely selection of men who made up his section of the 4th Croydon Light Infantry. Mavroleon, a fat man in his early thirties, seemed to be having an asthma attack. Forssander, a boy Norma recognized as the person who served her in the greengrocer's in the village, looked as if he was about to burst into tears. Gooderson, a red-faced, corpulent man who (surely?) was well into his forties, turned to his men and barked, "Where are your rifles?"

"We haven't got any rifles, sir," said Mavroleon.

Gooderson went into a threatening mime of what looked like a man hacking another to bits with a bayonet. "Rifles!" he barked. "Rifles!"

This sounded to Norma like a request to some invisible person to come out of the shed with rifles, but at first no one responded. Eventually Peckerley emerged, carrying a large cardboard box. It did not look heavy enough to contain rifles.

She looked at Hatchett and Lycett. She couldn't believe, somehow, that she had just told one of them she had got engaged to the other. And neither showed any urge to return to the subject. For a moment she was almost hurt by this typically male indirectness, and then she thought, Perhaps that is all I need to say. Perhaps we will never discuss the issue again. Perhaps, although things between me and Alec will never be the same, between the three of us nothing has changed. She knew that this could not possibly be the case. But it seemed to be how the two of them wished to behave.

It would be perfect, of course, if it could be like that. She looked across at the parade-ground.

Peckerley, to Norma's horror, was wearing khaki. Although to call what he was wearing a uniform seemed like a contradiction in terms. Norma had never seen so curiously individualistic a garment.

It looked as if it had been designed for some long-vanished race of giants. Its sleeves hung down almost to his knees, obscuring his hands completely, and its waist, designed to accommodate a gigantic belly, spilled over his webbing belt in khaki bunches. The trousers were clearly intended for a different soldier, one from a regiment that specialized in short people – the 8th Surrey Royal Dwarfs, perhaps – for they only just reached past Peckerley's knees. Gooderson was commenting on this fact, loudly, into Peckerley's left ear. "Do you know what you look like, Peckerley?" he was shouting. "Have you any idea what you look like?" Peckerley did not answer this. He was clearly not supposed to. "You look like a pregnant duck, Peckerley," continued Gooderson. "What do you look like?"

There was a short pause during which Peckerley registered that this was not intended to be a rhetorical question. "A pregnant duck, sir," he said, eventually.

"Exactly!" said Gooderson, pleased by the symmetry of this exchange. "That is exactly what you look like. A pregnant duck."

Given the right degree of encouragement, Gooderson could obviously keep up this sort of thing for hours.

"My father," Hatchett was saying, "was a chaplain in the 4th Croydons. It was probably that that sent him round the twist."

Lycett was giving his friend a peculiar look. In so far as either of them ever talked about their parents – and they didn't much – Norma had been able to gather that there had been some kind of tension between the two families. In fact, the introduction of this subject seemed to make for far more tension than the question of which of them was or was not going to marry her. Perhaps that was right. She had always known she would marry one of them. Bigamy was not legal.

The thought of living in a house with both Lycett and Hatchett brought a smile to Norma's face, perhaps because it seemed so completely unshocking, but neither of them noticed it. Lycett was looking at Peckerley, who was unpacking his box in front of Gooderson, and his face was troubled.

She wouldn't be able to call him Lycett when they were married. It would make him sound like a dog.

"At least," said Alec, his jaw still tense, "he had the guts to fight. Which is more than mine did."

It was Alec, not Hatchett, who was upset by this conversation. That was curious. As Peckerley unloaded what looked like more extraordinarily shapeless uniforms (wasn't he a little young to be in the Territorials? Surely they wouldn't give Peckerley real bullets?) she saw Alec turn away then clench and unclench his fists, something he did when he was working himself up to make an awkward speech. Why should he be so upset about Hatchett's father? Or his own father come to that?

She didn't like the idea that there was a real or serious rift between Alec Lycett Junior and Alec Lycett Senior; she was going to marry him. She hadn't thought of his family at all when he asked her. She didn't know them well enough to do so. But she was going to have to get to know them now.

"Look, old man," Alec was saying, "I mean . . . you know . . . we are both . . . and . . . you know, I and Norma and . . ." this, thought Norma, is how Hatchett and Lycett have an intimate conversation " . . . and . . . well, really, you and I and Norma are . . . you know, but . . . I just I mean . . . I feel I know you feel but I do feel I actually do feel and you feel too but . . . you know . . . well . . . me and Norma but . . . you know . . . you too in a way!"

"Yes, Alec," said Hatchett, with a pale, sad smile. "You and me. And Norma too, of course. But you and me. Very eloquently put, if I may say so."

Alec thrust out his hand to his friend. Hatchett looked at it slowly. He seemed to be examining it for traces of dirt, like some strict matron at a boys' school, checking to see if the bad boy of the class had washed his hands. Then, almost as if his mind was not on the job, he took hold of it and pumped it vigorously.

"And now," said Lycett, for he was Lycett, suddenly, now, the companion of her childhood, "I must go and play at soldiers." He turned to Norma and became Alec again. His eyes were flickering bruises in his face and he looked the way he had when he had touched her arm, suddenly, on the way back from the church. She felt the urge to put out her hand to touch him, to reassure him that whatever it was that seemed to frighten him (for his hunger for her, she could see quite clearly now, was a kind of fear) she would be the one to make it go away. "See you in the Queen Vic at seven?" he said.

"That would be lovely, Alec," she said.

Hatchett was looking at the two of them. Alec moved towards her. For a moment she thought he was going to kiss her cheek but at the last minute his lips swerved and encountered hers. Just a slight brush but she could smell him, feel his breath on her. Hatchett stood a little way off, his pale blue eyes fixed on the two of them. And she was aware of his gaze, even when Alec's lips were actually on hers.

"Goodbye, then . . . er . . . darling," said Alec and, clearly shocked by the boldness of this last word, turned on his heels and marched smartly towards his regiment.

"Where is everybody?" said Mavroleon.

"Late," said Forssander, in a small, morose voice. He was a tall, thin youth who seemed to have a secret sorrow. Alec had thought at first it might be something to do with a woman. But it was hard to believe Forssander would ever get close enough to any woman to allow her to make him miserable. It wasn't, anyway, a great sorrow that the man carried around with him, more a minor ache, as if he had just suffered the death of a pet of which he was not particularly fond.

"At least," said Gooderson, with a rare flash of wit, "that would show they could all do something at the same time."

They were, thought Alec, an uninspiring bunch. What was it the

Duke of Wellington had said of his soldiers? Something about not knowing whether they frightened the enemy but they sure as hell put the fear of God into him. This lot put the fear of God into Alec Lycett, but not for any of the right reasons. What frightened him was their obvious incompetence, publicly acknowledged cowardice and complete lack of physical fitness. There were still only about fifteen of them.

Alec seemed to be in charge of Mavroleon, Forssander, Peckerley and a few keen but extremely stupid lads from the other side of the village. Forssander had already announced that he had a phobia, although whatever it was terrified him so much he dared not say its name out loud. Mavroleon had just been asked to touch his toes and had fallen over, while Forssander had imploded on his fourth press-up. They were now gathered with the others, in a circle, on the grass behind the TA shed being taught hand-to-hand combat by Gooderson. Hand-to-hand combat, he thought, was all they were going to be capable of if some weapons didn't arrive soon.

The war still did not seem real to Alec. Although he supposed he ought to feel all those things that war seemed to engender in young men – solemnity, uplift – all he could think of was that, for the first time in his life, he had come first. He had got the girl. And Hatchett, poor, dear, lovable old Hatchett, had lost. He wasn't, by the look of him, a good loser.

But this wasn't going to change their friendship. Keeping up their friendship somehow made sense of things. Particularly of what had happened with both their fathers. Thinking about the unfortunate moment, just now, when they had touched on that time, Alec ground his teeth into his jaw. He didn't want to think about his childhood. Or to witness Norma seeing him do so. Thinking about Lucius brought back guilt, anger, shame, and now a terrible pity for his defeated rival. When he thought about it, Hatchett had never had a chance. The poor boy in the rich boy's house.

"In order for you to succeed," this was his own father speaking now, "you have to cut out the other fellow. Life is a war, Alec. A war."

It certainly was now. He tried to concentrate on Gooderson.

"I am a German," Gooderson was saying to Mavroleon, who looked prepared to believe this completely, "and I am coming at you. I appear to be unarmed but I may be carrying a knife. What do you do?"

There was a pause.

"Run, sir?" said Mavroleon.

With a terrible shriek, Gooderson hurled himself at Mavroleon, flexing his fingers as he did so. *"Schweinhund!"* he yelled. *"Schweinhund! Englischer Schweinhund!"*

"No-o!" yelled Mavroleon. "No-o-o-o!"

"Ja! Ja! You die, English pig!" yelled Gooderson, as he closed on the thirty-two-year-old filing clerk. He seized Mavroleon by the neck, hurled him to the ground and straddled him, still screaming in pidgin German.

"I surrender!" bleated Mavroleon.

"Nein, nein!" screamed Gooderson. "You die, *Englischer* peeg! I steb you viz my knife like so! Ha! Ha! Ha!" And, forming his right hand into a fist, he drove an imaginary blade into the plump centre portion of Mavroleon and twisted it round and round, howling fragmentary insults in heavily accented English.

When he had finished he clambered off his man and faced the rest of them. "By the time I have finished with you," he said, to the members of the 4th Croydons who were present, "I want you all to be killers. I want you to be at such a pitch that we will have to unleash you on the Germans in order to stop you tearing yourselves to pieces. I want you to be mad dogs. I want there to be no pity in your hearts. I want you to be devoid of mercy."

"We will be, sir!" said Mavroleon, who was still lying on the ground. He rolled over on to his side and appeared to compose himself for sleep.

Alec wasn't sure that anything would be capable of turning Mavroleon into a mad dog. He might, he decided, be quite irritable if deprived of sleep and regular meals, but "quite irritable" wasn't going to stop Hitler, was it? Absurd though he seemed, Gooderson had a point. No, although he might have suffered a pang of guilt about Hatchett just now, there was simply no other way it could have been, ever. If he was honest with himself it had been like that from the beginning, from the days when he and Hatchett and Lucius had played cricket in the big garden at Albion House.

Gooderson had called out Peckerley from the ranks. "Right, lad!" he barked. "I am a German sentry!"

Gooderson took his Wehrmacht roles seriously and made some attempt to differentiate between them, to give each character a little twist, to make it come alive for his audience. His sentry was a very different character from his insane knife-wielder. He gave him a sort of rustic twist, a yokel-at-play look that compelled sympathy, even mild laughter from the watching infantry. He was a man, you felt, who would rather have been at home minding his cows in Lower Saxony than wandering around waiting to be killed by savage Englishmen. As he strolled around the field, Gooderson hummed a little tune to himself. "I am armed," said Gooderson, "but I am looking in the other direction. I want you to creep up on me, lad."

Play-acting, of course, of the kind Hatchett loved, was more important in life than Alec had previously thought. When he had asked Norma to marry him he had had an overwhelming sense that he was in a drama of some kind, but whereas before he might have felt outside it, now, like Major Gooderson, he had somehow been transformed by events into a credible character. War, thought Alec, would be the making of him, of all of them. All he had to do was play the part properly, just as he had judged that declaration to Norma up there in the field on the way from church. If he –

"Lieutenant Lycett," Gooderson was saying, "are you with us? Are you keeping your eyes open?"

Just as he came out of character, abandoning the whistling and the village-idiot-stares-at-new-surroundings routine, Peckerley leaped on him with a truly bloodcurdling cry of rage. "DIE!" he yelled, as Gooderson fell, like a poleaxed tree. "DIE!" he yelled again, as he rubbed his commanding officer's face into the earth.

"Get off, Peckerley," grunted Gooderson. "I wasn't ready."

"That, sir," said Peckerley, "was the whole point, wasn't it?"

"This," said Gooderson, dusting himself down, "is serious. You don't know how serious." He pulled himself up to his full height and glared round at his men. "We are leaving for an unknown destination tonight," said Gooderson. "I have been given sealed orders. The Territorials are on the move. In fact, we are almost the last of the Terriers to be on the move. But at last we are on the move."

"Where are we going, sir?" said Forssander.

"I can't tell you that," said Gooderson. "It is a secret destination. If I told you it wouldn't be secret, would it?"

"Do you know, sir?" said Mavroleon.

"I told you," said Gooderson, "these are sealed orders."

"Someone must know, sir," said Forssander. "Otherwise how will we know we have got to where we are supposed to be going?"

"Someone does know," said Gooderson, unwilling or unable to reveal whether he was that person, "but they haven't told us yet. They probably won't tell us even when we get there. Or even when we have been there for however long we are going to be there. We may never know where we are. Security, as I do not have to remind you, is paramount."

"Will anyone ever tell us where we are?" said Forssander, plaintively.

Perhaps, thought Alec, his phobia had some kind of geographical implication.

"I can't tell you that," said Gooderson sternly. "It may well be that we don't perform well enough to be entrusted with that information. It is very much up to you. As I said, the really vital thing is that the Germans don't know where we are. And one way of keeping that information from them is to keep it from us. We leave at nine and you have from seven thirty – when we break – until nine to prepare what you need for the journey to . . . where we are going."

Things, thought Alec, were getting serious rather more quickly than he had expected them to. Feeling a little like a child in one of his classes, he held up his hand. "Sir," he heard himself say, "I have to meet my . . . er . . ." he enjoyed saying this next word ". . . fiancée at seven and . . ."

Gooderson, who didn't really like Alec, enjoyed this. He rounded on him, tucking his swagger stick into his armpit as he did so. "Well, she will have to wait, my young Lieutenant, won't she? In fact, all your wives and sweethearts and families are going to have to learn to wait. From now on your wives and mothers and sweethearts are going to be the British Army. You are going to live for the British Army. You are going to sleep, wake and dream about nothing else, and by the time I have finished with you, you are going to be an immensely cruel and efficient fighting machine. You tell your fiancée there is a war on, young man!"

The 4th Croydons were now crowding round Gooderson, asking questions. A lot of them, thought Alec, sounded even more like schoolboys (and rather younger schoolboys) than he had. "Sir, sir, when do we go, sir? Are we going from the station, sir, or will we go by lorries, sir? Sir, why is it so quick, sir, why couldn't you tell us earlier, sir? Are we going abroad, sir? Sir . . ."

Only Peckerley, a boy who never seemed to bring his parents to school (Alec sometimes wondered whether he even had any) and who had belonged to the institution even more wholly than he or Hatchett, sat a little apart from the others, asking no questions, staring ahead of him.

He looks, thought Alec, as if he had left already.

And maybe I have left too. Or left something behind. Left behind Alec the second-rater. I am no longer in the shadow of Alec Senior. I am a soldier with a job to do and a girl to come back to. That was the sweetest thing. He had (at last cliché was not merely acceptable but almost mandatory) conquered the heart of the girl of his dreams, and when it was all over, by Christmas, he would return and marry her. He had come of age at last and when he said goodbye to her tonight, the farewell would somehow make their union seem all the more real.

And when I do marry her, he thought, with a grin, Hatchett can be my best man. Because the best man lost. No no no no. Won. The best man won – the lesson that losers find so difficult to learn.

6

Hatchett, Norma and Rachel did not stay long outside the TA building.

"I have to get home to Father," said Norma, as they turned away and walked back up the hill. "I imagine my stepmother is going to feel upstaged by the outbreak of war. She always likes to be the centre of attention."

"You're very fond of old Loosebottom, aren't you?" said Hatchett.

He said this quite without thinking, and for a moment he thought Norma was going to let it pass. But she turned her acute gaze on him and said, "I beg your pardon?"

"Er . . . some of the boys used to call him . . . er . . . your father that," said Hatchett, "God knows why. It bears no relation to any . . . er . . . physical quality he might or might not have and . . ." His voice guttered out. She was still looking at him. She was not smiling.

"You and Lycett," she said, "are both quite incredibly childish. Did you know that?"

"Yes," said Hatchett, although he could not resist adding, "although that is no way to speak of your fiancé."

Norma looked at him and, at last, she smiled. "You'll always be Hatchett and Lycett to me," she said, "and I quite like childish people, actually. I quite like children for that matter. And . . . er . . . Dennis . . . I am sorry if . . ."

"If what?" said Hatchett.

"Nothing!" said Norma.

There was an almost companionable silence. Norma's revelations had winded him at first. There had been a moment when the expression on Alec's face, a sort of puppyish ecstasy, had filled him with a desire to rip off his friend's ludicrous beret, stuff it into his mouth and beat him to death with his ridiculous boots. But almost immediately he had come to see that he, Hatchett, would never have been able to ask the bone-crunchingly simple question that had won Norma for Lycett. She and he were too similar. Love, thought Hatchett, was principally about not having a clue what the other person was really like. How else could you be so stupid as suddenly to decide that you wanted to spend the rest of your life with someone else? How, in God's name, could you think you knew what you would feel about them when you were, say, thirty? Or forty? Or fifty? Or, like Hatchett's mother, hobbling around in wizened circles?

You didn't know. You hadn't a clue. Only something as stupid as love could make you imagine you knew.

He was better off as her friend. He always had been her friend and he always would be. Friendship didn't wear out like romance. It never required the sacrifices of judgement that love seemed to demand. In friendship your partner's weaknesses, whether they be snoring or an unpleasant laugh, were grounds for discussion, not rupture.

"I was wondering," said Norma, who seemed to have changed her mind about visiting her father now she had been reminded that he was married to her stepmother, "if we should pay a call on Mabel Hughes."

"Why on earth would we do that?" said Hatchett. "She always reminds me of one of those French hags who brought their knitting to the guillotine."

"She is a little odd," said Norma, who always defended all of her girls from attack, "and she was unhealthily keen on Everett, I thought. But she is clever and moral, in a strange kind of way."

"What does 'moral in a strange kind of way' mean? Immoral?" said Hatchett. "You really want to find out why she said that about Everett being murdered, I suppose, don't you?"

"I suppose," said Norma, looking ahead at Rachel, who was absorbed in the antics of a bee moving around the flowers in the hedgerow, "I want to introduce Rachel to somebody. Mabel is a bit of a leader and it would be good for Rachel to make friends with her. I want people to be on her side. I am terrified she will let something slip."

Hatchett found time to be amused at Norma's ability to conceal her true motives from herself. Or, at least, to arrange them in an order that represented her in the best possible light. Women, of course, were taught to be more serious about being good than men. Lycett was a little like that. And this concern to be moral ruled them with a quiet insidiousness Hatchett did not always notice in men.

"I will come with you," he said, "although for different reasons."

"And what," said Norma, going into one of their Scottish routines, "might that be, pray?"

"I have decided," said Hatchett, looking over his glasses at her and speaking in a deliberately silly voice, "to investigate the murder of Alice Everett."

"If it was murder," said Norma. "And how do you propose to do that?"

Hatchett spread his hands. "I deescuss zer case," he said, in his Hercule Poirot voice. "I watch. I listen. And like zer Hercule Poirot so loved by your friend Jacqueline Rissett, I use zer leetle grey cells. Everett is dead. *Eh, bien!* Perhaps it is murder! By someone she knew! A teacher, perhaps, or a pupil at the very school where we instruct zer young!"

Norma looked at Rachel sharply. She was still absorbed in her insect but, catching Norma's eye, she broke off and walked back to join them.

"There is something going on," said Hatchett, in his normal voice, "and, as you say, I suppose we need to know what the class is thinking."

Rachel tugged at his sleeve. "Jacqueline Rissett worships Mabel Hughes," she said. "I have discovered this. But she is frightened of her also. I do not know why this is except . . ." here she shrugged ". . . Mabel is very clever. There is a big secret between them but I do not know what it is."

"There are always big secrets among schoolgirls," said Hatchett. "To listen to Mayhew you would think something supernaturally strange happened when we were in France."

"Perhaps it did," said Rachel. "You found me."

That seemed to close the conversation for the moment. But it decided Hatchett that going to see the Hugheses was a very good idea. As Jacqueline was close to Mabel, she was the one most in danger of finding out their secret. Perhaps she already knew. Didn't Jacqueline Rissett live somewhere near the Hughes girl? Hatchett straightened his shoulders, drew in his breath, turned and headed for South Croydon.

The Hughes family lived in a narrow street, in almost the last terraced house of a row that was the last dribble of the city before the stretch of open countryside that lay between Crotchett Green and Croydon. As the trio made their way round the edge of a cornfield and into a meadow, where a lone figure scythed at the long grass, Hatchett looked back at the church steeple, the school clock tower, the huge elms that stood on the long lawn that separated the boys' school from the girls'. Nothing has changed, he thought, and yet everything has.

He was hoping they weren't going to go to the Hugheses' place via Alec's street, which was almost the next one to it, but Norma seemed determined to do so. As they got closer to where his old friend lived, Hatchett felt the need to make it absolutely clear that, as far as he was concerned, Norma was free to marry the King of Siam. "Over there," he said, "is Lycett's house. I must turn my eyes to the wall. A tiny piece of me dies when I see the abode of my hated rival."

"Don't be silly, Dennis," said Norma.

Hatchett's tone reverted to the conversational. "You would have thought," he said, "that Lycett's old man would have stumped up a bit more cash than for one of these properties. The Alec Senior is loaded."

"Perhaps," said Norma, "he wants Alec to make his own way in the world." She gave him a careful look and added, "Did your families not get on?"

"Oh, my mother was always round there," said Hatchett, "but I don't think Papa would have approved of Alec Senior. My father was a great moralist, by all accounts. Which is why I am almost sure he disappeared with another woman." He met her eyes. "I wonder how you will get on with Alec's father, Norma . . ." he said.

"I am sure I shall get on with him perfectly," said Norma, "and if I don't I shan't really care. I am sure Alec wouldn't ask his father's permission. Any more than I would expect him to ask mine."

"I don't know," said Hatchett, "he is quite old-fashioned, is Alec. Did he go down on one knee to ask you to marry him?" Norma did not answer this. Hatchett looked over his glasses at her. "Did he go down on one knee to ask you to marry him?" he said again. Still she didn't answer. He turned, abruptly, into Hamish the Notary. "Miss Lewis, I must beg ye tae answer the question."

"Dennis!" said Norma.

"I just wondered," said Hatchett.

A small voice penetrated his consciousness. "Actually," said Rachel, "he did. I have been forward dispatched but have to the road returned and so seen this. At first I thought he was tying up his shoelaces but later it was clear to me that in England men are expected that they do this."

"Don't they do it in Germany?" said Hatchett.

"In Germany," said Rachel, with a short, satirical laugh, "they grab them by the hair and they bang them up against the wall."

Hatchett, as always, was enjoying his conversation with Rachel. She responded well to his type of interrogation. Hadn't Norma said her father was a scientist? Probably a teacher of some kind. "So this," he said to her, "happened on a deserted stretch of road. Did other people see it?"

"They have gone in a field!" said Rachel.

"Rachel!" said Norma.

Hatchett winked at Rachel.

"I saw that!" said Norma.

They had passed by Alec's house without comment. Half-way down Fairmead Passage Hatchett had glimpsed it on the other side of the road. He marvelled, once again, at the comparative squalor in which so many rich boys lived. Lycett, of course, wasn't a rich boy yet. He wouldn't really be a rich boy until his father died. Then he was going to be a really rich boy.

Hatchett found he was looking at a girl coming towards them. This wasn't like him. Hatchett rather disapproved of people who looked at girls. And yet it was impossible not to look at her. She was young, just on the edge of being an adult. But her hair, her lips, her, well, Hatchett, her breasts – say the word – compelled the attention. It took him three separate looks to establish once and for all that this actually was Jacqueline Rissett. And she was – surely not but she was – wearing lipstick, a substance classified, at Saltdene School, alongside cocaine and the music of Louis Armstrong. Where on earth was she going?

When she saw Hatchett she was overcome by furtiveness. She looked suddenly like a pickpocket going out on the night shift. She wasn't even wearing glasses, he thought, which might have explained why, when she saw Norma, she very nearly collided with a lamp-post. She and Rachel didn't appear to greet each other at all. Odd, thought Hatchett, how wary children are of each other. So little of their lives is under their own control that they can never really trust anyone. Which might, of course, help the cause of secrecy as far as Rachel was concerned.

"Where are you off to, Jacqueline?" asked Norma.

"Nowhere, Miss Lewis," mumbled Jacqueline, "just out." She turned to Rachel, as if seeing her for the first time. "I hear you're coming to Saltdene," she said. "That will be fun."

"Yes," said Rachel.

"You will be taught by your auntie," said Jacqueline, without the trace of a smile. Rachel inclined her head gracefully.

"Well, Jacqueline," said Norma, in a brisk tone, "we are off to see Mabel Hughes. You and she must come over and visit Rachel. Help her settle in." Jacqueline did not respond to this remark. "She's your friend, Mabel, isn't she?" said Norma. There was a pause. Jacqueline still didn't answer. Norma gave Jacqueline's face a sudden and devastating inspection. "So long as you take that muck off your face you will be very welcome."

Jacqueline very nearly curtsied before making her way off down the street.

Hatchett liked this fierce side of Norma's nature. It was part of her natural honesty. He had always been slightly suspicious of people who, like himself and, indeed, Lycett, were slow to lose their tempers. But he was surprised by the intensity of her response.

"Did you see the warpaint?" she said, as Jacqueline marched off. "And why should she be so worried about our going to see Mabel? The girl is up to no good. She had pounds of stuff on her face. She is probably afraid that Mabel will tell what she is up to. Miss Hughes is very strict about boys."

"Some people," said Hatchett, with mock pathos, "don't need warpaint. Some people have beautifully clear complexions and jet-black hair and . . ."

"Stop that at once, Dennis," said Norma, with a slight grin. "I will have you know I am practically a married woman." She turned to Rachel. "Has Jacqueline a boyfriend, Rachel?" she said.

"I do not know, Auntie," said Rachel. "I only just got here."

They were in Mabel's street now. Several of the houses here, Hatchett noted, had sandbags piled up against the doors. At the front of the house opposite, an elderly man was nailing up his windows with great thoroughness. The Hugheses, however, looked as if they had been aware of the implications of the Prime Minister's broadcast for longer than anyone else in the street. The sandbags here were piled up beyond the sills of the lower windows. The windows themselves had not only been blacked out from the inside but barricaded with bricks and what looked like barbed wire. There had been a number on the door, but it had been carefully painted out – presumably to fool any members of the Hitler Youth with specific orders to search out and destroy the inhabitants of 23 Kitchener Avenue, Croydon.

Norma rang the bell. A voice from deep within the premises called, "Who is it?"

Hatchett was tempted to bark out a few words in *Hochdeutsch*, just for the pleasure of watching the occupants hare out of the back door, down the garden and over the back wall in the direction of Croydon.

"It's Norma Lewis, Mr Hughes," Norma was shouting through

the letterbox, "from Saltdene. I said I would call round to discuss Mabel's plans for the future."

She was far more capable of tact, that mild form of deception, than Hatchett had thought. When she allowed herself to make free with the strict moral code she had set herself she became, however, more, not less, attractive. That was just what Hatchett did not want. She was colouring up at her social falsehood and her cheeks were showing off the colour of her eyes and ... Damn this, Hatchett! You are not here because you cannot bear to be apart from your best friend's fiancée. You are here because ...

Why was he here? Could he bear to be apart from her? No, he couldn't. Yes, he could. No, he couldn't. Yes, he could.

A face appeared at the door. It was not, thought Hatchett, a human face. It had pig-like qualities. Which is to say there was a snout of some kind but it was more like a disappointed elephant's trunk than a snout. And the eyes, round and circled with black, like a panda's, made him think for a moment that Mr Hughes (for he was somewhere inside this artificial head) had been amusing himself by walking around the house in a diver's helmet.

Then he realized. It was a gas mask. All the Hugheses, Mrs Hughes, Master Hughes, a tiny cowed boy of five, and Miss Hughes, who were gathering behind Hughes *père* in the gloom of the narrow hall, were wearing gas masks. What made it even odder was that the sallow-faced man Hatchett recognized from the church, he of the blue suit and nasal voice, who was standing a little behind the family, was presenting a naked, unadorned face to the visiting company. And he would have been greatly improved by the wearing of a gas mask. Perhaps, thought Hatchett, he was from some government department sent house-to-house to make sure that people were wearing these things properly.

Hatchett was damned if he was going to wear a gas mask. Except, possibly, to an orgy of some kind.

Mr Hughes wrestled his off his face and stared, accusingly, at Norma. "Is this a convenient time, Miss Lewis?" he barked.

"Don't be silly, Daddy," said Mabel, pushing back her mask. "Miss Lewis said she would call round." She stepped in front of her father and, her eyes never leaving Norma's face, gave her a smile of ghastly confidentiality. It was clear to Hatchett that here was a girl with a bad case of teacher worship. Perhaps she had simply replaced Love of Everett with Love of Lewis. It was also clear that she was the one in charge in this place.

Her mother, a short, blowsy woman with blonde hair, nothing like her daughter, bustled out in a manner that was almost professionally servile. "Don't mind him, Miss Lewis," she said. "He's been making us hide under the table for most of the day."

Mr Hughes certainly took a belt-and-braces approach to the coming conflict. In the front room all the furniture had been piled against one wall ("to minimize blast", as he was keen to explain) and, on the back kitchen table, at which they were invited to sit, were a torch, a whistle, three or four more sandbags and a brand new spade.

"This is Mr Mason," said Mr Hughes, as the sallow-faced man stepped forward to greet them. "Friend of the family. He works for a Government Department. Very hush-hush." Hughes obviously expected his visitors to be impressed by this. If Mr Mason, whose handshake was as limp as his suit trousers, was a spy, he was a very junior one, thought Hatchett. More likely he was a person who checked up on spies' expenses.

Norma gave them ten or fifteen minutes on Mabel's future, the obligatory five minutes on the war (the Hugheses all seemed to think it was a very bad idea, Mr Hughes expressing the view that it would be "bad for business") and a rather hair-raising session on Rachel's entirely fictional childhood in Calcutta, during which Mrs Hughes asked a couple of unanswerable questions about nuns. Finally, she swivelled round and gave Mabel the full benefit of her attention. "And how are you, Mabel?" she said.

Mabel stared at her unblinkingly. "You mean," she said, scraping back her already scraped-back hair and composing her hands in her lap like a Victorian chaperone, "why did I say what I said in church this morning?"

"Mabel!" said her mother.

"She is quite right, Mrs Hughes," said Norma, "that is partly why I came. I was concerned about you, Mabel."

Mabel nodded slowly. "I know," she said. "You care about all of us girls." She turned to her mother. "Miss Lewis is a wonderful teacher," she said. "She and Leafy and Miss Leach and . . ." she looked at the floor briefly ". . . Miss Everett are all wonderful teachers. They are good and kind and full of love for us. Except Miss Everett is dead, of course. She took me for Spanish. She was marvellous at Spanish. Sometimes to hear her you would think she actually was Spanish. Although she didn't look Spanish. But I suppose she could have come from northern Spain."

The thought of Everett prompted her to physical action. She leaned forward and took Norma's hand. A curiously old-fashioned thing, thought Hatchett, but a personality. Norma was quite right to try to get her on Rachel's side.

"I said she was murdered because I am sure she was," said Mabel. Her mother, who seemed to be even stupider than she looked, jumped up in her chair, put her hand to her mouth and squeaked, "My God!" before subsiding again. "Everyone is saying she was murdered, aren't they?" went on Mabel. "Shouldn't it be out in the open?"

People were starting to say this, of course. Someone in the staffroom had said only last week that they had heard Hornby, from the boys' school, was strongly tipped as a suspect, although the only reason given was that he had had a room quite near hers in the *pension* and he did have a very shifty look about him.

"You wouldn't take hyoscine hydrobromide in any other than very small quantities," said Mr Hughes, who seemed positively enthusiastic about the turn the conversation had taken. "Although, of course, if you wanted to murder someone it would be a very good way to do it. Very good." He said this as if it was something he had often seriously considered. "But I happen to know that Miss Everett was always very careful about dosage."

"And how," said Hatchett, trying to keep his voice as neutral as possible, "did you come to know that?"

"I am a chemist, Mr Hatchett," said Hughes, with quiet pride. "I am a pharmacist by trade. Miss Everett obtained the drug from me on prescription. From my shop. In a sense I feel responsible for her death. I am sure Mabel, too, feels responsible for her death."

"I do," said Mabel, "though not, of course, literally speaking."

"No!" said Hatchett, who felt a mad urge to giggle. Something to do with the overwhelmingly grim atmosphere of the house. It was as well, he decided afterwards, that he had not, because Mabel Hughes quite clearly regarded the death of Alice Everett as no laughing matter. Her eyes were still fixed on Norma's face.

"All sorts of people wanted her dead," she said. "I am sure that Mr Breeze had every reason to conceal their passionate affair from his wife."

This remark had a sensational effect on all those present. Mrs Hughes bounded up in her chair again, this time with three, not just one, my Gods. Even Mr Mason, of the sallow face and limp handshake, choked on his teacake. Hatchett was certainly horrified, although his revulsion at the thought of the physical union of A. Breeze and A. Everett was on aesthetic rather than moral grounds.

"They were kissing and fondling," went on Mabel. "They could not keep their hands off each other. Jacqueline Rissett saw them. Apparently."

"So," said Hatchett quietly, "Jacqueline Rissett told you this, did she?"

When she answered, Mabel did not look at him but at Norma. "She did," she said. "She said she had heard them one night in Everett's room carrying on like . . . animals. And it was funny because there was a time when I thought Jacqueline might . . ."

"Might what?" said Hatchett.

"Might have a stupid crush on Mr Breeze," said Mabel, "but she reassured me of that, I can tell you, Miss Lewis. She was horrified by what he was up to. She thought he should be prosecuted in the courts. It is pretty obvious that Mr Breeze murdered Miss Everett to stop his wife finding out!"

The upper fifth, now lower sixth, of Saltdene Grammar School for Girls, thought Hatchett, was a far steamier place than he had ever imagined. The schoolgirl mind seemed to steam and bubble with the force of a cesspit in hell.

"Miss Everett," went on Mabel, "was a beautiful person and a wonderful teacher. I feel sorry for what happened to her." She did not say whether this referred to the Spanish teacher's being humped by the chemistry master or given lethal doses of a known poison. Hatchett was fairly sure that Mabel considered the first option the more unsavoury of the two.

"I think, Mabel," said her mother, in the silence that followed this remark, "that is quite enough about this subject. The school . . ."

"The school must be informed!" said Mr Hughes.

Norma turned the conversation deftly towards her niece. It was funny, thought Hatchett, that that was how he thought of Rachel now. And her presence was altering his view of Norma: it seemed to make her softer, more maternal, in a way that Hatchett had never thought she could be. The brusque lines of the schoolmistress were being softened so that her face, her eyes and –

Stop it, Hatchett. She belongs to Lieutenant Lycett. You never wanted her anyway. Write out three hundred times "She is bossy. She is bossy. She is . . ."

"Jacqueline and I will take very good care of Rachel, Miss Lewis!" said Mabel, with devotional intensity. "And I am sure Elinor and Janet," here she gave a winsome little smile, "will be able to spare time from each other to make her very welcome too."

"Mayhew," said Norma, "isn't part of your little group, is she?"

Mabel did not respond to this, but cast her eyes down as if to say that she personally had no objection to girls who dropped aspirates, picked their noses and talked about periods in loud, unseemly voices but that as far as the others were concerned . . .

My God, thought Hatchett, am I glad we spared the time to negotiate poor Rachel's passage through this minefield!

Mrs Hughes asked if the school was to be evacuated. Norma said there were no plans to evacuate any pupils. Mr Hughes said he wondered if they might make an exception in Mayhew's case. Everybody, apart from Norma, laughed.

All four Hugheses and Mr Mason, who was treated with elaborate and deferential respect by Mr Hughes throughout the visit, accompanied them to the door.

"I hope you'll excuse me," said Mason to Rachel, as they stepped outside. "I couldn't place your accent when you came in, young lady."

Mr Hughes looked at him in undisguised admiration. "You can't pull the wool over Colin's eyes," he said. "Colin sees things that are hidden from us mere mortals. Colin knows Europe like the back of his hand. He went to Finland once!"

"Some people," said Rachel calmly, "think I am German, which is funny. My mother is Swiss, of course."

This was the first time anyone had ever mentioned Norma's sister-in-law, but Rachel did it with such aplomb that Hatchett could have sworn the woman was actually Swiss.

"If you were German," Mason said, with a laugh that showed a set of yellow teeth, "we would have to lock you up and throw away the key."

"I suppose," said Hatchett, smoothly, "we must be prepared to admit that not all Germans are bad. Goethe, Schiller . . ."

"Are they Germans?" said Mason, suspiciously.

"They are," said Hatchett, "or rather were. They're dead."

"Good!" said Mason, with quite extraordinary ferocity. "The only good German is a dead German!"

Well, thought Hatchett, as Rachel, Norma and he said their goodbyes a little further down the street, we are going to see a great deal more of that as the year plays out. People love to have something to hate, and now they have been given licence to fear and distrust millions of people whom they have never even met. Perfect! How good this will be for everybody! War seemed to have a horrible talent for simplifying things. It had certainly made relations between him, Norma and Lycett hideously clear. They were a couple. He was a gooseberry or a raspberry or whatever fruit into which couples turned people.

"You mustn't be late for your fiancé!" he said, because he thought generosity would make him feel better. It didn't.

And, turning on his heels, he walked away from her with every appearance of enthusiasm. He didn't even look back at her once. He was able to simulate indifference so successfully, he decided afterwards, only because he had started to follow a train of thought that interested him. For Hatchett, intellectual activity was the sovereign remedy for depression. He was puzzling over the fact that, because he wasn't a chemist and regarded the subject as an incomprehensible series of hideous abbreviations, he had not read a chemistry book since he was twelve. And yet the name "hyoscine hydrobromide" was curiously familiar. He had read it in some book somewhere, he said to himself, as he turned the corner of the street, and made his way back towards the solitary life.

Hatchett really was an infuriating man, thought Norma, as she studied herself in the mirror. Simple black dress. Stockings straight. No jewellery or makeup. Black shoes. Offer no encouragement to the enemy.

She was shaking, she realized. Her hands were shaking. Was this to do with the war? She didn't think so. She had somehow thought that when you got to the moment there would be some public manifestation of human or divine wrath. Everyone would be dashing through the streets, hunting down Austrian cake-makers or German sausage-manufacturers or there would be a hurricane or a thunderstorm or something, anyway, that said THIS IS A SERIOUS DAY!

But it was a day like any other day.

The reason she was shaking was because of Alec. Tonight would be the first night when she and Alec would be alone together, for the purpose for which men and women usually were alone together. What was that? she said to herself, a touch hysterically.

She knew she was being quite ridiculous but, even as she thought this, she reflected that she had spent too much of her life being not at all ridiculous. Too much time at her books. Too much time deliberately not encouraging men, until it had become a habit. Well, now she was going to encourage a man. She was going to encourage him and encourage him and encourage him until he . . . well . . . until he did what it was that men did when they were encouraged. She flushed even more hotly at this thought.

Presumably he would want to kiss her. He loved her. He would therefore want to kiss her. And Norma, although she was in her mid-twenties and widely considered beautiful (Doran had said she had the best legs in South Croydon), had never been kissed. A boy had tried to kiss her in her last year at Manchester University but she had dodged at the last moment and he had ended up banging his chin on her shoulder. One of her French teachers had put his hands on her shoulders during a seminar and she had asked him not to do it again. She was almost sure it had affected her marks. But she had never, for some reason, done that thing that people were always doing in cinema films. She had never tipped her head back against the left palm of some brilliantined oaf while he circled above her like a fly then swooped in to land on the soft bits of her face . . . all the while his right hand kneading her upper thighs like unproved bread.

She didn't like the thought of doing that but it was something you had to go through. Maybe it was that that was making her hands shake.

Presumably they had to start it. You couldn't suddenly drape yourself across a chair, jerk your head back and open wide. You shouldn't (or should you?) grab them back when they grabbed you, as she had seen Barbara Stanwyck do in one drama (a sin for which she had been severely punished). You shouldn't (she was sure about this) let it go on for too long, in case it led to Other Things, and it was probably necessary to break away and sit up every few minutes to examine yourself in a vanity mirror while saying, "Oh, Mr Lycett! You're mussing my hair!"

Saying this out loud to herself, even in an American accent, made her realize suddenly how much she wanted him to muss her hair, and once mussing had started how difficult it was going to be to tell him to stop. It was all very . . . she reached for an adjective and, as so often, found an inappropriate one – explosive.

Norma patted her soon-to-be-mussed hair back into place and watched it bounce, in a not unattractive manner, just above her shoulders. "Rachel!" she called.

Rachel appeared at the door. Although it was only half-past six she was already wearing one of Norma's nightdresses. She had come, Norma reminded herself once again, with absolutely nothing.

She had brought no books, no keepsake letters, no photographs, no objects of sentimental value, no objects of real value come to that. The only wealth she possessed was a gold filling in the left back molar, which Norma glimpsed every time the girl laughed. She didn't read books, apart from the occasional scientific text-book, which had somehow found its way into Norma's flat from school, probably from Mr Groenig, who was, she thought, a little interested in her. She didn't listen to Norma's wind-up gramophone. She didn't draw or take exercise or show any interest whatsoever in cooking or cleaning. Occasionally, if she thought Norma wasn't looking, she would cover sheets of paper with indecipherable calculations – mathematical symbols, Greek letters, oddly shaped brackets, exclamation marks that didn't follow exclamations, commas hung in space like flags and row after row after row of incomprehensible numbers. But when she had finished she screwed up the paper into a small ball, as if she didn't want anyone to see it.

If she threw away the ball of paper she would always consign it, not to a waste-basket from which, perhaps, someone might retrieve it and make some kind of sense of it, but to the bin outside, where it would soon be covered in potato peelings, tea-leaves, fragments of bread and half-chewed meat.

What Rachel thought about frightened Norma. Principally because she did not understand what it might be. One of the reasons she had studied languages was that she hated the idea of things being secret from her. Rachel had her mind on something beyond all this, but whatever it was, even if it wasn't actually secret (when Norma asked her once what she was writing Rachel had said it was nothing, some formula from her physics work at school), it was something about which she had been taught to be circumspect.

She was about to initiate another, probably fruitless conversation about this very subject, when Rachel said, "Please – where is Birmingham?"

"Why do you want to know?" said Norma.

"I have to go there," said Rachel.

"Why on earth," said Norma, "do you have to go to Birmingham?"

There was a long pause.

"To see someone," said Rachel, in a small voice.

"This person who might look after you?" said Norma. "This friend of your father's? Is that it?" Rachel didn't answer. "Is he a German?" said Norma. "Is he here illegally? Is that why you dare not tell me who he is? Do you think I would betray you to the police, Rachel? I mean, if he isn't doing any harm here why would I do that? Why is this person here?"

Rachel looked at her miserably. "I don't know, Auntie," she said. "I don't know what is safe to tell you and what is not safe. My father has told me to talk to no one about certain things. In Germany it is not safe to talk about many things. Even some questions of what you may say is . . . intellectual truth, I should say, truth about the way the world is, the hidden nature of things, are not possible to discuss. We use what you may say is a kind of code. And in my father's work he also uses a code. You understand? If he says to this man such-and-such, he and this man very well know that he means so-and-so."

"Er, yes," said Norma, who hadn't really understood a word of this.

"I am frightened to tell you, Auntie," said Rachel. "I am frightened to say what I can and cannot say. You are so kind to me. You give me a home and you take me in and you are a good and kind person. But now I don't know any more what I can and cannot say and even to you who has been so kind my tongue is tied and I am frightened although I am trying. I am trying to tell you, I swear."

The little girl, and she wasn't, really, more than a little girl, thought Norma – in some ways she was much younger than her own English charges – was crying now, great dry sobs. Norma crossed over to her and took her in her arms and let Rachel's head rest on her as the two of them stood in the darkening room. "You don't have to tell me anything you don't want to," she said. "You don't have to talk about any of the things that have happened to you. You don't have to worry about anything apart from being a little English schoolgirl just outside Croydon."

Rachel, breaking away from her and drying her tears, laughed through the last of her sobs. "I think," she said, "that that is enough to worry about in fact. I find Croydon a very frightening place."

Norma went back to watching herself in the mirror. Rachel went back to watching her watch her reflection. "You go to see Mr Lycett," she said. Norma grinned by way of answer. Rachel wagged her finger. "Ha!" she said. "Ha! Ha! Ha!"

Norma turned to face her. "Who is this person you want to see in Birmingham?" she said. "He is a scientist? Who worked with your father? On secret work? Is that it?"

Rachel shrugged. "On problems of physics," she said. "There are no secrets in physics. Apart from things we are too stupid to understand. These are secrets. So, as far as the average Reich official is concerned, the whole of physics is one big secret. For example, just now, because I am thinking of this work that my father has done and also this friend of his, also I am thinking of a formula that applies to the surface area of an object when it is expanding. That is not a secret. The surface area of a sphere increases more slowly with increasing radius than does the volume, as nearly r squared to r cubed. That is not a secret."

"It might as well be as far as I am concerned," said Norma. "Is it something to do with . . . with rockets or something?"

Rachel looked at her reproachfully. Then the two of them smiled. Norma went to sit on the bed, and, after a while, Rachel joined her.

"What kind of camp have they taken your father to?" said Norma.

"A camp," said Rachel. "They have camps for Jews. And trouble-makers. My father is both of those things."

"And what do they do to them . . . in those . . . camps?" said Norma.

"I don't know," said Rachel, bleakly. "I think perhaps they kill them."

She didn't look as if she was going to cry again but in case she did Norma kept her voice very gentle and soothing as she said, "I am sure they don't kill them, Rachel," she said. "I am sure they just . . . lock them up and . . . make them do dirty work and . . . dig roads like we do convicts . . . and . . . ." She was aware that what she was saying sounded increasingly feeble with each word. She had no idea, really, what life in Germany must be like for a girl like this. She couldn't begin to imagine it. She tried very hard to inject a note of hope into her voice. You could do that for people, even in a comfortable corner of England like this one, you could try to tell them that life wasn't as bad as it seemed, that . . . Before she lost confidence in her own optimism Norma said, "I am sure that you will see your mother and father again, Rachel. I am sure you will. There is some justice in the world, Rachel, I know there is. I am sure there is. Really."

Rachel looked at her. "If you say so, Auntie," she said. "If you say so."

Norma was going to be late. She settled Rachel with a pencil and a sheet of blank paper and, after a final self-inspection – this time in the long mirror in the hall of the flat – she set off down the stairs. Rachel called, "Good luck!" after her. As she went out into the front garden of Albion House, she looked up at the gabled housefront. She had been here as a child. She was sure of that. Perhaps she had even seen Alec here, although she could not be sure of that. The one thing she was sure of was that in those days there had been an elegant iron fence. The hedge was new.

The fact that she should have ended up here, where he had used to live, made her nervous, as if some pattern over which she had no control was working itself out. That was odd. It ought to reassure her, to make her feel that luck was with her on her engagement. Maybe she was a little more worried about the Lycett family than she cared to admit to herself.

She had heard enough from Alec to know that his had not been a happy childhood. Perhaps there had been a special misery about his home. Thinking about Albion House now, as she walked back down the hill towards the Queen Vic, she thought again about the woods behind it. High, intertwined oaks and chestnuts, and weird gaps in the trees, dank with moss, always made her think that perhaps the locals were right when they said they were haunted.

A car inched up the hill towards her. It was dark now. Norma had not really paid much attention to the blackout. She had completely ignored gas drill, air-raid shelters or the need to look out for German spies, loitering around the bus queue and trying to make conversation in halting English. It was only when she saw the twin feeble, shrouded beams of the vehicle's approaching headlights that she realized how dark the rest of the landscape was. Croydon, usually a swarm of tiny lights, was suddenly blanketed in darkness, strangely beautiful. There were no tell-tale ribbons of street-lamps, distant flickers from electric hoardings or the lonely glow-worm gleam of cars trekking home through the summer night.

And the blackout seemed to have intensified the silence. Somewhere, miles away, a man was shouting something, but his voice only emphasized the church-like quiet of the scene before her.

The Queen Victoria was a little way out of the village since an ancient by-law forbade all alcohol within two miles of St Mary and All Angels Church. Some locals referred to it, disparagingly, as a "roadhouse". But the Queen Vic was usually a respectable, well-lit beacon of light and noise in a stretch of near-suburban countryside. Tonight, however, it wasn't so much blacked out as completely and utterly obliterated. It was as if someone had wrapped the whole thing in dark velvet. Or, thought Norma, as she came down the lane and was unable to find it in its usual place, picked it up and moved it a few hundred yards to the right. That tree, on the left, standing out against the sky, should have been the one on the corner before the pub. And if the road was, as she thought it might be, curving to the left, then that five-barred gate that came before the apple tree that came before the hedge with the ditch in front of it ought to be arriving round about now, since they were what you usually saw just before you got to the Queen Vic, even as you heard a tinkling piano, a cracked voice singing something to its accompaniment, the distant noise of footsteps, a door slamming and shouted farewells in the darkness. But Norma did not hear them.

When the moon came out from behind the clouds and she finally saw the outline of the pub, its silhouette against the sky seemed as sudden, silent and wickedly distinct as that of some haunted house on a hill in a horror film. Perhaps, she thought, it was closed because of the war.

Then the door opened, there was a sliver of light, and a darkened figure slipped out and away down the lane. Signs of life. Someone was at home.

Norma wasn't the kind of girl who went to pubs unescorted. She went in jolly parties or with Hatchett and Lycett (nearly always the two of them). Although she had met Alec, once or twice, on his own, it hadn't been this kind of meeting. The nature of the day, the war, his proposal and the feeling that, suddenly, every time you did something it might be the last time you did it made her feel hectic, fast, although Norma knew she wasn't really a fast girl. But to meet a man *à deux*! That, she now realized, was as truly terrifying as it was truly exciting. She crept towards the dark door and put her hands to the cool metal of the quaint latch.

She was quite unprepared for the brilliance of the interior.

There were the same rows and rows of glasses and bottles alongside the mirror at the back of the bar. There was the same huge chandelier in the middle of the big, cavernous room, but tonight they seemed to have added more light, more glasses, more mirrors, in honour of the occasion, as if to announce their defiance to the coming darkness. Business as usual.

The fact that it clearly wasn't business as usual was what made the scene so eerie. For in spite of the wattage and the reflections, the full complement of three well-turned-out bar-keepers and the shine on brass, wood, pump handles, silvered mirrors and carefully polished tankards laid out for absent regulars, the Queen Vic was empty.

Well, almost empty.

There were two people at the bar. They were standing, no, thought Norma, they seemed to be trying to fuse themselves with its polished wood, since they were also in the middle of a shockingly public kiss. The man had his back to her and the woman was being forced against the edge of the bar, so that at first all Norma could see of her was a pair of hands wriggling all over the fellow's shoulder-blades and lower back as if they were trying to find a point of entrance. Then, in full view of everybody – well, Norma anyway – frustrated in this quest, they dived down further to give his behind a thorough, and rather distasteful, exploratory feel.

When they heard the door the pair broke apart.

Norma saw, as the woman straightened herself and went into that characteristic, jolly-hockey-sticks gesture of wiping her forehead with the back of her wrist, that the red hair, the freckles, the wide mouth and the spade-shaped chin belonged to none other than Jennifer Doran. It didn't surprise her, really. Jennifer was capable of that kind of behaviour. In talking about men she nearly always used language that might have been more appropriate to the subject she taught. They were "scrumptious", "mouth-watering" or "good enough to eat", and the less attractive ones "not very appetizing" or "hardly tasty". Norma had never disliked this side of Jennifer. It was the way she was and her directness – so different from Norma's cautious way with other people – was what made their friendship interesting. But seeing Jennifer actually snacking, as it were, made her stop and wonder.

All she saw of the man, at first, was the uniform. It took her a moment to realize that it was a Royal Air Force outfit and then she remembered that they were to be stationed at Saltdene. Perhaps this was the first of them. If this was how they were going to carry on she hoped there weren't going to be too many others. But then he turned round and she saw that the person in the uniform was Alec Lycett. Alec Lycett, who, as far as she knew, was nothing whatsoever to do with the RAF and who was looking at her as if he had never seen her before in his life.

He didn't express shame or guilt or even surprise at the fact that, after having proposed to her at ten forty-five, he should be caught doing unmentionable things to her best friend in the very pub where she had arranged to meet him. He just stared, sneering slightly, as if he had done something clever or brave. Jennifer started to say something but Norma did not wait to hear what it was. Without saying a word, because she could not think of one that fitted the occasion, she turned and practically ran for the door. She ran up the hill and did not stop until she was absolutely sure that no one was following her. She was terribly afraid she might cry –

something she hadn't really done since her mother died – and she did not want anyone close to her if she were to give herself up to the indignity of tears.

PART THREE

20 August 1921

"Can I stay? Can I stay?"

Hatchett's mother had come to take him home. He did not want to go home. It was only six o'clock. They were sitting in the big kitchen. Lucius, who was usually kept out of sight even for visits by people as unimportant as Mrs Hatchett, had been allowed down from his room. Maybe it was a treat because he was going away.

Now he knew that Lucius was a murderer, Hatchett watched him very carefully. He knew murderers were not like other people. What was strange was that Lucius walked and talked just like he normally did. Hatchett watched him very carefully, all the same, for the tell-tale signs. Probably, he thought, Lucius was so bad that he did not even show remorse. Not showing remorse, his father had said, was about the worst thing you could do and God would never forgive you for it.

"Please! Please!"

Hatchett's mummy looked at Lycett's mummy. Lycett's mummy looked at Lycett's daddy. Lycett's daddy looked at Lycett. Lycett looked at Hatchett. Hatchett put his hands together as if he was praying and fell to his knees. Everybody laughed.

"I don't see why not," said Mrs Lycett.

"If it's too much trouble . . ." said Mrs Hatchett.

She was always saying things like that. She didn't mean them. She didn't care how much trouble it was. She didn't want Hatchett at home because she had told him so. She was just being stupid and polite the way grown-ups were.

"It is no trouble, Mrs Hatchett," drawled Mrs Lycett. She gave Hatchett another of those funny looks she was always giving him. "We love having him, Mrs Hatchett," she said. "Don't we, Lucius?"

Lucius, who had been biting his lip and probably thinking about who to murder next, said, "No! We don't!"

All the grown-ups laughed. As they did when Lucius said things like that.

"He smells," said Lucius.

Alec's daddy came across to him. Lucius dodged his head but Alec's daddy didn't hit him, although, thought Hatchett, he well deserved it. As he raised his hand, Lucius's mummy seized him by the arm and said, in a low voice, "Alec! For God's sake! You and your temper!" She said this as if she really hated him.

Mrs Hatchett, instead of pretending this wasn't happening, which was what you were supposed to do, gave them both a good long stare of the kind she had lavished on the waxworks when they went to the Chamber of Horrors at Madame Tussaud's. "If it's not too much trouble," she said, blinking at them. "I'll pop back around bedtime with his pyjamas."

He had got his eyes from her, his father had said. And his clothes, too. Not dresses, but she made him things that looked as if they had come out of a jumble sale like she did. That was probably why his father had left.

"Hooray!" said Hatchett.

"Hooray!" said Lycett.

"Help!" said Lucius.

All the grown-ups laughed again.

"Lucius," said his father, "is going away to school today. And he is a bit upset. He'll miss us. Won't you, Lucius?"

"I won't miss you!" said Lucius.

It must be funny having an identical twin.

When he had first heard about it Hatchett had thought it would be ripping fun. You could turn up to school instead of the other person – although, of course, Lucius didn't go to their school – and no one would know. You could rob banks and then pretend it wasn't you but the other one.

But Alec had explained to him that it wasn't like that at all. It was actually the most horrid thing you could imagine, having another one of you following you around everywhere, copying you, making you feel like you did when you saw yourself in a mirror and thought, Oh, my God! That can't be me! And the copy of him, Alec explained, was a sort of bad copy. This was why, thought Hatchett, they had MADE IN BRITAIN stamped on things because it told you they were good and not cheap, inferior imitations. Britain was the best and the fairest country in the world.

If you looked closely, of course, there were bits of Lucius that were not at all like Alec. There was a wiggly bit on his left ear. There was a funny bumpy bit by one of his knees. And, although Hatchett had not had the chance to verify this, Alec said his willy was completely different.

His voice was the strangest thing. Once you knew it was Lucius instead of Alec – and that could take quite a long time – you could hear a sort of sneer in Lucius's tone that wasn't there in Alec's. Although, this was funny, once you had heard it in Lucius, sometimes you heard it in Alec's voice as well and you were tempted to say, "Gosh, you sound just like Lucius when you say that!" Which was not a good idea. Because the thing Alec hated most in the world was being told he looked or sounded like Lucius.

Which must have made life pretty hard, considering he was his identical twin.

The grown-ups had drifted away. Mrs Lycett was talking to Mrs Hatchett. Lycett's daddy was watching them. There was a funny expression on his face.

"Are you going to hang around us?" Alec was saying to his twin brother.

Lucius just stood there, clenching and unclenching his fists. Hatchett hoped Alec wasn't going to be too rude to him. He wondered how Lucius had got the petrol to pour on the tramp. And why the tramp hadn't woken up while he was pouring it and sounded the alarm. Hatchett had always felt particularly sorry for Archbishop Cranmer in history. Being burned alive must be horrible.

"I suppose," said Alec, "we won't have to put up with him after tonight. He won't even be coming home in the holidays. Daddy has a sister."

Lucius put the sneer in his voice. "Daddy Daddy Daddy!" he said. "You know what our daddy is, don't you?"

It was Alec's turn to clench his fists. "Shut up about Daddy," he said, "or Hatchett and I will jolly well bash you!"

Hatchett could not quite think how they were going to do this. Although they were identical in almost every respect, Lucius had some special strength, which meant he won fights. He didn't stop like most people. He went on and on and on until you surrendered, which you usually did. Well, of course, he was a KILLER. He was looking at Hatchett now with the sneer on his face as well as in his voice. "You and Wetlegs!" he said. "Fat chance!"

In spite of the horrible name, which was worse because it was true – Hatchett had once had a terrible accident at school and had had to try to flush his underpants down the lavatory – it was important not to get the KILLER too angry.

"Come on!" said Hatchett. "Let's play anyway. I'll be It. Hide and seek. Count from . . . from two hundred!"

Lycett's house was good for hide-and-seek. And two hundred meant he was going to try really hard. He could see that both twins were tempted by the idea. Instead of waiting for them to discuss it, which would have ended in an argument, Hatchett crossed the third finger of each hand over the index finger and chanted, "Fains I! Fains I! Can't catch me!" And shot off down the garden.

He looked back once at both boys. Obediently, they had each closed both eyes tight and were counting. "No looking!" said Hatchett. "Or I win!"

He had known where he was going to hide from the moment he had suggested the game. It was a very brave place. They would never, ever find him. He was going to go back into the woods. Even though they were haunted, probably by the ghost of the tramp, he was going to go. The excitement of the game meant he was not – to his surprise – afraid.

At least, not at first.

He ran straight down the lawn, turned right into the lower part of the shrubbery (in case either of them had cheated and was looking), then worked his way back through the bushes until he was by the gate that led out into the fields behind Albion House.

This was a dangerous bit. Once they had started out after him, there were plenty of places in the upper part of the garden from where you could see the gate. Seventy-five, seventy-four, seventy-three, seventy-two . . . Lucius, of course, was perfectly capable of cheating. A boy who could set light to a poor old tramp was quite up to missing out a few numbers while counting himself down in hide-and-seek.

Sixty-two, sixty-one, sixty . . . He was at the gate.

Hatchett slipped it open, closed it with dexterous quietness and, before he was down to forty-five, was running, full tilt, back to the woods where they would never find him. Now it was an adventure, he said to himself, he was brave, and from now on it would be easy to be brave.

Oh, their faces when they gave up!

To make it extra difficult, he was going to hide in the most dangerous place of all. The dark place, surrounded by brambles, where he had been so frightened earlier in the day. As he tore through the trees and, lowering his head, wriggled further and further into the heart of the wood, he felt like a soldier behind enemy lines. Ten – nine – eight – he had made such good time! – six – five – four . . . There was a spot just ahead of him where, behind a tall oak, was a third bramble bush and, with reckless disregard for the state of his clothes, Hatchett threw himself into it, pulled the branches behind him and settled down to wait. Three, two, one . . . zero!

It was the silence that made him afraid.

He had been fine before that. But when the silence started, and it did just begin like that, not creeping up on you the way silence usually did, it was like something you could touch, whispering things to Hatchett as the serpent whispered in the Garden of Eden. Things like – "They're not coming! No one will ever find you!" Things like – "Someone else will come! Out of the wood! Some . . . horrid . . . thing! Can't you hear it?"

But he couldn't hear it. Which made it worse. All he could hear was the silence and the ticking of his heart under his grey cotton shirt.

That was when he saw the handkerchief.

It was so strange because no one ever came to those woods. You never found litter here, newspapers or empty beer bottles or any of the things you sometimes saw on the Downs. So when he saw it really was a handkerchief Hatchett's first thought was that it must have belonged to the tramp. It looked like a tramp's handkerchief, all smelly and dirty and old and hardly white at all, which was why it had taken him so long to see it.

I've seen this before, he found himself thinking, this has all happened before.

He sometimes had the feeling that things had happened before. When he had that feeling Hatchett often wondered whether, if he did something, made some gesture, some amazing secret would be revealed to him. That the earth would open, as in that fairy-tale, and he would step down into a magical world where there were genies and treasure and extraordinary truths brought home to him by the thought that all this had happened before.

He couldn't have seen it before. Things didn't happen twice. But it seemed to him, as he crouched there in the bushes, that the handkerchief was a kind of secret sign. There were things like that in stories. You found a cup or a piece of paper or a handkerchief and it was a sign, a clue that told you a story if you looked hard at it. Sherlock Holmes would have looked at it through a microscope and found traces of the tramp's hair.

He was just thinking that he would go out there and get it to have a closer look at it when he heard them crashing through the woods towards him.

At first he could not believe it was them. Surely they wouldn't think to come looking here. Even if they were brave enough to go into the wood they wouldn't, surely, head straight for the place that was haunted. Now, suddenly, Hatchett was sure that the ghost that haunted the woods was the old tramp that Lucius had killed. It could be that he was hiding in the very place where Lucius had killed him. That patch of earth over there looked as if it had been disturbed. There was a sort of mound. Was that the tramp's grave? And was the tramp's hand about to claw its way up through the earth to retrieve the snotty handkerchief?

Perhaps it wasn't them. Perhaps it was the ghost. Or policemen looking for the tramp. Or burglars. Or other murderers. For a moment Hatchett felt like dragging himself out of the bush and giving himself up. His heart was pounding fast and his chest was crawling with sweat. Better to give himself up. Better to –

Then he heard Alec's voice. "He won't hide here, stupid!"

"Why not?" This from Lucius.

"Because I told him it was haunted. Maybe it is haunted too." This from Alec.

"Why?" said Lucius.

"You know why," said Alec. "You know what happened. It happened here, didn't it? So maybe it is haunted, come to that."

There was a silence. They couldn't have been more than a few yards away.

"You should never say those things about Daddy!" said Alec.

"I'll say what I like!" said Lucius. "I saw him. I saw him all weak and feeble and crying like a baby because she didn't want him. He wouldn't even have had the guts to –"

"Shut up!" said Alec. "You mustn't say those things!"

There was another pause. Hatchett could not have said how he knew this but he was sure that they were as frightened as he was.

"It was horrible. It was horrible when he screamed like that. He screamed and screamed and screamed," said Alec.

"I know," said Lucius. "I know."

Hatchett held his breath. It didn't even sound as if they were looking for him any more.

"You haven't told Hatchett, have you?" said Lucius.

"Of course not!" said Alec hotly.

"Daddy said we weren't to tell anyone," said Lucius. "He'll be in serious trouble. He hit him in the face." Alec said nothing. "He deserved it anyway," said Lucius. "He deserved it for what he did. He was disgusting. He was wicked." Still Alec said nothing. What had the tramp done? Hatchett wondered. The silence went on and on and on. It was Lucius who spoke in the end. "It's not true, anyway. It's not true that I did it. It's not true that I killed him. It's just what you want to believe. That's why you're sending me away. But one day I'll come back and I'll tell. I will. I'll tell everything."

Finally, Alec spoke, in a whisper: "No one will ever believe you," he said.

Hatchett was unable to bear it any longer. He was desperate to burst out of his hiding place, yelling at the top of his voice that he surrendered, he gave up and they could say they had won. But he knew that he had listened to things he was not supposed to hear. And so he waited until the twins crashed away from him. When he was sure they had gone, he crept out of the bushes and, because he was a detective now and this was evidence, he picked up the handkerchief. Too frightened even to look at it, he thrust it deep into his pocket and ran, as fast as he could, back towards the sunlight and the cool of Albion House.

Dennis Hatchett's Diary

6 November 1939

11.15 a.m.

Writing this in the staffroom, which has been overrun by women. There are pot plants and half-completed items of knitting everywhere. Mother said, darkly, as I set out for school this morning, "You'll be gadding about with young ladies now!" Perhaps this fear of predatory women dates back to my father's disappearance. I suppose a woman was involved. From what I have heard about him it seems likely. But how, in God's name, do you manage to conceal an illicit *amour* in Crotchett Green?

I have cut out all beans from her diet. Now she only breaks wind last thing at night, although then she gives a sort of Last Post *obbligato* with a bewildering variety of tones and registers. I am thinking of recording it and sending it to the BBC.

I'm sitting here and, though I don't like to admit it to myself, I'm waiting for Norma. I should really, of course, be teaching the upper sixth but as 8 per cent of them have disappeared into the Army there doesn't seem a great deal of point. Peckerley was the only one who was any good anyway. My bright hope is now a short-sighted, flat-footed boy called Archer, who keeps talking of his admiration for a poet called Rimbode and a medieval balladeer called Villain. I am pretending to mark one of his essays, entitled "What is Symbolism?" – a question he has attempted to answer in about a hundred and eighty words – but every time the door handle moves I twitch, preen myself, try to look dashing.

At the other end of the room Leafy Green, swigging as usual from one of her endless series of tonic bottles (she is a total hypochondriac), is deep in conversation with Mabel Hughes. As both of them are still in sensationally elaborate mourning for

Everett (Hughes is wearing what looks like a large black bag and what looks like a large black bow-tie), they are honouring the late Spanish teacher by conducting their conversation in hushed whispers. This is annoying because, from the little I can catch of it, it is riveting stuff.

"They don't believe me," I heard Mabel say at one point. "I don't know what it would take for them to believe me! You would think I was . . . Mayhew or something!"

Mayhew is still looning around muttering darkly about the things what she saw and the secrets what she will take to her grave but nobody takes her seriously. This is partly because she says she can't say what it was that she saw ("I would suffer for it, Miss Lewis!" she said to Norma. "There is a killer on the loose and I would suffer at the killer's 'ands!'"), and partly because she is generally thought to be (a) common, (b) melodramatic and (c) habitually untruthful, all of which, among Saltdene girls, adds up to a low-rent version of Cassandra.

"They will believe you, my dear!" said Leafy, closing one enormous paw over Mabel's stringy fingers. "I am sure the truth will out. I personally feel that men should never have been allowed anywhere near any of my girls. And now they are all over them, stinking out the place with their . . . shoes!" She shot me a vicious glance as she said this and, placing her enormous behind a little nearer Mabel on the bench, began to whisper.

I feel like pointing out that the girls actually came to Kirkby not the other way round but fear Leafy might beat me to death with her cane if I did so. According to Norma, Mabel has transferred her unhealthy attachment to Everett to Everett's best friend and every word the old bat utters makes the Mad Governess, as I have taken to calling Mabel, quiver with excitement.

There is no proof Everett was murdered anyway. It's just staff-room gossip.

Norma and Alec are now coming under its scrutiny too. Jacqueline Rissett asked Norma only last week if it was true that Mr Lycett was now engaged to Jennifer Doran, and whether I was going to fight a duel with the two of them. Norma tried to be diplomatic, but the last few weeks cannot have been easy for her. She walks into a pub and sees what she thinks is her newly bagged fiancé trying to impale himself on the domestic-science mistress (who is supposed to be her best friend). Added to which he seems, between lunch and dinner, to have joined the RAF and completely forgotten she exists.

It gets better. When she recovers herself enough to go round to said fiancé's house with rolling pin in order to cross-question him about memory loss, joining of Air Force, attempt to have public sexual intercourse with best friend on licensed premises, etc., it turns out that said fiancé has been shipped off to an unknown destination by War Office and may never come back until we have rolled up the Hun. Not that we show much sign of rolling up the Hun at the present time. The war is being prosecuted with the enthusiasm of a vegetarian booking a tour of an abattoir. It is my personal belief that people like Leafy or the Hugheses (and there are plenty of those in government) are just waiting to do a deal with Hitler so that we can send all the Jews to some desert island and get on with being racially pure English *Volk*.

Maybe Rachel poisoned that old trout Everett. I can't say I would have blamed her.

It fell to me, of course, to tell Norma about Lucius. Which I found almost impossible. I suppose I had thought of him as dead since he walked out of our lives nearly twenty years ago. Oh, I think about him quite a lot and I am almost sure Lycett does too. That weird business with the handkerchief. But, like Gambetta and the battle of Sedan, we never speak of it. I once started to ask whether what he had told me that afternoon – that Lucius had killed some poor old tramp – was true. But it was clearly a taboo subject. Which suggests to me that Alec wasn't making it up.

"Alec," I said to Norma, the afternoon after he was spirited away by the Army, "has a twin brother."

Her chin rather hit the floor at that point.

"But . . . er . . ." I went on ". . . he was sent away to school. Well, sent away for good, really . . . to relatives. He was never spoken of. They had always made a thing of keeping him away from people in the village."

"Is he disabled?" said Norma. "Has he got some frightful disease?"

"Not as far as I know," I said, "although he may have contracted one during his absence. But from the sound of it he is as perfect a replica of his brother as he was at the age of eight."

"Is he . . . is he . . . insane?" said Norma. "Or a monster of some kind?"

Women, of course, have a particular interest in the genetic history of those they love. I don't think, although she is a health-and-strength merchant, that Norma is a social Darwinist or, God help us, a fan of the eugenics movement. I think she was imagining Lucius as a sort of male Mrs Rochester, a dark family secret kept in a locked room. It was only as I spoke of him, for about the first time in twenty years, that I realized that although as a child I had been given the impression that there was something wrong with him, I couldn't actually think what it might be.

Apart, of course, from setting light to harmless vagrants.

That wasn't the point. I have absolutely no proof that he did anything of the kind. What was Lucius actually like? I was being asked for concrete memories and, as I thought about Alec's twin, I realized how little I knew of him.

"I thought of him as a monster when I was a child," I said, "but he's certainly not insane. He was sent to a school in Devon for 'difficult' children, but if you asked me quite why or how he was difficult I wouldn't be able to tell you. Maybe Lycett Senior just decided he was."

Lucius bullied me, of course, I thought. But maybe that was simply because he had been bullied by his father. The sneer, the carefully calculated superior pose – could that have been a defence against Alec Senior's unremitting hostility? I suppose my opinion of Lucius has always been informed by the fact that he might well have been a child murderer. But these are things I do not allow myself to think about, let alone confide to Norma. I tried to choose my words carefully.

"In fact, as I recall, he was very clever," I went on. "Very difficult but very clever. I don't think he's very . . . nice. He certainly wasn't very nice to me. But I suppose people can change in twenty years. He and his father hated each other, that I do remember."

"Jennifer Doran seemed very keen on him," said Norma, with a wry smile. "If they had gone on any longer I think the landlord would have had to turn a fire hose on them." She shivered slightly. "I still don't know whether she thought she was doing . . . that with Alec or Alec's twin."

"I suppose, on the physical level," I said, "there isn't much difference."

She looked as if she was about to slap my face.

"I don't know what she thought," I said. "I haven't talked to Lucius. I have no desire to talk to Lucius. Or to his pompous father. I don't know why he is back. I don't know anything about him. And I certainly don't talk to Doran. All she talks about is jam rolls."

"Jam rolls," said Norma gloomily, "can be quite an interesting subject."

So then she asked me to ask Doran for information about Lucius. Why she couldn't ask her herself I do not know. Doran didn't know much. All she did say was that Lucius was the most attractive man she had ever met, which, considering she met him for the first time at 5 p.m. on the evening in question and by early evening was practically eating him alive on the bar of the Queen Vic, is probably no less than the truth.

Norma then asked me to go and ask the Lycetts where their long-exiled and much-disliked other son might be. She has a horror of confronting things on her own account and seems to enjoy using me as a kind of interpreter in conversations with other humans, even when they speak the same language. But that wasn't why I refused to do it. I haven't spoken to Lycett *père* or Lycett *mère* for years. I don't think the father could forgive me for being cleverer than Alec, or for growing up into a passable human being, instead of remaining the snivelling, over-grateful little bastard I was at the age of eight.

There is an atmosphere of death and misery in that family. It was there, under the surface, in Albion House and it is still there in their new establishment. I don't know how Alec stands it. He did tell me once that he thought his parents had moved to "try to save their marriage". As if the house you lived in could really change the fact that you loathe and despise your partner! What is it Chekhov says? If you don't want to be lonely, don't get married.

The father is rumoured to have affairs. Or at least to have had An Affair. And probably the mother too. She always looked in serious need of something and it might well have been another man.

In the end, because Norma wouldn't leave me alone, I found out from Doran that Lucius was only in town for a few days. He was apparently being "psychologically evaluated" by some RAF team that is, even now, located in Saltdene School for Girls, after which he was off to learn how to be a fighter pilot. Which is where he is now. I suppose complete and utter sadists come into their own in wartime. Doran saw him before he left town and he told her that he hadn't seen Alec. He also told her that he had been sent away because he didn't get on with his father. I reported this conversation to Norma. I did not add that her fiancé's genetic double might well have been a fully fledged murderer at the age of eight.

So there she is – back in love with him, thanks to me. Desperate to see him, in fact, to explain things, to confirm her love, which, as is usual, has gained strength from his absence. Good old Hatchett. Doing your rival a favour.

Leafy and Mabel are still murmuring to each other at the other end of the staffroom. They look like a couple about to book a double room at a small hotel. Leafy is wearing a voluminous pair of black trousers, a gigantic black jacket, a black billycock hat from which is suspended a veil, suggesting she is some kind of professional beekeeper, and a pair of sizeable boots of the kind worn by policemen. She has taken to wearing black gloves, even during school meals.

"I loved Alice Everett so," Mabel has just said, "because she was such a kind, sweet, generous person and because . . ." this turned out to be the first half of one of the most wildly inaccurate sentences of the mid-twentieth century ". . . because she was so loving and such a marvellous, marvellous teacher!"

I think Norma once told me that Everett's method of teaching was to leave her girls alone with twenty-odd copies of *Basic Spanish Grammar* while she flicked through books about the Communist Menace.

"Perhaps," whispered Leafy, peering over in my direction to see whether I was listening, "Mayhew saw Mr Breeze doing something awful to Everett. And she is terrified, poor little thing, that Breeze will do away with her if she reveals her secret. I do know the man is an animal. An animal. A beast. I know things about him that would make your eyes water. I know for a fact that he . . ." Here she lowered her voice even further and whispered the filthy details into Mabel's ear.

"If only we could get some concrete evidence against him," Mabel said, "I'm sure if we keep our eyes and ears open we will be able to stop him doing the awful things he is doing!" And the two of them clucked away for minutes about how shocking it was that dear, kind, gentle, six-foot, muscle-bound Miss Everett should have been mixed up with such an evil pervert as the Kirkby School senior chemistry master.

From the way they were carrying on I was almost tempted to sympathize with the man. He lost my support by the simple expedient of entering the room and instantly reminding me of what a disgusting creature he actually is.

He has his martinet manner on today. A neat grey suit, sharp striped tie and horrid little black leather pumps with which he took finicky, dance-master's steps into the room. He smiled round at us, lifting his beaky little face as if he expected us to admire it. He is, I suppose, thought handsome by some. But one of those uselessly handsome men who trundles his face around as if he were a waiter and it were a redundant sweet trolley. That silly thatch of blond hair. That total lack of intelligence behind those fine, apparently thoughtful, blue eyes.

Within seconds Mabel the Mad Governess and Loopy Leafy had swept out of the staffroom as if they had just been told it was the site of a cholera epidemic. So I suppose he had performed some useful function. And now – oh, jolly, jolly good – Norma has come in, her black hair radiant about her shoulders, her clear complexion and square shoulders all helping her to look more than usually like a nice female athlete. Perfect partner for my best friend. Obviously. Obviously. Obviously.

12.30 p.m.
Still in staffroom. On own again. Natural state for Hatchett.

She still hasn't heard from Alec.

In fact, nobody seems to know where he is. The morning after he and the rest of the 4th Croydon Territorials disappeared so suddenly we did make some half-hearted attempts to contact the people in the British Army who might know where the various bits of it are, these days. This was a lot harder than you might have thought – something that I feel does not bode well for future encounters with the Nazi beast.

I ended up telephoning the War Office, who gave the distinct impression that they thought I was a German spy. There isn't, as far as I can tell, a recruitment centre in Croydon, although someone in the staffroom said there might be one in Streatham. The nearest thing to hard information came from the brother of one of Alec's comrades in arms, a person called Mavroleon, who used to be at Kirkby. I must say, if Mavroleon is anything like his brother the British Army is in for a very hard time. Mavroleon Mi thought they had been sent to Scotland.

"I just think about him all the time," she said in a low voice – Breeze was still in the room – "and . . ."

"And what?" I said.

"I don't know what . . ." she said. "This business of his having a brother. A twin. And not just any kind of twin. An identical twin. And then not telling me. It disturbs me. It makes me feel I never really knew him."

"They just don't tell people about Lucius," I said. "They just don't. It's one of those things."

"I don't know when I'll see him again," she whispered. "Whether I'll ever see him again. I love him so much, Dennis."

Dennis! I nodded sympathetically. Something about the absent soldier, I have noticed, makes a chap misty-eyed, even if his friend is not the kind who usually inspires those sorts of emotions. "He's doing vital work," I heard myself say. "He's defending the country!"

I wasn't sure that this was the case, of course. From what little I know of the 4th Croydon Territorials, they are probably wandering aimlessly round Britain rather than actively defending it. Breeze was now openly listening to our conversation. To let him know I didn't care if he was, I said, in a loud voice, "The important thing is that you love him and he loves you. Loving one person and being true to one person is, as far as I am concerned, the thing that makes us what we are. The permanence of love is bound up with the idea of keeping promises, holding to an intellectual idea, being able to agree that when we use words we mean the same thing by them."

This, I felt like saying to Breeze, is far too high-minded ever to be worth repeating by the Kirkby staffroom gossips. But it is what I think. Or what I would like to think anyway.

"Oh, Dennis," said Norma, "you say such beautiful things sometimes."

A moment after I had said it, of course, it didn't seem what I had wanted to say. It sounded, as usual, too schoolmasterly, too on the wrong side of pompous to be really interesting. And, if I was honest with myself, I didn't think it was necessarily true as far as she and Lycett were concerned. But it was what she wanted to hear.

It certainly set Breeze back a pace or two. He clearly thought it was aimed at him. After a little more desultory conversation about Rachel, to whom I seem to have become a sort of honorary uncle, Norma departed for a class, and Breeze, who had been watching me narrowly for some time, said, "You believe in love, don't you, young Hatchett?"

"I think I do!" I said.

"Maybe," smirked Breeze, "that is why you are still a bachelor. Young men in their twenties all believe in love. Later they find out it isn't as simple as that."

I did not attempt to answer this, but readdressed myself to Archer's attempt to explain Symbolism with a vocabulary that did not seem to contain any word longer than two syllables.

"Love is just a word for little girls to misuse," he said.

"Or," said I, frankly bitchy now (is a mixed staffroom having a bad effect on me?), "middle-aged lady schoolteachers?"

Breeze looked sharply at me. "What exactly do you mean by that?" he said.

"Oh," I said, "people are saying that you and Everett were –"

"Were what?" said Breeze, his voice rising to a squeak.

"You know," I said, trying to sound man-to-man, although that is a bit of a contradiction in terms when talking to Breeze, "er . . . rather keen on each other." I gave him a deliberately disgusting hand gesture designed to illustrate sexual complicity. It was entirely self-invented but I like to think it was the kind of sign language that would have been popular and instantly recognizable in the foyer of a Malayan brothel.

It certainly had a profound effect on Breeze. "Me and that disgusting old hag?" he said, moving with his usual effortlessness from bourgeois correctness to changing-room smut. "I would rather stick it in a meat-grinder. You are a cheeky boy, young Hatchett. Everett was a cow."

"*De mortuis nil nisi bonum*," I said, raising my eyebrows slightly.

"Everett," said Breeze, who clearly did not adhere to this principle, "was an ugly old lesbian whose only pleasure in life was manipulating schoolgirls. Who on earth told you I was playing doctors and nurses with *la* Everett?"

"I think it was Mabel Hughes," I said, "and she was told it by Jacqueline Rissett."

The effect of this was most satisfactory. He practically rolled his eyes, foamed at the mouth and fell on the floor. By which I mean that although he did not actually do anything resembling any of these things he gave the impression that that was what he might do at any moment. He recovered by skilfully deploying his parade-ground manner. Breeze is one of those men who has responded to war, not by joining the Army but by perfecting a manner in civilian life far surpassing any routines found among the High Command. He gives the impression of a man who has been issued with a rank so high that it can only be accommodated by civilian clothes. A bit like really top surgeons being called Mister.

I remained suave, pleasant, Hatchett the Gossip, the Young Man About Croydon. "I think I heard it from Mabel," I said, as if Hughes and I regularly took tea at some Sapphic dive in Coulsdon, "but I think she said that Jacqueline told her."

"Bitch!" said Breeze. "Horrible, stringy, mad, possessed little pervert that she is. If you believe a word Mabel Hughes tells you, Hatchett, you are a greater fool than I took you for. No wonder Norma went for your friend and not you! Hughes is a liar! She is an evil, twisted, half-mad lesbian bitch!" With which evidence of public trust in one of his pupils he strode from the room. Such was the violence of his rejection that I'm beginning to think that Mabel could be right. Everett and Breeze! What a truly ghastly thought. I know people have to find love in their own way. I suppose, to paraphrase Samuel Butler, it might have been very good of God to allow them to get together, so that they only had to make two people miserable instead of four, but . . . Everett and Breeze! The mind reels!

I suppose I'd better get back to Archer and Rimbode. I ought to do something. I can't see myself in the Army. But I have been mistaken for a Belgian, a Pole and a Dutchman. Maybe I should become a spy. Anything would be better than hanging around Croydon listening to Norma's troubles and desperately trying to fool her (and myself) that I am not in love with her. Well, I am not in love with her, am I? Am I?

Was Everett's death murder? Is Breeze a psychopath? Does any of this matter, when Hitler has walked through Poland and simply taken it, the way a killer takes another's life, without thinking of the consequences?

7

15 December 1939

"Now, shall we all try to concentrate?" Norma did not like teaching Rachel. Or, rather, she liked teaching Rachel, but she did not enjoy teaching Lower Six A when Rachel was in it, which she was all the time, since now, the lower sixth consisted of only one class and Norma seemed to be their full-time teacher.

The core of Lower Six A were the Misfits – Mabel Hughes, Jacqueline Rissett, Rachel Lewis (as she was generally known), Ruth Mayhew, Janet Frosser and Elinor Wreays. There was also, for reasons still not clear to Norma, a small boy with glasses called Potter, who had been told, or perhaps had decided unilaterally, that this was the place for him.

Norma took them for everything apart from physics and mathematics although, from time to time, even this was part of her duties. Today she had been called upon to deputize for the grievously overworked Mr Groenig, the Physics Master Who Knew Two Nobel Prizewinners. Since Mr Putter had joined the Navy, Mr Malpas the Fleet Air Arm, Miss Knorr the Women's Royal Air Force and Mrs Sitz the section of the school that had been evacuated to Norwich, he was the only person in the two schools responsible for cluing in young people on numbers and the natural world.

"What," said Norma, "is an atom?" She had not the faintest idea of the answer to this question.

Neither, however, and this may well have been why she asked it, had any of her pupils. Apart, of course, from Rachel. From odd, disconnected things she had said, Norma had gained the impression that Rachel was a girl who knew a thing or two about atomic and subatomic particles. Not in the way that most people she knew (Hatchett, for example) thought they knew about such things. "Apparently Rutherford – an Englishman, I'll have you know – has succeeded in splitting the atom," he would say. "Huge amounts of energy," he would add, waving his hands in the air, "have been released – and if we could use this energy the *Queen Mary* could sail five times across the Atlantic on only one ounce of nitrogen."

But if you asked Hatchett how exactly we were to use this energy, or what exactly he meant by "splitting the atom" (did they get the things out, allow them to roll around the laboratory floor then whack them with hammers?), he was silent and her mystification increased. From time to time Mr Groenig would try to explain some of the mysteries of the subject to her but his explanations only served to confuse her. In fact, when Groenig started to talk, Norma often became convinced that even he wasn't really sure what an atom was.

So perhaps she had asked the question with some hope that Rachel would enlighten her. If so, she was mistaken. She sat, like the other Misfits, waiting for Teacher to entertain her.

"Well," said Norma, "the atom is a very, very, very small . . . er . . . thing. This desk behind which I am sitting is made up of millions of atoms. It looks like . . . er . . . wood. But if we looked at it under a very powerful microscope, a very, very powerful microscope, we would see it is made up of millions and millions of tiny, tiny atoms. Like little balls. And inside these balls, it seems, so scientists tell us, are even smaller balls, which we call . . . er . . ." A word she had picked up somewhere, probably from Hatchett, surfaced in her brain. ". . . call . . . er . . . electrons." Did she mean electrons? There was another word Hatchett had used. ". . . or . . . er . . . neutrons!" This sounded right, somehow. Was there a flicker of interest in Rachel's eyes? "Neutrons," went on Norma, "are very, very, very small balls indeed sort of inside these other balls that are, as I said . . . er . . . atoms."

A breathless silence greeted this remark. She had better, she decided, move on to some other discipline. She glanced down at the notepad on the desk. It read HANDWRITING PRACTICE. What, in God's name, was that? At least it sounded easier than theoretical physics. She was getting increasingly confused these days.

"I would not say," Rachel was saying, in her increasingly convincing English, "that a neutron was a ball exactly. But neutrons are very useful to those interested, as you mention, Miss Lewis . . ." Rachel was very formal with her in class ". . . for those interested in fission."

The rest of the class were goggling at her.

"Oh," said Norma brightly, "and why is that, may we ask?"

Rachel shrugged. "For example," she said, "a neutron is bound to hit a nucleus eventually. It is not bothered by electrons, for example, and not repelled by a positive electric charge."

"Well," said Norma, "that is fascinating!"

"Fermi discovered this," said Rachel, as if this would somehow help matters. Who, in God's name, thought Norma, was Fermi? An Italian presumably. And weren't we at war with them, or as good as? She really was out of her depth with this girl. Before Rachel started to confuse her even further, Norma said, "Handwriting!" That is what it said on her desk. If only she could remember why it was written there. She had been feeling, recently, as if she was sleepwalking through her duties. Alec's absence, unreal at first, was now dominating her consciousness, and what he had written, instead of reassuring her simply –

"Yes, Miss Lewis!" It was Mabel Hughes, sitting ramrod straight as usual, her eyes, as bright as buttons, fixed on another adored teacher, and her long prehensile fingers folded neatly on the desk in front of her. "You are going to let each of us take our handwriting practice down to Miss Green in the day room."

Leafy Green was an ardent fan of General Franco, and Ernst Roehm, the head of the *Sturmabteilung* (for some reason her particular favourite among the Nazis until he had been killed in dramatic circumstances), but she was not your ordinary run-of-the-mill Fascist. She was a woman with her own individual vision and she was always keen to suggest that the failure of contemporary democracy was intimately linked to a decline in handwriting standards.

She always said that handwriting was the clue to character. "If you want to be beautiful, girls," she maintained, "write a beautiful script." It wasn't what you wrote that mattered, it was how you wrote it. And that did not refer to your feeling for the right placing of an adjectival phrase. It referred to the graphic quality of your Ps and Qs and Vs.

Leafy, like Everett and, it had to be said, Miss Leach, sought uniformity in her girls. She liked them to dress the same, walk the same and (most importantly) to write the same. For her, the standard formulation of a Greek E, an italic N or a cursive L or B was as important as wearing your Iron Cross on the right bit of the upper chest. All her girls wrote something called Green copperplate and they wrote it exactly the same. There were times when Norma wondered whether the Misfits were not all powered by the same central brain.

It was Monday afternoons that Leafy, surrounded by her pills and bromides and tonics (Hatchett always said there was a strong link between hypochondria and Fascism), would mark her girls' efforts, usually a short essay called something like " 'A healthy mind in a healthy body.' Discuss in relation to Spain and Germany."

"Of course I am going to do that, Mabel!" said Norma, with a brightness she did not feel. "Of course I am! Er . . . who is first?"

Mabel, who always made Norma feel as if she had done some-thing wrong, nodded, priestlike, and after a discreet pause, in which she was able to assume Norma had agreed to this move, filtered from the room like Jeeves.

"In the meantime," Norma continued, "Rachel can tell us more about the . . . er . . . neutron."

This was, by no standards, a successful lesson. Rachel, who was usually almost talkative when any scientific subject was raised, seemed to feel she had said all she had to say on the subject of the neutron. Eventually, in a tone that suggested the question was being dragged out of her, she said, "What else would you like me to tell you about the neutron?"

"Things that might interest us," said Norma.

"It was discovered in 1932," said Rachel, with a shrug. "Is that the kind of thing you want to know?" She said this in a manner that was almost hostile.

"Now," said Norma, frightened that her *protégée* might lapse, if alarmed or excited, into German or say something too revealing about her past (she should never have allowed the girl to discuss in public things that interested her), "what else was discovered in 1932? Can anyone tell me?"

There was an immense pause. Eventually Mayhew said, "A special kind of soap, I think."

Janet Frosser sniffed and said to Elinor Wreays, in a loud voice, "And I am sure *she* doesn't use it." Jacqueline Rissett said she thought contraception had been invented in 1932. Once again Norma found herself marvelling at the contradictions in the girl. Contraception indeed! She seemed so shy and quiet. Perhaps Mrs Rissett was progressive as well as overprotective. The two sometimes went together. She had better give the dreamy little thing a good talking-to about boys. Perhaps, thought Norma, she herself could do with something along those lines.

The lesson was now proceeding, as Norma's lessons sometimes did, from the significant to the inconsequential and apparently making no distinction between them. Her girls were, as her father would have put it, "wittering on" to no clear purpose, but there was some sense in that. It was only by these sorts of discussions that she got to know what they really felt or thought. She had got her ideas of teaching, of course, from her father and he always said that the job was to do with finding out what the pupils thought rather than telling them things and expecting them to commit them to memory.

Clearly this mode of procedure was not very popular with Rachel. She was now positively glowering at Norma, and Norma, not for the first time, began to feel irritated with her. Who did the girl think she was? Norma was doing everything she could to help her. She was breaking the law, for God's sake! Most English people she knew wouldn't lift a finger to help a stray Jew. They didn't like Jews. Only the other week Miss Leach had said she thought they all made a great deal of fuss about what was happening in Germany.

Norma didn't feel able to comment on this but she did feel Rachel could be a little less spiky, a little more grateful.

Somehow or other, while she had been thinking this and refereeing a lively debate between Mayhew and Jacqueline Rissett on whether gunpowder had been invented by the Chinese or the Arabs, Mabel Hughes had returned to the room, Janet Frosser and Elinor Wreays had left for a shared handwriting session with Leafy and Mayhew was scooping up her latest handwriting sample to take down to the Spanish mistress in the day room.

"What have you written, Mayhew?" said Norma, as the waif-like little girl passed her. Mayhew's face looked more than usually troubled.

"Just a few words . . ." she said, clutching her papers to her chest. "Nothing important, really."

"We have to write out things like proverbs or quotations or Great Truths today," said Mabel, looking round at the rest of the class, "and I wrote 'I have made you out of the fire a sword of ice!' It is from one of Hitler's speeches. It was Miss Everett's favourite." She jutted her jaw forward, as if daring anyone to contradict her. "My father says we should never have declared war on Germany. He says Hitler is basically on our side."

"As of last September," said Norma, carefully, "I don't think the facts will really bear that interpretation." She didn't want to demolish the girl in front of the rest of the class, even though Rachel was looking as if she was about to say something. This dangerously revealing piece of nonsense from Mabel was simply a repetition of something her appalling parents had said. But she was keen to move the subject away from what a nice chap Hitler was.

It was Mayhew who came to her rescue. "I have written," she said, staring round at the class in her best Gothic manner, "that I have seen what I have seen and in time I will reveal all." She clearly expected to be asked what she had seen but nobody obliged. "I know a few things," went on Mayhew, "about the murder of Miss Everett." She had announced, only last week, that she was going to "tell all to Leafy out of respect", but had not yet done so.

Mayhew never got down to detail in respect of her revelations, presumably because, when she announced to the world that they concerned her seeing Laura Stokes pick her nose, it came as something of a disappointment. But she certainly made a meal out of the prospect of them.

"I am sure you do, Mayhew," said Norma briskly. "Now, run along and we will get on with the lesson."

It was dark, now, outside. On the freezing football pitch, the giant Hs of the rugby posts straddled the grass mannishly and, at the back of the class, Jacqueline Rissett appeared to be trying to catch a glimpse of her reflection in the window. A strand of her black hair seemed to be bothering her. "If you want to pay attention to your toilette, Jacqueline," said Norma, "I suggest you do so at another time of the day." There was a lot of giggling at this and Norma, as she always did when she lapsed into sarcasm, felt guilty. As Jacqueline turned back towards her, blushing, she saw, once again, how the lumpish, rustic look she had had on the school trip was leaving her. Her gloomy twitches were becoming charming, sensitive tremors, and that cast-down look about the eyes was starting to resemble a rather attractive form of maidenly modesty. Now that her cheeks had some colour in them they set off those big, haunted eyes very well.

"Now, Jacqueline," she went on, softening her voice, "you raised a very interesting question in class just now and that is the whole issue of birth control."

There was nothing smutty about the way Norma discussed it. She had read Marie Stopes's *Married Love* while at university and, inspired by the fact that Marie – as she liked to think of her – had been the first female science lecturer at that establishment, she had been a keen exponent of her views throughout. But even though Norma's tone was as elevated as that of the author of *Wise Parenthood*, her introduction of the topic always brought out the girls in fits of giggles. At times it would have been almost impossible to grasp that Norma was, in a roundabout way, discussing sex. She had used the word once (Norma was a keen fan of D. H. Lawrence) and it had set the girls off howling like demented prairie dogs and wobbling like disturbed jellies. But even when, as today, she kept it on the theoretical plane, it gripped them like no other subject.

That, of course, was why she had introduced it. It diverted attention away from Rachel. Jacqueline was transfixed although, Norma noted, she did not seem to find the subject in the least amusing. "Terrified" was the word she would have used to describe the girl's expression. Janet Frosser and Elinor Wreays, now back in class, looked as if they had both just sat on an active fire hydrant. The boy Potter looked as if he had had a nasty accident in his trousers – and when Norma used the word "pregnant" the entire class quivered like corn in the wind.

"Rachel," Norma was saying, "what do you think of this question of birth control?"

Not a lot, the girl's expression seemed to say. But at least she wasn't frowning. Norma told herself, once again, that that was why she had started the class down this road and that the danger to Rachel had been averted. But really she knew she had mentioned these things because her mind was dwelling on them anyway. Since he had gone she had been unable to stop thinking about Alec in that way. Before, she had been aware of his hands, his eyes, the gentleness of his voice, but all these things were part of him, notes in the symphony of friendship. Now that he wasn't there, however, now that she didn't know where he was or when she would see him again, these characteristics came back one by one, distilled by absence into dangerous commodities. When she lay down to sleep at night and Alec came into her thoughts, it was his physical presence that seemed most potent, most real. She didn't simply picture them together, walking hand in hand through some meadow or down some river path but, entirely unbidden, moments of contact seemed to ambush these reveries. Now he had his hand on her shoulder. Now he was leaning across her and she could smell him – leather and harsh soap and a faint, enticing sourness. Now they were doing something they had never even tried to do – kissing. And he had his hands in her hair, which everyone said was her best feature.

"Miss Lewis," Rachel was saying (had she been speaking for long?), "Miss Lewis, I try not to think about birth control. I would rather think about the neutron."

The class seemed to find this hilarious. But Norma, shocked by the realization that she hadn't really been listening, that she had been standing in front of one of her classes dreaming like a lovesick girl, like . . . like Jacqueline Rissett, for God's sake! And she still could not stop thinking about Alec. Even though this might lead, she was well aware, to something she found it almost impossible to contemplate: the loss of control of a class.

It was the business with the letters that was making her feel like this.

She had written to him as soon as she had worked out how to address the letter, although even that had taken her about a week. It felt rather unreal writing LIEUTENANT ALEC LYCETT 4TH CROYDON TERRITORIALS – 1234567. It had taken her a week to find out what his number was and another three days to convince herself that it wasn't some grim practical joke being played on her by the British Army. Even allowing for the unnaturally ordered sequence, she could not believe there were that many people in the Forces.

Darling Alec,

Dear old Hatchett has explained to me why I thought I saw you kissing Jennifer Doran the night we were due to meet in the Queen Vic. I must say it came as a bit of a shock to discover you had a twin brother of whose existence I was completely ignorant.

There are so many things I need to ask you about your family when we meet. Even Hatchett is quite mysterious on the subject! But, and this is what I really wanted to say, what I felt on the day war was declared is what I feel now. What I have felt for you all the time, all these years, was love. It was and it still is. I cannot stop thinking about you.

My love

Norma

The response to this was less than satisfactory.

My darling Norma,
   It was so marvellous to

Roger   you. The night I was dragged off by

      hundreds of men with big

            willies   was the best
time of my life. I want your

      big   bottom my love!

            I feel my precious

      cock

                  until I   come

   on your belly in thick undergrowth.

Why am I talking like this?

   underpants
               My identical twin is a

   soapdish. And the men of this regiment are

huge and exciting and digging into my

      back passage even as I write this!
   All my love
      Alec

177

There wasn't much point in trying to reply to this. Whoever had censored Alec's letter had actually cut out the words with scissors so there was no clue as to what the offending words had been. One of the many confusing things about the letter was that Norma found it almost impossible to imagine how it would have looked if reconstituted. She ran alternative sentences through her mind, trying to think of what had given offence to the security people. Perhaps he had veered off from the subject of underpants into a precise description of the 4th Croydons' whereabouts or perhaps he had just felt the urge to lace his letter with random bursts of treason, defeatism, military secrets, etc.

Darling Alec [she had replied]

It was wonderful to get your letter but I fear the Army censorship made most of it completely incomprehensible.

Perhaps next time you should stay off anything to do with geography and, even if the war is getting you down, don't say anything to THEM, *whoever* THEY *are (are they reading this? I wonder).*

Tell me about Lucius. Why was he sent away? What did he do? Was it something awful? Hatchett is being ridiculously mysterious about it all but I am sure there is a perfectly simple explanation and I am dying to know more so I can know you better.

Jennifer Doran, whom I think I have forgiven for embracing a man who is the spitting image of my fiancé, says Lucius, once he had said who he was, didn't want to talk about his family at all. What a strange bunch you Lycetts are!

Have you told your father our news? I almost don't like to tell people but it will be impossible to keep it a secret I fear . . .

I miss you.

Your fiancée

Norma

Alec's reply was not helpful. It went:

Darling Norma,

Can you please please please send me back my
big hairy thing that goes

boing boing boing?

He did not even appear to have signed this one. Did the censor now consider his Christian name to be a subversive act?

She looked at the class. All of them seemed to be talking at once. Rachel was talking about neutrons to Elinor Wreays, who was nodding furiously. Janet Frosser was talking about pregnancy to Potter, who had gone very red and whose cheeks were bulging like a hamster's. Mabel Hughes was rapping on her desk, even more like a spinster governess than usual, and ordering everyone to be quiet so that Miss Lewis could talk. She was Miss Lewis. She must talk. "Order," she kept saying, "Order! Order! Order!" Alec was under orders. She, too, must give an order in order to keep order. How long had she been standing here gawping at the class thinking about Alec?

And now Jacqueline Rissett, who had gone down to see Leafy without Norma even realizing that she had, was standing in the doorway, her face flushed. What she was saying was –

"Miss Green is dead. She has been poisoned. I think it was probably strychnine."

"I don't think you should go in, Dennis!" said Norma.

Interesting, thought Hatchett, as he tentatively pushed open the door of the day room, that she should have sought his help. And used his first name, even if she was thinking of him so obviously as Hatchett. Good old Hatchett. Reliable, brainy, dogged, second-in-line Hatchett, the Fortinbras to Alec's Hamlet.

Norma put a restraining hand on his arm. "It's strychnine poisoning!" she said, "Apparently you go all sort of –"

"Dead?" said Hatchett, a touch impatiently. "And how do we know it's strychnine poisoning? Just because Jacqueline Rissett said it was? How does a nice English girl like her come to be so well up in the symptoms?"

179

"Apparently," said Norma, "it was in one of those Agatha Christie stories she keeps reading."

"I must say," said Hatchett, placing his hand on the door for the second time, "that up until now I never thought Miss Christie's work could have any practical application to the lives of her readers. But I suppose even the lowest form of literature has its uses."

"I think," said Norma, "we should call in the police."

"Zer police," said Hatchett, in his Hercule Poirot voice, "are useless! They 'ave not my leetle grey cells!"

He did this principally to annoy Norma, who, for the last week, had done nothing but talk about Alec as if he was some highly rated Greek god or a thinker on a par with Goethe or Leonardo da Vinci. Hatchett was determined to be generous to his absent friend but there were limits to his tolerance. Anyway, as with Everett, he was quite unable to feel anything about the death of this unfortunate, but highly unpleasant individual. Whoever was doing these things – perhaps it was someone with a grudge against Spanish teachers – they were not, in Hatchett's view, entirely devoid of sympathy. He could easily see why someone might want to do away with the pair of them.

He did rather alter his opinion when he opened the door of the day room.

Everett had been, in her way, a pretty sensational corpse, but her best friend was not to be upstaged in the bid to win the prize for Most Striking Last Attitude By a Murdered Individual. She had gone to meet the great headmistress in the sky in a position that made her look like Count Dracula in the middle of being impaled by a wooden stake. Her arms and legs were all over the place. Her mourning hat was perched, crazily, over one eye, and her mouth set in a diagonal scream that reminded Hatchett of the work of Edvard Munch.

She was surrounded, as usual, by bottles and pills and powders, and on the table in front of her was a selection of the girls' copperplate, scattered across the polished surface by the last crazy sweep her arm had taken as she struggled for breath. It was fairly clear what had caused the damage: next to her left hand, on its side, was an empty tonic bottle and in her right hand a silver teaspoon, held aloft at a slightly jaunty angle, as if it were a conductor's baton.

This, thought Hatchett, grimly, was fast becoming a pattern in his relationship with Norma. It seemed that wherever they were, there, also, were liable to be the fresh corpses of lady grammar-school language teachers.

With Norma still muttering about the police, he moved further into the room and saw that just before she died Leafy had been in the middle of composing a letter to her headmistress. Right up until the end Leafy's handwriting had remained immaculate. Hatchett read it aloud:

Dear Miss Leach,

I feel I must write to tell you that, although some members of staff have been pouring scorn on the rumours surrounding Miss Everett's death, I have reason to believe, from private information, that Everett was foully murdered.

I also have good evidence that the culprit was Mr Breeze, the chemistry master. He had, I am afraid to tell you, been forcing his attentions on her. Eggy told me more than once that he had said wicked and improper things to her and she was deeply disturbed at the idea of having to stay in the same hotel as him – especially in a foreign country!

He may even, I fear, have seduced or in some way attacked this brave, kind and lovable member of staff, whose beauty, both physical and spiritual, was such an inspiration to the other lady teachers of Saltdene.

Mr Breeze is a murderer and I can prove this because

At this point in her revelations strychnine had interrupted her flow rather seriously. The last "because" resembled the traces of a heavily inked spider doing a mating dance across the lower half of the page. It was only when he finished reading it that Hatchett noticed he had an audience. The door was open behind him and out in the hall he saw the anxious faces of Jacqueline Rissett, Ruth Mayhew, Janet Frosser and Elinor Wreays, who seemed to be locked in a wild embrace, and at the back, taller than the others, the austere, black-clothed figure of Mabel Hughes.

"I don't know why I said that," Jacqueline was saying. "It wasn't true about Mr Breeze. I was just being stupid and jealous. We all had mad pashes on Mr Breeze. It was just a silly thing I said to Mabel and I wish I hadn't. Mr Breeze is a wonderful man."

Casting doubt on the authenticity of this statement, Alan Breeze was one of the teachers joining the crowd out in the hall. His blond thatch of hair combed forward over his prematurely lined, beakily handsome features, he inflated his nostrils slightly as if to let the world know that he did not need the good opinion of schoolgirls but that, yes, they did think he was something rather special, and he was, wasn't he, come to that?

"There there, Jackie," he was saying, as he pushed his way through the crush towards her. "Those bitches were always against me!"

He rather wished Breeze had not heard his extempore reading of Leafy's last letter to her headmistress. With his cheap handsome face working away as he thrust both girls and teachers out of his path, he looked, thought Hatchett, not only capable of murder but also liable to think it quite justified in the case of persons who read out scurrilous accusations against him. Before Breeze could get to Hatchett, or to Jacqueline, however, the Rissett girl had wriggled to the front of the queue and was gazing at her former handwriting teacher.

To Hatchett's surprise, the first person to speak was Mabel Hughes.

She was shaking with anger. Her usually expressionless features were alive with a fury that Hatchett would not have thought her capable of feeling, let alone showing. She pointed her right forefinger at Jacqueline, like some *citoyenne* of the Revolutionary Republic of France, and loaded any amount of scorn, repressed anger and sheer hatred into her opening remark. "How dare you?" she hissed. "How dare you spread those lies about Miss Everett? How dare you do that, you wicked, wicked, wicked girl? You made me believe things of her I could hardly credit! You made me think she could be – could be – with – that evil, evil man!"

"I'm sorry, Mabel," said Jacqueline, "I just –"

"Come away from there, Jackie," said Breeze, and then he rounded on Mabel. "And you," he added, "can shut your poisonous little mouth!"

But Jacqueline didn't come away from there. She had got herself a ringside seat for the balletomanic Leafy's Last Position and it was working on her powerfully. Although, eventually, Norma and Hatchett moved her away, closed the door of the day room and announced that the murder scene was closed until the arrival of the police, something she had seen in the room was still causing her to mutter to herself. So odd and inward-looking and yet so intense was this self-communion that at first Hatchett was afraid the sight of the corpse had tipped her over the edge. She had always been a sensitive, overwrought girl, according to Norma, and the sight of Leafy, spreadeagled like someone who has just been done to death by the Inquisition, could not have improved her stability.

The rest of the girls were finally persuaded to move away. The hardest to shift was Mabel, who was still screaming abuse at Jacqueline in a manner that was most untypical of her. Hatchett, who had noted the girl's keenness on any lady teacher in sensible shoes, put it down to anger that the reputation of her beloved Miss Everett should have been so cruelly besmirched. But when she had been calmed by the arrival of Miss Leach, a woman whose footwear had never been known to be frivolous, he walked after Norma, who had taken Jacqueline out into the quadrangle under the Old School. She had had her arm round her and, although Breeze tried to follow them out, she gave him a glare of such intense hostility that the chemistry master gave up the attempt.

Teacher and pupil were sitting on the lower steps of the Old School, dimly lit from the one masked lamp at the head of the stairs. Although it was a bitterly cold afternoon and she wasn't wearing anything more than a thin dress, Norma was so intent on her charge that she didn't seem to notice it. Jacqueline's complexion (or was this simply the light?) seemed to have changed again. She had a yellow look about her, like someone suffering from a tropical disease, and as Norma held her close, the girl stared at the floor, still mouthing some mantra to herself. Hatchett moved closer.

"Now, Jacqueline," Norma was saying, "don't fret. Think about nice things."

Perhaps, thought Hatchett, unable for a moment to play the comedy of friendship, that was why he loved her. He loved her almost childish belief in the goodness of the world. He loved her oh-so-English out-of-doors decency, as completely natural as red pillar-boxes or policemen cycling home in the dusk. He loved the confident cut of her chin, her square shoulders, the bounce and sparkle of her black hair.

You didn't, thought Hatchett, deliberately indulging his feelings now, love people for the way they looked but for the way they were. If he was honest with himself he would have admitted that Lycett didn't really understand her, didn't see the heart of her. He, Hatchett, did. And now, although he knew he was not allowed to feel this, although it was a quite hopeless feeling that did no one any good, a feeling that he did not even want, he admitted, for a brief while, that it was what he felt, and he allowed himself to look at her, to want her, even though she belonged to someone else and even though he loved that person too.

He was within yards of them now, but they still hadn't seen him. Jacqueline was still muttering to herself. "She took a bromide," he heard her say, "and there was tonic in the bottle. That was how they did it in the book. That was how they did it in the book."

Hatchett stepped forward, and took her by the arm. The two of them got her back inside, where they met a large man with a black moustache who introduced himself as Inspector Roach of Croydon CID. "I had been meaning," he said, "to get in touch with you two young people. Weren't you the ones who found the corpse of Alice Everett?"

"We didn't exactly find it," said Hatchett, who did not like the man's tone. "I mean, we were just wheeling her along when we suddenly noticed she was dead. I don't think there is any proof that it was murder. Or that poor Miss Green was killed deliberately. It could have been a seizure of some kind, couldn't it?"

Miss Leach, wearing what looked like a Savile Row suit and appearing, as usual, out of nowhere, nodded firmly. She was clearly not anxious to have her girls bothered by a murder enquiry. "This," she said, "is very, very bad for the Spanish Department. It is also a very upsetting time for my girls. They have been exposed to men *en masse* for the first time in their lives and it has been a very traumatic experience for them." She nodded at Hatchett, of whom she only mildly disapproved. She had once said, without a trace of irony, that she felt she could talk to him man-to-man. "Mr Hatchett is one of the men who has had to expose himself to these young women, but he is a man of sensibility and, I am sure, has a point in regard to the danger of leaping to conclusions." She glared up at the balcony running round all four walls of the central hall, where Mr Breeze still seemed to be catching Jacqueline Rissett's eye. "I have a great deal of time for the male sex, Inspector," she went on, her light Scottish accent becoming more pronounced as she spoke. "I am a keen cricketer, and enjoy watching a game of football with the other fellows. But some men are not worthy of the name."

"Whoever did this," said Inspector Roach, "was a madman. There is little doubt of that. And there is little doubt in my mind that this was strychnine poisoning. I am a policeman, Miss Leach. It is my job to know these things. But we will catch this madman, Miss Leach, and we will hang him, make no mistake about it." He gave no indication of how he was going to set about doing this.

Hatchett felt a sudden, impatient desire to get Norma away from this ridiculous scene. He still could not feel anything about these deaths. They seemed as weird and disconnected as this war that refused to start, or his pal Lycett, who had made his proposal, wrecked Hatchett's chances then disappeared off the face of the earth. "I think," he said to the Inspector, "that Miss Lewis and I need to get her niece home. She has been very upset by all of this."

They looked up at the gallery, where Jacqueline seemed finally to have been cornered by Breeze. They were having an intense, whispered conversation. Mabel Hughes, still quivering with anger, was glaring up at them. Norma shook herself and, with real warmth, turned to Hatchett. "Of course we must, Dennis," she said.

*

If he wanted to sneak behind Lycett's back – and he now tried to fool himself that he wasn't really doing that but simply playing a game that might improve his self-esteem – there was no better way than to appeal to her through Rachel. Their unofficial visitor was perhaps the strongest link between them at the moment.

"Neutrons," he said, opening with what seemed like a harmless and uncontroversial remark, "fascinate me."

"Hatchett," said Norma, in withering tones, "thinks he knows about science but he doesn't."

"I am interested in it," said Hatchett. "I am interested in all forms of knowledge. We should all be interested in such things. Rational discourse is the most important gift we have. 'The mind is its own place and of itself can make a heaven of hell, a hell of heaven.'" This was Hatchett's favourite quotation, but Milton did not seem to have the same effect on Norma as he did on him.

"Mind, mind, mind!" she fumed suddenly. "All you ever talk about is mind. You're all mind. You're like a brain on stilts. You never talk about feelings, it's always reason, reason, reason. Well, sometimes people do things for absolutely no reason. They do things and they do not know why they do them. People fall in love, for God's sake, although I suppose you have never thought about that because love to you is just another subject for silly, masculine . . . jokes, isn't it?"

That unfortunate incident at the Gare du Nord still rankled. It had, Hatchett reflected, been a bad idea to propose to her then pretend he didn't mean it. Although, to be fair, at the time he hadn't actually meant it. Or, at least, he wasn't sure whether he had meant it or not. It was only after he had said he didn't mean it that he had started to realize he had, but he had probably only said it was a joke because he had thought she wouldn't take it seriously. And by then, of course, Alec had not only said it and meant it but also been taken very seriously indeed.

"He knows nothing about science," said Norma to Rachel. "He only pretends he does to try to make me feel small."

"I know what a neutron is," said Hatchett, hotly, aware as he said this that he didn't. He had better move on. "I know what an electron is, come to that. And while we are on the subject of reason I am not saying that I don't believe in love but that I think it should be founded on reason. I think that we . . ."

They were coming up to the school gates now. There, as usual, waiting for their daughter, were Mr and Mrs Hughes. Accompanying them was the sallow-faced man in the blue suit, Mr Mason. Once again, Hatchett thought, he was showing a rather worrying amount of interest in Rachel.

"Well, well, well," he said, with an oily smile, "the little girl I thought was a squarehead." And he looked round for a response to this remark, which, from the Hugheses anyway, he got in the form of outrageously loud laughter. It seemed that Mr Hughes shared Mr Mason's anti-German sentiments.

As soon as they had got Rachel clear of the school and the three of them were heading towards Albion House, Hatchett decided to return to the subject of nuclear physics, if only to annoy Norma. "So what is it that interests you about neutrons?" he said.

"I am interested in fission," said Rachel, "and what happens in fission. There are people who think the neutrons would multiply to cause other fission fragments, multiply like rabbits."

She obviously thought Hatchett would have some idea of what she was talking about, which, of course, he didn't, although he was not going to reveal that to Norma. He nodded sagely and said something along the lines of "I see" or "Of course" as if he was always chatting about fission fragments with Norma's pupils. Fission fragments of what?

Scientists, of course, had a way of admitting you into their thought processes as if you had been privy to the hundreds of man or woman hours that had got them to the exalted stage of thought at which they found themselves. He decided to take the human angle. At least it might prove to Norma that he wasn't a ruthless, cruel calculating machine – although secretly Hatchett rather fancied that idea. At least it would help him to put up with her droning on about Lycett's legs, hair, ears, eyes, way with the English language, etc.

"Was your father working on fission?" he said.

"In a way," said Rachel, in rather careful tones. She was still not keen on discussing what her father had been doing. "All problems of physics interested him," she went on. "Until the Nazis arrived he was a very important scientist. With the Nazis came something called Jewish physics."

"What on earth is that?" said Hatchett.

"Einstein, Hans Bethe, Lise Meitner, who was a hero to me. All great physicists. But Jewish. And Jews are stupid and dangerous and impure, as I am sure you have read in the newspapers, so Jewish physics is apparently no good. When the Nazis arrived they put some moron in charge of my father's department. He knew nothing about anything. But at least he wasn't Jewish."

Norma was still glaring at him. Why was this? Wasn't he supposed to talk to Rachel at all? Although he suddenly found that, now she had opened up (why now? did she want something? had she got something she wanted out of Norma?), he was desperate to find out what was really happening inside Germany. With each moment that passed he was becoming more and more aware of how ignorant he was about what was really going on inside the Reich. What he read in the newspapers didn't really describe what he was hearing from Rachel. Was that because such things weren't reported? Or because he didn't want to believe them? Or – this bore out what Norma had been saying – because you never really understood events unless you grasped what the people involved in them were feeling?

"I think," said Rachel, as Norma drew a little way away from the two of them, "that Miss Lewis is very upset about what happens to Captain Lycett. His letters are impossible to understand and all have holes in them."

"What kind of holes?" said Hatchett. "Logical holes?"

"Real holes!" said Rachel in an awed whisper. "Someone has made them look like Swiss cheese!"

Hatchett was intrigued by this thought and wanted to ask more but Rachel was jabbing her finger violently in the direction of Norma. "Go to her," she said, "and ask her about the Major Lycett. And tomorrow I have persuaded her we can go to Birmingham to see my father's friend. I do not like the way this Mr Mason looks at me and asks questions. I want much that you will come with us. I don't know why she does not want you to come with us. I feel safe with you there, Mr Hatchett. You are an intelligent person." Then, without a trace of self-pity, she added, "I am not wishing to be sent to a camp. I am frightened of what would happen to me. My father's work is very important, Mr Hatchett, and there are bad things in the wind. For all of us. You understand me?"

"I think so," said Hatchett, wondering at Alec's rapid promotion through the British Army, at the fact that this girl seemed involved in things that were clearly of rather more importance than her youth might suggest, and not least at the fact that she should think he had influence of any kind over Norma. He soon caught up with Norma, who was striking out in her best hockey-team manner towards the steep, twisting road that led down to where Albion House was folded into the hill above Croydon.

"Have you heard from Alec?" he heard himself say.

"What do you care?" said Norma, rounding on him fiercely. "Why do you pretend to care?"

"Norma –"

"Go away!" said Norma. "I hate both of you! I wish I had never clapped eyes on either of you! Go away!"

Hatchett started back towards Rachel. He looked at the girl. She was shaking her head in a decisive manner. She went into a brief, graphic mime that seemed to indicate that Hatchett should put his arms round Norma. After a pause, Hatchett did so. Norma started to cry. She smelt of soap and clean linen. "I don't know where he is," she said. "I don't know where he is. And I love him so much, Dennis. I love both of you so much."

"Yes," said Hatchett, patting her shoulder awkwardly, like a novice trying to burp a baby. "Of course you do, Norma." She seemed to relax then, and he almost asked her if he could accompany them to Birmingham the next day. Something made him decide not to. She trusted him and the feelings he had for her were not really those of a friend. It would be more honourable to wait until he was asked.

16 December 1939

A few hours later, before it was light, Lieutenant Alec Lycett crawled through undergrowth a few miles outside Yeovil.

Gooderson was doing something to his letters. He was sure of it. The man denied it: he had come up with some story about GHQ (SOUTH-WEST) sometimes just picking a letter out of the bag and chopping it up into little pieces just for the hell of it, but Alec, however sceptical he might be about the rationality of those in charge of the British Army, did not think they had yet got round to deliberately demoralizing their own men.

Although there were times . . .

He had wondered whether to demand that they be censored by the people above Gooderson – which seemed to be one of the rights not taken away from him since 3 September – but until he had proof that the ex-bank manager was doing what he was doing he didn't feel able to make a move. He was certain, however, that the letter in which he had asked Norma to send him a copy of his letters to her had been got at by Gooderson. Her reply had been: "Dear Alec, What is your hairy thing that goes boing boing boing? I am at my wits' end. I feel I need to talk to you and . . ." etc., etc. The truly ghastly thing about all this was that he had never needed to talk to her more urgently in his life. Lucius, for God's sake! She knew about Lucius. She had seen Lucius. Lucius was back in Crotchett Green, spreading lies about him, seducing local women and generally giving him a bad reputation. For all Alec knew he was running up bills on his account, insulting tradesmen and generally exercising the unlicensed power-of-attorney that goes with being an identical twin. Oh, how he loathed knowing that there was someone in this world who resembled him so exactly that no one else could tell the difference between them! What an insult it was to his already precarious sense of individuality! What a licence it gave to his double!

He couldn't write to Alec Senior about it. Or – he shivered at the thought – his mother. He couldn't talk to Norma about it because of Gooderson.

It was Gooderson all right. Gooderson was barking mad. Gooderson had secrecy on the brain. It was Gooderson who, in their first week of training, had tried to conceal the fact that the regiment was stationed at Yeovil. This was pretty difficult when, three hundred yards from the camp, there was a sign saying YEOVIL. One of Alec's first assignments had been to crawl out under cover of darkness (Gooderson was very keen on officers crawling) and cover the thing with a blanket.

He was showing other signs of being completely and utterly batty, thought Alec. He refused to use a lavatory that anyone else had used and had had his own personal mobile earth closet brought from Croydon. He spent hours devising *placements* for regimental dinners. He rarely spoke above a whisper (again for security reasons) and wherever possible used incomprehensible hand gestures to convey his meaning. One of the reasons they had been given so little warning of their departure for training, it turned out, was that Gooderson believed all orders should be concealed from the men for as long as possible. In an ideal world he seemed to expect other ranks to carry out his instructions before they had received them; as it was, he delayed their transmission almost until the point when they should have already been carried out.

Alec looked at his spade. He was fairly sure it was not standard Army issue. In fact, he was almost positive that no one in the 4th Croydons had what you might call an official digging implement. Peckerley, for example, had got something that looked like a gigantic trowel. Forssander and Mavroleon had spades that looked as if they had been forwarded to the regiment by some agricultural museum.

Terranby did not have a spade. At first Alec had thought that this was simply because there weren't enough spades to go round; then he had noticed they hadn't yet given Terranby a real rifle. Perhaps it had been decided, at senior level, that Terranby wasn't to be entrusted with any kind of offensive weapon. Perhaps when battle came they were just going to set light to him and roll him towards enemy lines.

Shouldering his spade, a squat, snub-nosed shovel that made little impact even on soft earth, Alec wriggled further into the birchwood. Their instructions, handed out by Gooderson at 0145 somewhere in this Godforsaken wood, were to dig in on a line north-west of the church.

But where was the church?

Alec had crawled towards something that had looked like a church some days earlier but on closer inspection it had turned out to be a deserted brick factory. He and Peckerley had got out the map and Peckerley, as usual, had suggested there was something wrong with it. Forssander had said that if you half-closed your eyes and imagined the sound of bells it looked quite like a church. The rest of the platoon, as they usually did, sat around looking depressed and muttering about lunch. Mavroleon had fallen asleep in the middle of a hawthorn bush and had to be beaten with twigs to wake him up.

And now here he was, scarcely able to see more than a few yards in front of him, his only guide a useless sheet of paper full of shabby typescript telling him to go to GQRMN MAPREF DDLI AT 0234 ACK EMMA and a map that was, after weeks of training, still as inscrutable as the Rosetta Stone. There was a church marked on the map, certainly, but was it the same church? There was a wood, all right, but was it the wood they were in? And what was the weird crinkly thing in the middle of the grey blob?

What was the war going to be like when real Germans started shooting at him?

He looked around for the other members of the platoon. A few yards to his left, Peckerley, irrepressibly cheerful as usual, was whispering to him. "I think, sir," he was saying, "that we should dig in. BLUEFORCE are in the region. I thought I heard Gooderson." This wasn't surprising. Gooderson, in spite of his obsession with secrecy, was a man who never neglected to disturb the odd twig when on night manoeuvres. The theory in the regiment was that it was his way of dealing with a deep-seated fear of the dark.

Whatever the reason, he generally made a noise like an elephant trying to uproot a tree while being pursued by hornets.

"Yes," said Alec, "tell them to dig in."

Perhaps his letters to Norma had been defeatist. He had droned on about crawling through the undergrowth and sliding down hills on his bottom, his anger at the fact that Hitler seemed to think he was cock of the walk, and the simple fact that a soldier's life was digging into your hole and hoping to fill your belly with some decent food. Maybe that was defeatist. Maybe all his fine feelings about the world were about to be mocked and twisted by people like Gooderson and – God help us – Lucius. Lucius, Lucius, Lucius. The last he had heard of him was when he was at Cambridge. His father had said he had gone abroad and they would never see him again. They had very nearly talked about the past, but Mrs Lycett had put a stop to that. He still remembered the way she had looked at Alec Senior across the dinner table, her eyes as hard and unforgiving as she had been all those years ago, when the thing in the woods screamed and twisted and blackened in the fire and when his father, who was supposed to be strong, cried like a child, like a baby.

He simply wouldn't tell Norma about Lucius. That was it. He would give her the bare facts. Stick to the outline. That was all she needed to know.

Peckerley, with his familiar keenness for carrying out Alec's orders, was throwing up earth with the enthusiasm of a dog burying a bone. At a rather slower rate, Terranby scratched feebly at the soil with the edge of his plate and then, whining to himself, slumped against a nearby tree. Mavroleon appeared to be asleep.

Forssander was crouched by a tree trunk. Something in the bushes seemed to have made him nervous. Perhaps, thought Alec, they contained the things that inspired his phobia – spiders, snakes, beetles, perhaps. Or perhaps it was bushes of which Forssander was frightened. His gaze was directed generally enough to suggest that that was the case. If it was, Alec had a certain sympathy with the man. Things could hide in bushes then leap out at you from them. Perhaps bush phobia was a life-preserving neurosis to have for an infantryman.

Alec, too, got out his spade and started to dig.

In some ways this censorship business was a blessing in disguise. He was pretty damned useless at expressing himself anyway. His sentences were probably a lot more interesting with the odd noun or verb lopped out of them. And what he had to say, what he ought to say, about Lucius was unsayable. He had never said it, not even to Hatchett. It was a secret he tried to keep even from himself, although late at night it came to him and tortured him and would not let him sleep.

You weren't supposed to have secrets from the one you loved. Secrets, as he knew from watching Mr and Mrs Lycett for the last twenty years, slowly poisoned every good thing about an affair. And part of him knew that if he was going to have a chance with Norma he was going to have to tell her the truth, the whole truth and nothing but the truth. That morning in church, on the day war was declared, he had known, with sudden and absolute clarity, that he loved Norma. Oh, before he might have thought he was interested in her. He might have flattered himself that she found him attractive or that he was ready to see exactly how interested she might be, but the moment when they walked away from the church had not been like that at all.

He had looked at her, as the church bells rang out, cracked and defiantly optimistic in the summer morning, and realized suddenly that he could be saved. It was, he said to himself, an echo of his religious period, but it was more profound and more serious. Love of another person could save you. Literally. If they loved you and you loved them, and if, as Norma was, they were a good and true person, then you in your turn had the obligation to be good and true. And, perhaps even more important, the chance of becoming those things. Not inhabiting the hell in which his prosperous parents had lived all their married lives. She loved him. He loved her. From now on it was going to be different.

It was love all right. But the trouble was that the words he used to describe this love were all words that had been used at him, by teachers or priests or parents. "Complete union with another," that appalling padre at college had said, more than once, "is a way of losing your self. And the self is what holds you back from real knowledge and understanding of the spiritual beauty of the world." He could laugh at poseurs like the college padre, who had left his hand on Alec's knee for rather too long in one tutorial, but there were other voices from his past that were harder to ignore.

No, he was scared of this love, and with good reason. It was serious. It had been, of all people, Hatchett's father who, in that frightening, hellfire sermon he remembered across all these years, had talked about love, its corrosive and purifying effects, its terror and its pity. "Love," Mr Hatchett had said, leaning across his pulpit, "is a vision of perfection, an apprehension of the marvels of God's work in the physical presence of another. If you betray that love, if you lie or cheat or fail your chosen partner in some way, then make no mistake about it, my friend, you are in hell and you will burn with the grief and the shame of it. Guilt is put there by God for a reason. It is to make us act morally – because without guilt and fear we are not capable of morality. Just you remember that."

Alec remembered Hatchett's father's face now, craggy, lined, the huge eyes buried deep in the face, the wild hair blowing around his temples like some Old Testament prophet. He was talking about his own guilt, of course, now Alec could see that. Dirty old bastard. But when he preached, he seemed to be talking about Alec and his own innermost feelings; and he preached now in Alec's head, saying, "You're not worthy of her, boy! You're not worthy! Not worthy!"

The trouble with this love business was that it made you so aware of what you were; if he was honest with himself, that was something Alec had been avoiding for the last twenty-odd years. He thought about not feeling things as he looked round at his platoon. There had been, it seemed to him, another world before he had started thinking this way about Norma. In many ways it was an easier place in which to live. You followed directions and obeyed orders; and other people did not fray your nerves. Love was being at the mercy of other people. It hurt.

Peckerley was crawling towards him. He jerked a thumb in Forssander's direction. The boy was now positively gibbering with fright. Alec, who had had to censor no fewer than twenty-four of his letters to his mother in Coulsdon (he never wrote to anyone else), recalled a paragraph from the last one: ". . . I am afraid that when we get to wherever it is we are going to actually fight the Germans there will be a lot of THEM all over the place and I shall not be able to be brave because of THEM and I can't even write what THEY are but you know Mum how I am with THEM and I just hope THEY don't make me ashamed to be British and to do my duty for my country and Croydon and you Mum of course to whom I send fondest . . ."

Perhaps it was people that scared the living daylights out of Forssander. Once again Alec felt a pang of sympathy for the lad.

"I think, sir," whispered Peckerley, "that you and I should take a look-see, sir. Our orders were to capture BLUEFORCE. And while we're at it we could give old Gooderson a bit of a fright, don't you think? I am sure he's round here somewhere. I can smell him."

Peckerley was right. Soon, as they crawled off in the gloom, Alec heard somewhere over to his left a noise that was either a group of badgers snuffling their way through a camp-site or the commanding officer of the 4th Croydons having a sitrep conference. They veered over towards it, and Peckerley, taking the lead as he often seemed to do in these operations, got up to a crouch and hurried, with extraordinary lightness, through the darkened wood.

If you had any degree of imagination, thought Alec, as he followed him, a few yards behind, even a wood outside Yeovil could be a pretty frightening place. Of course, he realized, it recalled that other wood, behind Albion House, and that afternoon, all those years ago, when he was so suddenly introduced to cruelty, death and betrayal. With each step, he seemed to hear an answering noise in the trees nearby. Peckerley, ahead of him, stopped, cupped a hand to his ear then, like the last of the Mohicans, flitted on through the wood. Lucius and he had moved like this, stalking imaginary targets, on the day when there was the fight and then the burning. Alec shook himself awake. Now, now was the thing, not the past. The matter in hand.

"Sir!" Peckerley was whispering in his ear. "Sir!" He was pointing ahead of them through the trees. About ten or fifteen yards away, the ground sloped steeply downwards, and there, in the light of the whitening sky, Alec saw BLUEFORCE or, to put it more precisely, the brains behind BLUEFORCE or, to put it even more precisely, the complete and utter idiot and madman who seemed to be in charge of BLUEFORCE. He was alone. His only companions at HQ seemed to be a copy of *The Times* and a bottle of claret. Colonel, as he now was, Arthur Henderson Gooderson 4th Croydon Light Infantry (Territorial Division) was in the act of lowering his trousers and reversing into the small mobile latrine that was one of his proudest possessions.

"It doesn't seem right, sir, does it," whispered Peckerley, "to attack a man with his trousers down?"

"It gives us a military advantage, Peckerley," said Alec, as Gooderson fumbled with his large white underpants, "but if we are going in I think we should do so before the situation has a chance to develop any further."

He was just about to move, when he thought he heard a noise in the bushes. Peckerley, more Indian scout than ever, stiffened, and then – surely copying some gesture he had seen in a cinema film – waved his superior officer on. They crept slowly at first, but just as Colonel Gooderson was lowering his behind on to the seat they rushed upon him, seized him by the neck and hissed, in unison, one into each ear, "You're dead! Sir!"

Gooderson struggled in a hopeless, flaccid sort of way – like an elderly fish trapped in a landing net. Alec saw at once that in his left hand was a wad of papers, presumably for use when he had finished on the latrine. As he grabbed the Colonel's left hand – Peckerley seemed to be saying something along the lines of "One more peep out of you and we will blow your head off, you German swine" – Alec caught sight of one large, official-looking sheet.

Gooderson had been holding it out level and its surface was covered with what Alec at first took for confetti. But as he pulled his superior officer's hand towards him, taking care to make sure it was still parallel to the ground, he saw that in fact they were cut-out words and phrases in a handwriting, big, childish, firm, that he

recognized as his own. He saw phrases he remembered writing . . .
". . . it is so hard to talk about Lucius, my darling . . ." or ". . . when
I realized I was in love with you I saw that my whole life had
changed or, rather, had GOT to change but my love . . ." and the
occasional isolated word. Quite often the word was "love" but
even more frequently – and this came as a surprise to Alec for he
hardly ever spoke of him these days, even to Hatchett – the word
was "Lucius". It seemed, now, in the early dawn, to stand out more
boldly than any other word in that alphabet soup of letters, so that
as he fingered the fragments of paper, in the lightening gloom, it
seemed to be set in capitals – LUCIUS LUCIUS LUCIUS.

Perhaps because he had his right forearm firmly round the
man's windpipe, Alec could feel no resistance whatsoever from
Gooderson. He didn't make a sound as Alec peered down at the
sheet of paper that was acting as a kind of tray for the mangled
residue of his love-letters to Norma, and saw that it was an order
of some kind, withheld as usual from the regiment by Gooderson
until the last possible moment. It seemed to be saying that the 4th
Croydons had been granted two days' leave from eight o'clock that
morning. Alec, who should have felt elated, not only at his victory
but also at the opportunity to talk to Norma at last, to explain all
those things from his childhood that had surfaced between them,
felt suddenly cold and afraid and lonely. So that there was doubt
and its shadow on his love for Norma, and it seemed to come from
that one word more noticeable than any other in the pile of cut
phrases scattered across their serving dish of Army notepaper –
LUCIUS LUCIUS LUCIUS LUCIUS.

8

"Rachel!" Norma was speaking, she realized, in a whisper. This was absurd. Who was going to hear them? There was no one else in the flat. From the unusual silence, there was no one else, as far as she could discover, above and below her in the whole of Albion House. Mr Shale, who lived underneath, might have been there, of course, but he had been completely silent since war was declared.

"Rachel!" She shook the girl awake. Rachel stirred and shivered and yawned and, as she often did before she was properly awake, muttered to herself in German.

"Rachel! We have to go to Birmingham today!"

Norma still didn't understand why she had not wanted Hatchett to come with them. It had not been easy to track down Rachel's father's friend and Norma had not been particularly eager to help her. She was frightened, of course, of doing anything that might attract attention to the girl, and heading off to Birmingham was, by Crotchett Green standards, a rather unusual thing to do. She wanted her refugee absorbed into Croydon.

She had finally made contact with Rachel's father's friend about a month ago. Frisch, his name was. There had been endless phone calls to any number of university physics departments before she located him. Norma hadn't spoken to him but Rachel had had several quite long conversations, both in German and then, more and more, in English. "German is not such a good language at the moment," said Rachel, "not only because of our memories of Germany but over here they want to put you in a camp if they hear it. Otto is very worried they are going to send him off to one. Mrs Peierls has prepared a shirt for him that will be easy to iron."

Norma didn't like to ask who Mrs Peierls was. She was nervous in the extreme about this long journey across England to meet a man she didn't even know. But that, surely, would have been a reason for asking Hatchett to come with them. That was what men were for, wasn't it? To organize train tickets, to look authoritative when officials were asking you for papers you didn't possess? Norma had never been so aware of the fact that, these days, everyone was supposed to have an identity card and Rachel didn't even have a passport. Once upon a time she had found English official uniforms reassuring. Now, even a ticket inspector seemed to threaten danger.

No, it would have been logical to ask Hatchett. She didn't ask him to come because he disturbed her. Last night, on the steps, when she had got up to take Jacqueline back inside, she had felt him look at her. She remembered now how uncomfortably aware she had been of the lower half of her body when he had looked at her like that, of the way her skirt rustled and swayed against her stockings. Well, a lot of men looked at her like that. But he wasn't supposed to. He had told her he was her friend. He had even made a joke of a marriage proposal. That was how serious he was about her! He had listened to her pour out her heart about Alec. He had said how fond he was of Alec, how much he missed him, how happy he was for the two of them. And then he had looked at her like that! He was not supposed to.

He was just being a man, thought Norma, as she flicked on the gas fire then busied herself in the front room, examining her packing for the twentieth time. He just wanted what another man had got. The thought that Alec Lycett had "got" her brought a pleasant flush to her face as she looked out at the winter landscape, sloping away towards Croydon in the thin December light. It was cold but no snow yet.

She saw Mason before he saw her.

It might, of course, have had something to do with Leafy's murder but her first thought was that he had come for Rachel. There was a policeman with him. A big, amiable, rather foolish-looking man whom she recognized from the village. Constable Potter, of course.

She was confident of her ability to manage him and, although she ducked out of sight at the window, she was tempted, when she heard the heavy pressure on the doorbell, to go downstairs and bluff it out. It was the sight of Rachel, coming through the door in her nightdress, that made her change her mind. She had seen fear on her face before, of course, when she first saw her on the boat and once when Mason had started quizzing her at the school play – in which Hatchett had given a bravura performance of Iago – but the terror she saw in her now was like nothing she had ever seen before.

"Who calls?" said Rachel. "Who calls so early? No one calls early!"

This was, as it happened, perfectly true. In fact, hardly anyone ever called late either. But there didn't seem any reason why, just because someone decided to press the bell at eight o'clock in the morning, you should automatically decide they were from the secret police. Although, thought Norma, as the bell sounded again, harsh, prolonged, angry, that was what they were, as far as Rachel was concerned. They would take her away and Norma would never see her again. She would cry probably. Cry like her mother had the last time she had seen her in the hospital and she would not let go of the side of the bed and she was kicking and screaming as she called out, "Goodbye, Mummy! Goodbye, Mummy! Goodbye, Mummy!" Her father and the nurse had had to drag her down the slippery corridor.

"Stay very still," Norma whispered, "and they will go away!"

"Who are they?" said Rachel.

"A policeman," said Norma, "and that horrible Mason man."

"They won't go away," said Rachel. "They will come in anyway. They will break down the door."

"This," said Norma, with what she felt might be misplaced confidence, "is England. We don't do things like that in England."

"You are sure of this?" said Rachel.

Another push on the bell.

"He is an English bobby," said Norma, "with a funny hat and a kind red face."

"He sounds," said Rachel grimly, "just like the man who took away my father."

But Constable Potter did not try to break down the door. Indeed, from his expression, Norma got the idea that he did not particularly want to be there in the first place. She could hear Mason whining at him and Potter's slow grumble of disagreement. And then they were gone. As soon as she saw them walk back up the lane the first thing she did was telephone Dennis Hatchett.

He was in his pyjamas. She could tell that from his first "hullo". He was also – this took slightly longer to work out – in the room with his mother. His voice always took on a slightly formal quality when he was with her. In all the years she had known her son, Norma had hardly exchanged more than a few words with Mrs Hatchett. She was a hunted little woman with a face that seemed subtly altered for the worse each time you saw her.

"Good," he was saying, in his brisk, schoolmaster's voice, "so you want me to drive you. I shall do so, of course. In the new MG!"

She had thought, somehow, that she and Rachel would be safer in a car. She was beginning to think like a refugee in her own country. This was ridiculous. The most dangerous thing about the journey would be Hatchett's driving. The thought of Hatchett's driving made her wonder whether she should have stuck to her original plan, but what she needed most of all, she now realized, was a friend, a supporter, a tough, reliable backstop sort of a person. Hatchett.

"Come up the lane," she told him, "and keep a lookout for that horrible little man who was at the Hugheses'. Mason. If it's clear just honk the horn and Rachel and I will come down." Mason and the policeman could have waited a little way down the road. Their departure might have been a trick.

"Rachel! Are you planning to go all the way to Birmingham in your nightie?"

"No, Aunt Lewis!" said Rachel, with a grin. Now she knew Hatchett was coming she seemed to have cheered up. While Norma finished off giving Hatchett orders – he quite liked being bossed around where practical things were concerned, perhaps because he had no real interest in them – Rachel put on her school uniform. She was curiously attached to it and would wear it even at the weekends.

"Tell me," she said, as she came back into the room, "do you think that Mr Breeze has poisoned Miss Everett? Or do you think Jacqueline Rissett has poisoned her because she is in love with Mr Breeze and resents his passionate affair with this ugly old woman?"

Norma, who had been unable to work up as much interest in the destruction of the Spanish department as she felt she should, was suddenly intrigued at this classroom-eye view of events. In so far as she had any kind of theory about the deaths she felt it was more likely to be connected to some feud between Green, Everett and Miss Leach. All three had the kind of intense friendships that Norma regarded as unhealthy.

"Miss Green has been horribly murdered," went on Rachel, in conversational tones, "because she has revealed the love of Everett and Breeze. Fingers of suspecting point to the chemistry master. But I find it hard to believe that Miss Everett and Mr Breeze are making sexual love. Miss Everett is surely a lesbian, as is Miss Green and, come to think of it, Miss Leach also is preferring to make love with women. Almost all the staff of Saltdene School for Girls are lesbians, Auntie Lewis, apart from yourself. Have you seen the film *Mädchen in Uniform*? It is very, very funny, I think!"

She had never known the girl talk so much. She must be excited at going to see her friend. But Norma was truly impressed by Rachel's grasp of the gossip at Saltdene School for Girls. And even more so by the level of her knowledge of the ways of the world. The first time Norma had come across the word "lesbian", in the sixth form, she had assumed it referred to an inhabitant of a Greek island.

"What I do not understand, Auntie Lewis," Rachel went on, "is why Jacqueline could say this thing about Everett and Breeze to Mabel, who is a very strict person for truth, I think. Although I have to say her truth is not exactly mine. I think she does not like Jews. To make mischief? Jacqueline is a kind person, I think. But she can be stirred by love passions. She all the time thinks of love passions. Perhaps it is Jacqueline who has poisoned Miss Everett. Perhaps Miss Everett has made her to do lesbian things with her and Miss Green and she has had a revulsion and done away with the two of them."

Norma, noting how much better the girl's English was when she talked about nuclear physics, held up her hand for silence. "Rachel," she said, "I think we should have a cup of tea before Mr Hatchett arrives."

Rachel grinned. "I think this will be very good for both of us," she said, "and you must remember that you do not have lover feelings for him. Although I think he is very, very handsome. Especially now he has shaved off his moustache."

There was some truth in this. Hatchett was greatly improved now that you could see his upper lip. But Norma did not want to get drawn into a discussion of whether Hatchett was or was not what her stepmother referred to as "feasible". She had the impression, sometimes, that Rachel acted as an advocate for him. While the kettle boiled for tea she went to the desk in the corner of the room and took out Alec's last letter – his response to her response to his asking her to send him a hairy thing that went boing boing boing.

Darling Alec [her response had been]
    I simply do not understand what it is you are writing
that makes them cut your letters,
literally, to pieces. What is it you want me to send to
you? I miss you and need to ask you
about so many things, but all I get in each letter is miles
of

this
    I love you

    Norma

She had been rather proud of this artistic way of letting him (and, perhaps, the swine who was cutting up his letters) know what it felt like to have the thoughts of someone you loved censored. But whoever was doing what they were doing to Alec's post, they were not impressed. When his next letter arrived she wondered why they hadn't just folded it up into a paper dart and lobbed it out of the window without bothering to send it to her at all.

> Darling Norma,
>   I wanted your

> bum

It was his writing anyway. She took the letter out, thrust it into her handbag, and walked through to see to the kettle. In the other room, Rachel was whistling to herself as she gathered together her things for the journey. It sounded like the slow movement of a Mozart piano concerto. She was rendering the top line of the orchestral part absolutely accurately, and preserving, with astonishing faithfulness, its bars of silence when the soloist was on alone.

Down below came a long blast on the car horn. Norma ran to the window. There, leaping out of a large green MG coupé, was Dennis Hatchett, looking positively rakish. He was wearing a huge black overcoat and an equally huge black Homburg hat. He was obviously hoping to look, thought Norma, like some Central European businessman who dabbled in espionage. But the middle-aged clothes – both hat and coat were several sizes too big – only made him look younger and more vulnerable. As she waited he leaped out of the car and, with one foot on the running board and the other on *terra firma*, bowed with mock ceremony. Then he pointed back down the lane and, raising both thumbs in the air, did a small circular jig in the middle of the road. The coast was clear.

Then, standing a little way away from the vehicle, he shovelled air in its direction, with both hands, in the manner of a salesman proud of his wares. Oh, God, thought Norma, who had put this fact out of her mind, he is driving.

Hatchett's favourite phrase as he pulled out, usually on blind corners or in the last few yards before the crest of a hill, was "Room enough for three!" "Room enough for three!" he would shout, as he swerved out from behind the lorry and into the path of the oncoming vehicle. The masculine, aggressive side of him, usually deflected by his lively sense of the absurd, came to the fore when he was behind the wheel of a car. As Norma hustled Rachel towards the door, forgetting about tea, she took one more look down at him as he stamped his feet round the car, driving one gloved fist into another gloved palm. Rachel was right about one thing. Without the moustache, he was a very attractive man.

"This," said Hatchett, with a confidence he did not feel, "is almost certainly the B1349. From there we shall cut on to the B2067 and that should bring us out on to a road, which I think is the B3894, which, if my calculations are correct, comes into the main A5 just outside Birmingham. It looks longer on the map but actually it's quicker. If we were on the A5 we would be stuck behind some lorry, which will not happen on this road. This road is empty."

That much, at least, he thought, was true. No one in their right mind would venture on to the B1349 (or whatever it was called) on purpose. It was a road that seemed hell bent on taking the longest possible distance between any two points along its length. Where it could bend, it bent. It did not just bend but, in order to prove to those foolish enough to use it that it was better to travel hopefully than to arrive, it turned back on itself, looped the loop and wriggled ecstatically backwards and forwards across perfectly flat pieces of country that your average normal road would have ignored in a mad dash for the horizon. It was a road, thought Hatchett, keen to express itself.

It was also dark. All of England was dark. On the A1 and the A5 and the A23, lorries crawled sheepishly through the gloom, their headlights shrouded; and along the roads that ringed the larger towns, factories and shops showed no sign of life. Vehicles groped their way forward in the blackout while others slept on their feet like cattle in a field. But the darkness of the B1349 – if it was the B1349 and not the B3034 or the A73467891B or even the private drive of some ogre who was going to eat them when they got to his front door – was like thick cloth. It seemed about to swallow the car whole.

"We are going to have to stay the night," said Norma.

"Of course we are!" said Hatchett breezily. "I have booked us into a commercial hotel. All three in the same room!"

He winked, rakishly, at Rachel. Really, this Homburg was having a very strange effect on him. He had not meant to say something quite so inappropriate. But Rachel seemed to find it rather amusing. Norma looked as if her first reaction was to laugh and, almost immediately, to be disapproving. Hatchett decided to talk to Rachel.

"So tell me," he said, "fission is going into the nucleus of an atom and splitting it. Am I right?"

Unknown to either Norma or Rachel, he had been talking to Groenig about this very subject a mere three days ago. At the time he was fairly sure he understood, but now he was also fairly sure that he was about ready to have it all explained to him again.

"Of course," he said, "the amount of energy liberated in such a reaction would be colossal . . . Is that the area in which your father was working?"

Rachel gave him a very careful glance. Hatchett was hoping to simulate a blend of ignorance and enthusiasm but she had rumbled that almost immediately. When she was talking about science Rachel betrayed an extraordinary directness, a unique simplicity that seemed to give rise to a clarity of language. Shamed into trying to express himself better, he said, "What I am saying is there are certain elements that seem susceptible to such a reaction – unstable, shall we say?, in some way. Uranium 238, for example?"

Rachel gave a brief, percussive laugh. "You do your homework, Mr Hatchett. Perhaps you are talking to Mr Groenig? He is an unusually intelligent man as are you also, I think. But I am afraid uranium 238 is not a candidate for fission. It is a common enough element so it would be handy if it was but it is not. It scatters fast neutrons, and for fission you need slow neutrons. My father was working on uranium 235."

"And uranium 235, you think you might be able to –"

"To what?" said Rachel, giving him a beady look. "If you must know, there is no possibility of fission, in the sense in which I think you mean it, as far as uranium 235 is concerned. Even if you had this chain reaction, let us say, with slow neutrons in 235 it would be like setting light to a pile of gunpowder. Uranium 235 is also very hard to get hold of and there are many other difficulties, which I will not detail here. My father has come to the conclusion, as many great physicists have also done, including Niels Bohr, may I say, that fission is not possible."

There was a pause. Rachel looked at Norma. It was fairly clear to Hatchett that she had not understood a word of this conversation and, for reasons of his own, he was quite content to leave it that way. Rachel, too, seemed to have noted Norma's lack of interest or understanding.

"In the sense in which I mean it," said Hatchett.

"Precisely," said Rachel. "So, Mr Hatchett, let us worry about other important things such as your delightful Mr Mason."

"And," said Norma acidly, "where we are."

It was at that precise moment, however, that, very much in the manner of a neutron arriving at the nucleus by a combination of gravity, electricity and sheer luck, Hatchett realized they were in a place that was almost certainly Birmingham. Things outside the car were still dark, but at least there were now differing degrees of darkness. Some of the dark things were now, probably, houses or even shops, and others, though they looked at first like lighter chunks of darkness carrying glow worms through the impenetrable gloom, turned out to be people wearing luminous cards in their hatbands, in a desperate attempt to be seen as they made their way through an uncharted forest of hidden kerbstones or lamp-posts that had given up being lamp-posts and transformed themselves into just one more thing into which you could walk.

The headlights showed what they had always showed since the darkness came in – an unresolved fragment of the road ahead – but at last at its edges there were signs of the end of the womb-like country darkness.

Not only that.

Although Hatchett had once had some vague plan of coming into the city somewhere near the university, he had long ago decided to settle for any bit of Birmingham or, indeed, any town or village where there might be people who could give him a clue as to where the hell Birmingham was. But as far as he could make out, from a half-glimpsed sign on a wall, the general feeling of buildings gathered round a green space and, finally, a small notice that read UNIVERSITY OF BIRMINGHAM, DEPARTMENT OF PHYSICS, they really were about to meet Rachel's friend, the mysterious Mr (or was it Dr? or Herr Professor?) Otto Frisch.

Hatchett had always imagined that great scientists did not spend their time bent over oddly shaped glass tubes heating up potions, but when he, Rachel and Norma pushed back the doors of the lecture theatre to which they had been directed, that was exactly what the great man appeared to be doing. He had also assumed, for some reason, that a man who numbered among his interests the attempt to split the nucleus of a uranium atom would look pretty serious about it. But Otto Frisch, a small, impish-looking man in his thirties, seemed, as far as Hatchett could tell, to regard the whole business as a huge joke.

"What do you think?" he said, when he had embraced Rachel, and Norma and Hatchett had introduced themselves. "The glass blowers made it up for me." He pointed towards a weird glass object that looked as if it had come straight out of a medieval alchemist's room. Hatchett tried to look as if he knew what it might be. He wasn't sure what kind of press Rachel had given him, but he suspected she had exaggerated his good qualities and, almost certainly, been overly kind about his grasp of Newtonian, let alone post-Newtonian, physics.

"Fascinating," he said. "So what are you cooking up here? Uranium 235?"

He was quite pleased with this remark, which seemed to pass for perfectly acceptable small-talk with Herr Frisch but, like anyone who has delivered a short, impressive-sounding remark about something of which he is almost entirely ignorant, he braced himself for the unanswerable follow-up question: "No, this is deuterium 90 and I am using Herschel's Exclusion Law – you will know the formula, of course, Herr Professor Hatchett."

Instead Frisch laughed. "Hertz," he said, "did it with neon. Why not? You are a teacher, Rachel tells me. You teach physics?"

"I'm afraid not," said Hatchett.

"There is just air in it at the moment," said Frisch, peering at his glass tube. "The idea is that the nitrogen sinks to the bottom."

Then, quite suddenly, he reverted to the personal. He said something rapidly in German to Rachel. Hatchett thought he caught the words "father" and "camp" but Frisch had a strong Viennese accent and was talking deliberately quietly. Rachel looked as if she might cry. The two embraced. Then Rachel started to talk, very rapidly, in German. Again, she was whispering and it wasn't easy to catch what she said, but Hatchett thought she might be telling him some more about him and Norma. Whatever it was, it seemed to go down well with Frisch. When she had finished he went across to Norma and shook her warmly by the hand. Then he did the same to Hatchett. It was his eyes Hatchett noticed the most. They burned with the curiosity of a child.

"I am waiting," he said, "to be sent to the Isle of Man. Unless I can prove I am invaluable. A policeman has come to see me and asked about whether I am to sit for an examination!" He looked at Rachel and then at Hatchett. "I do not know what I can do, Mr Hatchett," he said. "I do not know what any of us can do. This poor child has no papers."

The glass tube was not the only thing that had transformed this unassuming lecture room into a cave in Frankenstein's castle. Over in the corner was another maze of wires and beakers and next to it on the floor what looked like a large lead suitcase. Norma, who was bounding around the room in a distinctly puppyish manner, was asking Frisch what was in it. He seemed to be saying that, at the moment, there was absolutely nothing in it, but at some point in the future he was going to climb down a pothole in the Yorkshire moors and grope around until he found a substance called radon, an amazingly radioactive commodity only found deep in the earth, which he was going to pop into his lead suitcase and lug back to Birmingham by train.

Stinks! thought Hatchett. The romance of new elements! The sheer Heath Robinson effrontery of it all made him wish he had paid more attention all those years ago when Mr Vine had tried to teach him the basics of heat exchange and the laws of thermo-dynamics. Norma was asking intelligent questions about something called beryllium. She seemed to have become *au fait* with nuclear physics in record time. But, as Rachel interpreted questions, nodded furiously and shook her head with equal ferocity, he could see that, unlike either he or Norma, this girl actually understood this stuff. She seemed to be conversing with Frisch on almost equal terms.

And when a fine-boned man called Peierls wandered into the room, Rachel became even more voluble. Like him, she seemed interested in the mathematics of all this and, in this, clearly reflected an interest of her father's – after whom Peierls asked with intens-ity and affection. Within minutes, all three of them were pacing around the room, waving their arms and tossing out immensely long German words, interspersed with the odd Greek letter, and numerical calculations, all of which, for some reason, were done in English.

Norma came over to him. "They're talking about this fission business," she said.

"Indeed . . ." said Hatchett.

"All these neutrons that Rachel keeps going on about are the problem, apparently," went on Norma, "and they are trying to work out how much uranium you would need for them to hit the nucleus. It was what Rachel's father was working on."

"Of course," said Hatchett. "I imagine you are about to whip out the back of an envelope and work it out yourself. For someone with your grasp of the periodic table that should prove no problem at all."

"Why," said Norma, "do you feel this need to prove yourself intellectually superior to me? Is it just because of Alec?"

Women, thought Hatchett, had a unique way of making intellectual disputes personal. It probably had something to do with the way they could dissect someone's character with the thoroughness and strictness of a mathematical philosopher. Norma was mercifully free of a lot of the things that women of a certain kind did. Unlike Jennifer Doran she did not go in for eyelash-fluttering or ignorance-simulation – but she was certainly guilty of the capital crime of putting feelings to the fore. He did not feel jealous of Alec. Well, not very . . .

"Look . . ." he said, but she ignored him. Rachel, Frisch and Peierls had reverted to English.

"So," Frisch was saying, "let's assume for the sake of argument that with the Clusius tube we could make enough 235 to create a reaction not dependent on slow neutrons. How much would you need? No one has looked at the figures for fast neutron reaction with 235."

"Because no one has made enough!" said Rachel, with an air of triumph.

Frisch pointed, once again, to his weird glass tube. "How much would you need?" he said.

Peierls and Rachel were looking at him with the suspicion of any theorist asked a practical question.

"What's the cross-section for uranium?" Rachel asked. "The standard cross-section."

"Ten to the minus twenty-three cm squared!" said Frisch crisply.

"You could try," said Rachel, "plugging into his formula. Peierls's formula gives you the critical mass. Which for 238 is of the order of tons, but for 235 it will be different. If you plug ten to the minus twenty-three cm squared you get . . ."

Frisch was writing furiously. "That," he said, "is just what I was about to do . . ." His hand moved rapidly over the sheet of paper in front of him and then, abruptly, stopped. His face expressed something close to shock. He looked up at Peierls. He seemed to have forgotten Rachel was there. "It really is not very much at all," he whispered. "A volume less than a golf ball for a substance as heavy as uranium." He looked into Peierls's face. "But would a pound or two explode or fizzle?" he said. "The chain reaction would have to proceed faster than the vaporizing and swelling of the heated metal ball, no?"

Now Peierls was writing like a madman. Even if, thought Hatchett, Norma and he and Rachel had stood up on one of the desks and taken off their clothes, these men would not have noticed them. They hardly seemed aware any more of Rachel's presence. Her interjections seemed to have set them off on a course where she could not follow and, as he watched, Hatchett felt a familiar awe in the presence of those who, with numbers and equations, could predict or tame the passage of the natural world.

Peierls's face, too, was registering shock. "Four millionths of a second," he was saying. "Incredibly much faster than slow neutron fission. Eighty generations of neutrons before the thing starts to slow down. It gives you temperatures as hot as the interior of the sun, pressures greater than the centre of the earth, where iron flows as a liquid. The results would be staggering. If you could make enough 235 you could . . ." His voice faded away.

There was an expression on his face Hatchett thought he recognized. He had seen it on the face of a man at Cambridge who wrote rather good poems and, more often, on the face of Jack Sarrat, who wrote music and played so beautifully. It was a kind of awed disquiet at the way the world seemed to be.

"With a hundred thousand Clusius tubes," said Frisch, "you could produce a pound of reasonably pure uranium 235 in a matter of weeks."

The two men stared at each other. There was a long, long silence. They still did not seem to be aware that there was anyone else in the room at all.

"It looks as if," said Frisch eventually, "after all, an atomic bomb might just be a real possibility."

Up until this moment, no one had mentioned bombs. They had been free with the word "fission", and once or twice Hatchett had heard the words "chain reaction", but immediately the word "bomb" had been spoken Hatchett saw that that was what the discussion had been about from the beginning. He had just been too stupid to grasp the fact. But neither of the men had seemed inclined to admit the direction in which their thoughts were leading them either. This, thought Hatchett, had been equally true of Rachel. He couldn't work out whether it was simply that they were so concerned with the problems of physics that they did not wish to consider any kind of practical application.

The two scientists had gone into a kind of trance, and they seemed, to Hatchett, like wizards or magicians, playing with spells that were so old and strange they could enchant or destroy the world. But as they came out of it, they seemed to notice there were others in the room and, like people awaking in a strange place, to look about them in fear and confusion. What had broken their concentration was a sudden noise outside. Someone was wheeling a heavy object along the path that led through the gardens immediately beyond the window. Peierls flicked a glance in that direction. But it was Rachel who spoke. "You must understand," she said, "that in Germany also they work on fission. Heisenberg has the *Uranverein*. They work on the separation of 235. My father has things that I must tell to Otto about this question. Things about the German work. This is the secret I have been entrusted to tell him. But until I have done so it has not been safe to tell you. I am sorry I have not been able to be candid but really it is safer. They are talking about a devastating device. That can have the power to destroy whole cities. That would turn mile after mile of our planet into a desert. And those who did not die in the blast would die from the radiation. Yes, yes, yes. An atom bomb. It is about this subject I must speak with Otto. A question of life and death – you understand me? Because if we do not build one – they will."

Long afterwards, when he was working at Bletchley, Hatchett gave much thought to this business of secrecy.

Right up until the moment when Peierls glanced, first at the window and then at Norma and him and Rachel, there had been no hint that any of this might prove dangerous if reported to the wrong people. Scientists, he decided, were like lovers, never knowing the moment until it came. Like Norma and Alec, who had suddenly seen the world differently at 10.45 on the morning of 3 September, Frisch and Peierls had been visited by divine chance. And if, at times (Norma had been quite right to charge him with jealousy), he found it hard to believe that Alec hadn't been playing some kind of double game, plotting an assault on the woman who was supposed to be their mutual best friend, he only had to think of the raw wonder on the faces of those two men when they became the first on the planet to realize that we could now make weapons so powerful they could destroy it totally.

"Well," said Frisch, eventually, "we'd better tell Oliphant about this."

"I think we better had," said Peierls. His eyes flicked over in the direction of Norma and Rachel and Hatchett.

"I think," said Frisch, slowly, in response to his colleague's unspoken question, "that for someone in Rachel's position, it may be useful for her to know something she shouldn't." Peierls started to laugh. "Come to think of it, Rudy," said Frisch, "this discovery could be of some use to me in my struggle to be acknowledged as a useful citizen of this country. Knowledge is Jewish self-defence, didn't you know?"

Hatchett, even if he wasn't quite in the Frisch-and-Peierls league, was a rational intellectual. And all through the dinner the five of them later shared at the home of Peierls's entertaining Russian wife, who laughed almost as much as Frisch and organized the washing-up with military thoroughness, the conviction grew in him that the likes of Mr Mason would not be able to harm someone who was privy to such a terrible secret.

It was only when he and Norma and Rachel were installed in a miserable bed-and-breakfast on the outskirts of town – having parted from their new friends in a mood of embraces, kisses, handshakes and optimism – that it occurred to him that this was precisely what the idiots who seemed to be in charge of the war would try to do. He went to bed afraid, not only for Rachel's immediate future but for the future of all of them. He stared into the dark and thought about the day when such terrible discoveries would bear fruit; for the terrible weapons engendered by the rational enquiry of two charming and humane individuals would fall one day, he felt certain, into the hands of the cruel, the deranged and those who rule with no respect for the lives of their fellows.

While Norma, Hatchett and Rachel were with Frisch and Peierls, Alec was sitting in the back of a lorry, the fragments of his letters to Norma cupped in his hands.

Forssander, Mavroleon and Peckerley were sitting opposite him on a large coil of rope. They had thumbed down the lorry somewhere near Salisbury Plain on a roundabout full of lost soldiers. Forssander was looking at the rope with his usual hunted expression. It obviously wasn't the thing about which he was phobic; otherwise, presumably, he would be gibbering and slavering away in a corner of the truck, but there was something about it he clearly did not like. If, thought Alec idly, you were phobic about knots, for example, then you would be afraid of rope because it could easily be turned into knots and also, presumably, of ships because ships had ropes and ropes had knots and . . .

He yawned. He was falling asleep again. He mustn't do that. He was going to see Norma soon. He must be wide awake.

"It won't make any difference, chum," said Lucius. "You are what you are, no matter how hard you try. No matter how much you pretend. You are second eleven, Alec. No matter how much you suck up to Daddy. And remember, this time you are going to have to tell her the truth!"

Mavroleon, as usual, was asleep. All fifteen stone of Mavroleon could sleep anywhere. He could sleep at attention. He could sleep at ease. There were those who said he could sleep while presenting arms or marching. Certainly – Alec knew this for a fact – he could hold apparently rational conversations while sleeping soundly. He didn't say much. His vocabulary was usually limited to one word, but he sounded almost sensible. It was when he was awake that the trouble started.

"Where are we, Mavroleon?" said Peckerley, who enjoyed sleep-talking with him.

"Croydon!" grunted Mavroleon.

"Are you sure you're in Croydon?" said Peckerley.

"Croydon!" grunted Mavroleon.

"I think you're asleep," said Peckerley.

"Croydon!" grunted Mavroleon.

"All right," said Peckerley. "Can you name a small town to the south of London on the way to Brighton on the A23?"

"Croydon," grunted Mavroleon.

"Good!" said Peckerley. "Now, I want you to think very hard before answering the next question."

"Croydon!" grunted Mavroleon.

"I want you to give me the name," said Peckerley, "of a town in the south-east of England, where you were born and brought up, that gives its name to our regiment and also begins with C and ends with N."

"Croydon!" grunted Mavroleon.

"Now, one more question, Mavroleon – and if you answer it correctly you get ten pounds. Are you asleep?"

"Croydon!" said Mavroleon.

"Peckerley," said Alec, "stop it."

Peckerley looked across at his superior officer with a concern that suggested that it was he, not Alec, who was the elder. "Bet you're looking forward to seeing Miss Lewis, sir," he said.

"I am, Peckerley!" said Alec.

"I always thought," said Peckerley, "that Mr Hatchett was a bit sweet on her." He grinned engagingly. "But I don't think women are his thing, really. He's more into things like Mallarmé and Latrine, or whatever his name is." Peckerley poked his nose out of the flap of the lorry's awning into the freezing night. "Think this is Croydon," he said. "Smells like Croydon!" He looked back at his former games master and grinned again. "Let's hope they've bumped off some more of the staff – what?"

"It gives us all something to talk about," said Alec.

One of Hatchett's recent letters had begun

HIDEOUS MURDERS IN GIRLS' SCHOOL
SPANISH TEACHERS SLAIN
CHEMISTRY MASTER SUSPECTED

Over the page Hatchett had begun his letter, as he usually did, with a lengthy parody. His letters hardly ever touched on the personal.

> *The story of the death of ALICE EVERETT, a blameless spinster, from poison, has been closely followed by all at SALTDENE SCHOOL FOR GIRLS. Was it indeed murder most foul, or was it the result of strain brought on by taking a mixed party of schoolchildren across the Channel? If the "old bat" was "topped" by a person unknown, who is he, or, indeed, she? Was it devil-may-care ALAN BREEZE? He is certainly rumoured to have been her lover by enigmatic, stern and sensationally gloomy MABEL HUGHES! Or was it suppressed romantic JACQUELINE RISSETT, who told MABEL that BREEZE was EVERETT's steamy lover, and who now denies it? Tensions run high in the lower sixth, and the form "prole" RUTH MAYHEW whispers that she holds a key to the identity of the MURDERER! But beware of MAYHEW, and indeed of incipiently lovely JACQUELINE RISSETT, who is now making strange remarks about the bravura death performance of EVERETT being predicted by a mysterious "book". A book of instructions perhaps? "How To Kill Schoolteachers" (Collins, 4/6d). And what, meanwhile, does HEADMISTRESS LEACH think?*

> *PS How are you, Lieutenant?*

> *PPS Don't worry about Norma and Lucius. Apparently the RAF have sent him to Scotland, from where, according to Doran, he is liable to be sent on one of those missions from which you are not expected to return.*

> *PPPS The best man won. Can I be yours?*

Hatchett's letters were not, of course, entirely impersonal. In among the drawings

Hatchett

Lycett

the impromptu quizzes

Loosebottom is (a) an African rectal disease; (b) a Croydon Latin master; or (c) a slang term for an attractive naval recruit?

and the maps

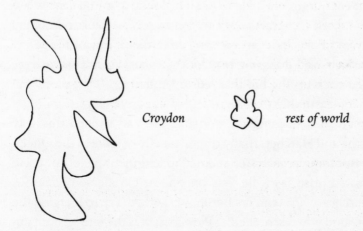

Croydon   rest of world

there were scattered sentences that served to remind him of their long friendship and of how precious it was to him. One letter began, "Dear Oldest and Best Pal," and then, as if ashamed of this emotional tone, went into blank verse for two pages. Another simply started, "Hey, Lycett of the Lower Fourth!" and it was this, for some reason, that almost reduced him to tears.

The lorry was slowing. Alec scrambled across to where Peckerley was sitting and opened the side of the cover. "Where exactly are we?" he said.

"Croydon!" said Mavroleon.

Whereupon there was a squeal of brakes, a grinding crash, an end of forward motion and Alec saw that that was indeed where they were. And not just anywhere in Croydon either. They were not perched on a slice of Coulsdon or cast up on the edges of Purley Way, they were on the main road, at the foot of the hill leading up to Crotchett Green. Ahead of them, against the sky, was the outline of Kirkby School. Away to their right were the last streets to trickle into the open country and, beyond that, the aerodrome. But Alec did not look in that direction. As he eased, stiffly, out of the lorry, he kept his eyes on a dark patch of wooded country just below the line of the hill's crest. That was Albion House. That was where Norma would be. It was only six o'clock. He wouldn't even bother to call. If she wasn't there, he would wait until she was.

Aware, somehow, that this was going to be an even more important encounter with the woman he loved than the time when he had proposed to her, Alec shook Peckerley by the hand, joined with him and Forssander in carrying Mavroleon out of the lorry, still fast asleep, and dumping him by the roadside, still fast asleep, and turned back up the hill that led to his fiancée. That word still gave him a pleasurable thrill.

It seemed to take longer than usual. He had walked this way with Norma and Hatchett many times, usually *en route* to the Queen Victoria. But tonight each step seemed to lengthen the journey. He felt, to his surprise, as if he was on one of Gooderson's famous forced marches. ("Pretend it's Berlin, Peckerley! Try to imagine the ground around you is scorched!") Perhaps it was the kitbag, containing, as it did, five tins of Spam, six pairs of underpants, a woollen jersey, numerous shirts and an Army-issue weatherproof garment that resembled an elephant's cape. Or perhaps, he reflected, as Lucius once more pressed himself into his thoughts, it was guilt.

"Of course it's guilt, Alec! Of course it's guilt, Daddy's darling!" Lucius was saying, dressed, now, in RAF uniform, his jaw set in a determined fashion. "You ruined my bloody life by sucking up to Father! There was never anything really wrong with me! My only crime was to try to be myself in a family that is simply evil! Talk about perfidious Albion, old boy! Talk about hiding dark secrets from the world! Do you really think you can get away with not telling Norma?"

Someone had been careless in the Queen Victoria.

From the far-left ground-floor window, clearly visible now in the moonlight, they had allowed a yellow chink of light to escape. It spilled out carelessly into the night, mocking the blackout in its small, grubby way, while, above, the stars burned on carelessly, ignoring the war. From within Alec could hear the sounds of singing. A single female voice – a contralto, he thought – was singing a popular song. Alec followed its Edwardian sonorities, tried to resist it and, as usual, found himself quite undermined by the catch-line – "There's a boy coming home on leave! There's a bo-oy coming home on leave!"

By the time he had put his hand to the door of the pub, the singer was asking someone to wish her luck as he waved her goodbye. But the words of the first song were still in Alec's head. They had acquired, somehow, a new and rather threatening tune. There was something repetitive about it, a percussive, death-march feel to the noise the words made in his brain as he pushed his way to the bar. "There's a boy co-oming ho-ome on le-eave! There's a boy co-oming ho-ome on le-e-eave!"

The crowd in the pub didn't know there was a war on. Or, rather, they knew there was a war on but they were celebrating that it was happening somewhere else. Someone was talking about the Finns. Apparently the Red Army was being nasty to them. Alec, who had no idea about how, where and why the war was being fought, apart from the transparently ridiculous Yeovil sector, tapped his half-crown on the bar and waited.

Mick seemed surprised to see him.

This was unusual. One of the things about the landlord of the Queen Vic was that he seemed to have no concept of the passing of time. You could go away on holiday or to university for a couple of months and, on your return, Mick greeted you with exactly the same combination of wary indifference and unstated awareness of your deep and personal inner problems that made him so popular with his regulars. You could have gone out to buy a bag of chips or sailed round the world on a home-made coracle, Mick's quasi-formal nod of greeting made it clear that anything happening outside the pub wasn't really happening at all. As well as lacking all sense of the passing of time, Mick had no politics, no preferences of any kind in matters of food, décor or the character of his customers; indeed, the only flicker of an attitude he ever displayed was on the subject of the weather, a phenomenon about which he could become almost eloquent.

"Blimey!" he said. "It's you again!"

"How do you mean 'again'?" said Alec. "I've been away since September."

"Oh, have you?" said Mick, giving him a broad wink. "Have you indeed?"

"Yes, I have!" said Alec, faintly offended that he had made so little impact on the man.

"Say no more!" said Mick, as he pulled Alec's pint. He winked again. "I suppose," he said, "you're on secret work. I mean, one day you appear in one uniform, the next day another." He leaned forward across the bar. "It must be very confusing being in the Army and the Air Force at the same time. But no one could say you weren't serving your country, Mr Lucius! Or testing your skills, sir!" Another smile, and then another wink, this time openly lubricious. "I hope you and Miss Doran have a very nice evening! I assume she will be in later?"

Alec opened and shut his mouth several times. What silenced him wasn't simply the difficulty of explaining that he had been mistaken for his twin. It was a feeling in his neck. A feeling he remembered vividly from his childhood. It started in his neck and then, like neuralgia, rippled out to his shoulder. Then – and these were quite definite physical symptoms – a heat rash crawled across his knuckles and into his wrists. More than a rash, really. A feeling that the skin was on fire. It was when it was at its most acute that he knew Lucius was actually in the room. He thought, as he had often thought in childhood, that he could feel every step his twin took as he made his way towards the bar. He thought – no, that wasn't true – he knew exactly when Lucius was reaching out towards him to tap him on the shoulder. In fact, even before his brother spoke, he had a pretty good idea of what he was going to say. For although they had not seen each other for nearly twenty years, although as far as the family was concerned Lucius didn't really exist, he was Alec's flesh-and-blood double, as real as the beer-stained wood in front of him. Alec turned before his twin's hand reached his shoulder, caught the blue RAF uniform, saw the familiar mirror image of himself together with that indefinable something that wasn't him at all and heard it say, "Well, well, well, well, well. I hear you are to be married, little brother!"

9

"Lucius," said Hatchett as, the following afternoon, his MG rounded a corner on the Brighton Road at nearly fifty miles an hour, "always called Alec 'little brother'."

"Why did he do that?" said Norma, who did not really want to know this fact. "I thought they were identical twins."

"He came out a few minutes ahead," said Hatchett, "and never stopped alluding to the fact. He used to call Alec Number Two. A nickname that has dual significance for small boys."

"I don't want to hear about when you were small boys," said Norma. "All you talked about was bottoms. It's all you still talk about. I don't think men ever grow up. Not really."

"We have two lives," said Hatchett. "The Life of Innocence. And afterwards the Life of Sex. It is impossible for us to reconcile the two."

He was always saying things like this. They sounded impressive until you thought about what they meant. What on earth did he mean by the Life of Sex? Hatchett, as far as she could see, led the Life of Homework Marking.

Sex.

It was a word Norma now prided herself on being able to pronounce publicly without going red or giggling the way Jennifer Doran did. When Jane Dewley, or "Dewlap", as she was known in the staffroom, had bought quantities of expensive underwear it was Jennifer who had shrieked, "It's a waste! The night of the wedding they will all be ripped to pieces!" and Norma who had blushed at the remark. But now that she was a girl who was going to hang on to a lieutenant's arm, she thought, she would probably have to make an investment in lingerie on her own account.

"We are all animals," Hatchett was saying, as he wrenched the wheel to the left. "Love has pitched his mansion in the place of excrement."

She really did not enjoy it when he talked like this. But the prospect of talking about both literature and sex at the same time filled him with such obvious pleasure that it seemed unfair to try and stop him.

"Sex," went on Hatchett, breezily, "is the stuffing in a relationship. It is, as it were, the meat and potatoes. Without long, hot and strong sex there is no real marriage. We are animals and must go to each other in the dark, like animals."

"Really," said Norma, not sure whether this last remark was intended humorously or not. "I am not sure whether you should talk like that in front of Rachel."

"I know all about sex," cackled Rachel, from the back of the car. "In Yiddish there are three hundred words for sex."

"Are there?" said Hatchett, with tremendous keenness.

"Probably," said Rachel.

Hatchett laughed. His eyes twinkled behind his glasses with benign, schoolmasterly pleasure. Norma turned to look at the landscape. Today the sun had returned. Although it was still cold, and yesterday the sky had seemed pregnant with the possibility of snow, today they drove through an austere winter light. From the bare trees and rough black-earthed fields, Norma turned to look at Rachel. She was staring at nothing at all, absorbed in her own thoughts, her black hair shrouding her face. What was she thinking about? Bombs that could blow the world apart? Her parents? Norma understood now why she had been so secretive about them.

But the weight of her knowledge didn't seem to burden her. Like Frisch and Peierls she was a supremely practical person; now, probably, her mind was occupied with some problem of physics that Norma wouldn't understand even if it was explained to her, but it made Rachel quite content, able to forget the immediate difficulties and past miseries of her life. Norma remembered something she had said, quite early on after her arrival, when Norma had been almost an hour late for some appointment to meet her by the war memorial in the village: "It's all right, Auntie, I can think anywhere."

To her surprise, the Rachel business had now bound her closer

225

to Hatchett. She had tried, she realized, to keep the girl to herself. But this journey through darkness to that extraordinary meeting with the girl's brilliant friends had taught her that Hatchett's pedagogic side, something that had irritated her in the past, was really why she liked him so much. As he scanned the road ahead and drove, at speed, on the right-hand side round another sharp bend (although they had come from the north they seemed to be approaching Croydon from the south), she saw how dependent she was on his concern for and knowledge of intellectual issues. It was a shame, really, that she couldn't love him in that way. Whatever "that way" was.

"We are," said Hatchett, "a long way from home."

It was often hard to tell whether Hatchett was speaking metaphorically but, as they had just passed a sign that read CROYDON 5 MILES, on this occasion, he probably was.

"We blunder around," he went on, "ruled by emotions we cannot control. We do things and we do not know why we do them. There seems to be no relation between our reason and the acts we regard as most important, most 'human', if you like. That is why we end up with lunatics like Hitler running the place. Everything should be amenable to reason."

Even, thought Norma grimly, as Hatchett took a wrong turning, braked, tried to reverse, stalled, restarted, accelerated and stalled again, car-driving. What she said was, "I'm afraid I don't think love is amenable to reason. It's there, suddenly. It wasn't there between me and Alec when I went into church that morning. It was there when we came out. I don't think we even know why we like people, let alone love them. I like you. I don't know why but I do. You are childish and bossy and conceited and terribly, terribly arrogant in any kind of discussion, but I like you. If you had shaved off your moustache six months earlier I might have married you . . ."

"Ah!" said Hatchett. "Now we're talking!"

"Do not be stupid, Hatchett!" said Norma. "You cannot marry me! You are Alec's best man!"

"So I am!" said Hatchett, deflated by this obvious truth.

In the back, Rachel laughed, throatily, once again. "You two," she said, "are always talking about love. But you have never kissed."

"That," said Norma, slightly wearily, "is because I am engaged to someone else."

"Exactly!" said Rachel. She was definitely more argumentative and more cheerful, thought Norma, since her active involvement in a discussion of a weapon that would be capable of devastating the planet.

"Engaged! But you talk about love with Mr Hatchett! This is more interesting than engaged! Engaged is just a form of words! Engaged is like a treaty or some politician's promise!" She stopped suddenly. "I am sorry," she said. "This is none of my business. You are very kind to me and I interfere with your lives in this way. It is nothing to do with me. I am sorry. Typical Jew. Always poking the nose in when not wanted."

"Rachel," said Norma, trying not to sound too like a Sunday-school teacher, "I take it as a great compliment that you feel easy enough with myself and Mr Hatchett to say exactly what you feel when you feel like saying it. I want you to feel at home with us. This is your home."

After this remark all three were silent. They were coming into Crotchett Green now. A country mansion came up, behind a huge, well-ordered privet hedge. Beyond it the sports-field and a row of red-brick labourers' cottages. And then the traffic lights by the undertaker's, where Mr Japp, as usual, was looking mournfully out of the window at the passing prospective trade. That was where Norma saw Mr Mason. He was standing with the Hughes family on the far side of the road, and immediately he saw the car, he waved and, with fussily simulated friendliness, trotted over. As usual, he was wearing the blue suit, and still looked like a man who had been kept in a government storage vault for ten years and only just been taken out to be put to practical use. The Hughes family followed him. Mabel walked a little way away, as if she did not wish to be seen with them.

Oh, well, thought Norma, the lights will change, and in a matter of moments we will be able to accelerate away from here.

"Well, well, well," said Mason, lowering his face to the window, "the little threesome again."

"Yes?" said Hatchett, not bothering to conceal his aggression.

Mason peered into the back of the car. "Hullo there, young Rachel," he said. "How is life at your . . ." he paused, leered and then continued ". . . your auntie's?"

"My auntie and I," said Rachel, "are very well. We have not caught any diseases."

"My, my, my," said Mason, with an offensively stagy chuckle, "you do express yourself in an interesting way!" Then he looked at Norma, and this time his tone had an edge to it. "I was talking to PC Potter," he said, "and we were saying that . . . you know . . . there being a war on and all . . . you know . . . and . . . well . . . we really need to check papers, you see."

Would the lights never change? Was there something wrong with them?

Hatchett leaned across Norma and said, with a confidence he did not feel, "Of course. The silly girl lost her passport, as you know. We think it's just mislaid and as soon as we track it down we'll bring it to the station and she can get her ID card. If necessary, we will just have to get her birth certificate. But I must say I think you are being a wee bit bureaucratic, Mr . . ." He pretended to forget the man's name and then, with infinite contempt, pretended to remember it ". . . Mason."

"I am forgetting my head next, I think," said Rachel, with what to Norma sounded like a chillingly authentic German accent. The lights had still not changed. And now, beside Mason, Mabel Hughes was looking more than usually sepulchral. She was, as far as Norma could see, in mourning in triplicate. 'Leafy' and Everett, her outfit seemed to say, were worth more than just a double dose of funeral weeds. Not only was she wearing a black blouse, a black hat, black stockings, black shoes and a black veil, but each half of her had sprouted various black items. Pinned to her left breast was a black paper rose and, to her right protuberance, she had added a black brooch.

"One is for Leafy," she said to Norma, catching the direction of her gaze, "and the other is for Alice." She quivered slightly at the post-mortem licence of being able to use her favourite teacher's first name. "I am very worried," she went on, "about Jacqueline. I think she may be shielding Mr Breeze. I think he may have placed her under awful pressure. She is such a sweet and impressionable girl. Everyone is saying that Mr Breeze is going to be arrested at any moment."

"Tell me," Mason was saying to Rachel, thrusting his sallow face unpardonably deep into the car. "Your mummy and daddy. What part of India did you say they were . . ."

Mercifully, at last, the signal changed from red to yellow to green. Hatchett let in the clutch and the MG bounded forward. In the offside mirror, Norma saw Mr Mason jump clear. In the back, Rachel was shaking. "That man . . ." she started to say, and broke into rapid German.

"It's all right, Rachel," said Hatchett. "They'll take for ever. And by the time they get round to moving, Frisch will have been in touch with someone. They won't want to lose someone who knows what you know. Who else will tell them what the boys in the Dahlem Institute are up to?"

"You think?" said Rachel.

"My God," said Hatchett, "I feel rather uncomfortable knowing it. I wish no one had ever told me about fast neutron fission of uranium 235. It's not the sort of information that should be entrusted to your averagely stupid grammar-school languages master."

Actually, Norma realized, Hatchett understood rather more than he let people think. But she knew what he meant. She wished she had not heard what she had heard yesterday in Birmingham. But she had. A bomb that cracked open the seeds of nature. A thing of unimaginable force. As she looked out at the winter landscape, she thought once again of how provisional the world seemed when it gave up its secrets. Perhaps the reason we held on so desperately to things like love and friendship was because the real inner life of things was so unstable. She thought about a couple she had met who had flown in an aeroplane from Croydon to Le Bourget. Half-way across the Channel the craft had developed engine trouble and gone into a steep dive. "I love you!" the man had said to his wife, clutching her hand.

But how was that supposed to help?

They were about two hundred yards from Albion House when she saw Alec. He wasn't in uniform. He was wearing a heavy overcoat and swinging his arms in a way that seemed familiar and yet, at the same time, unexpected. Hatchett slowed, sounded his horn and Alec turned, with a slight air of impatience, as they slowed to a stop beside him.

Norma pushed open the heavy door and held out her hand to him. She wanted, suddenly, to throw herself into his arms but realized, as she thought this, that she had no clear idea of how to set about doing such a thing. Instead, she stood there foolishly, as if she was inviting him to a garden party, while in her head she played a picture of the two of them falling together in a jumble of arms and hair and lips and eyes.

Wasn't he supposed to throw himself into her arms? They were engaged, for God's sake. It was going to be in the *Croydon Advertiser* as soon as Alec had talked to his father. If this was the case, if she hadn't dreamed the whole thing, why was he standing there looking as shifty as a partially submerged frog? Had his mind been turned by Basic Training? Had bayonet practice unhinged him?

"Alec?" she said, more tentatively than she thought she would ever say that name. "Alec?"

He was still looking decidedly fish-like. Had he met someone in the Army? No, you couldn't meet someone in the Army. It was all men in the Army. Unless, of course, Alec was actually one of Them. An Oscar Wilde or something. It was possible. It was conceivable, if not possible, that Hatchett and Lycett had been, to use Hatchett's phrase, "at it" for years. The face was the same. The hair was the same. The eyes, nose and ears were all quite clearly Alec Lycett's. But there was something decidedly odd about his expression.

She thought at first that it was shifty. She thought at first that his eyes were flickering away from her and towards Hatchett because the two of them shared some terrible secret. Hadn't Hatchett hinted as much? But then she realized that Alec was looking at Hatchett as if he had never seen him before. No, not quite that. As if he had seen him but years ago, on the top of a bus somewhere.

It was this expression that most interested her. It was, she decided, something to do with the mouth. The mouth and the eyes. Something had happened to Alec's mouth and eyes as a result of being in the Army. That was it, thought Norma, that was it. He was suddenly something Alec had never been. It was only as she saw this that she realized her fiancé had ever been lacking in this quality, but as she perceived it, she also saw that it was such a huge and important difference it could not possibly have been wrought by the simple expedient of crawling around the English countryside with Major (or was it Colonel?) Gooderson. This not-Alec thing wasn't Alec. It never could have been Alec. She had got Alec completely and utterly wrong. She didn't really know who Alec was at all, since he never had been, she now saw, what he was now. Confident. That was it. The not-Alec thing was confidence. She should have seen that but she hadn't. And now it was too late. Too late for what? Norma could not have said. But it was too late for it, all right. Far, far too late.

"Are you Alec?" she said to Alec.

"No," said Alec, "I am not Alec. I never have been Alec and I never will be Alec."

"No," said Norma, in slow, awed wonder. "You are Lucius, aren't you?"

"I am," said Lucius, with what was really rather a winning smile, "and you must be Norma. I have heard a great deal about you."

He looked past her and cracked out a mock-salute for Hatchett's benefit. "Hullo, Wetlegs!" he said.

"I no longer answer," said Hatchett, with a scowl, "to that name."

"Frightfully sorry," said Alec, who wasn't Alec at all, of course, but still looked so like him that he might as well be. "Old habits die hard." He gave a brief, ironical mock-bow. "It seems that you grew up into a real human being," he said. "I had you down for a toad of some kind. Or a small marsh-dwelling animal that is better avoided."

"I must say," said Hatchett, who had not moved from the driving seat, "I am surprised you survived. I would have thought that someone like you would have provoked someone like me into justifiable homicide years ago."

"Well, well," said Lucius, with what sounded like quite a genuine laugh, "I am sure you and I were more alike than either of us knew, Hatchett, old bean. Tough in our own way. And, talking of homicide, I hear there is quite a lot of it about the old place, these days. Two lady teachers in the village. Did you do it, Hatchett? Murder, murder, murder . . ." his voice trailed away and he looked at Hatchett with something that seemed a little like compassion ". . . the story of all our lives."

He said this in a way Norma didn't quite like. It was curiously unmelodramatic. But its quiet seriousness made it all the more chilling. Why should murder be the story of all their lives? It certainly had an effect on Hatchett. He pursed his lips rather primly – which he usually only did when he was disturbed by something – and glanced across at Norma to see if she had noticed. Which, of course, she had, although she made sure that he hadn't noticed.

"What," said Hatchett, "are you doing here?"

"I'm on leave," said Lucius. "I start flying in a week or so. Thought I'd make my peace with the parentals."

"Oh," said Hatchett, "and did you?"

"No," said Lucius, after quite a long pause. Then he said, "I told the truth. And they didn't believe me. It was that simple." He shrugged wearily. "They didn't believe me the first time either."

"Anyway," said Hatchett, "by 'here' I didn't mean . . . Croydon in general. I meant this particular patch of road."

Before he answered this question Lucius looked at Norma. Now that you knew he wasn't Alec it was hard to see how you had ever thought that that was who he was. He had developed, almost instantly, a whole repertoire of things that seemed quintessentially Lucius – a slight bulging outwards of the head just above the ears, a funny, sardonic little smile – and now she knew that the heavy coat and the rather tramp-like shoes were not and never could have been Alec's choice, it was hard to believe she had ever thought they might have been. Alec, she saw for the first time, was ridiculously fussy about his shoes. He went around in things that made him look like a waiter.

"I'm on my way to Albion House," Lucius was saying. "That's why I am on this particular patch of road."

"And why," said Hatchett, "do you want to go there?"

"Oh," said Lucius, "*nostalgie de la boue*, don't you know? I hear you teach French, Wetlegs. Sorry. Not allowed to call you that. Why aren't you in uniform? Couldn't they get one to fit you?"

"I am not in uniform," said Hatchett, "because there is something wrong with my heart."

It was the first Norma had heard of this. It certainly silenced Lucius. He looked at Hatchett for a long time, but it seemed to Norma that he wasn't seeing what she was seeing when she looked at him.

"I thought," said Lucius, eventually, "I would take a look at those woods at the back of the house. Stroll through them. Relive old memories. You remember how we used to play there, Wetlegs."

"Stop," said Hatchett, through clenched teeth, "using that name."

Lucius had pushed his face even further in through the window. Hatchett suddenly leaned across and seized him roughly by the collar. Norma noticed the brute strength in him, the way he was transformed by his anger. Lucius reached up his hand and tried to dislodge the other man's wrists but Hatchett only pulled him tighter and tighter until his face was forced against the window. Lucius seemed to be finding it hard to breathe. "Sorry, old boy," he said. "No offence."

Hatchett let him go. "You'd better get in," he said gruffly. "I suppose we can't stop you wandering around in a wood but I suspect you'd better do your wandering and then bugger off."

Lucius clambered in next to Rachel. He didn't look like a monster, thought Norma, but, then, monsters were quite good at pretending to be nice people.

Rachel was looking at him, wide-eyed. Lucius gave her an

encouraging smile. "Genetically," she said, as the car pulled away, "you would appear to be a perfect match with Lieutenant Lycett."

"I'll say!" said Lucius. "We're identical! But there, I'm afraid, the resemblance ends." He laughed, quite loudly, at his own joke. Then he held out his hand. "There's a scar there," he went on, pointing to the knuckle. "And here, on the side of my neck, is quite a deep cut where Hatchett and my brother stuck something into me just before I was sent away. So, you see, although I am like Alec, life has marked me in a different way. My brother has led what you might call a charmed life. It will be interesting to see how he responds to the challenge of the times. Stirring times, eh, Hatchett?"

Hatchett did not answer. Far below them, on a bend in the road, Albion House came into view then disappeared as the car rounded another bend.

"Why did they send you away?" said Norma.

"What did Alec tell you?" was Lucius's response.

"He didn't tell me much," said Norma.

Lucius made her feel uncomfortable. He wasn't anything like she had imagined him. His charm, which neither Alec nor Hatchett had bothered to mention to her, was curiously unsettling. She was able to see why Jennifer Doran had found him so irresistible. She, Norma, found him attractive. Well, he was identical, for God's sake. The mocking, detached way he looked at her made her feel hot, awkward.

"Why," she said, feeling a sudden urge to make friends with him, "were you sent away? Didn't you get on with your father?"

"Oh dear," said Lucius, "he hasn't told you anything at all, has he? I don't think he has told the dear father and mother anything either. My father is a very weak and stupid individual and my mother is an equally stupid and self-regarding bitch who cheated on him. That's something Alec doesn't really want to believe although he, too, pretty much knows it to be the case. I personally prefer Spitfires."

"You would think," said Norma, "that twins would get on. I mean, they have so much in common."

234

She was aware what a foolish remark this must seem. But, to tell the truth, being in the car with a full-scale replica of her fiancé was depriving her of all talent for rational conversation. And the hostility from Hatchett to Lucius was so violent, so confusing and inexplicable, that it had made her question whether she had known him or Lycett at all, all these years. Lucius leaned forward and spoke softly but with such passionate feeling that Rachel, usually able to ignore adult conversations when they did not specifically concern her, stared frankly at him in wonder.

"Imagine," said Lucius, "someone doing an . . . an impression of you. Someone mimicking your voice, parodying your gestures, but never getting them quite right. I like the remark of that poet who said he thought he could always do a better parody of his own work than anyone else. From my very earliest years I can remember this person doing a horribly good impression of me, a sort of caricature or parody, and yet never acknowledging it. I mean, imagine going into a shop and the man leans over the counter and leers at you and says, 'How are you, little man?' and you realize this ghastly inferior imitation of you has been in this shop and relished being patronized by this idiot. You know, as everyone knows, that you are unique and interesting and difficult and clever, and yet the world makes absolutely no distinction between you and . . . that!!"

He pointed forward as he said this and Norma saw that he was indicating Alec, sitting in his Army uniform by the front gate of Albion House. Just for a moment, influenced, as it is hard not to be, by the last person speaking, she saw him through Lucius's eyes, and caught a droop about his shoulders, a lost look about his face, as he turned towards them. But then the car stopped, Alec got up and she was running towards him down the road, her arms outstretched, waiting to be caught up and swept away.

He smiled at the sight of her. A big, healthy Alec Lycett smile that she thought was going to turn into something else – an embrace? a kiss? – but just as she reached him, as his arms, in fact, were reaching out for her, a voice behind her froze him. It was Lucius. "Well, Alec," he said, "ready for our walk in the woods?"

Alec looked over her shoulder as Lucius climbed out of the car and his face dropped. She saw things in it she had never thought to see there – fear, a sort of distaste for things of which she had always thought him free, and an inward-looking expression, a sort of petulant concealment that was all the more frightening for being totally and completely unexpected. "Are you all right?" she said.

"I'm fine," said Alec, and at last he reached for her and put his arms round her. "It is so good to see you – I have missed you so much. There is so much I have to tell you." But then his arms fell away from her and his gaze returned, once again, to the mirror image of himself over her shoulder.

"It's good to see you," she said, feeling suddenly cheated of something, although she could not have said what it was. Hatchett had come up near them and was standing a little way away. But she could feel the tension in him: like a dog sensing the presence of a rival, he stayed still but tensed. Once again she was acutely aware of how aggressive he could be. It was as if he was guarding Alec from his twin, waiting for a fight to start, almost willing Lucius to make the first move.

"It's good to see you, Lycett," said Hatchett, in what was nearly a growl. "I have been taking good care of her."

"Yes," said Alec, his eyes still on Lucius. "Yes! Thanks!"

"You two still share things!" Norma heard Lucius say, behind her. "First conkers and now women. Do you take turns on her?"

Norma decided that Lucius was not, after all, a nice person. She turned and, for the first time, saw his RAF uniform under his coat. Alec had said that the RAF were all very conceited. Alec still wasn't speaking.

Lucius was looking at him quizzically. "We were to take a short walk in the dear old woods behind Albion, were we not?" he said. "Wasn't that the arrangement we made last night? After our cosy little chat about the days long ago. Ah, the days long ago!"

Alec looked at Hatchett then and, for some reason, spoke to him, not to Lucius or to Norma. "I said I'd do that," he said, rather helplessly, with an expression Norma did not understand. "I said I'd . . . you know . . . talk to him and . . ."

"Talk to him if you want to talk to him," said Hatchett. "If you want to. After all, he is your brother. I am afraid I think he is absolute poison. But if you want to talk to him you talk to him."

"Here we go again," said Lucius, with a funny kind of sneer that made Norma dislike him even more. "Dennis Hatchett! Principal Private Secretary to Alec Lycett! Why are you trying to advise him, Hatchett? You know he has to talk to me. He ought to talk to this girl of his but he hasn't got the guts, has he?" He turned to Alec, and for a moment he looked terribly, terribly sad, as if some wrong had been done to him but he would never say what it might be. Norma found she was almost liking him again. "What have you told her about us, Daddy's darling? Have you even started on our family? As far as I can see Pater has never even heard of her. Are you going to go public on this engagement, old bean?"

"I don't think," said Alec, "that we have any more to say to each other. Not really."

Lucius looked from Hatchett to Alec and from Alec to Norma and when he spoke again there was something like compassion in his tone. "Well, Alec," he said, "I won't rock the boat if you don't want it rocked. There really are more important things to worry about. The jolly old Nazis for a kick-off."

"What should you have told me, Alec?" said Norma. "What is he talking about?" But Alec did not say anything.

Lucius walked into the group, his big overcoat swinging behind him. "Hatchett and Lycett and Loosebottom's daughter," he said, chanting the words as if they were a nursery rhyme, "fell in love with each other much more than they oughter. But when the brave soldier was up and away, bespectacled Hatchett stole his sweetheart away."

Suddenly Alec broke away and went for his brother, but before he could get to him Hatchett grabbed him and pulled him back. Norma thought Alec was going to cry out but he didn't. He allowed himself to be held by his friend as he stared, with a hatred Norma could not begin to understand, at the twin in the blue uniform. When Alec's breath had slowed and he was calmer, Hatchett said,

237

"You are a disgusting person, Lucius. You know nothing about real love or real friendship."

"I know something about them, Hatchett, old bean," said Lucius, and once again Norma, hearing a real human note in his voice, found herself unable to dislike him as much as she suspected she was supposed to. "I know they are very hard to find," he went on. "In fact, I am pretty sure there are no such things at all in this life. That was drummed into me at an early age." He opened the gate to Albion House, and walked a little way into the dismal December garden. Above him, the darkened windows of the house peered down suspiciously, like an animal waiting for the attack.

"I shall go through the woods on my own," he said, "and then I will leave and no one will ever see me again." He turned to Norma. "Get him to try to be honest," he said softly. "Get him to try to tell you what we are really like. Get him to try to say what really happened between us. If he is to have any kind of chance he'd better start by telling you the truth." There was a silence. Then, in sing-song rhyme, he added, "Poor Lucius Lycett went up in the sky. Since his pa didn't like him, he decided . . . to die!" With which, without a backward glance, he walked round the side of the house, off in the direction of the woods that began on the far side of the meadow behind it. Norma had always been a little afraid of Albion Woods, as they were known, not only because people said they were haunted. She remembered seeing them as a little girl and dreaming of what it might be like to be left out there, cold and alone, with no one to feed you or clothe you or tuck you up in bed. And now that she lived in Albion House they still scared her. They glowered up at her from her bedroom window, as if they concealed the dark and frightening things you found in fairy stories, as if they were preparing to haul themselves up by the roots and march in on the house to stand around it in a deadly crescent.

"What did he mean by 'rock the boat'?" said Norma to Alec, when Lucius had gone. "What are you supposed to tell me? What was all that about what 'really happened' between you?"

"Nothing," said Alec. "Just stupidity, that's all. I've told you everything there is to know about me and Lucius. We just hated each other, that's all, from the day we were born. And then he was sent away. There is nothing to tell about me and Lucius. Really, there is nothing to tell at all."

"He is a poisonous character," said Hatchett, quickly, "and he always was. I remember why I disliked him so much now. He would do anything to stir up trouble between you and Alec, Norma. Do not listen to anything he says."

"It's wonderful to see you, darling," said Alec.

"Yes!" said Norma. "Yes, it is!"

And she meant it. She did not ask him any more questions. But although she could not have said why or how, things between her and Alec Lycett had changed, and the little time they were due to share together no longer seemed so precious.

20 *August* 1921

"Lots more lemonade!" said Lycett's daddy. He was being, as usual, really good fun.

Hatchett's daddy didn't say much but what he said was pretty gloomy. Once he didn't say anything for three days and when he finally did say something it was, "There is going to be a war!" Last time he had said this, according to Mrs Hatchett, it was in 1913, and he had turned out to be absolutely right.

It was because he was a vicar that he was so depressed. That was why he was so gloomy. That and because he believed in hell. He talked about hell on Sundays sometimes. He leaned over the pulpit and waved his arms and said if you did something wrong you would burn for ever and ever. He had shown Hatchett a painting of hell. There were horrible things coming out of eggs and faces that weren't faces and things that were half human and half monster. The pain of it wouldn't go away, like when you had toothache. It would go on and on and on and never stop.

Perhaps that was why he had run away. Perhaps he had done something wrong and he was frightened God would catch him and send him to hell.

The funny thing was, Lycett was more frightened of hell than Hatchett. There was a little bit of Hatchett that, even when his father was preaching in church, didn't quite believe what he was saying. Or, rather, a little bit of him that believed that he – and his father – would not go to hell even if everyone else did.

"Thank you, Mr Lycett," said Hatchett, whose manners, when he remembered them, were very good. In some ways he felt, as he held out his cup, they were almost too good. It was as if he was creeping to Mr Lycett – which was probably what the KILLER was so cross about. But with Hatchett, it was usually a question of either being extra polite or not being polite at all. There was no middle ground somehow.

"Delicious lemonade!" he added, for good measure.

A car was coming for Lucius later in the evening. Hatchett was glad the grown-ups said he could stay the night and sleep in Lucius's bed. Lucius, of course, had made a fuss about this.

"One more sandwich, then!" said Mr Lycett.

Mrs Lycett, as usual, was looking at him in a funny way. She was always looking at him in a funny way. Perhaps, thought Hatchett, my fly-buttons are undone. Or my glasses have slipped down my nose. He avoided her gaze and concentrated on Mr Lycett, who liked you to eat and join in. "I'd love some!" said Hatchett. "Fish paste are my favourite!"

This wasn't actually true. Fish paste came a long way down the list of things that Hatchett liked. It was about on a level with football and custard. But because Mr Lycett liked you to like things, Hatchett put an extra dose of schoolboy into the way he said "favourite". He sounded, he thought, a bit babyish, which, up to a point, grown-ups liked.

Even as he said it, though, he suspected he might well have overdone the babyishness. If he carried on like this he was going to start lisping. A quick, sharp look from Lucius told him that he had spotted this and, to cover his tracks, Hatchett did a bit of Funny Chewing. He puffed out his cheeks like a hamster and brought his two front teeth over the front of his lower lip so that he looked a little like a beaver. Adults liked that too – in moderation.

"My goodness," said Alec's daddy, "you look like a hamster!"

"How thweet," said Lucius, very quietly. But not so quietly that Alec's daddy didn't hear.

"For God's sake," he said, rising from his chair and looking as if he might hit Lucius, "can you not try to be nice for one moment? You are going away tonight! Can't you try to be nice for one moment?"

"No," said Lucius, softly.

For a moment Hatchett thought Mr Lycett was going to hit

Lucius. He got up from the table looking as if that was exactly what he was going to do. But Mrs Lycett put her hand on his arm. "Please, Alec," she said, "if you want to punish someone punish me."

Mr Lycett looked at her. He did not look as if he liked her very much. Then he sat back down, heavily. He turned once again to Hatchett. "Can you fit one more in?" he said.

"Hatchett," said Alec, "will burst. He will explode!"

Alec's daddy seemed to find this very funny. Because he did, Hatchett accepted another fish paste sandwich. He did some more Funny Chewing.

"Come on!" said Mr Lycett. "Hatchett the Champion Chewer!"

He and Alec started to clap. Mrs Lycett looked cross. Hatchett started to chew in time with the clapping. This was quite hard to do but it seemed to make Alec and his father laugh. So Hatchett did more of it. They clapped more. They clapped faster. Hatchett chewed faster. To make them laugh more, he put both hands up to his nose and began to stroke an imaginary pair of whiskers. Mrs Lycett got up. For a moment Hatchett thought she was going to cry. Instead she screamed, "For God's sake, can't you leave the poor little bugger alone?"

"Bugger" was a rude word.

Alec and Mr Lycett stopped laughing. Mr Lycett just looked at Alec's mummy. Then he said, "You're a fine one to start talking principles. You're a fine one to take up the cudgels on behalf of kindness."

Then he said they were all to go and play. But this wouldn't be garden play. They would have to go upstairs and do quiet things. If they were good and didn't fight – this was said with a warning look in Lucius's direction – they would be allowed out later to play cricket on the lawn. Lucius loved cricket. So, as it happened, did Hatchett. Cricket, at which he was no good at all, was one of his favourite things. It was unfair that Lucius, who was so horrible, should be quite so good at it. But one of the many good things about cricket was that even if you were no good you could still spend a long time hanging around the boundary or the pavilion before people discovered how useless you were. One by one they got off their chairs and filed out into the hall. When they had gone Hatchett could hear Alec's mummy and daddy shouting at each other. He couldn't hear what they said. He knew what they were talking about, though. About how the tramp was murdered and he burned like someone in hell.

It was important, Hatchett decided, to keep on being polite to Lucius. They were a long way away from the grown-ups upstairs. Lucius could easily lock him in a cupboard – as he had once done, in fact – or try to push him out of a window. Murderers quite often got away with it. Lucius had already managed to do so. This would encourage him to try it again.

Thoroughly scared now that he was almost alone with a murderer, Hatchett said, "Why are you going away, Lucius?"

He said this in a nice way. But Lucius just scowled. "Why do you think?"

"I don't know," said Hatchett. "Perhaps you need . . . broader horizons!"

He was quite pleased with this. But Lucius, for some reason, seemed to find it comical. Deciding to capitalize on this, Hatchett went on, "I mean, Croydon is frightfully limited. It is not the centre of the universe, is it, old bean?" This was something his father had said. This was, perhaps, he thought, why his father might have left. When he wasn't talking about hell and God and war, the Reverend Arthur Hatchett quite often talked about broader horizons. He said he would have been really happy to have been born in France because they had wine there.

Lucius, however, didn't seem to find this last remark funny. "I am going away," he said, his scowl becoming even more pronounced, "because my father hates me. And my mother won't stand up for me because she is too busy hating my father. I am going away because my brother . . ." Here he stopped and gave Alec a look of such hatred that Hatchett wished he had never started the conversation.

"Where were you hiding?" said Alec, when they got to the games room.

Hatchett thought it probably wasn't a good idea to tell them that he had been hiding in the wood. Once they got on to the subject of the wood, it would be horribly easy to get on to the subject of murder and that might give Lucius ideas. "I know," he said, "let's play chess."

This was a good idea. Lucius liked chess because he always won. The Lycetts had a big carved wooden chess set, which was always set out on the table by the window overlooking the garden.

"How are we going to play chess with three of us?" said Alec.

"You can play Lucius," said Hatchett, "and I'll be your adviser."

"That," said Lucius, who was already walking over to the board, "should make my job even easier."

"I'm going to go outside," said Hatchett, picking up a white pawn and a black pawn, "and I am going to put one pawn in one hand and one in another and you both have to say which hand you think it is in and the one who guesses right chooses his colour."

"That," said Lucius, "is stupid."

"Why is it stupid?" said Hatchett.

"Because," said Lucius, "it has to be one of the players who puts the pawns in his fist." He was, thought Hatchett, trying to cut him out of the game. He was always doing that. "Suppose," Lucius went on, in acid tones, "we both pick the same hand."

"You're not allowed to," said Hatchett. "One picks first and then the other chooses."

"So how do we decide who chooses first?" said Lucius.

Games, thought Hatchett, began a long time before they actually started. And games involving the Lycett brothers never really stopped. He knew, however, that he had to be involved. Not only because he hated to be left on the sidelines, like when they picked those teams at school, but also because if he wasn't there to see fair play they would be trying to kill each other within minutes.

"I know," said Alec. "I'll put a white pawn in one fist and a black pawn in the other and Lucius has to choose and if he wins then he chooses first and then Hatchett can go outside and put one white pawn and one black pawn in each fist and then Lucius, because he has won the first round, has to guess and if he is wrong then the other one, i.e. me, gets to choose although I will know probably because it obviously won't be in the hand that Lucius chose because he lost."

Everyone thought about this for a moment. Hatchett was beginning to think that this was rather more fun than actually playing chess. "What would be fairer," he said, "would be that if Lucius chose wrongly then I should go out of the room again and swap the pawns around, or not as the case may be, and come back and then the second person would not necessarily know which pawn was in which hand."

"Playing chess with you two," said Lucius, yawning, "is like playing chess with a couple of old women."

"I am ninety-two!" said Hatchett, sucking in his cheeks and doing a hunchback impression. Alec laughed.

So, after a while, did Lucius. "All right, then," said Lucius. "Off you go, Hatchett!"

"Actually," said Alec to his brother, "you can choose. I don't mind."

"What's got into you?" said Lucius, giving Alec a sideways look. "Why so friendly all of a sudden?"

"You can choose!" said Alec.

"Are you feeling guilty or something?" said Lucius.

"Why should I feel guilty?" said Alec.

"You know why," said Lucius.

"Why," said Alec, "are you always so horrible?"

"You're beginning to sound like Daddy," said Lucius. "I suppose because you're his favourite you'll end up just like him."

"I will not," said Alec, with a passion that surprised Hatchett. "I was nice to you and all you can do is be horrible."

"Oh, for heaven's sake!" said Lucius, sweeping the chess pieces off the board with his forearm. "Stop being stupid all the time!"

"Put the pieces back!" said Alec.

"No!" said Lucius.

"Put the pieces back," Alec went on, "or we'll bash you! We'll both bash you!"

In a minute, thought Hatchett glumly, they would be on the

floor trying to strangle each other. That, of course, was how any game usually ended up with the twins. If they had actually started playing it would probably have been worse. Once, Lucius had tried to gouge out Alec's eyes with his knight because – he claimed – Alec had touched a piece then refused to move it. And other games were worse. Once, he shuddered at the memory, they had tried to play skittles. He very much did not want them to fight. It was frightening even watching them. Lucius bit his lower lip, went white and drove his fists into Alec again and again and again. He nearly always won. And now Hatchett knew he was a murderer he realized this was probably only the beginning.

It was this that made him say, just as the two of them were squaring up to each other, "I found a handkerchief. In the woods."

They both stopped dead.

"I hid in the woods," said Hatchett, "in a really thick bush. That's why you didn't find me. I heard you coming but you didn't find me."

There was an awful silence, now, in the room. Lucius looked at Alec. Alec looked at Lucius. Hatchett had said the wrong thing. All he had wanted to do was to stop them fighting but now he had said the wrong thing and it was somehow worse than it was before.

"What kind of handkerchief?" said Lucius, slowly.

"A white handkerchief," said Hatchett, "a really old one. It had been there for years, it looked like."

"Whose handkerchief was it?" said Lucius.

"I don't know," said Hatchett. "It was just an old handkerchief. It could have belonged to anyone. It could have belonged to some . . . tramp or something."

Why had he said that? Lucius would know now. It was such a stupid thing to have said. Lucius would know and he would be in trouble and something terrible would happen. Lucius was looking at him really strangely, and Hatchett did not like the look in his eyes. Why had he blabbed that out? Why was he such a chatterbox? People always said he talked too much. He just said things without thinking. His father had always said that.

"Well," said Lucius.

He looked at Alec. Alec looked at him. It was suddenly – as it was sometimes when he was alone with them – as if the two of them could read each other's thoughts. They were talking even though they weren't saying anything.

When Lucius spoke again his voice was dangerously quiet. "I think," he said, "you had better give the handkerchief to me."

"Why should I?" said Hatchett. "It's my handkerchief. I found it. It belongs to me."

"Give it to me," said Lucius, as he walked over to Hatchett. He spoke in a soft but nasty voice. Hatchett looked at Alec. But he could see from Alec's face that, suddenly, he was not on his side against Lucius.

"You had better give it to him," Alec said. He sounded frightened. It was something to do with the murder, Hatchett was certain now. Maybe Lucius would know now that Alec had told him. Maybe he already knew that Hatchett had heard the two of them talking when he was hiding in the bush. Maybe he would want to kill him because he had evidence against them. Hatchett put his hands in his trouser pockets. He pulled out the crumpled handkerchief. He hadn't really looked at it before. But there was a stain on it. Was the stain blood? Was it the tramp's blood?

"Don't look at it!" Lucius was saying sharply. "Just give it to me! Now!"

Hatchett started to look down at the handkerchief to try to see what it was that Lucius did not want him to see. But he remembered, just in time, that Lucius was a murderer. So he did not even glance at it. He would just give them back the handkerchief, then Lucius would stop looking at him in this horrible way. And Alec wouldn't be so scared.

"Give it to him!" Alec said, in a harsh, cracked voice.

"I am!" said Hatchett, as he passed it over. "I'm giving it to him!"

Lucius snatched it and thrust it deep into his pocket. He turned and looked at Alec. Alec looked away.

"Now," said Lucius, "we can play chess!"

But Hatchett didn't say anything. He had thought Alec would back him up about the handkerchief. But he hadn't. He could see that Alec was scared because, after all, Lucius was a murderer and it was important not to get him too angry. But he could have said something or been a bit nice. One thing you learned, if you didn't have any brothers or sisters, was that however much they fought, in the end, brothers and sisters always stuck together. He couldn't help feeling that Alec had let him down. In fact, as he started to collect up the chess pieces, he felt he was in danger of doing something you should never do if you were a boy, which was cry. You were on your own, really, thought Hatchett, as, when the board was tidy once again, he picked up two pawns and tucked them into his fists, keeping his back to the twins. There was nobody who would stand up for you but you, when it came down to it.

PART FOUR

Dennis Hatchett's Diary

14 February 1940

8 a.m.

It's Valentine's Day but I'm not sending any. I suppose the rest of the world are still exchanging coy little messages, though. Love makes the world . . . well . . . grind to a halt in my case. Perhaps Alec, wherever he is, has poured out his heart to the girl he loves.

My first letter from him, which I have put up on my mantelpiece, read,

Dear Hatchett,

I have been in

a   large bowl for three months and

they have put   sprouts

up my backside

the whole of the Army   is   sniffing

Peckerley's underpants and I am

developing   his

knob   which is

short, greyish in colour and

makes a squeaking noise when you run it along the

floor.

Best

Alec

That was before he rumbled Gooderson's rather personal approach to censorship. Alec's letters are now being sent to Yarmouth to be censored, for some reason, and the boys in East Anglia clearly take exception to Lycett raving on about censorship since when he strays on to that topic the holes start appearing in the writing paper once again. He has also taken, in his letters to me, to using a code we used when schoolboys, in which the initial letter of each word reads off a crib to the writer's Real Thoughts. "Good old Oswald does everything really slowly. Oh, no! He ain't such a friendly auld trooper. But! Up Midriff!" means GOODERSON HAS A FAT BUM. Poor old Alec clearly devotes so much time to devising sentences that sound credible in this code that he has almost given up trying to express whatever it is he wants to say. Assuming he has anything to say in the first place. Also, nearly all his letters are about five thousand words long.

Ah, secrecy! Careless talk costs lives! Hitler will send no Warning!

As for me, I have made approaches to the intelligence services, in the shape of my old friend Duncan Heap, one of the stupidest people ever to get into the University of Cambridge. I asked him how you set about becoming a spy and he said, tapping the side of his nose as he did so, "I am not supposed to tell you that because if I was a spy I would want to keep it a secret but, seeing as you have asked me, the way you make an initial approach is to ask someone like me. If you see what I mean." He stopped and a look of panic spread across his face. "My God!" he said. "That's what you've just done. Have I given something away? I suppose I will have to do something about this." He then rushed from the room and I have not seen him since.

One of the few coherent sentences I did get out of Lycett's letters said, more or less, that since Lucius surfaced again he has been quite unable to talk to Norma as he feels he should. He says he wanted to tell her something when he was on leave – surely not about Lucius? why should she need to know that? – but he "hadn't got the guts". It's his family, I suppose. He is scared of introducing her to them.

I am not sure, since meeting him again, that we were quite fair to Lucius.

I am writing this in the kitchen as Mother has commandeered the living room. She is sitting bolt upright on the sofa, in her coat and hat. When I asked her why she was dressed like that, she said, "Someone is coming to take me away!"

I must say that I could not help thinking that this might be very good news for both of us – but when I asked her who they might be, she said, "Hannah Croft!" As Hannah Croft has been dead for fifteen years I do not think this is very likely.

Miss Leach is due to make an announcement today. It is popularly supposed to be about the murders. She spent yesterday afternoon closeted with Mayhew who, since Leafy's death, has not stopped issuing bloodcurdling press releases along the lines of "I know what I know and soon I shall tell all!" What I don't understand is why the murderer – whoever he or she is – doesn't bump her off, instead of the members of staff in whom she chooses to confide. I am assuming that that is why Leafy got her tonic laced with strychnine (still no clue as to how it got into the bottle).

But, then, murder is no more rational than love or war or the behaviour of subatomic particles. Maybe Mayhew is the murderer. Maybe she entices female members of staff with her "secret" – some wild claim about who killed Everett – and then kills them in case they ask her to substantiate it. The staffroom rumour is that (a) Leach is about to make an announcement about Breeze, since he is the People's Choice as far as culprits are concerned and (b) say something about Leafy's last letter. Norma heard this from the head herself, and as she, like Leafy, is a keen fan of graphology, that is the most favoured rumour as to why we have all been gathered together.

I personally quite like Rachel's theory – that this is all bound up with some lesbian feud. "Gentleman Jim", as she is generally known among the male staff, may well be about to tell us she bumped off the two of them as a result of a lovers' tiff.

Have just gone in to tell Mother that Hannah Croft has been dead for fifteen years. She said, "I know that. But she'll be along soon anyway." As I was on my way out she asked me how the war was going. From a few of the things she said, I think she was talking about the first conflict rather than the one going on at the moment.

Have decided to leave her in her hat and coat. Perhaps someone will come to take her away. Never did get close to her, really. Always wanted my hellfire preacher father and he wasn't there. Poor little orphaned Hatchett. Violins, please.

11 a.m.

Waiting in staffroom, hoping Norma will turn up. I should be taking the upper sixth, or what is left of them, for a course of instruction on someone Archer refers to as Hugo Victor. But I do not wish to teach the upper sixth. I want to see Norma. I want to talk to her. I want to find out how she feels about the war, about Rachel (of whom more anon), about Alec and, most importantly, about *moi*. Groenig was in a moment ago and he says the rumour among the girls is that "Gentleman Jim" is indeed about to make sensational revelations on the subject of handwriting. He, like everyone else, is sure that Breeze did it.

"Chemistry," he said, "is a subject only engaged in by prospective poisoners! Anyway, the man is an anti-Semite!"

11.50 a.m.

My patience has been rewarded. Norma! Immediately I heard her step outside I decided to let the upper sixth's encounter with Hugo Victor wait.

Of course, we talked about Alec. Or, rather, she talked about her feelings for him.

"You see," she said today, "until I found out about Lucius I think I thought Alec was a straightforward person. I mean, I think that was what I loved about him. I've always seen him – I don't mean this to sound rude – in sort of opposition to you. There were two ways of living – the Hatchett way and the Lycett way. One was dark and complicated and troubled." I put my hand up at this point and made my Ogre of Lapland face, which went down quite well. "And the other was . . ."

"Well . . . Lycett, really!" I said, with a bright smile. She laughed again. A very good sign that.

"But you see," went on Norma, while somewhere below us the upper remove – presumably – started pelting each other with pellets and over in Europe the Wehrmacht prepared to move on yet another defenceless *mittel*-European country, "you see, that was the very thing I thought I loved about Alec. And that is what he clearly isn't. I mean, I want to be with him – even more now I know how wrong my idea of him was – but I do have to face the fact that when I am with him I may not like what I see. Not really."

I nodded sagely at this. Some of my evident satisfaction might have shown in my face because she went on, "I mean, I know I will, really, because I do love him. And love means that you are able to make things work, doesn't it? Love means sticking to someone in sickness and in health and for richer and for poorer and all of that. But . . . do you love someone first and then find out about them? Or do you find out about them and, out of that discovery, learn to love them?"

"Love," I said, looking her in the eyes, "is a look in the eyes."

She thought about this for some time. It is a very good sign when women play back your own opinions to you and what she had just said was, almost word for word, a rerun of a speech I had made to her on the Old Field football pitch about two months ago. I decided not to press home my advantage. She shivered slightly then, and said, in a whisper, "I keep thinking about his brother. I keep thinking about Lucius. Something about him and Alec sort of . . . frightens me. I couldn't say why. Alec was quite different when Lucius was here. He hardly talked to me at all. If I asked him about their childhood he just stared at me as if he had never seen me before. And Lucius was . . . well . . . he was charming in a way. He wasn't how I imagined him at all."

"People," I said, "are never how you imagine them. That is why most love affairs go so badly wrong."

I was rather pleased with this *mot* but she did not appear to pay it much attention. Finally she got out Alec's last letter to her. He has, apparently, been writing much less since his last leave. It read,

Darling Norma,

I love you. That ought to be enough, oughtn't it? I sit at your feet and smother you with kisses. The kisses turn to butterflies and the butterflies fly in and out of your hair and your hair curls about my face like the caress of a loving mother. Future and past meet in you. They are destroyed and reborn and wonderful and strange. I will tell you all one day. I swear I will for my love for you is powerful and real.

I miss you

Alec

"Is he all right?" she said. "It doesn't sound like him at all."

"Maybe," I said, "he copied it out from somewhere."

"In some ways," said Norma, with a nervous laugh, "I preferred them with holes in them. Sometimes gaps in sentences can be rather eloquent."

"Maybe," I said, "he is having a nervous breakdown. Or perhaps he is just trying too hard. It's often easier to express yourself if you are really insincere."

"Perhaps," she said, with a smirk, "that is why you find it so easy."

She obviously slightly regretted this smart remark. She sat for some time looking at her hands and then she said, in a soft voice, "Have your feelings for me changed?"

"No," I said, "and they won't change. They won't change whatever happens. There is nothing I can do about them. I thought I could but I can't. And you were asking me about love just now. Well, if you want to know, for me love is something that is defined by its inability to change."

She looked at me for a long time, and then, in a tone of voice quite new to her, she said, "I thought he was strong, you see, but

256

there are times when I think he isn't. And I don't think I could tolerate that. I don't even know what I mean by 'strong'. Maybe it is just this thing about him that I don't yet know. When I find out what it is I'll be all right. We'll be all right." There was a silence. She went on, "I love him, Dennis. I'm sure I love him. I just don't know what that love means any more. I don't know where he is or what is happening. I'm frightened."

Then we talked, as we so often do, about Rachel.

Frisch, to whom I talk on the telephone, says he is in touch with some committee, via his boss Oliphant, and that "very soon" he thinks we will have the "highest possible clearance" for Rachel. I do find the man's intense practicality very reassuring but my great fear is that Mason – who also seems to be cross-questioning Mabel Hughes and Jacqueline Rissett about Rachel – will get there first. I even had the paranoid fantasy the other day that Mason might be a German spy, trying to worm atomic secrets out of the girl. This is, of course, absurd, but gives you an idea of the pressure placed upon one simply by knowing the things she knows.

"I've got so fond of that girl," said Norma.

"Me too," I said. And patted her hand. Sexless Hatchett once again. It is not how I feel.

1.30 p.m.
Writing this in the Queen Vic, whither I have repaired with notebook and pencil. Working on a poem. It begins,

> *say citizen of what strange land*
> *you knowingly rehearse the ancient code*

I think this is supposed to be about parliamentary democracy, but it might well turn out to be about espionage or Egyptology, for all I know. It is not, anyway, about Norma. I am totally incapable, I have realized, of sentimental effusions about people, even those I think I love.

Miss Leach did not turn up for dramatic announcement re murders. Breeze said she had probably been murdered. Even I thought this in bad taste. Although, I have to say, if I had to choose three members of staff to bump off, those three would be top of the list. Perhaps someone is on a mission to stamp out lesbianism, Spanish teaching and graphology at Saltdene School for Girls.

We all hung around the gym – where Gentleman Jim had chosen to make her revelations. Breeze, who was wearing tennis shoes and a rather loud sweater, vaulted ostentatiously over the horse. He seems positively to relish the role of Principal Suspect. After about twenty minutes someone said we should go and find her. Norma had the bright idea of finding out where she had been immediately before the meeting. It turned out she had been taking the Misfits for netball practice down by the Old Field. And – this caused several raised eyebrows – Breeze had "looked in on them to lend a hand". Or, as we say, to watch schoolgirl breasts bobbing up and down under their gym slips. A deputation consisting of myself, Groenig, Breeze and Norma set out to find the girls, who were all waiting in Lower Six B for a talk on What To Do If We Are Bombed.

There they all were, sitting primly at their desks: Mabel Hughes, Jacqueline Rissett, Elinor Wreays and Janet Frosser – who seemed to be sharing a desk – Rachel a little apart from everybody else, as usual, and a very frightened-looking Mayhew. I asked them all when they had last seen Miss Leach. It appeared that after netball she and Mayhew had wandered off alone because "Mayhew had something to tell her". I hauled the girl out of the class and the four of us surrounded the poor little creature like a group of gangsters demanding protection money.

"What were you going to tell Miss Leach, Mayhew?" I said, as gently as I could.

"Nothing, Miss!" said Mayhew, who, since the schools were combined, has had constant problems with the sex of her teachers.

"Listen, Ruth," I said, "we want to help you. If you really do know something about what is going on then you should say it."

"I don't know nothing, Miss," said Mayhew, her eyes fixed on my face. "I'm an ignorant girl, I am. I don't know nothing about nothing."

I looked back in at the rest of the girls. I could see that Breeze was studying them too. There was something quite horrible about his expression. He is up to something. And I wonder whether that is the secret of the murders. We are now all behaving as if Miss Leach has been done away with, which I feel is a little premature. She may have just got fed up with her life and walked out of it – the way my father did.

My favourite theory of the moment is that the murders are a kind of group enterprise by the lower sixth, led and directed by Mabel Hughes. There are precedents in the work of Agatha Christie, I seem to recall. Isn't there one where an entire pullman car gets together to bump people off, thereby leading Raymond Chandler to suggest that the solution is so ingenious that only an idiot would guess it? Murder is a horribly simple affair in real life. Isn't it?

9.30 p.m.
Mother is still next door in her hat and coat, waiting for Hannah Croft. I really ought to get her to bed.

I have just done a real bit of war work. I addressed the Crotchett Green Literary Society on the subject "Are We At War With German Culture?" The title was mine and I expected a pretty sensational turnout. I think I thought we might see Roland Oliphant organizing a public bonfire for his Wagner 78s or, perhaps, Peter Lymne publicly wiping his bottom with pages from Goethe's *Elective Affinities* – I myself have used it for just that purpose before the outbreak of hostilities and gained considerable satisfaction from so doing. It was a rather expensive edition.

God, how I loathe talk about love! What a metaphysical trick of novelists who seek to sound significant!

They were on the edge of their seats, even though there were only about ten or twelve of them. Norma and Rachel turned up, as did Mr and Mrs Hughes, Mabel, the mysterious Mr Mason and Jacqueline Rissett and her ever-dutiful ever-gloomy mother (Groenig says the father ran off with a bearded man from Colchester, but Groenig has an even filthier mind than mine). About half-way through, to my consternation, Mr and Mrs Lycett arrived.

I do not know why they go around together as they so obviously loathe each other. They sat throughout with arms folded, never speaking to each other once.

I keep thinking about Lucius and trying to imagine what he really was like all those years ago. His reappearance on the scene seems to have altered Alec's relationship with Norma quite seriously. I worry that in a sense I have used him to get what I want as, perhaps, I did all those years ago. I am sure I was so fond of Alec that I really did not want Lucius to get close to him. The Lycetts, anyway, left without speaking to me. I think they blame me for introducing Alec to Norma – even though I didn't.

"Beethoven's father," I began, "was Dutch. Wagner's mother – although the fact is not well known and, indeed, for a long time was deliberately concealed from us – was half Welsh. Goethe, Brecht and Hebbel had Swiss blood, while Brahms's father, and at least three of his cousins, hailed from the Auvergne. What does this do for our idea of nationality?"

While they were still digesting this sensational news, I leaned forward across the lectern so conveniently provided for me by our highly suspect vicar – who was at home with his friend Cedric – and said, "None of these facts, of course, is true. But in war truth, as someone remarked, is the first casualty. I want to argue tonight, however, that the cause for which we are fighting means it is important to respect truth and to respect all aspects of culture, even if that culture has been appropriated by the hyenas who now strut around Germany. Facts about nationality, so often, are not expected to be 'true' since national and racial boundaries are always being blurred – by war and by love. And yet our ideas of what a nation is, like our idea of what love is, are necessarily constrained by what I would call morality. It is Immanuel Kant, the greatest moralist of all time, in my view, who said, 'Handle so, dass du die Menschheit, sowohl in deiner Person, als in der Person eines jeden andern, jederzeit, zugleich als Zweck, niemals bloss als Mittel brauchest' – 'Treat Humanity as an end, not as a means to something else,' is how I would translate that.

"And yet here in this room I feel almost ashamed to be speaking

German, even if I am saying, as I now want to, '*Dieser Imperativ ist kategorisch . . . Dieser Imperativ mag der Sittlichkeit heissen,*' which I would translate as, 'The only thing we must obey is moral law.' Even if I am saying 'moral' things I am supposed to lower my voice because I speak the hated language of people who are trying to kill us. Well, not all Germans are trying to kill us. Our respect for what is good and truthful and honest about German culture is precisely what we are fighting for, which is why, when we deal in propaganda as we all must, we try at least to make it bear some relation to what is real.

"'All is fair in love and war,' says the old proverb. Well, it isn't." I stopped and stared straight at Norma as I said this. In a sense, I suppose, I was apologizing for my shameless attempt to outman-oeuvre Alec earlier, and I think she could see from the passionate tone of my delivery that I wasn't simply making an abstract point. "Love is morality!" I went on. "War is morality. Otherwise both activities are, instead of the highest expression of humanity, the very lowest. Anyone who says, as pacifists tried to do at the start of this conflict, that war is simply beastly is missing the point. They are in the position of those who argue that physical love for another person is, by its very nature, contaminating. We have to keep both activities as clean and simple as they can be rendered – not an easy task. We have to be true to one another even when we are bent on each other's destruction. We are not at war with German culture, ladies and gentlemen, we are at war on its behalf. We are fighting for the right not to feel ashamed when we speak the German language, a language that I, for one, am not ashamed to say that I love. But how – how, ladies and gentlemen – are we to do this?"

I noticed that Rachel was watching me with unusual keenness. And that Mr Mason, who was in the row behind her, was watching her. So I wasn't really surprised when she answered my rhetorical question out loud: "*Ja, ja!*" she stammered. "*Aus so krummen Holze, als woraus der Mensch gemacht ist, kann nichts ganz gerrades gezimmert werden.*"

I rose to this rather well, I thought. "Quite right, Rachel!" I said, in my best pedagogical manner. "'Out of the crooked timber of humanity no straight thing can ever be made!' Kant again! You were paying attention last week! But we have to try! We have to make the attempt!"

I went on for about another fifteen minutes but by then I had them. I could have been in the Sportpalast and not the Crotchett Green Church Hall. I personally always like to be able to see the whites of the eyes of every member of the audience.

Afterwards there was weak coffee and cakes. Mr and Mrs Hughes and the odious Mr Mason made a beeline for me. Although I signalled for Norma and Rachel to join us they huddled in the corner with Jacqueline and her mother and Mabel. Mason said, "I found your remarks most interesting. Not everything in German culture is hateful, is it?"

I had the impression, I don't know why, that he was testing me out – waiting for me to make some unwise anti-government remark so he could have me locked up as a Fifth Columnist, so I turned the conversation to propaganda. We ended up talking about this Nazi-run radio station called the New British Broadcasting Corporation. They play a lot of Elgar and patriotic tunes and try to make out that the green fields of England and the Union Jack are all, essentially, Nazi. Which, perhaps, they are. Mason, of course, was shocked by this. I made him even more uncomfortable by reminding him of how much Elgar hated the "Pomp and Circumstance" march being made into a patriotic tune.

I noticed he kept looking over at Rachel as we spoke. I hated him suddenly, although I knew that this was unfair of me. It is "patriots" on both sides – I say to myself – who are the enemy. Mason will be the first to have Rachel shipped off to some camp or packed off in a ship so that she can be torpedoed. All for the sake of neatness. But, of course, we want to win, don't we? And for that we need a certain measure of ruthlessness. As we left, Mrs Rissett took me aside and said, "Jacqueline is worried about Mayhew. She thinks someone is trying to kill her."

I said, rather more brusquely than I intended, that a lot of people were trying to kill a lot of other people and that we all had to try not to think about it.

11.45 p.m.

Writing this in bed. Mother finally asleep. Parted from her hat with great difficulty. Norma rang at around ten, to tell me that Miss Leach's body had been found down on the Old Field, near where she had taken the Misfits for netball. She had been strangled, it appears, with her own belt. Very soon we shall have no female staff left. We talked about the murders but I must confess that I was more interested in trying to find out what she feels about me.

IO

28 May 1940

"There is," said Inspector Roach of Croydon CID, "a madman at work in the school. We had hoped for a quick solution but it hasn't happened."

"Do you think," whispered Hatchett to Norma, "his moustache would look good on me?"

Norma tried to look as if she had not heard this. It was not a time for levity. She had never been particularly fond of Miss Leach. It was hard to feel positive about someone whose only positive quality was masculinity but she had not deserved to die quite so early in her career. And she had been an excellent headmistress.

"First of all," went on Roach, "we thought it was a madman. Then we decided it was a revenge killing of some kind. Then we thought it was a madman again. And that is what we think now. It may be more than one madman. Or madwoman. It may be a group. We don't know, but we are going to find out."

Roach's preferred detection technique was to make vaguely threatening remarks to large groups of people. He was now pacing about the stage of the Old School, looking as if he was hugely enjoying himself. When he got to the very front of the stage, he produced Miss Leach's belt and waved it above his head. "This," he said, "is the latest murder weapon. A leather belt. Used to choke the life out of a woman whose only crime was that she taught Spanish. We are also working on a theory based on the fact that all the murdered women taught Spanish. We think this may be a link. Maybe whoever did this had some kind of problem with Spanish."

It was no good. Norma simply couldn't get interested in any more murders. It was as if you were only given a finite amount of interest in horror and destruction. And whoever was slashing their way through the staff of the Saltdene School for Girls, Croydon, had some serious competition over the Channel.

The Maginot Line, about which Hatchett and Peckerley had been so confident, didn't seem to have been of much use. As far as Norma could make out the Germans had simply gone round the end of it. And the Germans didn't kill people in the finicky English manner so popular in and around the grammar schools of South Croydon. These chaps just drove large tanks into towns and blew up anyone who tried to argue with them. They were not the kind of Germans Hatchett was always on about – sensitive souls who liked using long words ending in -eit. They were squareheaded slobs who really enjoyed shooting people. They were also worryingly good at it. Now they were parachuting into the Low Countries disguised as nuns, now they were sneaking across rivers on cunningly designed portable bridges, and now (right now, as a matter of fact) they were squeezing what remained of the British Expeditionary Force into a narrow area round Dunkirk. From where, if someone didn't do something about it pretty sharpish, they were going to be driven into the sea.

"Poison and strangling," Roach was saying, "is what we are dealing with! Make no mistake about it!"

Norma looked along the row. There were murmurs of disapproval at Roach's performance.

The disastrous events in Europe had reformed alliances within the school, as well as between nations. Leopold of the Belgians had been transformed, overnight, from a gallant little minor royal into a pathetic, grovelling coward. Mr Breeze, from being for some time the possible lover and murderer of Alice Everett and the almost certain murderer of Leafy Green, had suddenly become a heroic figure around whom people might gather.

Alan Breeze had a boat. A thirty-three-foot yacht. Norma, Jennifer Doran and Hatchett were going down to Eastbourne with him, and Hatchett and Breeze, answering a call from the BBC for small craft to rescue what Jennifer described as "our gallant lads", were going to sail across the Channel to Dunkirk. These days, Jennifer spent most of her time knitting. She had accumulated a vast collection of socks, legwarmers and cardigans, which she sent off, on a daily basis, to the War Office.

There was, thought Norma, a distinctly naval aspect to Breeze this morning. He had rolled, rather than walked, into assembly. In the quadrangle she had watched him lick his finger and hold it up to see from which direction the wind was blowing. Under his left arm, she noticed, was a small peaked hat. He was wearing white trousers. Where on earth did Hatchett and he think they were going? Henley Regatta?

"Anyone," Roach was saying, "anyone who knows anything about this affair must . . ."

Somewhere out there in northern France was her fiancé. Somewhere among the tanks and the guns and the planes was Alec Lycett. There were moments when she thought she might force her way on to Breeze's boat and make the crossing with them. She couldn't be any worse a sailor than Hatchett, who had managed to overturn a rowing-boat on a local lake after only two minutes of the sixty for which he had paid.

There had been a time, just after that odd meeting with Lucius – who now, according to Jennifer Doran, was flying Spitfires – when she had doubted her feelings for Alec. Their three or four evenings together before he went back to the regiment had been oddly stilted. He had kissed her, very chastely, twice, and on the last night he had held her very tightly round the waist. All of that had been very exciting indeed. But every time they seemed about to have a really close conversation, he shied away from it. When she asked him about Lucius he simply said he did not want to talk about his twin. Once or twice he had become almost angry, as if she was prying into something that she had no right to know.

For Norma, conversation and embraces were almost as important as each other. But though their conversation was full of the word "love" – Alec seemed to use it every other minute – it all reminded her of that distinctly odd, artificial letter he had written her. Since he had gone back, her letters to him had been, she now realized, rather similar in tone to the kind of thing Hatchett might write. They were decorated with drawings:

St. Norma of Croydon
($\frac{3}{8}$ ths actual size)

N ⟵ ♡ A (troo)

and odd pieces of doggerel:

Schadenfreude   by N. Lewis
Can I SEE anothers woe
And nor feel a pleasant glow?

But now. Now. Absence and virtual silence (she hadn't heard from him for a month) made her heart hunger for him more and more. She seemed suddenly to be right back on that September day when he had proposed to her. She wanted to write letters that were hopelessly romantic, that ended with showers of black kisses down the page and unreasoning sentences that said love love love and need need need over and over again.

Inspector Roach appeared to have finished. The acting headmistress of Saltdene School for Girls (for so he had been described by the local paper) was Andrew Veitch, MA, Oxon. He was now standing on the stage in academic gown and mortarboard with standard-issue headmaster's cane (what on earth was he doing with that? had he been using it on a boy? or was it a last-ditch method of defence against the Nazi Beast?), and waiting for the two minutes of silence he seemed to need before opening his mouth in public. Breeze and Jennifer Doran, who were at the end of the row, got up to go. Hatchett and Norma followed suit. Veitch looked down into the hall, a faint trace of displeasure appearing on his face.

"Mr Breeze! Miss Doran!" he neighed. "Mr Hatchett! Miss Lewis! May we ask where it is you are going?"

Breeze drew himself up to his full five feet two inches, snapped out his peaked hat and planted it firmly on his head. "We are going to the rescue of the British Army, Headmaster," he said. "Do not wait up for us!"

There was something quaint, absurd and yet impressive about this. A whisper started from pupil to pupil and from master to master. Norma caught a glimpse of Rachel's white and frightened face turned towards them. And then someone, quite without warning, started to sing:

> *"O hear us when we cry to Thee*
> *For those in peril on the sea."*

All over the hall came the scrape of chairs being pushed back across the highly polished floor. Miss Lilywhite, who had a fine soprano voice, came in with a descant and Hatchett, who had a lusty bass and knew all the words of all the hymns, growled out his answer to it. Voices all over the hall came in, but the senior modern-languages master sang above all the rest as Norma and he, Breeze and Jennifer Doran made their way out on to the steps and down into the quad.

> *"O Trinity of love and power*
> *Our brethren shield in danger's hour . . ."*

Norma turned as they reached Hatchett's MG and heard now the massed voices of the school, thundering together in that slightly desperate plea to Almighty God, whose arm doth bind the restless wave, to reach out and somehow pull back brothers, fathers, uncles or good friends from the cruel embrace of Hitler's army. She looked up as she climbed into the car and saw that her girls, the Misfits – Mayhew, Jacqueline, Mabel, Rachel, Janet and Elinor – had come out on to the balcony and were waving furiously after them as, behind, in the hall, the combined voices of both schools beat out the verses of the hymn.

"O hear us when we cry to Thee
For those in peril on the sea."

If it isn't Mr Breeze, Norma found herself thinking idly, as Hatchett double declutched and his engine made a noise like a tub of iron filings being dropped into a meat-grinder, it is possible that one of my girls is a triple murderer.

But once again it didn't seem to matter. Even Breeze, pushing his absurd hat back on to his head, had a vaguely heroic aspect to him. Once again he wet his finger and thrust it out of the car window. "She blows easterly," he said, as Hatchett hurtled the car round a corner and down towards Godstone and the A22, "but there is southerly in her, too, I'll wager!"

Did Breeze know anything about sailing? It was his father's boat, Norma had heard. If he didn't he had acquired a large and impressive vocabulary of matelot-flavoured language in order to cloak his ignorance. Ever since putting on the peaked hat, his speech had undergone what was, quite literally, a sea-change and almost every word or phrase he uttered seemed to make some kind of gesture in the direction of the briny. "Yarely! Yarely!" he muttered, as Hatchett swung the car right and his passengers were driven into the comfortable leather of the seats. "Port your helm!" he cried faintly, as they came out to overtake on the third blind corner in a row. Sometimes he would slip in what seemed to be dialect words of doubtful provenance – "Slow with yer beamsills! Sprit that blockitt!" – and by the time they had reached East Grinstead he had acquired what was almost certainly a West Country accent.

Jennifer was rising to the occasion in her own way. Once, at the beginning of the Ashdown Forest, she wiped her forearm across her forehead in her best Land Girl style, looked out at the misty outlines of the trees and said, in a thrilling contralto, "Hitler will rue the day he tried to take on our gallant lads!" But even if it was as absurd as Breeze's performance, the context made it impressive. War had a habit of dignifying even the most clumsily expressed feelings, and the thought that, with each mile, they were getting closer and closer to an army in danger as well as to the man

Norma loved, made her companions' gestures and poses somehow appropriate and admirable.

Hatchett, crouched over the wheel, his face and shoulders tense, was as much like Mr Toad as ever. But now he was, as the book might have it, a Terrible Toad, a Toad of War, a Toad to Put Fear into the Heart of the Hun. He put quite a lot of fear into the hearts of his passengers. He almost collided with a milk float in Nutley. Just outside East Hoathly he nearly reduced the civilian population by five when he ran through a red light, his only warning being a cry of "Coming through!" At Lower Dicker he swerved to avoid a fox and very nearly destroyed a horse.

Norma felt a terrible exhilaration at it all. So what if Breeze was a triple murderer! So what if Jennifer Doran was even sillier than she had always thought she was and, to cap it all, had made a fool of herself with Alec's twin brother! So what if Hatchett was probably not, and never had been, entirely honest with her about his feelings! So what if Alec had gone distant and unreachable ever since Lucius came back! They were all foolish, hopeless, messed-up creatures and they had nothing to lose any more! War was making them into their true selves – brave, foolish, living in the moment.

And Norma allowed herself, once more, the delicious illusion of love. She was a woman with a sweetheart – she used the word consciously to herself, savouring its slight absurdity – and he was somewhere there over the grey Channel, a handsome lieutenant fighting for his country and the woman he loved and was, one day, going to marry.

Alec Lycett still had his spade. He had his bolt-action 1914 Lee Enfield rifle, which so far he had not managed to fire. He had his tin hat and his pack, and he had Gooderson's binoculars. Gooderson, poor Gooderson, was not going to need them any more. Alec had the last set of typewritten orders he had received, and although they were five days old there was a certain comfort in them. They said things like '0945 proceed to QRSTE 4312874 and JOIN DOUBLEFORCE ATTACK SW'. They had a jolly, confident ring to them and, although they bore no relation whatsoever to what had actually transpired on the day in question, they at least reminded him of the days when he believed that a soldier had some control over his destiny.

There had been an attack south-west. But it had petered out by the time they had managed to join it. Along the road they had met a lot of tired, frightened and often wounded men, who said they were what was left of III Corps. Alec had not the faintest idea who III Corps were or what they were doing there or in what direction they were headed but there seemed little point in Gooderson's plan of trying to carry on through them, like incoming commuters pushing against a tide of office-workers leaving at the end of a long and difficult day. One of them – who wasn't from III Corps but a completely different battalion that should have been, he thought, at Boulogne, or maybe Dover, although he thought Dover was in Jerry hands – told Gooderson that everyone had orders to retreat, in good order, in the direction of Dunkirk.

Gooderson, as Gooderson did, went on about Sir Ronald Adam's headquarters and Sir John Gort's tactical move on the north-eastern salient and the need to re-group but, by now, no one paid any attention to anything that Gooderson said. Alec's only concern was to get the hell out of wherever they were and into somewhere where there were a few British soldiers who had the faintest idea of what they were supposed to be doing.

"My leg hurts, sir," said Peckerley.

"Chin up!" said Alec.

The tanks had come out of nowhere. One minute they had all been trudging through open country in eerie quietness. The next, two squat shapes had come out of the trees over to the right of the line they had joined. The 4th Croydons had never been a very large regiment. There were those who maintained it wasn't really a regiment at all, but an unaffiliated bunch of Territorials who were only really trained to dig holes. What was left of them had been absorbed, by now, into the flood of soldiers going north and Alec didn't know many of the faces near to him on the road. Mavroleon,

Forssander, Gooderson, Peckerley ... that was about it. It was Peckerley who had said, when he saw the tanks, "They're ours!" and Peckerley who had been hit in the foot by a fragment of the shell that had thrown Gooderson up in the air and blended him, his uniform, his swagger stick and his sitrep folder with the soil of northern France. After that people had started running. Some had run towards the tanks. Alec and Peckerley had sheltered in bushes on the other side of the road while Alec tried to dress Peckerley's foot. The last he had seen of Forssander was a glimpse of him running towards a group of German soldiers, yelling, "I surrender!" They had let him get about fifteen yards away and then the youngest-looking of the Germans, a blond boy of about Peckerley's age, had shot him in the chest.

The column of men headed north didn't stop moving. They didn't even try to go much faster, for the very good reason that most of them were too exhausted to be capable of doing such a thing. It was as if they and the tanks inhabited a different world in which neither could consider the possibility of seriously affecting the other. Then, for a moment, Alec, who had watched all this from the bushes, had the impression that the armoured vehicles were about to turn their guns on them. But something seemed to be happening in the fields from which they had come, and several of the Germans, who were talking into telephones a great deal (they had things, like telephones and cars and shiny new-looking weapons, that Alec had never seen in his entire period of service with the British Army), shouted to the other Germans and the whole crowd of them beetled off in a completely different direction.

He waited in the bushes for quite a long time. Soldier after soldier passed on the road but Alec didn't move. It was Peckerley, in the end, who said, "I suppose we'd better get moving, sir." Still Alec didn't stir. Perhaps, he thought, he was a coward. Somehow it had never occurred to him that he might be a coward.

He and Peckerley were still waiting in the bushes, although the Germans were long gone. Alec wasn't sure, now, what they were waiting for. It felt as if they were waiting for the war to end.

Whatever they were waiting for it was a long way off and, perhaps, impossible ever to achieve. Perhaps they were waiting for night to come and blot out this horrible scene.

"Croydon!" said a small, snuffly voice to his left. Alec turned and saw Mavroleon, stretched out on the grass, his boots making the two sides of a V, his rifle still clutched in his right hand. How had he got there? He appeared to be asleep. He had slept through the voyage out. He had slept through the advance on St Aines-les-Oiseaux, or whatever it was called, and through the retreat from Bethanie-sur-Plonkières or whatever name that truly ghastly place took upon itself. He had slept, as far as Alec could see, while actually marching for Dunkirk. And he was asleep now, stretched out on the spring grass of Flanders or Picardy or whatever it was supposed to be. If you forgot the uniform and rifle, he could very well have passed for a French peasant on his lunch break.

Peckerley leaned over him. "Tell me, Mavroleon," he said, "where you would rather be in preference to this flat and uninspiring section of northern France. Think carefully before answering."

"Croydon!" grunted Mavroleon.

"Now," went on Peckerley, "can you tell me the name that you would like to see on the next road sign that we encounter as we march away from this scene of devastation?"

"Croydon!" grunted Mavroleon.

Peckerley, thought Alec, as he peered through the bushes, was either very brave, very stupid or very mad, or perhaps some combination of all three. He wondered whether he, Alec, was in danger of losing his marbles, for as he looked across the rough grass it seemed to him that Forssander appeared to be moving. Surely he could not have survived that bullet? He was moving, though. He was definitely moving.

His being wounded somehow made it worse. How, in God's name, was he going to get back to Dunkirk with two wounded and one narcoleptic soldier, all of whom were his responsibility? He looked away and looked back. Forssander stirred again. Oh, Jesus! Next to him, Peckerley seemed to have seen it too. "I think, sir," he said softly, "that we should go and get him."

"Yes," said Alec, "I suppose we should." There was a break in the endless flow of soldiers. As far as Alec could tell there were no Germans in the vicinity. "Let's go!" he said. But his legs wouldn't move. He was a coward. He knew now that that was what he was. It was just like the other time, all those years ago, with Lucius, just the same. He was a coward. There he was wetting his pants just because a few Fritzes wanted to blow his head off. Talking of wetting one's pants, he was dying for a leak. But it didn't feel safe to point Percy at the scenery when so many hostile soldiers were still out there, just waiting to get a glimpse of his todger. Peckerley appeared to be crawling in the direction of Forssander. He really had better follow him.

His legs still didn't seem to be working.

He tried thinking about Norma. He had done quite a lot of that since the shooting started. In books soldiers thought of their loved ones' faces when going into battle, but when he tried to summon up hers, together with the kind of phrase that went with such things – angel of light, merciful mistress, that kind of thing – he failed to do so. He could not connect any of this with what had gone before. Alec Lycett, if there still was such a person, was completely and utterly different from the bright young lieutenant who had walked out of church on the morning of 3 September.

"Sir!" Now he really had to start moving. "Sir!" Alec forced his legs, stiffly, across the grass. Away on the road to his right, he could see another ragged column of men approaching. One step, two step, three step – "Sir!" At last, after what seemed an age, he was up with Peckerley and Forssander. Forssander was lying in an untidy heap, his rifle away to his right. Peckerley was holding his hand.

Forssander seemed pleased to see him. He didn't seem unduly bothered that someone had made a large hole in his chest. He was looking off into the grass, a weird sort of calm on him. Perhaps Peckerley had given him morphine. Perhaps it didn't hurt to be shot. Not as badly as Alec thought.

"There's a lot of THEM here, sir," whispered Forssander.

"A lot of what?" said Alec.

"THEM, sir," said Forssander, "the things that frighten me. THEM!"

"Ah," said Alec.

The column on the road was getting closer. They must move.

"I can even say it now, sir," said Forssander, with what might equally well have been a smile or a grimace of pain. "The word doesn't bother me any more. And before, it frightened the life out of me. Just to say it or hear it said or see it written down. The word is 'worms', sir. It was worms that I was scared of. But I'm not scared of them any more. I can say it, sir. 'Worms!' There you are. I can say it."

His eyes closed and, breathing more shallowly now, he did not seem to notice as, from the grass, a fat, prosperous-looking worm crawled up on to his hand and wriggled its way up towards the dark entrance to his khaki sleeve.

"We'll have to leave him, Peckerley," said Alec. "I'm afraid there is no choice."

Peckerley bit his lip. He seemed about to argue the point. The column on the road was getting closer. To distract the boy more than anything else, Alec suggested they went back and wakened Mavroleon. But though they slapped his face, pulled his ears, tickled him and shook him thoroughly Mavroleon would not wake up. He would not even, for the first time ever, utter the word "Croydon". And, when they finally hauled themselves up and joined the river of soldiers headed for the coast he was still lying out on French soil, snoring happily, his pudgy hand still clutching the rifle that he had never fired and probably never would.

Breeze and Hatchett were long departed.

The day was wearing on. Jennifer Doran and Norma Lewis were standing on the same spot where they had watched the two men push Breeze's father's yacht *Hearts of Oak* out into the stirring sea.

"They are so brave!" Jennifer was saying. "They are so brave!" She gestured, slightly querulously, in the direction of Le Touquet. "All our boys are so brave! And Hatchett and Alec and Breeze and Peckerley! They are . . . well, they are . . . our boys! They are going into . . . into . . ." She shook herself like a dog coming out of water and her red hair fell away from her freckled face. "Into . . . into the heart of battle!"

"Yes," said Norma. "I suppose they are."

She looked out into the grey Channel. It was rather peaceful. The barbed wire that was so in evidence further down the coast didn't seem to have got as far as Poundsea, where *Hearts of Oak* was kept. Someone had told her you could see the flashes of the guns back at Dover, but down here she felt as if she was in an off-season holiday resort. Even as they were pushing them out into the water, Norma had felt she was seeing off two friends for a weekend jaunt rather than to the prospect of being shot at by Germans.

"It's funny," said Jennifer. "Lucius is so like Alec."

Indeed, thought Norma, that is usually the case with identical twins. But, in a way, she was rather glad that Jennifer had raised the subject. It had acted as a kind of censor on their intimacy for the last few months. And one of the things she valued about her friendship with the dom-sci mistress was being able to say absolutely anything to her. If they hadn't found themselves in the same staffroom, they might not have sought each other out. As it was, theirs had started out as a relationship based on the realization that, although they were very different, both felt the same way about quite a lot of the things involved in being female. Clothes and food, for example.

But perhaps not love.

Until she had seen Jennifer enjoying what she described as "great yummy slices of Lucius", Norma had found her directness about what she called "chomping on men" rather charming. Jennifer divided men into three categories – the first eleven, the second eleven, and what she called the Scratch Team. Norma had always suspected she put Hatchett in the Scratch Team, although they were careful not to discuss him. But, since Lucius, Jennifer seemed to feel she had conversation rights over Norma's fiancé.

Norma decided to tackle this issue, and said, "I don't really like talking about Alec. Or his brother."

"Oh!" said Jennifer, looking slightly put out by this news. She had, after all, been discussing practically nothing else since December of last year. "Oh!" Her voice rose slightly, a sure sign that she was about to ask for what she termed "great slices of love" from her friend.

"I'm not as clever as you are, Norma," she said, "and I hope I haven't done anything beastly. I mean, I know I tuck in quite a lot . . ." There was a fractional pause, which Jennifer seemed to take as strenuous denial that she did anything of the kind. "But I felt Lucius didn't sort of really . . . think Alec was his dish of prawns, as it were. And I think you said you thought Alec thought Lucius wasn't his . . . cup of tea, as it were!"

"I think I did," said Norma.

Once she had started to find Jennifer irritating, she seemed to notice more and more things that she had presumably always done but now seemed publicly disfiguringly present in almost all of their encounters. Reminding you of what she had said and what you had said by way of return was only one of them.

"I think I did say that," went on Jennifer, "and you said what you said as well. And I suppose it is not the sort of thing that is very easy to . . . digest, as it were. I didn't like to think of Lucius sort of nibbling away at Alec's reputation, as it were!"

"No," said Norma drily, "I find it rather hard to stomach."

"I mean," continued Jennifer, "I thought it was peculiar of him. And although, as I think I said, he was and still is, I suppose, a really delicious, scrummy sort of man I don't think I like him hating Alec like that because Alec is a complete poppet as well as being rather mouth-watering into the bargain, as is Lucius, of course, looking exactly like him as he does and vice versa!" She gave Norma a quick, sly, sidelong glance. "Anyway," she said, "you have first bite at flavoursome Alec because you are engaged to him, as I think you told me, and I said, 'Well done, you!' and you said, 'Thanks!', didn't you?"

"Yes," said Norma.

"And now here he is braving shot and shell," said Jennifer, "and it must be so hard to keep the relationship sort of . . . real. For you, I mean. Because, of course, you have a sort of picture of him to drool over, as it were, but he's not there, is he? Or he's not here. You are here and he's . . ." Jennifer waved energetically towards the French coast ". . . somewhere over there!"

"Yes," said Norma, "that's about the size of it." She turned away from the sea to look down the promenade. A line of Girl Guides staggered along, led by a fat woman with an armful of blankets. Such a grey day and so peaceful!

"We will just have to wait!" said Jennifer, knuckling her blue eyes in a way that she presumably thought looked girlish. "We are women!"

Norma did not attempt to deny this. You had to love, she thought, because you wanted something permanent. Hatchett was quite right about that. Love was just another notion – like Rachel's formulae.

Now, looking back out to sea, she started to face the question that was really bothering her. This business with Lucius. Why had he been sent away? There were times when she wondered if her first thought hadn't been correct and the rather distinguished, charming RAF pilot she had met wasn't the victim of some ghastly mental disease that sent him out, at night, to suck the blood of strangers or strangle unfortunate servant girls.

"Anyway," said Jennifer, who seemed to have been talking rather a lot while Norma was thinking, "you're going to get married, which is delish and moreish, and have lots and lots of babies, which is also a wonderful thing to get your teeth into. While I'm sure I never will. Nor will I ever hear from Lucius again, which is unfair as he's definitely first eleven and even more of a dish than Alec, which I hope you won't take amiss because of course they are both nutritious and nourishing in the extreme and, of course, very similar, I mean totally similar, I mean identical really in almost all respects, apart from one or two obviously, and I am talking like a silly goose, I know, because one of them . . ." here she looked up at the sky and shielded her eyes as if she was looking into the sun ". . . is up there and the other one . . ." here she tried a big heroic gesture of the kind seen in some nineteenth-century portrait of a Revolutionary heroine ". . . is . . ." the sweep of her arm took in

the whole of the Pas de Calais and Upper Normandy as well
". . . over there!"

Norma looked at her. "Yes," she said, "I know."

II

Alec and Peckerley were surrounded by the sullen, private faces of retreat. There were more and more soldiers, but although they knew none of them and although they all seemed to be from different regiments, there was hardly any exchange of information. They had passed lorry after lorry, car after car, as they made their Stuka-haunted journey north, towards the perimeter of Dunkirk. "I don't know," said a voice behind Alec. "I haven't got a fucking clue, mate."

Even a few weeks ago, he might well have turned round and asked the man to watch his language, but over the last four days he had come pretty close to using the F-word himself. It really did seem the only one appropriate to the situation. Minute by minute he could feel himself sinking lower and lower. He had tried to be honest. He had tried to be first eleven. But he wasn't first eleven.

Hatchett was working against him. He knew that now. Oh, he wrote letters that were funny and began "Dear Old Bean" but he was working against him. He was his best friend – if that meant anything any more – but he was quite clearly working against him. Once jealous thoughts came to you it was impossible to stop them. It started the New Alec, who was in a sense the Old Alec only more honest about it. New Alec wasn't like Alec Senior at all. New Alec cursed and raged and saw the reality of the situation he was in.

"F— it all," he muttered to himself, as the ragged column clattered past a closed café. Down a side-street to his right, he saw a small fat Frenchman in a beret, eating a raw onion. If he was disturbed about the fact that the British Army all seemed to be passing him, headed in the wrong direction, he showed no sign of it. A few yards further down the road a fat woman in a pinafore looked morosely back at Alec. It was not the sort of look he had expected to receive from an Allied civilian whom he was trying to save from the squareheads. What was she doing there anyway? Did she like being divebombed by German planes?

As he was thinking this, a Stuka screamed in from the east and, as it climbed away, dropped its load on a row of houses about sixty yards down the street. It had overshot the column by a long way, but the noise and the theatrical suddenness of its appearance were enough to send them scattering for the shelter of the houses on the other side of the road.

"There's never just one of the bastards," muttered Peckerley, as they huddled against a stone wall, "they're like bloody buses. You wait for ages and then there's –" Once again, that hideous whine, like a giant insect, and once more an explosion, this time, mercifully, even further to the west of the road than the one before. This time they limited themselves to a comprehensive strafing of something that looked like an allotment. Then the plane followed the other one up and away to the north, where the harbour lay. "Three . . . Perhaps," said Peckerley, "it was just high spirits."

Once they were sure there were no more planes, the two of them staggered back towards the column. "Once we're out of here, sir, and safely back in Croydon," said Peckerley, "you and Miss Lewis are going to go at it like the clappers. It's going to be so good!" Peckerley, too, thought Alec, had changed. He even managed, from time to time, a jolly kind of coarseness, although you could tell he was still that curious anomaly, a highly sensitized rugby player. He was also, it seemed, almost completely without fear. The more people fired at him the more he appeared to like it. Even now, when his face was white with pain, he maintained a cheerfulness that Alec found almost irritating. "I expect," he said, as they followed the line into the town, "you sort of keep her face before you, don't you? Something to come back to, sort of thing."

Well, he tried to, he tried to. But it didn't always work. And that frightened him.

The mass of men in front of them seemed to have disappeared. Now, within sight and smell of the sea, little groups of soldiers were making their way through the rubble, the craters and the abandoned vehicles. Alec tightened his grip on Peckerley's shoulder and struck off to his right past a squarely built café. Everything about it seemed intact, although just in front of it a road sign leaned at a crazy angle to the blasted earth. But almost every roof tile had been blown out by the impact of the shell, giving the Café Belle Vue the air of an old lady surprised in her hair-net. More quickly than he would have thought possible, they were looking at the beach.

Over to Alec's left was a group of British soldiers, who looked as if they had just walked off the parade-ground. They were stepping out smartly along the promenade in the direction of a tent and a Union Jack that looked like the nearest thing to an administrative centre for miles around. Beyond them was a grim and unusual sight: lorries, trucks and almost every kind of mobile vehicle, armoured and otherwise, were stretching out into the sea in an improvised pier; they were skewered into each other, nose to tail, like mating dinosaurs. Crawling over these, like children scrambling on rocks at low tide, were the distant figures of soldiers.

At first Alec couldn't think what they were doing there. Were they proposing to swim to Dover? Then, in the grey Channel light, he saw the ships. There were destroyers and what looked like a passenger ferry, stalled further off in deeper waters. But closer in, around the abandoned vehicles, were swarms of smaller craft – dinghies, and even what looked like a motor launch. As Alec watched, a distant figure hauled itself over the side of one of them as, leaning perilously over to one side, the vessel put out to sea.

At that moment the planes came over again. Peckerley and he flattened themselves against the beach wall. Norma, he thought, Norma! He had heard somewhere that people about to die repeated the names of loved ones, like a prayer. But the awful thing was that this prayer, like all the other prayers, didn't work. All there was was the fear. There was no use in chanting her name like the name of a saint because it was just another name. And with the fear came the other doubts and secrets that had haunted him for so long. His brother and his mother and his father, and the whole sorry mess that he had still not even begun to talk about truthfully. He never could, of course, any more than he could ever tell her about this horrible, stomach-loosening terror he felt now. So that after a few feeble repetitions her name was drowned out by the only words he now knew – "I don't want to die. I don't want to die. I don't want to die."

"Are you the thirtieth?" said the man next to him.

"No," said Alec, "we're the fourth Croydons."

"Blimey!" said his companion. "Never 'eard o' them!"

"We're about all there is left of it," said Peckerley, with tremendous cheerfulness. "We're working on a new motto 'omnes mortui sint'!" The man didn't get this. Peckerley obliged him with a translation. "'All the bastards are dead'!" he said, brightly, "Or, perhaps, 'Maybe all the bastards are dead' – we're not quite sure, hence the subjunctive." The man looked at him as if he had taken leave of his senses, which perhaps, thought Alec, once more, Peckerley had.

"We," said the second man, "were supposed to deliver some tinned food to Boulogne. But we haven't got any fucking tinned food, have we? In fact, as far as I can make out we haven't even got fucking Boulogne so with your fucking permission we are going to fuck off out of it." And, muttering about the absence of the RAF, that was exactly what they did.

Lucius was in the RAF.

No wonder there were none of the bastards to be seen. They were probably all swaggering around some aerodrome in Scotland smoking pipes and using words like "crate" and "prang". Lucius, now he thought about it, was exactly the sort of arrogant bastard who would join the RAF. Just so as he could sneer at his second-eleven brother doing all the work while he swanned around some Scottish airfield picking up loose women and drinking beer from a silver tankard.

Down on the beach a Stuka dropped its load and the blast, muffled by the sand, threw up a cloud of dust.

"I think we had better follow them, sir," said Peckerley. Alec peered over the wall. There was a craft that looked like a giant dinghy, or a sawn-off ship's lifeboat, bobbing on the water about fifty yards out. In the stern was a civilian boy nine or ten years old.

What the hell was he doing here? He didn't, thought Alec, look English. A refugee in the wrong place, like everyone else on this damn beach. "Come on, sir!" Alec couldn't move. The fear had paralysed him. He crouched in closer to the wall, lowering his head. It was Peckerley, in spite of his wounded leg, who grabbed him and yanked him to his feet.

The two of them wove across the beach and waded out through the water towards the boat. There were surprisingly few soldiers on it. Alec couldn't work out how this might be. But a fat man in the prow was rowing desperately hard, anxious to be away, and did not slacken his pace when he saw Alec and Peckerley. "Taxi!" called Peckerley, breezily. The man – there were two other oarsmen who did the same – did not stop rowing. For a moment Alec thought they were not going to make it and then the vessel rode back on a wave and he and Peckerley were grabbing at the sides of it.

For some reason, he didn't hear the plane come over. All his energy and attention were focused on getting into the boat. And he never found out quite where or how the shell landed, but he was aware of one person – it sounded like a child – screaming, and then everything went dark. There was the sea, but he was only aware of its restless permanence, rocking him to sleep while the madness of the world went on around him. He thought he saw Norma's face but it was a long way away. She was saying something. He couldn't catch what it was. Before he had the chance to try to decode it he felt himself slipping away with a sense of peaceful regret. "I never really knew you at all," somebody with Norma's voice who wasn't Norma at all was saying. Then a dark shape rose up to meet him, a figure shrouded in black that reminded him of a phrase Hatchett was fond of quoting: "Here it is at last – the distinguished thing."

"Pretty soon," said Breeze, "we should be seeing a sort of long finger of land on the port bow."

Hatchett peered round him. He saw nothing that looked anything like land. He was rapidly coming to the conclusion that Breeze

284

was not a lot better at navigation than he was reputed to be at teaching chemistry. All Hatchett could see was heaving, grey-green waves.

The Channel wasn't the only thing that was heaving. He had gone through the stage of vomiting up food, left behind the phase of sicking up yellow bile and now he was just puking for the hell of it. He had lowered his broad shoulders and thick neck over the side of the boat and prayed for a German shell to put him out of his misery. He went through the routine of nausea once more and, as he pulled himself back up to the vertical, saw land on what must be the starboard side of the boat.

When he pointed it out to his companion Breeze looked at it narrowly, as if he suspected France of having sneaked round the back of him, like the Nazis, in order to cut off his line of retreat. "It shouldn't be there!" he said, in shocked tones. "It may not be France at all!"

It certainly looked like France. It reminded Hatchett of a rather pleasant little resort near Dieppe where he had spent a fortnight a few years ago. There were no signs of soldiery. In a field beyond the beach a man sat on a tractor, gazing at the sky. He looked French. He was wearing blue dungarees and a beret. Perhaps, thought Hatchett, they could pull in for a short while to ask him directions. It would be good to be on dry land.

"Where the hell are we?" he said to Breeze.

"Ready about!" said Breeze who, for long stretches of the journey, had communicated by obscure seafaring commands none of which Hatchett had understood. He pulled the rope he usually pulled when Breeze said this and the yacht, moving its length into the swell, heaved round in a full circle.

Did Germany have a navy? And, if so, where was it? He really should have done some research into this kind of thing before he set sail with this lunatic. He had decided in the course of the hours he had spent with Captain Breeze that being a triple murderer was probably the least of his faults. They seemed to be heading north again. Perhaps they were going home.

"I know," said Breeze, suddenly, pushing his peaked hat back on his head, "that you think I killed Everett. And Green. And maybe Gentleman Jim into the bargain."

"I'll be honest with you," said Hatchett. "I no longer care who killed whom. As far as I am concerned Roger Ackroyd could have strangled Hercule Poirot. All I want is to stop feeling sick."

"Jacqueline Rissett," said Breeze, "accused me of having an affair with Everett simply because she was jealous. The silly little thing is in love with me."

This was the most interesting thing Breeze had said to him since they started their journey. As the boat ploughed back down the Channel, this time with France on their left, Hatchett tried to concentrate on it.

He was unable to do so. All he could think about was that they were probably going in the wrong direction. The whole idea of Dunkirk, as far as he could gather from the wireless, was to get out there and bring back a few of our boys. It was not a cheap excuse for a day trip to Cherbourg. And, to add to his feelings of guilt, everything about France looked extremely pleasant and peaceful. He did not want to be remembered as one of the small boats that had got lost and ended up in Berck Plage by mistake.

"It was Jacqueline Rissett who killed them, I am sure," Breeze was saying. "I can't go on protecting her for ever. I thought at first someone put her up to it. I felt sorry for her. She has some passionate schoolgirl crush on me."

"Enough to want to kill Everett because she thought you were having an affair with her," said Hatchett, suddenly thoughtful. He stiffened slightly. If Breeze had known him better he might have been alarmed by the tightening of the mouth and the small, owlish nod that followed this remark. When Hatchett was teaching, this was the gesture his class feared most.

"She was wildly jealous," said Breeze. "Those sweet little girls are full of evil passions. And if you dig any deeper you'll find even your precious Miss Lewis's little niece is no saint. You don't really know much about women, do you, Hatchett? They will kill for passion. They are swept away by passion. Women need love!"

The sea, thought Hatchett, had an even worse effect on Breeze than did watching netball practice – an activity for which he was famous throughout both schools. He clearly thought the fringe of a war zone was just the place for a man-to-man chat about girls.

"You don't know women," went on Breeze. "I know women. When you are my age you may know women. Possibly. Maybe you will not know women. But I do know women. I love women, young man, I worship them." He was actually licking his lips. If he went on like this much longer, thought Hatchett, he might well stimulate himself to the point where he was coming down the boat after the senior modern-languages master. This was not what was meant by the Dunkirk spirit. "When they yield to you," said Breeze, doing something complicated with a rope, "they are, as you will discover, so . . . so . . ." he cast about for the *mot juste* and, with a small spasm, found it ". . . open. I love that. You won't understand this business until you understand that."

"I don't believe," said Hatchett slowly, "that any of the girls who took their work in to Miss Green could have doctored the bottle of tonic without her seeing it. So, I repeat, how did the strychnine get into the tonic? And if you're talking about motive, you seem to have one. Especially if, as might be the case, you are not being entirely truthful about Jacqueline Rissett. For all we know you might have . . . encouraged her. Perhaps she touted the story of the highly unlikely love affair between you and Miss Everett to draw suspicion away from the two of you."

Breeze's face changed. The careful control he cultivated, especially in his role as captain, started to break up and, underneath it, Hatchett saw a rather ugly, frightened little man.

"I'm a happily married man, boy. And while we're at it, haven't you slept with Norma Lewis?" Breeze said. "Or at least thought about it? Don't pretend you're above all this, Hatchett, because you're not. You're a little prig, you are. You have some idea that we're all good little English people and that makes us all right." Here he leaned forward in the boat and seized Hatchett's arm viciously. For a moment, Hatchett thought he was going to try to pitch him over the side. His face worked angrily. "Sex," he said, in combative tones, "is at the heart of these murders. Sex is at the heart of everything. The reason Hitler is attacking England is because he hasn't had enough sex. The reason you are here with me on this boat is because of sex. You want to impress the woman you love and have sex with her. It is the great principle of the world, my little friend."

Hatchett was almost sure he had heard the distant noise of guns. But he wasn't thinking about where he was any more. Appalling as Breeze was, there was some kind of truth in what he had just said. Hatchett had been pretending, since the autumn, that he was an English gentleman. That his code of honour forbade him to feel things for the woman to whom his best friend had proposed. Well, the chemistry master had a point. This wasn't a time for gentlemanly behaviour. Hatchett recalled a picture of Halifax and Hitler standing on the steps of some building in Berlin. You could see from the way the tall English aristocrat peered down at the Reich Chancellor, as if he was some amusing little man he had just met at his club, that he thought there really was a chance for dialogue with this barking lunatic. He, Hatchett, wasn't like that. He wasn't like Alec Lycett. He wasn't a gentleman. He always had been and always would be an outsider.

And he was no longer going to sit around and let Alec assume he had won Norma when she was so obviously the wrong girl for him. He was no longer going to be good old Hatchett who was prepared to let the local rich boy marry the woman he himself loved just because, like a cricket bat or a toy train or a favoured bed in a dormitory, he had bagged her first. If ever Hatchett got out of this he would go and get Norma. And if, as he hoped, Alec was somehow there as well, then if Hatchett did manage to step out of character and sweep up the girl, Alec would just have to accept it. If he couldn't then it wasn't much of a friendship. At the very least he had the right to make his feelings clear to the two of them.

"Sex," Breeze was saying, "is OH, MY GOD!!"

This last remark was prompted by the sight of a German plane about a mile up ahead of them. It seemed, as far as Hatchett could tell, to have somewhere to get to and, if it was equipped with guns

288

or bombs, it did not seem interested in wasting them on two English grammar-school teachers. It flew off into the mist and beyond it, now, was the definite, audible sound of artillery.

The boat, however, came upon them as silently as a funeral barge. It was a mastless longboat, the size of their own vessel, but there didn't seem to be anyone at the oars. Indeed, there was only one man standing on it. He was at the prow, looking ahead of him. There was something Arthurian about his posture. He might have been gazing into the mists of Avalon as the vessel bore down upon Breeze's yacht in deadly silence. His face was white but there was a streak of blood across his left cheek.

Behind him on the boat was a *grand guignol* arrangement of bodies. Hands draped over the side of the boat reached hopelessly for things they would never touch. Heads lay at an unnatural angle. Bodies sprawled without ease and faces wore the empty grin of death or the extreme pallor of a sleep that was indistinguishable from it. It was a ship of fools, drifting, lost in the Channel, and the one other upright figure, at the tiller, at the back of the boat, clung to it more for support than anything else for it was bloodied beyond all recognition. It took Hatchett a long, horrified stare to confirm that it was Peckerley.

The figure in the bow was Alec Lycett.

"Oooh, look!" said Jennifer Doran. "That one's had a bit of a pasting!"

They had seen boats, back in towards the town, where there was barbed wire and crowds of soldiers thronged the promenade. But out here, on Breeze's private beach, Norma and Jennifer had seen nothing for hours. They had been standing, scanning the horizon and seeing nothing but crowds of non-combatant gulls.

The boat she was pointing to was some way out. It seemed almost too tired to attempt a landing. Its mast looked like an abandoned toothpick. It had been broken off half-way up and hung at a crazy angle to the vertical. There were sails but most of them seemed to be scattered across the deck. There was only one occupant standing; but he was an extraordinary sight.

Alan Breeze had exchanged his peaked hat for a circular tin helmet. In his right hand he held a revolver and, slung over his shoulder, no fewer than two rifles. If he had been naval on the way out, thought Norma, he was now definitely in the army. As the yacht bumped on to the pebbled beach he waved his revolver menacingly in the direction of the shoreline.

"No funny business!" she heard him bark. "Back away now! Military personnel aboard! Wounded soldiers here! Back off!" Raising his revolver in the air he loosed off several shots. A small boy on the road above them squawked like a chicken and ran off in the direction of Dorset. "Casualties present!" said Breeze again, "Request assistance!"

"Mr Breeze!" called Norma, as the boat grated up on to the beach. "It's me! It's Norma Lewis!"

Breeze leaped on to the pebbles. The only casualty was his tin hat, which fell forward across his face. For a moment he staggered wildly, waving the revolver in front of him, then thrust up his helmet with the point of the gun. Still with the pistol waving in front of him, as if he expected the Germans to have got to Eastbourne ahead of him, he advanced up the beach. "Casualties!" he barked. "Wounded men here!"

Perhaps he thought that talking as if he was on a short-wave radio would enable him to be heard by more people than were in the immediate vicinity. To Norma's horror, he loosed off another shot. This one seemed to go surprisingly low. It whined past her head and struck a bus shelter up on the road.

"Sorry about that!" said Breeze, unsteadily. "Sorry now! Wounded men here! Back off!"

"Mr Breeze!" called Norma. "It's me!"

Breeze stopped. His jaw started to twitch. "Miss Lewis!" he said. "We have casualties!"

No one was moving on the boat. Neither Jennifer nor Norma made a move towards it. Although she had only looked once in its direction, Norma knew she did not want to get a closer look at its cargo. Breeze was still waving his gun around as if he had landed not near Eastbourne but in the heart of occupied Europe. He was lining up his sights, now, on a large clump of seaweed. "I'd like to see the squareheads suffer!" he was muttering. "I'd like to see them bloody dance!"

With which he emptied his revolver into the seaweed. It jumped around, thought Norma, rather satisfactorily, as if it were a sentient being. And Breeze, who seemed calmed by this unprovoked assault on a vegetable, allowed his gun to hang, limply, at his side. "We don't make war on women!" he said. "We don't make war on children!"

Breeze seemed to intend this remark for the benefit of Jennifer Doran. He was looking at her suspiciously, as if she was some trap, laid to entice him. Norma was worried, for a moment, that he might decide to open fire on the domestic-science mistress, for he raised his gun arm and seemed to be pointing it in her direction. Instead he let it fall again and started to cry.

Norma had only seen one man cry – her father, after her mother died. She couldn't understand how something as puzzling as death could make a grown-up face collapse like that. Her father's grief had come from somewhere deep within him, Breeze's tears drizzled on to his face, quietly wrecking it, happening to him in spite of himself.

It was only then that Jennifer and Norma went down towards the yacht. There were two or three dead bodies in it, one of which was the horribly mutilated remains of a quite young child. When Jennifer saw it she turned away and vomited on to the damp shingle. Alec was in the middle of the boat with his arms round Peckerley. Hatchett was on the other side of the boy. Both men were unharmed but Peckerley had caught something – a bullet or a fragment of shrapnel – in the chest. Alec and Hatchett lifted him and laid him very gently on the beach. All the right bits of him seemed to be there, thought Norma, trying very hard to stay calm and be of some use, but there was this hole in his chest.

"The planes," said Alec, in a dull voice, "they were firing at the people in the water." There was something different about him but Norma couldn't yet tell what it was.

"We ought to get Peckerley to a hospital . . ." she said.

Only then did Alec seem to see her. "Norma," he said, "what are you doing here?" His eyes turned to Jennifer Doran. "Jennifer," he said, "you're here as well."

"Yes," said Jennifer.

"Then we're all here," said Alec. "That's good."

Norma knelt down on the beach by Peckerley. He looked up at her. "There was a boy on the boat," he said. "He was only a boy. He was Dutch. Or Belgian. And the planes took off his legs. His lower half. And he just kept screaming, over and over again, 'Finish me off! Finish me off!' Over and over again. Like that. 'Shoot me! Shoot me!' And I shot him, Miss Lewis. I finished him off. Did I do the right thing?"

"Yes, Peckerley," said Norma. "You did the right thing."

There was a pause and, in the same whispered tones, Peckerley started again. "There was a boy on the boat," he said. "He was only a boy. He was Dutch. Or Belgian. And the planes took off his legs. His lower half. And he just kept screaming, over and over again, 'Finish me off! Finish me off!' Over and over again. Like that. 'Shoot me! Shoot me!' And I shot him, Miss Lewis. I finished him off. Did I do the right thing?"

"That's all he says," said Hatchett, speaking for the first time. "He says it over and over again. That's all he says."

"Yes, Peckerley," said Norma. "You did the right thing."

"I think," said Hatchett, "the Royal Sussex is where they're taking them."

Norma nodded. But all three of them knew, without saying, that it was too late for hospitals. Peckerley's breath was coming in great, harsh gulps. He looked up at Hatchett and he seemed to be struggling to see him clearly. "I'm so tired, sir," he said. "I'm so tired. I'm sorry, sir. I'm so sorry."

"What are you sorry about?" said Hatchett.

"About Cambridge Entrance, sir," said Peckerley. "I'm so sorry."

Hatchett squeezed his favourite pupil's hand. "There's time," he said. "You'll get there. One of the brightest and best. Pure alpha. Didn't I always say it?" He stroked the boy's hair with a tenderness Norma had never seen in him before. "*Cet honnête flamme*," he said, in a voice as low as Peckerley's, "*au peuple non commune*. You'll get there."

After that none of them spoke. There was only the sound of the waves breaking on the beach. They must have knelt there for longer than they knew, for though it was still light when the boat had come in, it was almost dark when they stood up and looked down at the boy. The spirit had gone out of him. Although Norma took a moment to realize he was dead. She looked round for Alec but he was sitting further up the beach, slumped against Jennifer Doran. He looked as limp as a discarded doll. Hatchett and Norma were the ones who closed Peckerley's eyes for the last time. They stooped to do that and they stood again, apart from each other. They still did not speak but were aware of each other and, all around them on the cold and empty beach, of the sound of the retreating sea.

12

"I will not," said Breeze, "hand in these weapons."

Norma had been trying for some minutes to disarm him. But the chemistry master, who had managed to get hold of quite an assortment of small arms, including what looked like a Mills bomb and a wicked-looking Bowie knife, from the bodies in the boat, clung to them like a suspicious toddler to a new toy.

"When the sausage-eaters come rumbling up the A23," he said, "I am going to be ready for them."

While they discussed what to do with the dead, Breeze paced up and down the beach, still brandishing his revolver. Sometimes he would wheel round suddenly, as if he was being stalked by an invisible enemy. Once or twice, usually just when everyone thought he was not going to do it again, he would loose off a shot and make them jump.

If he was the man responsible for strangling her headmistress and poisoning the rest of the Spanish department, it was probably, thought Norma, not a good idea to let him wander around quite so heavily armed. Once or twice, she tried to catch Hatchett's attention but he was preoccupied with the boat and the bodies in it. After a moment when she thought he would do something unusual for him – display emotion – Hatchett had become brusque and practical.

"I think," he said to Alec, who nodded dumbly in agreement, "we should simply push the boat back out to sea. I don't think Breeze is going to have much use for it any more."

A shell had taken off the cabin and part of the port side of the yacht. It was a miracle they had got it back at all. It was curious, thought Norma, how dead bodies seemed to bring out the best in Dennis Hatchett. If you had a corpse on your hands, Hatchett was the man to deal with it – from lady teachers to eighteen-year-old schoolboys. If she thought like that about the thing that lay on the beach – she still couldn't think of it as anything to do with Peckerley – it helped her to deal with the obscenity of it. What was needed now was callous practicality. Because there were going to be more dead bodies. It was, she thought, as if Alice Everett was the graveyard equivalent of the first swallow. More and more people were going to die in ways too horrible even to think about. Why get upset about the fact that Peckerley was young and rather sweet? What difference did that make? War was going to sweep away the young and the pleasant, the old and the embittered, and there was –

"Give us a hand, Norma!"

This was from Alec. He and Hatchett had their shoulders to the stern of the yacht. He hadn't really looked at her since the boat had landed. He kept glancing at Hatchett as if something about his friend had started to worry him. Norma added her own weight to theirs and the wretched craft started to bump down into the ebbing tide. As the water took it, Breeze marched stiffly towards the sea and stood, briefly, to attention. Then he unshouldered one of his rifles, pointed it to the sky and fired three shots. Then he came to attention again. "God rest their souls!" he said. Everyone looked at him.

After that there was the question of what to do with Peckerley's body. Breeze seemed to think they should push him out to sea as well, although he didn't suggest how they would get him to float. He became, in fact, quite animated on the subject. He seemed to think someone should try to get hold of a Union Jack and that they should "do the thing properly". Norma took him to mean that they were to wrap the poor boy in it. Alec played no part in any of these discussions. As soon as the boat was in the water he sat on the beach, staring at the shingle, not talking to anyone.

"We ought," said Hatchett, "to try to get him back to Croydon."

This, thought Norma wildly, was a kind of leitmotiv with Hatchett. His Universal Panacea for the Death of Intimates – ship the body back to south London. Of course, she thought, as Hatchett and Lycett began to wrap their pupil's body in scraps of sailcloth salvaged from the yacht, ill people, like animals, always seemed to think they would get better in familiar surroundings.

Alec still didn't seem to be looking at her or talking to her.

When they had trussed up Peckerley like a mummy, they somehow got him into the back of Hatchett's MG. Hatchett fussed around the body in a way Norma found almost unbearably touching, trying to make sure the face was visible and that the boy was sitting in what he called a "dignified posture". When she got in next to him it was hard to believe that he wasn't going to turn to her and make one of those bright, eager, Peckerley jokes or engage her in some topic he found passionately interesting and important. Breeze was still pacing up and down the beach waving his revolver.

"Shall we leave him here?" said Norma.

"I suppose," said Hatchett, "we ought to get him back. I'll speak to him." He went and took Breeze by the arm, pacing up and down the beach with him, talking in a low voice, before steering him in the direction of the car. Alec watched them. He was sitting in the front passenger seat. Norma and Jennifer were in the back, with Peckerley between them.

"How have you been?" he said, finally.

"Fine," she said. "I've been fine."

Jennifer leaned forward and stroked his cheek. "Poor Alec," she said. Then she turned to the body that lay between them and, to show she had as much compassion for the dead as for the living, she began to stroke his cold cheek slowly. "Poor Peckerley," she said. "Poor, poor Peckerley."

"He died for his country!" said Breeze.

"Get into the car, Mr Breeze," said Norma, unable to keep the anger out of her voice. Patriotism, which had seemed so uplifting and necessary this morning, was now, somehow, a less attractive proposition. Peckerley was supposed to go to Cambridge and win prizes and cups and be loved by people. She wasn't supposed to be sitting next to his corpse as it leaked blood into a sailcloth. Breeze climbed in and, winching his leg over hers, joined the party in the back seat.

"How have you been, Hatchett?" Alec was saying as they pulled away.

"I've been fine," said Hatchett. "Do you want to talk about . . . what happened?" Alec said he didn't want to talk about any of that.

Why wouldn't Alec look at her? Had she done something wrong? Norma tried to remember her last letter. She went over the days they had spent together during his leave. He didn't seem to be looking at Hatchett either. What had Hatchett done wrong? Pulled him out of the sea. Was that one of the sort of favours strong men were not supposed to be able to accept?

"Thousands are getting away, it seems," said Hatchett. "It's an extraordinary thing." He looked sideways at Alec, who, staring out of the window at the English countryside, did not seem disposed to take up this conversational baton.

Jennifer had dropped her right arm, in a cosy, conspiratorial manner, round Peckerley's shoulder. She turned to the boy and in a way that suggested she had somehow failed to notice he was dead, said, "You did so bravely, Peckerley! You did so well!"

How did she know this? thought Norma savagely. For all she knew the boy had been hiding in a ditch, blubbering, when whatever it was had torn his chest apart. What was she going to do next? Jam her hand up his jacket and start feeding him lines as if he was a ventriloquist's doll? Was poor, poor Peckerley going to tell them all not to mourn for him because a piece of him was forever England and beneath this dust was a richer dust concealed? And if he really had thought something so stupid, dead or alive, that made it all right, of course, did it? Perfectly bloody all right.

When no one accepted his offer of a debate about the progress of the evacuation, Hatchett glowered over the wheel and put all his energies into driving. He drove, thought Norma, with what was now deliberate carelessness. It was as if he wanted to show his friend that life in the south-east of England could be quite as dangerous as in the front line of battle. Indeed, there was something of the invading army about the way he forced the big green MG coupé to bounce through sleepy villages, rear up on two wheels across dangerous curves or blast through East Grinstead like the man in the poem who had a banner with a strange device and was not going to stop for anyone. They bore down on Coulsdon like the wolf upon the fold. At any moment, Norma felt, poor, poor Peckerley was going to sit up and ask his old French master to slow down.

And Alec still did not speak to Hatchett. He stared ahead of him as rigidly as his fallen companion.

"We'd better tell his parents," said Hatchett.

Alec spoke at last. "Funny thing is," he said, "I've never met them. I can remember an address where we sent a letter once but that's all."

"We'd better try that," said Hatchett.

Alec nodded.

Breeze spoke for the first time. "We should have given him a military funeral," he said, "like we did those other poor bastards."

"We didn't give them a military funeral," said Alec, in a tone that was quite new to Norma, harsh, wounded, almost self-hating. "We pushed them out to sea in that rotten dinghy of your father's."

"A soldier," said Breeze, "has the right to a soldier's death."

"Listen," said Norma, suddenly very angry, "if you think that murder in large numbers to the sound of military music is more acceptable than the kind of murder we punish by hanging, then –"

Hatchett was signalling to her to keep silent. When she did so he twisted back over his right shoulder (Norma was sitting right behind him) and whispered, as he juggled the wheel, "I wouldn't antagonize him. I'm fairly sure he murdered all three of them. It's a nasty business. And I'm afraid your girls are mixed up in it too. He's a twisted little creature. There's going to be a terrible scandal." He indicated the chemistry master, who, oblivious of what was going on around him, was running his index finger along the edge of Alec Lycett's bayonet. "He may be a perverted murderer," went on Hatchett softly, "but he is a heavily armed perverted murderer and should therefore be treated with respect."

"That's a disgusting thing to say!" said Norma, more loudly than she intended.

Their conversation suddenly became embarrassingly public.

"It was more or less Chamberlain's policy towards Hitler," said Hatchett, "which I seem to remember you supporting."

"It's all murder," said Norma miserably, hating him for his cleverness, "all pointless bloody murder."

"Peckerley did die for his country, Norma," said Hatchett gently. "There is nothing to be ashamed of in that."

Angry now with herself, and angrier still with Hatchett for, once again, divining her inner feelings and making her express them against her will, Norma flushed scarlet. "What are we going to do with his body?" she said sharply. "Do you suggest taking it to his parents? Leaving it in their front room? Or wheeling it round in a barrow and dumping it in the front garden of a local conscientious objector to shame him into doing the decent thing and going out to die 'for his country'?"

"Is that a dig at me?" said Hatchett.

"It's easy to be patriotic when you're a non-combatant," said Norma, regretting this remark as soon as she had made it. Hatchett became ominously quiet.

"Poor, poor Peckerley!" said Jennifer, and, once again, she leaned forward to stroke Alec's face. Norma wished she would stop doing this. And not only because it did not improve Hatchett's driving.

"I think," said Breeze, eventually, "we should all drive to his people's place and let them know he died a soldier's death. And that . . . er . . . he is in the car if they want to view him. But if they don't we can just pop him round to the undertaker's and tidy him up a bit. He looks a fearful mess at the moment."

"Poor, poor Peckerley!" said Jennifer, reaching forward to stroke Alec's face again. She now seemed genuinely confused, not only about who was dead or alive but who they actually were.

Alec didn't look as if he really registered this.

When they finally got him home, Peckerley's parents did not seem very interested in the fact that he had been killed in battle. It turned out, after Hatchett had spent ages working the conversation round, as tactfully as possible, to the subject in hand, that they hadn't really brought him up. As far as Norma could make out they had got rid of him as soon as decently possible to a distant relative. For the last two years the boy had been living on his own, which perhaps went some way to explain why he had been so keen to

299

join the Army, and why he had always been so reticent about them. But it didn't explain their dimness, their self-absorption and their complete lack of interest in anything that did not directly concern their immediate welfare.

"I felt," said Hatchett, as he and Norma went back towards the car after their visit, "that this was the first time they had been told we were at war with Germany. I suppose there are a few people who haven't yet been told."

"What's the matter with Alec?" said Norma suddenly.

He had said he wouldn't come into the house with them to see Mr and Mrs Peckerley. He had sat in the car, while they were inside, staring ahead of him listlessly, his handsome face bereft of all expression.

"We don't know what happened over there," Hatchett said, "and I suspect we shouldn't ask him about it."

"What's Alec like?" Norma asked Hatchett, abruptly. "What's he really like? I mean – is this what he is like? Really?"

"He's a complicated character," Hatchett replied. "It's very important for him to be a good person." Then, grim-faced, he had driven back into the village.

And now the five of them (six if you included Peckerley) were parked outside Japp and Smudge, the Crotchett Green undertakers. It was early morning.

"Right," said Breeze, who, to Norma's intense relief, had been persuaded to leave everything, apart from a few pistols, his Bowie knife and a Mills bomb, in the car, "who's going to take him in? Shall I?"

Norma looked around at the village. The things that normally made it so familiar and reassuring – the little houses, the lime trees or the measured ritual of tradesmen opening their shutters in the morning light – were suddenly lurid, unreal. Crotchett Green had become a stage set staffed by actors while events unfolded, not so many miles away, on the other side of the Channel. As she watched, Mr Japp, his features as usual expressing cautiously optimistic sympathy for anyone who might want to avail themselves of it, emerged to open the curtained door to his funeral parlour. "Who knows?" his plump face seemed to say. "Who knows what may be round the corner? Is there life after death? It is possible, you know!"

Norma had known Mr Japp all her life. She could not help thinking that he had already worked out that war with Germany was a tremendous business opportunity. People dying in large numbers simply had to be good for anyone in his line of work. Well, they had something special for him this morning, she thought bitterly. The first son of this particular English village to die in battle. Japp didn't look as if he was working out percentages, but he must have studied the war memorial put up after the last time we tried this method of settling international differences. There were liable, she thought, to be even more names on the next one, assuming there were enough local citizens left to erect it.

"Has the Army been informed?" was all the undertaker said, as he moved tentatively towards the back of the car.

"I don't think there's much point in telling the Army," said Hatchett. Perhaps Japp, thought Norma, was keen to link up with Army Burial Liaison, or whatever they were called, and prove his competence in disposing tastefully of the remains of patriotic English manhood.

"I think," said Norma, "we just want him not to look . . . the way he does . . ." She was trying to fight back this terrible anger that had not left her since that moment on the beach, a feeling that made her want to say shocking, wounding things simply to see if they would make her capable of feeling.

"Indeed!" said Japp, peering into the back of the MG with professional circumspection.

"We want you to bury him!" said Norma, whose shoulders were now shaking with her suppressed rage at the stupidity of it all. "Or do you suggest we take him home and wait until your staff arrive? Or write off to the War Office to enquire about the correct procedure for civilians to adopt when reclaiming undischarged corpses? Or shall I leave him here in the main street of the village and lie over the body screaming and screaming and screaming to remind all of you people that, when all the flags and the attitudes are over with, this is what war is actually like?"

"We would be happy to act for the military," said Mr Japp, with some dignity, addressing his remark to Alec as the one man in uniform, although with a nervous glance over in the direction of Breeze, whom he obviously suspected to be some kind of guerilla. "Mr Running did something for the RAF down in Croydon." He turned, with some dignity, to Norma. "You're obviously upset, Miss Lewis, I can see that," he said. "I actually knew the boy myself and understood he was liable to go to Cambridge on a scholarship. He did a holiday job for me."

His face was wobbling, dangerously close to an unprofessional display of emotion. And now Norma, too, was crying. She was leaning against someone and crying the way she had never cried since her mother died all those years ago. The someone wasn't Alec although, even as this was borne in on her, she realized she wanted it to be. It was Hatchett who held her in his arms. And when she looked up she saw that Jennifer Doran was holding Alec to her and that he, too, appeared to be in tears.

"This is not very English of us," she said.

"You don't always have to be so bloody English!" growled Hatchett.

"But I am English," said Norma, crying again and, in spite of herself, repeating Hatchett's adjective, "I am bloody English."

She felt better after she had been able to cry. For a while all five of them were positively cheerful with each other. Then Norma noticed that when Jennifer was talking to Alec she wasn't doing what she normally did when talking to anything in trousers, i.e., screwing up her face tightly, keeping her eyes locked on the man's eyes all the time and laughing at everything he said. She looked serious. That was disturbing enough, but when Norma said, in a moment of sudden panic, "I've just realized! I've left Rachel alone in the flat!", it was Jennifer who suggested that Hatchett run her home while she, Alec and Breeze went off together.

Rachel, she realized, was almost a child of their shared imaginations. As if inventing a history for her, and having to stick to it, paralleled the act of bodily creation. Hatchett gave her the quick, quizzical look that she knew meant "Has Mason done something you don't want to tell me about?"

And although she wanted Alec to say something, he didn't, and she heard herself saying, "Yes, yes, yes. Of course. Will you be all right, Alec?"

"He needs to sleep," said Jennifer, answering for him in low, thrilling tones. "He needs to rest and forget all that he's been through." She was, thought Norma, as much an expert on Alec as she appeared to be on the rest of Our Gallant Boys. Who were all, presumably, just as he was – helpless, haunted, hopeless, totally at the mercy of the cloying ministrations of people like Jennifer Doran.

Hatchett and Lycett carried Peckerley out of the car.

Breeze marched alongside them and, for a moment, Norma thought he was going to loose off a few more shots. But instead he obliged them with a stand-to-attention while the body was taken into Mr Japp's parlour.

"Well, then," said Alec, when the two of them emerged.

"Well, then," said Norma, and thought, *I am engaged to be married to this man. Why am I looking at him as if he were an exhibit in a zoo? Why aren't we alone together with him pouring out his heart to me? Because I am not the kind of person in whom people confide. I am a peculiar, rather clever, cross English schoolmistress and I am not really sure I love anybody at all, apart from my mother and father and my mother died years ago. Once you cross the line that divides companionship from love, the smallest action defines you. If I go home now with Hatchett, it will mean something horribly important. But whoever I go home with, it doesn't look as if it will be Alec.*

"I am going home," said Breeze, "into the bosom of my family. Back to the fold. I pray that what we have seen will stay with us. And I pray that when these German swine do come, as come they will, when they . . . slither up through Dorking and Leatherhead with their . . . vileness, I pray Alan Hector Breeze will let them know who is the real master race."

Now that she knew Breeze was a Hector, it seemed to explain a lot of things about him. Before climbing back into the MG he fired three shots into the trees on the far side of the village green. Rooks, rather than Nazis, flew up in a black shower against the lightening sky. They all got back into the car.

303

Now, to her surprise, and she could not work out quite how it happened, Jennifer and Alec seemed to end up in the back seat with Breeze and she ended up next to Hatchett in the front. Jennifer seemed suddenly to have developed a knack for appearing at Norma's fiancé's side as if she had been painted in there by one of those tricks of photography. Norma had only to look away for a second, with Jennifer at least fifteen yards away from Alec, and when she looked again there she was, all five foot six of her, craning her head up towards his face like a baby goat looking for food.

There didn't seem to be much Norma could do about this. She had never been good at creeping up on men. As far as Norma was concerned, you faced men square in the face. She was powerless against this slithering-under-their-guard business.

When they got to Alec's house, near the aerodrome, she wondered if she was supposed to leap into the back, gaze into his eyes and offer to help him up the stairs to bed. But she found herself unable to do so. When Jennifer got out with him, arm round his shoulder as if she was some form of government nurse, and said, "I'm just going to see if he's all right," with a girlish smile in Norma's direction, Norma found herself saying, "Of course! Of course! Of course!"

"Norma," said Alec, as he stood on the pavement.

"Alec," said Norma.

Alec looked at Jennifer, as if he expected her to tell him what to say. "I'll call you in the morning," he said.

"Yes!" said Norma.

"I am so tired . . ." said Alec.

"Yes," said a woman's voice. "I know."

To her surprise, Norma realized it was Jennifer Doran and not her that was speaking. Then Hatchett was driving the MG back up the hill towards Albion House. They didn't speak for some time. At last Hatchett said, "I see Miss Doran made her move."

"What on earth do you mean, Hatchett?" said Norma. "What on earth do you mean by that? Made her move?"

"Nothing, Miss Lewis," said Hatchett, with a shrug. "Nothing."

"No," said Norma, "nothing you say means anything at all. And you still haven't told me why you aren't in uniform. You pretended it was your heart on one occasion. But you haven't got a heart, have you? You've got a piece of machinery that pumps your blood around, that's all."

"It's a valve in my heart," said Hatchett. "It's not serious but they won't have me."

"I bet," said Norma, savagely, "you haven't even tried."

They were at Albion House now and it was dark.

"I'm sorry I said that," said Norma. "*Is* it serious?" Hatchett shook his head. "I am glad it kept you out of the Army," Norma went on. "I don't want you in the Army. I don't want anyone I love in the Army."

"No," said Hatchett. "I can see the sense in that." She fell against him then and started to cry. He put his arms around her. They stayed like that for a long time.

"What did Lucius do?" said Norma. "Why did they send him away?"

"I think," said Hatchett, "that he may have killed someone, but don't repeat that to anyone, for God's sake."

"No," said Norma. "No, no, no, no!"

She didn't believe him anyway. Killed someone? Why? When? When he was eight or however old he was when he was sent away? She would never get to the bottom of the mystery of what was going on between these two. But whether it was true or not she was strangely eased by this confidence of Hatchett's. Like Rachel, it was another bond between them.

"Murderers," said Hatchett, "look just like you and me. In fact, some of them look a lot more plausible than me." He folded his two front teeth over his lower lip, narrowed his eyes to slits and, by some extraordinary sleight-of-hand, managed to retract his hair into his scalp. "I sleek only to bracken leputation of fliend's flamily in order gain unfair advlantage over fliend in lespect of fliancée!" he said.

"Is that really true?" said Norma. "If it is, say it again without the Chinese accent."

"It isn't true," said Hatchett. "I thought it might be but it isn't. I couldn't work against Alec. The man is shell-shocked or whatever they call it these days. Isn't he?"

"I suppose," said Norma. Then she said, "Would you like to come up for a moment?"

Hatchett placed the thumb and forefinger of his right hand deep into his mouth, then inserted his left thumb and pulled it in a diagonal line across his face. He hunched his back. "I would like to come up, Esmeralda," he said, "but I am so ugly! And you are so beautiful!"

Norma laughed. "Actually," she said, "you are one of the most attractive men I know. I want you to come up and say goodnight to Rachel. She loves talking to you."

He did not need to be asked again. And Norma was glad of it, for the moment she got inside she knew there was someone else in her flat apart from her illegal refugee. The door was slightly ajar and she must have heard the raised voices, but as she pushed open the door she knew who it was because that whining voice had been troubling her dreams for weeks.

"So we need to see some documents, really," Mason was saying. "We need to see proof that you are who Miss Lewis says you are, because strangers in our midst, as it were, even if they are vouched for, can be a problem. You see, you just appear and . . ."

That was as far as he got, but quite a lot of what he had said was indistinct. He had only got as far as "documents" when Hatchett heard him and he had only got as far as "proof" before Hatchett did the thing with his shoulders that he did when boys hadn't done their homework. And by the time the man got to "Miss Lewis" Hatchett was half-way across the room. On "strangers" he seized him by his coat collar, on "midst" he grabbed him by the seat of his trousers and by "vouched for" he had up-ended him, his face on to the carpet, and was propelling him across it as if he were some kind of cleaning device.

"You are messing," Norma heard him say, "with things you do not understand. You have no basis for the allegations you are making. You are breaking the law. You seem to have forgotten that in this country people are deemed to be who they say they are until you can prove otherwise and until you have some rather better qualification than some lowly job in an unimportant ministry, I suggest you bugger off. Bugger right off, old thing!"

On the second "bugger", Hatchett kicked the door further open and hurled Mason, face first, down the stairs. After which he slammed the door and crouched by it, his right hand to his right ear like someone in a pantomime attending to noises off. There were none.

"That seems to have got rid of him!" he said eventually, brushing his palms against each other briskly. "By the time he finds out enough to move against us we have to hope our friend Frisch has sorted Rachel's papers out. I really wouldn't worry about him, Norma."

He said this with reassuring confidence. And Rachel, as she often did when he was near, gave them the benefit of one of her rare but beautiful smiles. Norma tried to look as if she had absolute faith in what he had just said. But, if she was honest, she didn't really have faith in anything any more – especially not in the idea that there was a kind of justice in the world that somehow, against all the odds, asserted itself and rewarded the kind instead of the cruel, the good instead of the irredeemably evil.

20 August 1921

"Can I bowl? Please? Can I?"

They were playing cricket now out on the lawn. Alec hated it when Hatchett wanted to bowl. He always threw at least two or three wides, which lost them runs. Although the two of them together should have been able utterly to defeat and squash Lucius and make him beg for mercy, if Hatchett bowled too much he had a chance of winning.

Alec very much did not want Lucius to win.

"In a minute, Hatchett! I will have two more overs and then I promise you can bowl." Hatchett looked sullen. "You are fielding very well," said Alec. This was not strictly true. Hatchett had already dropped one catch and allowed the ball to trickle through his legs into the flower-bed by the wall, which was an automatic six. But it was important to keep up the morale of the team.

"Just move in a bit," said Alec, as he measured out his run from the wicket. "He may lash out and we can catch him." Hatchett, who was frightened of getting the ball in his face, which quite often happened when Lucius was batting, moved a pace or two forwards. He still looked sullen. Alec had only been bowling for twenty minutes!

"It's my bat and my ball!" said Alec.

Lucius leaned on the bat and yawned. "And your stumps, even though you don't seem able to hit them!" he said. He looked across at Hatchett, who was standing with his legs wide apart, trying to look keen. "Get on with it, Alec!"

"I am getting on with it, thank you!" said Alec.

Although it was late, it was surprisingly hot in the garden. He was about to wipe his forehead with the handkerchief, when he remembered that Hatchett wasn't supposed to see the handkerchief.

Lucius had taken him on one side just before they went into the garden and thrust it into his hand. "You take care of that," he had hissed, "and try not to let your stupid little friend see it or we will both be in serious, serious trouble!" Then he had gone on and on and on about how he was the one in charge and Alec had to do what he said, as if he was a master and Alec was his pupil. He was the stupid one, thought Alec, as he rubbed the hard ball against his trousers. He would take a really long run and bowl a really fast one and get him out and Lucius would be served right.

He wondered whether there was any blood on the handkerchief. There would have been some from where the evil swine had been hit, he remembered now, because Alec had seen him wipe his forehead with the handkerchief. He had seen him throw it away as well but afterwards he had forgotten about that. Alec wiped the ball against his trousers once more.

"Move in closer!" he yelled to Hatchett. Hatchett moved about an inch.

Alec liked the fact that they always played at his house. He had been over to Hatchett's once or twice but they didn't have any garden to speak of. Once Hatchett's father had come out of his study and put his hand on Alec's head. He was afraid he was going to bless him or something, like he did in church, or give him that thing to eat like he did with the grown-ups because they had been confirmed. He would not now, of course, because Hatchett's father was gone and was never coming back, not ever.

Alec swung his arm round in a circle. Sometimes he was a fast bowler. Sometimes he bowled off breaks. Sometimes he bowled leg breaks. Sometimes he bowled googlies. Sometimes, because he wasn't really that good at cricket, he just ran up to the wicket and hurled it at the other chap's face. Today was going to be one of those days. He turned and got his brother in his sights.

He shouldn't really have told Hatchett what had happened in the woods. He hadn't, of course, told him everything. But he had told him enough. Perhaps he should start to suggest that what he had said had not been true. Hatchett didn't look as if he had believed it anyway. Come to that, Alec wasn't sure he believed it. He thought back, now, to that afternoon, and it seemed like a series of horrible, disconnected images. There was screaming and there was blood and there was fire, although he could not have said in what order they came. And there was his father's face! Oh, the way he had cried!

"Are you bowling or just messing about?" said Lucius.

By way of answer, Alec took two more paces, wheeled round and, driving his left arm down at the ground like the piston of a steam train, ran towards the bowler's crease, which was marked with one of his father's old jerseys.

When he let fly the ball he grunted the way Frobisher did at school but the ball was a full toss. Lucius squared up to it and connected, meatily, with the centre of his bat. The ball rose up in the air, away from Lucius on the off side. It climbed so steeply that it came back at a narrow angle down towards where Hatchett was standing, blinking up at the summer light, moving his hands this way and that as the ball began its seemingly endless journey downwards.

"Get under it, Hatchett!" called Alec. It was a thing he had heard other people shout. But it didn't seem to make much sense to Hatchett. He was doing a weird little dance, tottering up to the ball's line of descent then backing off. As if he thought this might help him, he began a sort of circular prowl around the places where he thought the ball might land and, while getting himself into the correct position to receive it, he occasionally took his eye off the ball altogether. Finally he settled for a stance that made him look like a Roman matron begging a cruel emperor for her husband's life. He stood, his behind stuck out, face screwed up against the light of the sky, and waited for the ball to come to him.

It didn't.

It seemed finally to have settled on a spot without reference to Hatchett, about six feet to his left, and as it bore its way down through the air with agonizing slowness it was hard to believe that Hatchett, hands cupped desperately against thin air, could not see what everyone else could see.

But his eyes, Alec noted, were firmly closed.

Hatchett was braced as if for some terrible impact. He had made the imaginative leap necessary to believing that at any moment a hard circular object was going to smash against his fingers and that was all he really seemed to feel he needed to know about the next few seconds. Although Alec was now screaming at him to move left or right or backwards or forwards or, indeed, in any direction that would take him away from what was so obviously the wrong place, Hatchett remained at attention in his Agrippina Pleads for the Life of Agrippinus Maximus pose.

He remained at his post long after the ball had landed. Perhaps he thought it was going to rise up and, with a hop, skip and jump, move sideways into his waiting hands. Perhaps he thought it was still up there, somewhere, and that for as long as it was he should be in readiness. Perhaps he had been turned to stone by the Wicked Fairy of Cricket as a lesson to all in how not to catch a ball. Whatever the reason, thought Alec, he was jolly, jolly stupid.

Sometimes he really hated Hatchett.

When he looked at his face, as he did now, he thought, naturally, of that other face with blood all over it. He thought of the way the face had screamed and the noise it had made as the flames licked at it, blackening and twisting like the fires of hell. Hell would be like that. You would be in hell if you had done wrong but it wouldn't ever be over like that burning, it would be burning that went on and on and on.

He couldn't ever say anything to Hatchett about any of this.

That made it worse, of course. Hatchett was his absolute best friend. But the only person he could talk to about it was the person who always said he was second, second, second. Perhaps it was part of the punishment to be alone with Lucius and this information for all eternity.

"Well," drawled Lucius, "shall I run or something? To liven things up? Or is your friend going to get round to picking up that ball?"

"Why don't you shut up, Lucius?" Alec shouted. "Why don't you ever stop being so horrible to my friend? Why are you such a bully and a – a tyrant?"

"Oh," said Lucius, leaning on his bat again, still not deigning to run, "so you're the nice one, are you? You're the nice Lycett, are you? And you stand up for all the good things and everyone loves you, do they?"

"Let's get on with the game, shall we?" said Alec, frightened of the turn this conversation was taking. He went over to Hatchett, who was still standing stock still. He seemed to be in shock. Alec picked up the ball and patted his friend on the back. "Jolly bad luck!" he said. "You tried jolly hard!"

"Do you think?" said Lucius. "I thought you were supposed to put your hands where you thought the ball had a reasonable chance of being instead of flapping around like a penguin with its eyes closed."

Alec knew it was dangerous to say what he said next, because there was always a chance that Lucius would tell things however dangerous they were. But he could not help himself.

"You're a bully, Lucius!" he said. "You're a bully and a thug and I am glad you're going away. You don't belong here and Daddy says he never wants to see you again and you won't be part of our family and it serves you right."

Lucius poked at the ground with his bat. "One day," he said, "I'll tell your little friend what you are really like. I will. And then we'll see."

"Shut up, Lucius!" said Alec. "Shut up!"

But, of course, he knew Lucius would never say. He wouldn't dare. He was family. He was his twin. He was tied to Alec hand and foot. He couldn't move without him. He couldn't have a thought that Alec didn't know about. In a way it made it worse – although that was why the secret was safe. It showed how horribly close the two of them were.

"I know what you're really like, Alec," said Lucius. "That's what you don't like. I can read your thoughts. I can see right inside your head. I am your twin and don't you forget it. I am your double and I know just how weak and cruel and bad you are. Never forget that."

Alec turned back to his wicket. He looked over at Hatchett before he began his run up. His friend looked as if he was about to cry. Although he probably wouldn't. Hatchett was quite brave, really. Soon Lucius would be gone and it would be like it had always been. One of the reasons he had to be sent away was because of things like he had just said. You couldn't trust him not to go around telling lies and getting them all into trouble, Daddy had said. Well, when he was gone it would be like it always had been. They wouldn't have to think or worry about any of these things. And Hatchett and he would grow up like two brothers and play cricket in the garden of Albion House, which was the best place in the best country in the world, and sometimes he would let Hatchett bowl probably too.

"Prepare to die!" said Alec. And ran up to bowl.

PART FIVE

Dennis Hatchett's Diary

16 June 1940

11 a.m.

Taken to peering at Mother through gap in door to living room. She is sitting on the sofa staring straight ahead of her. Today she is wearing her hat but not her coat.

2.30 p.m.

Mother still in front room in same position.

2.45 p.m.

Frank Phillips was on the one o'clock news with the news that the Man with the Ridiculous Moustaches and Even More Ridiculous Hat, i.e. Maréchal Pétain, has, like many Frogs before him, got down on his knees and kissed the arse of the Germans. France has fallen. The country of Voltaire and Debussy is no longer our ally. *Je m'en fous.*

The French do not make good allies. As far as they are concerned France is the centre of the world – or, to put it more precisely, the centre of the world is usually located in the stomach of the Frenchman who happens to be thinking about the question at the time.

A bloke I knew at Cambridge called Shorter reckons he can get me into Bletchley Park. They apparently need people who can do German crosswords. Some kind of codebreaking? You sit around all day with a lot of mathematicians – a breed I have always rather liked. I asked him whether I could try out my theories on probability and he replied, "The trouble with your theories on probability, Hatchett, is that they are all totally improbable." Still, encouraging.

Since Peckerley's death I have tried again to join up. This time I lied about my medical condition. Unfortunately they listened to my chest. No one will have me as an active soldier. As well as being partially heartless I have flat feet, appalling eyesight and an obviously awkward attitude to authority. I have had to channel my anti-Hitler feelings into participating, unofficially, in the campaign to re-orientate road signs in order to confuse invading Germans. I dug out an impressive chunk of metal, which Carter Wilson and I pinched when on a French exchange some years ago. It reads simply, CHANTEMERLE SUR LOIRE 12 KMS. That should really fox them. I and a couple of fifth-formers fixed it into the earth on the main road leading to Dorking.

Peckerley.

I don't think I have ever felt angrier about anything. I can't stop thinking about the poor boy's face. I have one thought in my head at such moments. I write it out now, alone in my room – I fucking hate Germans I fucking hate Germans I fucking hate Germans. There. So much for Immanuel Kant. He was a complete Kant, if you ask me. Feel better now. Funny. I don't feel at all scared.

Alec died too, in a way. God knows what happened. Maybe nothing at all. Maybe he was always waiting to die in just that way, from the inside, slowly. It started when he moved back home, after the week he spent in the psychiatric hospital. I went over to see him one beautiful summer afternoon.

Norma visited him two or three times in the hospital. Each time he turned his face to the wall and would not speak to her. She came out crying on more than one occasion. I, in spite of recent resolve to pursue object of affections without compunction, tried to make her feel better about him. Better check on Mother.

3 p.m.

Mother now in hat and coat. Could not face talking to her.

Where was I?

Oh – at the Lycetts' new house. I say "new" although they have lived in it for fifteen years. To me Albion House is still theirs. It smells of them, intimidates me the way their family once did.

I think it was the first time I had called on them since before I went to Cambridge. It was only as Mr Lycett answered the door that a thought occurred to me. He and his very angry, frozen solid wife might be a little angry at the ugly little boy who, in spite of his lack of a father, grew up to do quite well. His manner was deliberately distant.

"Alec doesn't want to see anyone," he said.

From upstairs I heard Lycett's voice. He sounded, for a moment, just like he used to do at Cambridge.

"Let him up, Father," he called. "I want to see him."

Mr Lycett stepped aside and I walked into the prosperous, high-ceilinged hall. The new Lycett house is on the road south out of Crotchett Green. There is even a picture of some distant Lycetts on the wall, looking, I thought, like so many people in old paintings – nervously androgynous. Quite a lot of them had distinctly shifty chins, and their mouths, on the whole, were too small. I peered at one nameplate as I walked past, to check that it really did say SIR SEPTIMUS LYCETT, BART. He looked as if he had done something very shameful indeed but was damned if he was going to let anyone know what it was. I did not give Alec's dad the satisfaction of being asked who he was or how he got the Bart.

Alec was in bed, staring out at the beautiful summer day. His room is on a level with a huge chestnut tree, decked out in green and stirring in the slight breeze like some galleon easing its way out of harbour. As I came in he said, "How are we getting on with Loosebottom's daughter?"

The childish nickname eased things between us. On the floor by the window was what looked like a length of lead piping to which someone had fixed what was either a bayonet or a carving knife or some subtle combination of the two. While I was wondering how to answer his question, Alec indicated it satirically. "It's called a pike," he said. "The male parent is in the LDV. This is apparently what is going to hold back the squareheads."

He turned his face to the wall then, some memory distorting his face. I remembered how he often used some such circumlocution to describe his mother and father. Mrs Lycett was, usually, The Mother, and his father, more often than not, "Mr Lycett" – the quotation marks indicated by a quizzical tilt of the head. That superficial calm and comfort I remembered as a child was really nothing more than a family with money.

"Loosebottom's daughter," I said, "is still as stuck on you as ever."

"Is she?" said Alec. "It's funny, I don't think she is." He rolled over and stared at the ceiling.

"I think," I said, "Norma would like it if you just talked to her. Told her what the trouble is. She really thinks she has done something wrong."

"She hasn't done anything wrong," said Alec. "She shouldn't think that."

"She does," I said.

"Do you remember Loosebottom?" said Alec. "Coming in in that ridiculous gown of his and sort of sweeping it round himself as if it was a toga. And that day he got us to parade around the Main Hall to represent different nations of the empire. I covered my face in bootpolish. Because I was South Africa. And you wore a Mountie's hat because you were Canada. It was not a successful hat, Hatchett."

I grinned.

Then he said, "We have to grow up, Dennis. We have to stop pretending we are twelve years old. This is the real world we are in. It's a quite horrible place, I assure you. It's an ugly, terrifying place but it is where we live."

"What happened in France?" I said.

I shouldn't have said that.

His face darkened. "Nothing," he said. "Nothing at all. Tell me, you haven't by any chance caught sight of my dear, dear brother, have you?"

"I haven't," I said, with surprising ease.

"He came home for a few days," said Alec, "and then he just disappeared off the face of the earth. The Pater says he's flying planes. Fully qualified Spitfire pilot. I think they are in danger of making it up. But now – he's just . . . disappeared."

"People do," I said. "My father did."

"He did indeed," said Alec, his eyes shifting away from mine, "and mine stayed around. Every step of the way. Do you know something? I absolutely loathe my father. I loathe the smell of him. I loathe his . . . masculine odour. I wish he would die. I really wish he would hurry up and die. You'd better go, Hatchett."

Obediently – some things about our relationship never change – I set off for the door. I was half-way there when he propped himself up on his elbow and, just for a moment, he gave me a look of such desperate misery that I wanted to go back to the bedside and do the thing that English men like us never, ever do. I wanted to put my arms round him and tell him it was all right. That I loved him and he was my friend. But of course I didn't.

"I love her," he said. "I love Norma so much. But it's no good, old bean. It is no bloody good. I don't know why. It is just no good." He paused for a long time and met my eyes, steadily, in a way he has not done since he was back from France. "I'm no good," he said. "You'd better tell her the engagement's off."

Then I left. He can bloody well tell her. But I suppose I will have to.

3.30 p.m.
Off now to meet Norma at a tea-shop in the village. Looked in on Mother. She has not moved, still in coat and hat. This is a world record for immobility, I feel. Had not the heart to tell her no one is coming for her.

6.20 p.m.
Norma was with Rachel, and Jacqueline Rissett, whose complexion has gone very yellow indeed. Could she have jaundice?

The good news is that it seems my bluff with the odious Mason is not going to be called. Frisch rang and told Norma and Rachel he has got clearance for her with some very hush-hush senior guy called Tizzard. He is off to Liverpool about some mysterious business of his own. He is making arrangements to put Rachel down for some scientific niche or other. The effect of all this on her has been dramatic. She was very chatty with Jacqueline and the two of them went off for a girlish rendezvous with Mabel Hughes, with whom they now seem very friendly. They both talked, as all the girls do, of the murders: although the current favourite is Mr Breeze, Rachel's theory that Miss Leach was "strangled by a lesbian with big hands" is proving very popular, although she had to explain to Jacqueline what a lesbian was. Even when she had explained Sapphism, Jacqueline did not seem to believe in or fully grasp the concept.

Just before they left I said to Jacqueline, "You know, after Miss Green was killed, I thought I heard you say something like 'It was just like it was in the book.' Do you remember saying that?"

Before this moment she had been fairly cheerful. But she went pale when she heard this. It was obviously the wrong thing to say. "I don't," she said quickly. "I have no idea what you are talking about."

"Jacqueline," I said gently, "I was sure I heard you say it."

"Oh," she said, laughing nervously, "it was just a stupid idea I had. That these were . . . you know . . . sort of copycat murders. Out of books. But it was a completely stupid idea. I don't know what put it into my head. Shall we go, Rachel?" She seemed absolutely terrified.

Why would that be?

When they had gone I went straight into it. "He wants to break off the engagement."

She looked at me. I don't think I've ever seen Norma look hurt before. She has always been very good at concealing her disappointments. For a moment I saw exactly what she was feeling. I saw not only her vulnerability but also her desperate desire that I should not see it. I looked away, like someone not wishing to intrude on a funeral. When I looked back she was quite composed.

"Well, Mr Hatchett," she said, "I suppose I shall just have to put up with the attentions of more unappealing bachelors."

I inclined my head. "Indeed, Miss Lewis," I said, "I intend to form the nucleus of a queue. After a decent period of mourning for the snub this . . . animal has inflicted on you I shall be round with flowers. And I have already acquired a list of your hobbies from among your acquaintances."

"I have no hobbies, Mr Hatchett," she said, "unless you count knitting small blobs of wool, coating them with vinegar and hurling them at passing strangers."

"But I do the same," I said, "except that I use fragments of rubber instead of wool and household cleaner instead of vinegar."

"Why, Mr Hatchett," she said, pulling herself closer in to the table and nibbling a tea-cake, "we must pool our resources." She stopped suddenly. "I did love him, Dennis. I mean, I think I still do. Do love him."

"I know that," I said. "And I love him too, of course. Terribly fond. Just am. Always have been."

"I know, Dennis," she said.

"Dennis!" I said.

"Dennis," she said. "Dennis! Dennis! Dennis!"

"Norma," I replied. "Norma! Norma! Norma!"

Which made us both laugh.

9.30 p.m.

I watched Mother for nearly a quarter of an hour just now, through the crack in the door, wondering whether I was sick in the head as I did so. I do feel extraordinarily remote from her. I suppose because I always feel she came between me and my father. Or perhaps because she is a narrow-minded Lancastrian woman whose only mission in life is to get people to scrape carrots the same way she does.

10.00 p.m.

Gone back for another look at Mother, who is sitting in exactly the same position. What age has in store for us! Really the kindest thing to happen after you lose your teeth (Mother's are displayed prominently in a jar next to her and she makes a habit of "popping them in" when anyone comes into the room) would be to be hit by a truck. Like all old people, the years have simplified her, stripped her down to her basic qualities. I think it is probably her that holds me back from really being myself with Norma. Oh, I can be charming and helpful and funny (sometimes) and even, in a subtle way, lecherous, but I can't be me.

323

11 p.m.

Went back in to see Mother and found out why she is not moving.
She is dead.

13

15 August 1940

"Did you think," said Norma, as she and Hatchett walked into Old School, "that you heard a shot?"

"I am always thinking I heard shots," said Hatchett. "The Germans are about to invade us. I was sure I heard a group of men sing the 'Horst Wessel Lied' on Croydon station the other day."

"I am serious, Hatchett," said Norma.

He looked at her over his glasses. It was a stiflingly hot day. Hatchett was wearing an oversized white Panama hat and an open-necked shirt at least two sizes too big for him. He looked seedy but also glamorous in some indefinable way. He was sweating freely. "Ah," he said. "Serious! This is serious, then!"

Hatchett seemed to see the prospect of a German invasion as a huge joke. The other day he had walked into the butcher's in Crotchett Green and, in a heavy Berlin accent, had asked the way to the Houses of Parliament. As the man behind the counter was new and hadn't met Hatchett before he was very nearly arrested. In the Queen Vic the same evening he asked, in a Viennese drawl, for "a pint of your English beer, landlord," and then asked if there was a good place nearby where a man could bury a parachute.

"From where did it emanate?" said Hatchett. "Was it on the roof? Do you think they may have landed on the roof?"

"It came," said Norma, "from the staffroom."

"Ah," said Hatchett, "they are shooting each other now. I thought it might come to that. Shall we go and investigate?"

Without waiting for an answer he swerved across the hall and started up the stairs to the Minstrels' Gallery two at a time. Norma scampered after him. "I hope," she said, in what she realized was rather a peevish tone, "that it isn't another murder."

"I was rather hoping," said Hatchett, as he stopped and looked back down at her, "that it would be. Perhaps another full-scale assault on another school department. A lot of us feel the mathematics boys need a touch of thinning out."

"I mean," said Norma, "that if it is another body it seems rather awful that we should be the ones to find it. People are beginning to talk."

"About what?" said Hatchett. "About the fact that we are always stumbling across dead bodies or about the fact that we are always . . ." here he pushed out his teeth and did his Chinese face ". . . together?"

"About both," said Norma.

"Let them talk," said Hatchett. "Teachers' corpses have brought us together and only teachers' corpses can tear us apart." With these words he strode down to the staffroom and yanked open the door. Norma was still some way behind.

There was a silence.

"I wouldn't go in there if I were you," said Hatchett, eventually.

"Don't be ridiculous!" said Norma. "What is it? A dead body?"

"It is," said Hatchett.

"Who is it?" said Norma. "Is it a member of staff?"

"It is," said Hatchett. "That is exactly what it is."

"Is it a man or a woman?" said Norma, feeling as if she was embarking on the first round of a game of Any Questions.

"It is a man," said Hatchett.

"What," said Norma, in level tones, "is his name?"

"His name," said Hatchett, "is Alan Hector Breeze."

Norma's first, rather callous, reaction was that she was glad it wasn't anyone else. There were male members of staff – Groenig, for instance – of whom she had become rather fond. Her second thought was that this probably meant that Breeze was not the culprit, but then Hatchett said, "It is suicide of a rather flamboyant kind. At least, there is a note in what looks like his handwriting. I really wouldn't go in there if I were you."

Had Breeze impaled himself on a wooden stake? Managed to pull off the first self-administered beheading in recorded history?

Had he hanged himself and done something awful in his trousers? Norma, like the man in the play, had supped full of horrors recently and there were times when she thought that the only emotion left to her was curiosity. That was about all she felt as she pushed past Hatchett and had her first look at the principal suspect in the Croydon Girls' School Murders.

Hatchett had not been exaggerating.

Mr Breeze was in full academic dress. He wore his mortarboard, his academic gown, his MA gown, his BA gown, his Northampton-shire County Cricket Club tie, which he was not entitled to wear, dead or alive, his dark suit, his white shirt and his frankly unpleasant Italian leather shoes. The neatness of his outfit was only marred by a red stain issuing forth from under the mortarboard. Hatchett tiptoed across to it and lifted it off as if it were the cover of a serving dish or a tea-cosy.

It was only then that Norma saw the revolver. It was on the floor, just below his right hand, where he must have let it fall just after drilling a hole in his head.

He had, she decided, made a surprisingly neat job of blowing out his brains. He was, of course, known throughout the school as a fastidious man, who weighed sodium chloride or brewed up dishes of potassium permanganate with fanatical neatness. He had also tactfully placed his suicide note at the other end of the table, so that Norma could read it without getting too close.

It was not, however, one of the great suicide notes. It did not have the lyric sweetness of DONE BECAUSE WE ARE TOO MENNY or the stiff-upper-lip charm of that chap who walked out of the tent in a blizzard and told the rest of the team not to wait up for him. It began in capitals:

IT IS A FAR FAR BETTER THING I GO TO THAN FROM WHICH I HAVE COME!!!!!

and then proceeded to demonstrate that misquotation was not the only one of Alan Hector Breeze's literary vices.

Dear Fellow Members of Staff,

I must apologize for using the staffroom for the purpose for which I am about to use it and for inconveniencing your schedules even more than they have been already.

I shall not be teaching again this term or any other term for that matter. For by the time you read this – assuming something does not go wrong with the revolver – I shall be dead. In fact, even if something does go wrong with the revolver I shall be dead because I shall find another way to end my life. I will gas myself or cut my wrists or take poison or throw myself out of a window or under a bus or possibly attempt a combination of some or all of these things. And I will leave this note where it will be discovered.

If I throw myself under a bus, for example, I will make sure it is on my person. If I gas myself I will place it by the stove – assuming a stove is what I use – and if I throw myself out of a window or hurl myself into machinery where my body may be so hideously mangled as to be unrecognizable or if I drown myself, which is another possibility, I will probably post it to some reliable person like a bank manager or a priest or an accountant.

I want people to read this and know and understand the real Hector Breeze, not the sham who played the part of "family man". The real Hector Breeze (the name my mother always called me) is not a very nice person.

Hatchett looked up from their shared reading of this missive. "Neither was the sham Hector Breeze, come to think of it," he said. They bent their heads back to the letter.

He was brought up by loving parents in the town of Ipswich and from an early age showed some aptitude for science, although the finer points of physics still elude him. He came to Croydon in the early autumn of 1931 –

Hatchett looked up. "What is this?" he said. "A farewell message or a novel? Or a curriculum vitae?"

Although it did not seem polite to skip through a suicide note,

Norma was strongly tempted to do so and she did not complain when Hatchett turned over the first of its seventeen pages and, muttering about it being important to get to the point, even in the matter of Last Words, ran his eyes down the paragraphs of fussy, spidery writing:

> *perhaps I will put a bag on my head and suffocate myself or possibly*
> *weigh myself down with stones or a heavy object and drown myself in a*
> *river, canal or reservoir, although I cannot immediately think of one that*
> *would "do the job" that is sufficiently easy to get to.*

He did not stop until he reached the words JACQUELINE RISSETT. At which point the manuscript deviated into something resembling poetry:

> *Oh, Jacqueline,*
> *The luminous whiteness of your thighs,*
> *The hot intensity of your secret parts,*
> *The lovely gash between your legs,*
> *Like butter and daisies and sweet white wine!*

Norma was in favour of skipping this but Hatchett seemed keen to study it thoroughly.

> *Oh, in that hotel room,*
> *Yes, that hotel room,*
> *There was no other,*
> *My love,*
> *We made love all night,*
> *All night in Paris,*
> *I emptied myself!*

Hatchett lowered the letter and looked at her over his glasses. "This," he said, "seems to be fairly self-explanatory."

"I don't think so," said Norma. "I am sure this is just . . . unhealthy fantasy. He makes himself sound like some . . . plumbing device. And I am sure that Jacqueline . . . I am sure that none of my girls would but I am positive that Jacqueline . . ."

"Jacqueline what?"

"Jacqueline couldn't . . ." said Norma.

But she thought of the time she had seen Jacqueline out on the street the night they went to see Mabel Hughes. Perhaps Jacqueline could. With the uneasy feeling that Rachel had been more accurate than she had thought about the overheated atmosphere among her girls she skipped on through the letter:

'electrocution is quick and is used in the USA as a method of execution and although I cannot think of a device which'

until she read the following:

'You killed them, didn't you, Jacqueline? Once I knew it was all exactly as it was in the books and, oh, my Lord, it was I who introduced you to the books, who read you those books, I knew it had to be you. It was too much of a coincidence for it not to be you, my darling, and I blame myself!'

After that there were another eight pages of rambling insanity. But the phrase sparked off something in her memory. Something that had happened after Miss Green's death and that Hatchett had brought up that afternoon in the tea-shop when he told her Alec didn't love her any more.

"The books," Hatchett was saying, almost to himself, "it is all in the books . . . What books, though?"

"I suppose," said Norma, "we'd better go and ask her."

"Indeed," said Hatchett, "but I am sure it isn't her."

"You are?"

"Because of Rachel," said Hatchett. "Someone who could do something good and kind, like helping Rachel in Paris, couldn't kill like this. It could be Breeze all along and he's trying to shift the blame on to her. But the worrying thing is . . ."

"What?"

"There is something eerily familiar about the method of these murders," said Hatchett, "even if I can't quite put my finger on what it is." He gave a bleak little smile. "Books can be very dangerous things," he said. "If I hadn't made Peckerley read all that romantic French poetic rubbish he might never have . . ." Hatchett shook himself and touched her lightly on the arm. "Are you all right?"

"I'm fine," said Norma. "I'll come with you and find Jacqueline. I think we should speak to her before anyone else does. Although first we'd better tell someone about . . . this."

She knew, of course, that he wasn't really asking about the murders. He was talking about her and Alec. She didn't want him to do that. She wanted them to be friends, to talk about their common pursuits, even if it involved them in playing detectives with her pupils. But as she carefully replaced Breeze's note in the envelope, she remembered how horribly entangling doing anything with Hatchett was liable to be.

Norma took one last look at Mr Breeze as they went out into the corridor. What was it that was missing in a dead person's face? She didn't like to use the word "spirit" but it was really the only one that would do. But spirit could go out of the living too. That, she said to herself, was what was happening to Alec Lycett.

It was Jennifer Doran who had done this to him. The last time Norma had gone to see him in the psychiatric hospital, where he stayed after he came back from Dunkirk, Jennifer had been sitting at his bedside cooing at him as if he was a Higher Infant and not a grown man. When he left the hospital and came back to school – there was talk of his joining another regiment but he did not yet seem to have done so – Jennifer always sat next to him in the staffroom, and at lunch breaks they would walk, arm in arm, round the edge of the cricket pitch, Alec with his head bowed, Jennifer whispering words of comfort in his ear. Every third sentence of hers began with "Alec thinks . . ." and yet, it seemed to Norma, since he had come back from France that was precisely what Alec had not been doing.

"Mr Groenig seems to be on his way to the staffroom with some marking," said Hatchett. "I do not feel he is in a fit state to encounter Mr Breeze. Wait here!" Surprised at her obedience, Norma leaned against the wall and listened as Hatchett broke the news to Mr Groenig. He seemed rather keen on "nipping in for a quick peek" but gradually Hatchett seemed to be persuading him against the idea. As she was waiting a boy called Fitch came up the stairs from the other side and walked, purposefully, towards the door of the staffroom.

"Don't go in there!" called Norma sharply. "There's a dead teacher in there!" Fitch gawped at her. "Another one, miss?" he said, in awed tones. "Who is it this time? Is it Mr Cavendish the geography master? Is it Miss Hornbeam?"

"It is . . . a member of the Science Department," said Norma. For some reason she did not want to give out Breeze's name.

"They're going down like ninepins, aren't they, miss?" said Fitch, his pale face full of concern.

"Fitch," said Norma, "Mr Hatchett and I are going to have to find the police. I want you to stay here by the staffroom door and just in case anyone tries to get in you are to tell them there is a dead body in there and no one is allowed in."

"Yes, miss!" said Fitch eagerly. He now seemed quite excited at the thought of more teachers dying.

Norma was not at all sure he would carry out this command. By the time they got back he would probably be selling tickets for admission. But Hatchett was already striding off towards the music room and she ran after him.

The music room was on the ground floor, at the end of a narrow passage that snaked off from Old School. But even before they got to the passage Norma could hear the sound of someone hitting the drum, aimlessly, without definite rhythm. Someone else was pounding the keys of the piano in much the same style. There was something angry and unresolved about the noise. It scraped at Norma's nerves as she followed Hatchett down the stairs. He turned to her as he pushed open the door to the music room.

As they entered Janet Frosser turned round from the piano. She

332

was one of those girls who had no talents and, as if to compensate, spent much of her time trying to acquire what her mother called "accomplishments". There had been a ghastly few weeks, back in 1936, when she had tried ballet. When she saw Norma, she pouted, shook out her fingers and carefully lengthened her neck. "We're doing a concerto, Miss Lewis," she said. Norma looked round but could not see Jacqueline or Mabel. Nor, to her concern, did Rachel appear to be there.

"Tell me," said Hatchett, "was Jacqueline Rissett in here?"

Janet and Elinor looked at each other. There was a brief moment of conspiracy between them, as if they were in unspoken conference about whether or not to release some information they obviously shared.

"She was with Mabel Hughes," said Elinor, "but they went off. Jacqueline and Mabel spend all their time together now. And Rachel tags along. She was with them too. They're plotting something at Jacqueline's house – down by the aerodrome."

Janet Frosser studied her nails. "Why are you asking?" she drawled. "Is it some vital matter of national importance?"

"Mr Breeze," said Hatchett, "has just shot himself in the head." For which he was rewarded by the rare and yet satisfying sight of Janet losing her composure.

"No!" she screamed, throwing herself into Elinor's arms. "No! No! No! No! No!"

"Yes," said Hatchett, slamming the door behind him as they left and marching decisively off towards the hall. Since his mother's death he had been a different person. He was far more confident and, this was curiously disconcerting, apparently quite uninterested in Norma. No – not uninterested, interested but not in that way.

Once upon a time this was how she had wanted him to be. Now that this was how he was behaving, she was piqued. It added an edge to their friendship, which had never been there before. Norma found herself, sometimes, doing something she had always hated in other women – playing the coquette. She seemed to be looking sideways at Hatchett in a rather girlish way, as if she expected him to give her a role.

"You go into the head's office and phone the police," said Hatchett. "I will go and find Jacqueline."

"Very well," said Norma. "Hatchett is in charge!" She really must stop calling him Hatchett. But it was hard to break the habit.

Hatchett practically ran out of the building, but Norma did not hurry back out to Mr Veitch's office, on the other side of the quadrangle, where the nearest telephone was to be found. She did not want to think about the fact that the murderer might be found among her girls. If you allowed your mind to dwell on such things they would block out all other thoughts.

So she walked very slowly out into the fake Gothic cloisters. And almost the first thing she saw was Alec Lycett standing in his cricket whites with his back to her about twenty yards away. She suddenly felt like looking at him, staring at him really hard as if he was a painting in a museum. It wasn't just his blond hair, blue eyes, his near-perfect jaw or his expression of quite staggering frankness. All that would not have been out of place in a Nazi propaganda poster. What Norma found attractive about him was a fragility, a sharpness that you didn't always notice in the things he said. He seemed, she thought, as if he needed a bit of looking after, but that once you had started the treatment he would manage quite well on his own. Just like the kind of pupils she most enjoyed teaching. Something of a misfit.

She had dodged behind a pillar in order to look at him, so when he turned to his left, towards Old School, and the sun caught his hair, he still didn't see her. She had an uninterrupted view of his profile as his expression changed. It was extraordinary. The light seemed to go out of it. That element of submerged cheek was drowned out by some unseen care. His shoulders hunched. His hair lost its sparkle. Following the line of his gaze Norma's eyes alighted on Jennifer Doran, who was coming down the hall steps in a gigantic green hat and a red dress that did not flatter her figure. She looked, thought Norma, rather like a carrot.

'Oh, Alec!" she said, in a babyish voice. "Are 'oo sad?" If this was the way they talked when alone, thought Norma, no wonder they chose to wander deserted stretches of the school playing-fields.

Alec, to her surprise, did not march up to her and thwack her round the mouth. Instead he said, "Bit sad! A 'ickle bit sad!"

"Don't be sad, baby," said Jennifer, reaching over to him and placing a wrist on each of his shoulders.

This move shocked Alec into some semblance of normality. The next time he spoke he was no longer trying to sound like a rubber duck. "Actually, Jennifer," he said, "I was thinking about me and you. And how . . ."

"How you're what, yummy umptious baby dear?" said Jennifer.

"Oh, about my family. Things I should have told you about my family. And things about . . . about what happened in France."

"What about what happened in France?" said Jennifer, trying unsuccessfully to sound as if she was interested in the reply to this question. "What did happen in France, dear?" she said. "I don't understand it."

It's not that hard to understand! thought Norma. People killed each other in very large quantities for no good reason at all! It's what happens in wars!

Jennifer moved her hand up and stroked his hair. "Men are so scrumdiddlyumptious!" she murmured. "So lovely and mouth-watering and . . . tasty!"

Alec didn't seem to be listening to this. He was staring over her left shoulder, as if waiting for another, slightly more articulate woman to show up. "We should get married," he said, in a voice that suggested a completely different form of activity – washing-up, perhaps, or tidying the drawers in the spare room.

"We should!" said Jennifer. "We should!" She spoke very lightly, as if she was frightened Alec might wake up to the implications of what he had just said and change his mind. "That's a very good idea!" she went on. "And now let's go and play cwicket, shall we?"

"Yes," said Alec, in his soupiest voice so far, "let's play cwicket!"

Suppressing a desire to leap out from behind the pillar yelling, "No, let's play CRRRRICKET!" or "Why don't YOU play cricket and I'll watch?" or "Not in that DWESSSSS, Jennifer!" Norma retreated into the hall as the happy couple, hand in hand, walked towards the main gate of the school. You thought you knew people, she said to herself, but you didn't. Not really. To her surprise, she did not feel any jealousy towards Jennifer at all. If that was all that was going on between them – baby-talk, marriage proposals and complete unawareness of and indifference to each other – then it presented her with no difficulties. That wasn't the Alec in whom she had once been interested.

Norma strode purposefully across the quad towards the covered stairs that led up to the head's office.

She almost had her hand on the great brass handle when she heard the noise of the aeroplanes. At first she didn't think anything of it. There had been planes overhead ever since Dunkirk. Once, she and Hatchett had gone up on to the Downs and watched a dog-fight – two planes high up in the blue, circling each other. The unreality of the encounter (they looked like two insects) had made a gladiatorial game of the moment when one craft (the German, as it happened) veered away, smoke pouring from its side. She had been unable to connect it with death. She had tried to imagine Lucius up there among the clouds, with his handsome face and reserved manner and permanent sneer of a smile. But that didn't help. She had tried to remember Peckerley but that didn't work either.

How horribly strange it was that even the moment when she had been served up with the corpse of a favourite pupil had not made the war in any degree real. Poor Peckerley's dreadful wounds had been grafted on to him by some absent conjuror; he came, complete with death, out of nowhere, or from nothing, anyway, that Norma could understand. But this noise, transfixing her as she turned from Mr Veitch's door, was, she knew, almost from the moment she heard it, meant for her. It had a bass authority that she connected with her father's voice at its sternest. It was a growl as menacing as Churchill's voice on the radio and it drew her, in spite of the urgent task before her, out through the quadrangle and across the lawn.

Saltdene School for Girls was famous for its view. Rebecca Proud, an awkward girl who had edited the school magazine in 1935 and joined the Blackshirts a year later, used to say that it was the only thing that made up for the awful uniform and the low quality of the teaching. Ever since the school had been founded, it had been such a prominent feature of the prospectus that there were those who said the buildings must be a ramshackle collection of hovels since no one dared put them on display to prospective parents.

It was, thought Norma, the sort of view that might well have moved Wordsworth to dash off a sonnet. The distant houses sparkled in the August afternoon. The grasses and lush trees in the foreground set off the ragged sequence of houses that was Croydon, far below her, making it glitter like the silver city in some fairy story. The afternoon sky was clouding up from the west as Norma looked up, trying to locate the source of the sound.

It took her longer than she had expected, partly because they were flying so low. She wasn't particularly good at judging distances but she would have guessed their height at not much more than a few thousand feet. These were not like the other planes she had seen. Up to now they had come singly and had seemed to inhabit a world as closed as that of medieval chivalry. These planes were shoulder to shoulder, like a rugby scrum, and they were larger, heavier-looking.

Her first thought was that they were reinforcements of some kind – some of "our boys", to use Jennifer Doran's phrase, perhaps from up north. There was something quietly purposeful about the way they ambled through the air, in the manner of cows going home after a hard day nibbling grass. Idly, Norma wondered if she could spot Alec's house. And, indeed, Jacqueline's. They were down there by the aerodrome somewhere, part of the cosy, suburban sprawl that, despite a year of war, was still England.

As she thought this, a long trail of what looked like vases trickled out of the belly of the aircraft at the head of the formation. It reminded her of the sort of disgusting birth process found among an unusually charmless species of insect. Behind the first set of vases came another. And now, behind her, were people from the school, Mr Groenig and Miss Bellamen, the thin Classics teacher. There was, also, a small group of fifth-form boys. Like Norma they were gazing in wonder at these strange clean white objects, scattered like spores from the huge steel ships, grazing the afternoon sky.

They were not landing. That was the curious thing. They had somewhere to get to; they unloaded their cargo and passed on to the south, towards the coast. It wasn't, Norma realized suddenly, anything like birth, as more and more of the white things filed downwards through the summer air. These steel birds were defecating on Croydon, doing their ugly, metallic business on the peaceful green of southern England, then flying on home. And "home", Norma understood, with a sickening lurch of the heart, was not here but Germany.

Of course, she thought, as the first bomb exploded – they're after the aerodrome.

The noise, when it came, curiously delayed by the distance, out of time with the flames and smoke like an awkward dancer, was louder than she had anticipated. It was as if someone had dropped a huge plate on a stone floor then tried to muffle the sound. But somehow the contours of the sweeping hill below her picked it up and bounced it back to her with such force that the watchers around her on the hill could not help but understand that the tiny houses suddenly snuffed out with smoke and flames contained people, like them, who only a moment ago had been safe and sound islanders to whom the sky was always friendly.

"I am being a Warden for Air Raids!" Mr Groenig was shouting, his English, noticeably more impeccable since the opening of hostilities against his native Austria, suddenly deserting him. "I must become a fire engine and report to seniors!" With which he disappeared off down towards the centre of the village. Miss Bellamen looked as if she had had a stroke. Her jaw appeared to have been yanked open with the aid of a fishhook. One or two of the boys seemed positively excited and enthusiastic about the Luftwaffe's efforts against their home town.

Norma could think of only one thing. She forgot about Mr Breeze, and about poor Fitch still stationed at his post outside the staffroom. Where was the cricket pitch? Wasn't that near the aerodrome as well? Alec, Hatchett, Rachel – all the people who meant most to her in the world were directly in the path of the bombs. She gazed down as the last of the planes turned low, dropped their terrible message and grumbled off after their fellow conspirators, and she saw that the worst of the damage seemed to be not on the airstrip itself but on the houses that were bunched together around it. Out on what looked like Purley Way whole streets were flaming and, already, in the far distance, she could hear the noise of cars and sirens.

Without a word to any of the people round her, Norma turned and ran down the narrow lane that fronted the school. She would try to find a taxi. She would manage to trap a bus. But whatever happened – even if she had to commandeer someone else's bicycle – she would try to make sure her girls, and especially Rachel, were safe.

14

Hatchett and his bicycle swooped down through the woods on Crazyman Hill towards the aerodrome. He was thinking about Breeze's letter. Books . . . books . . . books . . . it's all in the books.

Well, of course, for him it always was. It was a shared enthusiasm for Auden and Lawrence that had deepened his friendship with Norma when he was at university. One of the main reasons Lycett had backed out of his engagement, he felt sure, was because he had come to see he wasn't up to Norma's intelligence. In Alec's world, women were expected to be gifted with other things – second sight, the ability to read dreams, cooking, and knowing what men were thinking. Easy in Alec's case because all he ever thought about was sport, sex and himself. He hardly ever read a book.

Books, books, books . . . the murders were in the books . . .

Everett had been poisoned with hyoscine hydrobromide, Green with strychnine, and Leach strangled with a belt. There might be some kind of pattern to this. And yet murder was not, whatever Hercule Poirot might think, akin to a crossword clue. The very fact that he could approach the crimes in this spirit was probably why, as yet, Norma had shown no sign that she was prepared to allow him to step into Alec's place. She found him too cold, too calculating, too crudely masculine when it came to the emotions.

And yet these murders were entirely to do with the emotions. The feelings of these girls, smothered by uniforms, respectability, Englishness, were in fact as violent and uncontrolled as anything in a Jacobean revenge play. If he could begin to understand the emotions behind the thing then . . .

Jealousy. It was, he felt sure, something to do with jealousy. What he had felt, if he was honest, about Alec all along and had never admitted. Jacqueline was having an affair with Breeze. Someone was jealous. One of Miss Lewis's girls was a murderess.

That, now, was an inescapable conclusion. There was no one else left from the trip who could be a likely suspect. Why had he not talked to Mayhew? Her Gothic warnings might have something in them. What about Rachel? Was she a factor in the business? She had arrived on the day of the first murder. Hatchett was sure it was nothing to do with her personally but . . .

Hatchett thought about Rachel. She had come among them burdened with a secret that, he now knew, was more terrible than anything he could imagine. Perhaps he had been wrong in thinking that these were very English crimes, inspired by sex or revenge. These were unusual times. A bomb that could blow whole cities apart might inspire any number of murders. Had Everett, perhaps, discovered her secret? Was she a German spy? Were they all German spies? Had they been bumped off by British Intelligence in the form of Alan Breeze (British Stupidity more like)? What the hell was –

Then, as he rode out of the trees, the sky above him burst into flames. It must, he realized afterwards, have been thousands of feet above him, but at the time it seemed as if the bomb was exploding in his face. He wasn't aware of the sound. In fact, the first noise that affected him was somewhere between the crack of a giant whip and the roar of a huge wind throwing itself against the walls of a tunnel. It seemed an entirely natural phenomenon: as it blasted him into the middle of something that felt like the upper surface of a giant hedgehog but turned out to be a hawthorn, he heard metal hitting the earth and thought of rain, saw fire and light and had a vision of a thousand suns.

All around him the undergrowth was fizzing. He must move. He must move now.

He could think of no clearer illustration of the wasted energies of war than the sight of his bicycle. It must have taken him nearly five minutes to clamber out of the bush, feel himself all over to make sure he was still there then drag himself back to the road; but when he did so he was greeted with something that was closer to a philosophical conundrum than a method of transport. The Hun might not have made much impact on him but they had made a hell of a good job of his two-wheeler. An avant-garde sculptor might have created such a thing, thought Hatchett, and carefully labelled it THIS IS NOT A BICYCLE. The front wheel was the shape of a partially melted rhombus. Some hooligan appeared to have whiled away the time he had spent in the bushes by yanking out the chain and trying to lasso the handlebars with it. The spokes of the rear wheel were as splayed as a bad boxer's teeth. The saddle appeared to have melted.

Something salty was trickling into his mouth. He put his hand up to it and saw that it was blood. Ahead of him, to right and left, the bracken was burning, and down below now he could see the thin lines of houses fanning out from the aerodrome. Fairmead Passage, where Alec lived, was immediately recognizable because the gasworks lay at its northern end. They seemed to have missed that but the rest of the street was ablaze.

He must report. He must report to the Auxiliary Fire Service. He was a member of the Auxiliary Fire Service. He would need a helmet. Or should he report to the Home Guard? He was also in the Home Guard. He was pretty sure he was in the Home Guard (had he, he wondered, got concussion?). He would need strong shoes. He would need a big brown pair with toecaps. Perhaps he should go into town and buy a pair of shoes. By the time he had done that the whole of Croydon would probably be alight. My God, said Hatchett to himself, as he gazed at the scene below him, why us? What did we do wrong? What has Goering got against South Croydon?

The curious thing was, throughout all this he had been quite unaware of aeroplane noise. First, of course, there had been the singing of the wind on his bicycle – and now, he realized, something had happened to his ears. He felt as if he had just dived into a swimming-pool. There was also a ringing in them. A frantic, desperate jangling, as if a lone campanologist was trying to warn the whole nation of imminent invasion. Of course, that was what they were going to do, weren't they? When the Germans landed they would ring the church bells. Maybe that was what was happening. If they had come through the Dorking gap it wouldn't take the bastards long to get to Croydon.

The ringing in his ears got louder. It seemed to be coming from behind him. There was another noise too – a heavy vehicle roaring down the hill. German armoured vehicles were notoriously fast. Perhaps an entire detachment of Panzer Mark IIIs were bearing down on him. Wondering what the ethics of this were – did they automatically shoot civilians? had he got time to improvise a white flag? – Hatchett turned and saw a man in a huge blue cloak and an enormous coal-scuttle helmet, rattling a large silver bell fixed to the front of a red lorry as he bore down the hill towards him.

It was only when the truck screeched to a halt that Hatchett recognized Mr Groenig. "Hatchett!" he said. "Hatchett! Is that you?"

"Bombs!" said Hatchett thickly.

"Ascend, please!" said Groenig, holding out his hand. Hatchett ascended. Groenig seemed to be enjoying himself. The physics master was notoriously short-sighted but he was rising to the emergency well. Indeed, only someone who had as little idea as he about what was in front of him could have driven with the panache he displayed as he turned the wheel hard to the right, veered off the road, bumped over a heap of blazing gorse and smashed through a five-barred gate to rejoin the track.

"What were you doing there?" said Groenig.

"Jacqueline Rissett . . . Rachel . . ." said Hatchett. He was concussed or something. He recognized one of the firemen nearest to him. For some reason this fireman was wearing an even stranger costume than Groenig's. He seemed to have a helmet but it was not as other helmets. It was made of some kind of green cloth and didn't seem to offer much more protection than a schoolboy's cap. It was, he realized suddenly, a schoolboy's cap. He was a bit big for a schoolboy. He was all in white, thought Hatchett, as the fire engine bounced off the road again on to another bumpy path. Like an angel.

In the distance was noise. The noise of bells and screams and what sounded like cracking wood and falling masonry. He looked up at the peculiar fireman's face. He was an angel, Hatchett decided, who had come to take him away. He had the face of an angel. Blond hair, blue eyes, a good chin and remarkable ears.

He had ears that were very like Lycett's. And his voice, when he spoke, was quite incredibly like Lycett's. But it was only when he lowered his face into his friend's that Hatchett realized this was Lycett. He was fully kitted out in cricket gear. All he needed was pads and he was ready to bat. What on earth was he doing on a fire engine?

"I am so sorry," Alec was saying. "I am so sorry, Hatchett. About everything."

What did he mean by this? Norma? As he gazed up into the handsome, troubled face of his friend, he saw that Alec was, in a sense, an angel who had died and gone to heaven. For something had changed him utterly.

"I just made a mess of it," he was saying. "I ruined it, Hatchett. Oh, Jesus, you have got to be good in this life. Your poor old bloody father was right enough about that. I haven't been good. I'm second eleven, Hatchett, and that is the truth of it!"

"Well, one good thing you could do is stop squeezing my shoulder, old man," said Hatchett. "It is a little bit painful at the moment."

"I am – I am so sorry, Hatchett. All I think about is myself! It's true! And I think I did wrong to Lucius. You see, I have been having these feelings about Lucius and it is so complicated! I want to tell you about it all! Oh, Hatchett, I love you! And I love Lucius! And I love Norma! And I love Jennifer!"

How long, Hatchett found himself thinking, has he been out of the bin? And should he not, perhaps, be sent back in there smartish? Perhaps they should all be sent there. Explosions, thought Hatchett, as they rounded a corner and found a whole street on fire, explosions on paper, in the heart, in the head and now in the peaceful suburbs. Jesus, what an almighty mess!

The fire engine had stopped. Groggily, he got to his feet. About thirty yards over to his right he saw Jacqueline Rissett's mother, her hands falling away from her face, her mouth like an open wound, howling, "My little girl! My baby! My little baby! She's in there with her friends! With Rachel and Mabel!"

Jesus indeed, thought Hatchett. Rachel. Rachel. He staggered

344

out across the street aware of the heat and the terrible noise of screaming and, with Groenig shouting orders, he followed Alec.

Alec's house was on fire. Not only that, it appeared to be lacking a chimney, most of the roof and a substantial part of the façade. It was unlikely, he thought, as he looked at it, that his reproduction of Botticelli's *Venus* would have survived. He was just wondering about whether his selection of cups, including the Kirkby Grammar School Swan-Hargreaves Trophy for the Most Number of Wickets Taken in a One Day Away Match, had stayed the course, when the screams of the woman over to his left resolved themselves into comprehensible English. "Jacqueline!" the woman was shouting. "My baby! Jacqueline! Jacqueline!"

Until he understood that the woman screaming was Jacqueline Rissett's mother, the scene in front of Alec had not made any kind of sense. He had approached it, he realized afterwards, as a fireman rather than a home-owner. As he turned and looked at her face, though – the mouth stretching out like water on a polished surface as her hands beat out a rhythm at her sides like the wings of a trapped bird – he understood that he wasn't any more of a visitor here than she was.

That was when he started to run. He didn't ask permission. He didn't pause to collect a helmet or an axe. He simply lowered his head and ran for the blazing building. In his white studded boots, white jersey, shirt and trousers, he looked as if he was beating his way to the crease and his right arm stabbed down at the ground while his left forearm worked across his body, for all the world as if he was about to throw down a bouncer; but the sport Mrs Rissett thought of as she saw him breast her front gate and thunder towards the flames wasn't cricket but swimming. "It was like watching someone do a perfect dive!" she said afterwards. "The door had been blown off its hinges by the blast, you see, and it was on the path in front of him and he sort of bounced off it like a diving board. The smoke closed over his head like it was water."

As soon as he was inside the hall Alec heard the crying.

It was a girl's voice but he could not have said whose. Pain had

345

almost deprived it of humanity. It sounded, he thought, as he started up the stairs (it was coming from the rear bedroom of the house), like a fox in a trap. It was one word over and over again. But it was only when he was outside the room that Alec realized it wasn't an English word. It sounded, he thought, like German. As he strained his ears to catch what it said another voice – one he recognized as Mabel Hughes's, came over the top of it: "You'll be all right, Rachel!" said Mabel. Her voice, even in the middle of a burning building, had the icy competence of a professional servant. "You must be very calm! And listen to Mabel! Mabel will look after you! And Jacqueline!" Then, as he muffled his face in his jersey, he heard her say, in a kind of whine, "Mabel looks after you all! You know she does, don't you?"

The front bedroom was alive with fire. The curtains drooled redly, while the carpet belched smoke. No sense going in there. The box room, which lay between the front and back upper rooms, its door closed, seemed locked in urgent, private communion with the visiting monster. But the way to the back room was clear. Alec ran towards it.

The first thing he saw was Mabel Hughes. At first he thought she had grown another leg. Then he realized there was another body underneath hers. A beam from the roof (still attached to the far corner) had fallen across her upper chest, pinning her to the floor. It had caught the edge of her chin and she was bleeding badly. But she seemed eerily self-possessed. She looked at him as if he was an importunate tradesman. "You're Mr Lycett!" she said. "You're engaged to Miss Lewis!" She lowered her voice to a whisper. "Miss Lewis is a marvellous teacher! Miss Everett was a marvellous teacher! We are so lucky to have marvellous teachers!" she said. She jerked her head to the left and, directly underneath her, Alec caught sight of Jacqueline Rissett, her face that ghastly shade of yellow, her big, gloomy eyes half closed as if in sleep. What had she been screaming? And why was she speaking German?

"It's OK," he was saying as he tugged at the beam. "I'll get you out!"

The smoke seemed to have eased. The fire, capriciously, seemed to like or dislike patches of floor or wall: it took diversions and while at times it gobbled furniture or carpets whole, at others it decided to take an easier route, to dally over a delicious slice of bedspread or munch grimly at a chunk of chair-leg. In this moment of lucidity, Alec looked up and saw that if he dislodged the beam he might sever its connection to the roof and bring the whole place falling in on them.

There was no way round it, though. The girls were jammed into the side of the bed, which was sharp up against the far wall. He would have to move it. Alec stooped and, bracing his back, seized the end of the rafter. It was warm to the touch. Above him, through a jagged hole in the ceiling, he could see the roof, a smouldering attic piled high with boxes. If he got it wrong all this would crash round them like the walls of the Philistine Palace in Gaza. Alec Agonistes, he thought, as he heaved hard. "Mabel! Jacqueline! You must roll away from the bed!" Mabel was still looking at him in that detached, watchful way she had. "Now! You have to roll away from the bed!"

All this was happening so slowly!

It seemed to take minutes for them to move – and all the time he was pushing up against the end of the beam, forcing it back into the outer wall of the house as he allowed it a few inches' clearance above Mabel's right shoulder. Somehow or other the two girls slithered away from under it and, to his relief, when he wedged it back in place, nothing above him seemed to move. Alec grabbed both girls and, putting one under each arm, dragged them back towards the stairs.

In his absence, the fire had started on the banisters. It was dining, a touch pruriently, on the spindles; it was nibbling the thick, polished rail with hundreds of tiny flamelets that seemed to burn with the regular blue of a gas jet. They're like flowers, he thought, as he bump-bump-bumped Jacqueline and Mabel to the top of the stairs, crocuses or bluebells or . . .

Who had been speaking German? And what was it Mabel had been saying as he came up the stairs that were now wrapping him in fire on the downward trail? "You'll be all right, Rachel . . ."

There was someone else back in the bedroom. Of course, it was Rachel. The funny little girl Norma said was her niece yet who didn't seem, somehow, part of her family at all. The odd little thing. She was the one who had been speaking German. As he bump-bump-bumped his way closer and closer to the smoke-filled hall he leaned over and shouted through his jersey at Mabel, "Who else is there? Is there someone else back in the bedroom?" Mabel just stared at him, her eyes empty of expression. Then she said, in a flat voice, "My daddy says there's something not quite right about her."

Then they were out in the front garden. Alec had dropped both girls on to the grass and was himself on his knees, choking for air. He turned, once again, to Mabel. He didn't really know, any more, what he had heard and what he hadn't heard. "Is Rachel in there?" said Alec. His mouth felt as if someone had thrust a piece of paper down his throat then set fire to it and his lungs were dying in his chest. Mabel's eyes fixed on him. But she gave up the attempt to speak and fell back on the grass. Alec saw two or three people running up the path towards them. One of them was Mrs Rissett. He didn't wait to find out what they had to say but, without a backward glance, sprinted into the burning house. Whatever she was or wasn't, Rachel belonged to Norma, and Norma, he had known, all the way between the burning landing and the smoking hall, was the woman he really loved.

Hatchett was pointing the throbbing hose in the direction of number twenty-four when he saw Alec run into Jacqueline's house.

He felt a little like a urinating giant. Or, to put it more precisely, a small man holding on to a giant's penis while he relieved himself. He was spraying the Nazis with his bulging snake. He was weeing on the Boche. It felt good. As he thrashed the foam this way and that he felt a crazy urge to scribble with it on the sky and, to his shame, experienced the exhilaration he had felt at Dunkirk: something to do with being close, but not too close, to danger. All around him members of the Auxiliaries were dragging out lengths of hose and rushing backwards and forwards between the burning houses. Labatt, also known as the Village Idiot, was belabouring the front door of the only undamaged house in the street with his axe. Groenig, his helmet cocked over one eye and his cloak flapping behind him like Dracula's, was barking orders – in a mixture of German and English – to the few people who would listen to him.

"Number twelve," said Welch, the Fireman Who Desperately Wanted to Drive, "is done to a bloody crisp!" Hatchett followed the line of his gaze and, with a jolt, remembered that there were people inside these buildings. The extraordinary pointlessness of what had just occurred struck him forcibly. The money, the time, the effort, the thought, the planning, the care, the love that people put into killing each other, he thought, as he moved slightly closer to Jacqueline's house.

Fortunately he was not directing the jet of water anywhere near the front door when Alec emerged with the two girls in his arms, otherwise he might have knocked him straight back into the flames.

He looked, as usual, sickeningly perfect. Just for a moment, Hatchett thought he understood that sneer Lucius had perfected all those years ago, on the afternoon when he and Alec had come in from the wood behind Albion House. He must have felt overshadowed by Alec. It was Alec, after all, who had displaced him in Alec Senior's affections. All that stuff about being older, stronger, better was the desperate talk of someone who had been left behind. And now Lucius was in the RAF. Shed not a tear for Johnny Head-in-Air. More and more, as their lives unfolded, Hatchett was ready to see Lucius as the victim.

Oh, he was still dazzled by Alec. But just as civilized behaviour could sometimes only be enforced by its direct opposite, so affection, of the kind he felt for Alec, could only survive, or grow stronger, by acknowledging that what one sometimes felt for boon companions was pure dislike. There was something so cockily perfect about the way Alec emerged from the flames, his profile unsinged, his blue eyes raking the crowd as if expecting the approval that greeted his overs, his innings, his goals, his tries and his final sprints. You golden English boy, thought Hatchett, as the throbbing snake he clutched in his hands pulsed out white water in Alec's general direction (was there some unhealthy Freudian significance in the fact that he was now spraying the life-saving fluid dangerously close to his old friend's upturned face?). You stuck-up, good-looking, morally untarnished, returned not-quite-war-hero – why don't you hop off back to the war zone and get yourself killed for King and Country as soon as decently possible, leaving the field clear for the rest of us shabby mortals to get on with our lives and have a clear run at your girlfriend?

Alec had laid the two girls, one of whom seemed to be Mabel Hughes, out on the grass, and, very, very slowly, started to get up again. He really was, thought Hatchett, a very good-looking man. Blast him! Uncomfortably aware, now, of the sexual jealousy that had eaten away at their friendship, Hatchett jerked his hose wildly off to the right and very nearly blasted Mr Groenig off his feet. What was the man doing now? He wasn't, he surely wasn't, going back inside the house, was he? That was the kind of thing people did in propaganda films, wasn't it?

He bloody was.

As Hatchett watched, Alec went up the garden path towards where the front door would have been if it had not been smouldering on Mrs Rissett's lawn. Without looking to right or left he walked, almost dreamily, into the burning house and disappeared from view. "Alec!" Hatchett heard somebody cry, and then again. "Alec!" He turned to see Norma, standing a little way away from the fire truck, next to Mrs Rissett. "It's Rachel!" she screamed at him. "Rachel's in there!" Hatchett did not wait to ask questions. He laid the pulsing tube of water gently on the ground. He didn't feel particularly brave. Neither, by the same token, did he feel particularly frightened. He simply knew that now, as of this moment, he had no alternative but to follow Alec Lycett into the burning house. Which was what he did.

15

"What," said Jennifer Doran to Norma, "is happening?"

She was still wearing the red dress and the large green hat. And her manner was still that of a well-bred ignoramus watching a sporting event from the safety of the boundary. Somewhere along the way she seemed to have acquired a pair of white gloves. Perhaps, thought Norma, this was what she thought you put on for a bombing. She was, as so often at social gatherings, peering over Norma's shoulder in the hope of seeing someone more interesting. As Norma watched her, Jennifer fluttered her chubby fingers at one of the firemen, who, although he was half-way up a ladder with a large hose, seemed glad of her attention. By now quite a large group of people had gathered. "I think I know him!" she said to Norma, and then, "He's rather delish! Where's Alec?"

At first, Norma could not bring herself to reply. It had taken her so long to realize she disliked Jennifer that she now had no way of letting her know that she did. Not, she thought bitterly, that she seemed to be equipped with any technique for letting people know what she felt about them. She certainly hadn't managed very well with Hatchett or Lycett, had she? Eventually she said, in a level voice, "Alec went into Jacqueline Rissett's house and rescued Jacqueline and Mabel Hughes and then he went back in because my niece is trapped in there. Hatchett went in after him. So now they're both in number twenty-two."

They both looked at number twenty-two. It was not an address to detain any right-minded individual for long. Most of the roof seemed to have gone. The chimney breast looked as if it might topple into the street at any moment. The front downstairs parlour, which Mrs Rissett had kept for best, swirled with smoke. The hall and what you could see of the stairs were crackling merrily. "Oh, no!" said Jennifer, and then, in case Norma hadn't heard, she added, "Oh, no! No! No! No!"

She met Norma's dry eyes with her incipiently moist ones. "He proposed to me this afternoon," she said to Norma. "He wanted me to become his bride!" Overcome by this form of words she began to sob freely on behalf of both of them. "I know you loved him, Norma," she said, "but he wanted me to be his bride. We were to be man and wife. I loved him so much and he is trapped, trapped, trapped in the rubble."

"He may be trapped in the rubble," said Norma, with a slight touch of acid in her tones, "but we don't want to use the past tense until we have evidence that he is actually dead."

Jennifer held her gaze for a moment, then went off once more into floods of tears.

Norma looked at Mrs Rissett's once spotless hallway and saw a standard lamp lean drunkenly against half a table. On the wall behind it a mirror had grown a spider's web of cracks. Cautiously, aware that behind her Mr Groenig was shouting something, she moved closer – so that she could see up the stairs. The smoke hurt her eyes, but not enough to stop her noticing that a large pile of debris on the upper landing appeared to be moving of its own accord.

It was then that she heard Hatchett's voice. It seemed to be coming from inside the rubbish. "Keep calm!" it said. "There is no need to panic!"

As she watched, through the remains of what must have been a wardrobe came Hatchett's helmet, like a seal breaking the surface of the water, and, in due course, Hatchett himself, with his glasses, his strong, cherubic face and his air of slightly puzzled intelligence. "Leave in an orderly fashion!" he said, and then, "Norma! What are you doing here?" He was clutching a leather-bound, looseleafed book. A diary of some kind?

In spite of herself, Norma found she was laughing. "Hatchett," she said, "what are you doing there?"

"It makes a change," said Hatchett, "from trying to explain the use of the subjunctive to people who think that a mood is something you have if your dinner doesn't arrive on time."

"Where is Alec?" came Jennifer Doran's voice behind her.

"He's somewhere up there," said Hatchett.

Jennifer clutched Norma's arm. "You mean . . ." she said ". . . he's . . . with the angels . . ." All around her the fire seemed to have died down. Perhaps that was why they were the only people there.

"No," said Hatchett, "I mean he's . . . up there. In the bedroom."

That was when Alec Lycett appeared out of the smoke billowing around on the landing. His cricket whites were blackened with soot. His blond hair was streaked with ashes. And in his arms was the girl Norma had first seen on the cross-Channel ferry a year ago. Rachel's curls lay in the crook of his elbow and, as he stepped carefully down the stairs, Alec stroked them tenderly away from her face. "She's OK," he said to Norma. Then he took her out into the light and laid her on the grass.

"Darling!" squeaked Jennifer, running at Alec like a rugby player going in for a tackle. "Darling!" She very nearly knocked him over as she leaped towards his now vacant arms. "Darling darling darling Alec!"

Norma knelt down by Rachel. Mr Groenig, she realized, was on the other side of her. Hatchett seemed to be standing a little way away, his face buried in the book he had rescued from the house.

"Is she all right?" said Norma to Mr Groenig.

"She'll be fine," said Mr Groenig.

Rachel's eyes opened. *"Ich komme gleich!"* she said. Then she spoke more German. It sounded long and complicated.

Mr Groenig listened to it with interest. "Yes," he said gently. "Your niece speaks excellent German."

"She isn't my niece," said Norma, with a wonderful sense of relief at the way Rachel's terrible secret had saved her from internment. "She's Jewish. She's a refugee from the Nazis and she has no papers, but it's OK. We are getting papers for her."

"It's OK," said Mr Groenig. "I know all about Rachel. I teach her physics. Or, rather, she teaches me. As it happens my uncle knew people she knew in Germany. She, of course, had not told

353

me anything until Hatchett heard it was safe from Otto Frisch but now I look forward to having conversations with her on many subjects. You have a remarkable girl here, Miss Lewis. She is something very precious indeed. She understands things I have tried all my life to understand. She will do great things in science, I know she will. You should be proud of your niece. Even if she is not your niece."

"I am," said Norma, feeling deep shame that she had ever doubted the girl, "I really am. And if she wants to be my niece, then I would love to have her."

"Yes," said Groenig, "and perhaps I am no longer the Funny Foreigner with the Big Nose!"

"You are a funny foreigner with a big nose, Mr Groenig," said Norma, "but I love you for it." And she stood up on tiptoe and kissed the old man on the cheek. He flushed with pleasure. Then Hatchett came up behind her and said something about taking the girls to the hospital, and after that Norma, too, felt in danger of betraying her emotions, so she stood a little away from the rest of them until she felt quite composed and able to be the person they expected her to be.

Dennis Hatchett was looking at Jacqueline Rissett's diary as he paced up and down the ward, waiting for her to wake up. His tin hat was perched on his head. The left-hand strut of his glasses had snapped and one lens clung unaided to his substantial nose. His hair had been blown in countless different directions then set in a series of tufts and tangles that gave him the look of an owl that had been woken too soon. But no one questioned him or tried to stop him. Even when not actually teaching, Hatchett had the natural authority of the schoolmaster.

Jacqueline, Rachel and Mabel had been put in beds next to each other. Rachel, too, was asleep. Only Mabel, her black eyes on Hatchett's face, was sitting up, straight and composed. She watched Hatchett and Jacqueline like some anxious, over-correct chaperone. She doesn't, thought Hatchett, like me. He was not sure if she liked any kind of man.

354

Norma was next to Rachel, stroking her forehead and whispering to her. She made a good nurse, he thought. Just the job to wake up to – cool hands soothing your brow and starched white linen crackling in your ears as you came round after the operation. He opened Jacqueline's diary, burnt at the edges by the flames:

1 September [he read]
HE was coming out of the staffroom today. HE smiled at me and I smiled back. I am sure other people know about US but I don't care. I don't care that Everett is dead. It served her right for snooping. She was a wicked woman I think. When I see HIM I go all hot and think about that room in France with the blinds drawn and the heat outside in the street. What we did wasn't bad. It wasn't. Things you want so much can't be bad.

15 December
I'm very frightened. Both murders were exactly as they were in the books we read. And for a moment I thought they were our secret, that it meant somehow that only we knew about them. But, of course, any number of people could have read them and had the idea. I should never have said that to Mabel about HIM and Everett. She is so angry with me. I did not think she would be quite so furious. When she is angry she can be really frightening.

He flicked through the pages until he found:

15 February
All three murders the same thing! The belt now! All in the books! All in the books! The books we read!

The word ''books'' was underlined heavily wherever it appeared.

It was most likely that Breeze was trying to shift the blame away from himself, thought Hatchett. He simply didn't believe a girl like this could have done it. Now that she was asleep you could see the yellow in her face more clearly. Her mother had said there was something wrong with her liver. She wasn't strong enough to strangle Gentleman Jim. Although it might have been that she and Breeze were in it together.

No, no, no, no. He had made her his accomplice in an entirely different crime, one over which the poor girl had no control. He had not been an inspiring individual, had Alan Hector Breeze. In a way Hatchett felt guilty at disturbing her, but someone would have to break the news and it might be that he would do it more tactfully than most. At any rate, he did not feel inclined to judge the poor little thing. She was waking up now. A delicate fluttering of the eyelids. Mabel Hughes leaned over and hissed at him, "She's not well enough to be disturbed!"

"She'll be all right, Mabel," said Hatchett. "I only need to talk to her for a couple of minutes. You get some rest."

Mabel showed no inclination to do anything of the kind. She leaned up on one elbow and glared balefully at him as if she expected him to club her friend to death.

Hatchett moved his chair round so that he was presenting her with his back but he could still feel her looking at him. "Jacqueline," he said softly, "Mr Breeze said you read books together. What books did you read?"

She was hardly awake yet.

"Jacqueline," said Hatchett gently, "we know all about you and Mr Breeze. We know what happened. We know that is why you told Mabel that Miss Everett and Mr Breeze were . . ." Jacqueline's eyes were terrified. Hatchett touched her arm. "It's all right, Jacqueline. You didn't do anything wrong. He did something very, very wrong. You didn't. We just want you to help us."

"Love is a beautiful thing, Mr Hatchett," said Jacqueline, in a tiny voice. "You told us that."

"Did I?" said Hatchett, wondering where and when he had done so. "If I said it it must be right, mustn't it? I'm a teacher. Look – I'm afraid Mr Breeze is dead." Jacqueline's eyes widened. She lost control of her mouth. She pawed at the sheet, pathetically. Hatchett, trying not to allow himself to be influenced by her large eyes, her look of a helpless puppy and the misery in all the lines of her delicate face, talked on without really knowing what he was saying.

"The thing is, Jacqueline, he left a letter and the murders, you see, are something to do with the thing we were talking about ages ago in that tea-shop, you remember? When you said or, rather, I said you said something about it being 'just like in the books'. What books, Jacqueline?"

"Dead?" she said, starting to cry. "He can't be dead. And . . ." she looked about her wildly ". . . what do you mean 'in the books'? What books? What are you saying? He can't be dead, can he? Why are you saying those horrible things? What books are you talking about, you stupid man?" Her voice was rising in pitch. Behind him he heard Mabel Hughes say that he must go, he was upsetting her. She would call the sister.

"I am calling Sister!" hissed Mabel. "You shouldn't come here and say those things to her!"

Hatchett turned. The sister, in full sail, was coming down the ward towards him. He had better go. The new, sensitive Hatchett had not made much of a success of his first outing. Norma was getting up and Rachel still appeared to be asleep. But it was Mabel who held his attention. Her black eyes were as alive as a cat's and she was practically spitting as she said, "I heard you! I heard what you said! You were talking about dirty things, weren't you? You were saying bad things like she said about Miss Everett and Mr Breeze! But I don't blame Jacqueline! I don't blame poor Jacqueline because she was led astray, wasn't she? By a man. Don't think I don't know about Mr Breeze because I do. Because Miss Everett was right – all you men think about is one thing and one thing only! You're horrible, dirty, disgusting, and we don't want anything to do with you and it's all your fault that poor Miss Everett was killed, isn't it? Because you started a dirty rumour!" She was screaming now, as Hatchett and Norma beat a retreat down the ward, pursued by a very angry-looking sister. "Get out! Get out! Get out!" yelled the normally so-correct Mabel Hughes. "Get out! You . . . dirty . . . horrible . . . disgusting . . . man!!"

Hatchett and Norma walked together out of the hospital and down into the still-burning fringes of the town. They didn't say anything until they were in the car and driving away from the hospital. It was Norma who spoke first, as she looked across towards Purley Way where columns of smoke were still rising in the summer night.

"The only books that Breeze and Jacqueline Rissett had in common," she said, "were Agatha Christie. All they read were Agatha Christies. It was Breeze who persuaded her to read them."

"Good God!" said Hatchett. "I never thought of that! I shall have to read some."

"If you're interested in murder," said Norma drily, "I am told they are remarkably informative on the subject."

The two of them drove, in Hatchett's MG, back towards the scene of the bombing. "I can't believe," said Norma, after a while, "that Jacqueline has anything to do with any of this." Hatchett stared moodily out of the window. She wished now she hadn't said that thing about Agatha Christie. Agatha Christie didn't have anything to do with real-life murder. Agatha Christie was like the crossword puzzles that Hatchett loved so much. Anyway, he never read Agatha Christie. Hatchett only read great literature, preferably in French or German. They were getting closer to the aerodrome. In one house, the whole front wall had been surgically removed, leaving the upper rooms undamaged but exposed to general view. A large black Labrador was sitting next to a dining-table, still laid for the evening meal. There was no sign of anyone else. They turned into Alec's road. The firemen were gone. Here and there shattered-looking groups of people stood or sat talking quietly.

"She was in love with him," Hatchett said quietly. "Love makes you do strange things."

"And all those other people?" said Norma. "This was done by someone . . . I don't know . . . someone truly . . . wicked!"

"All we have in the way of motive," he said, "is the business with Jacqueline and Breeze."

"Did you see Mabel?" said Norma. "Her eyes? The way she screamed at you? I knew she was fond of Everett but I didn't know she'd . . ."

"She'd what?" said Hatchett.

"Oh, I don't know," said Norma. "I think people like Everett and Breeze are two of a kind. Twisted schoolteachers who get children and teach them to conform to their – their ways."

"You mean their sexuality?" said Hatchett, as he pulled the car into the kerb. "I thought all schoolteachers did that. You're probably right, though. Everett and Mabel Hughes's relationship was quite as sick as Breeze and Jacqueline's. Two mad females!"

She heard a voice at the open window. "Who's a mad female? Is it you, Norma?"

It was Jennifer. Still wearing the hat and with Alec at her side. Hatchett sighed to himself as he climbed out of the car. "Could you and Mr Hatchett give me a lift?" said Jennifer to Norma, with suspicious brightness.

She's jealous of me, thought Norma. Why, in God's name, is she jealous of me? She's tied him hand and foot and now she's frightened I'll steal him. I don't want him. Everyone has made all this far too complicated to be any fun. She stepped out of the car.

"I fear, Jennifer," she said, with no sense that she was outmanoeuvring a rival, "that I said I would do some things for Mrs Rissett."

"Are you staying, Alec?" squeaked Jennifer. "I have to be at the school." Alec glanced at Norma again. "Yes," he said, "I'm staying."

What does he want? thought Norma. He's up to something.

"Well," said Jennifer, "kiss me, fiancé!" Alec dutifully negotiated her hat. Jennifer put both arms around him and, while Norma and Hatchett looked away, she massaged his back vigorously. As she climbed into Hatchett's car she gave a series of tiny waves and, as they drove away she turned several times, a white, blurred face at the darkened window.

Alec and Norma walked back down the gutted suburban street.

"I had this feeling," he said, after quite a long silence, "just now. After you and Hatchett went to the hospital. I had this feeling that Lucius was dead."

"What kind of a . . . feeling?" said Norma.

"A sort of . . . impression of an absence," said Alec. "A sudden emptiness all round me. And then, although I felt ashamed of it because I knew what the emptiness meant – I mean, I knew it was Lucius – I felt a great relief. Up there, somewhere up there. They shot him down, Norma. I know they did."

"Well," said Norma, rather more brusquely than she had intended, "let's wait and see, shall we?"

"You got close to Hatchett while I was away," said Alec.

"We talk," said Norma, "about . . . Rachel, about the murders, about things . . ."

"Do you . . . care for him?" said Alec.

"It's hard to tell," said Norma.

"It is," said Alec, with some keenness, "it is hard to tell."

Norma realized, to her horror, that this was one of the longest conversations they had ever had – at least, one of the longest conversations (bar the one that led up to and away from his proposal of marriage) about what either of them felt. "It's horrible," he went on. "You see, now Lucius is dead – I do know he is dead, Norma, I just know it – now he is dead it's like I can see myself clearly for the first time. I look in the mirror and there is just me – at last. I always wanted to tell you, you know, about my childhood and about Lucius and I wonder whether . . . whether now I can."

"What exactly did happen with Lucius?" said Norma, as if they had discussed this matter before. It was odd, she thought, how many of the things she knew about Alec she only knew because of Hatchett. There was a sense in which he seemed almost present throughout the conversation. Alec turned to her and for a moment she thought he was going to speak. Not in the way he usually spoke but as if a whole rush of words was going to be loosed from him, as if he was going to babble like a Pentecostal preacher, scream, shout, laugh, confess, do all the things that Lycetts never did.

But he didn't. His face got an odd, mask-like look. A look she remembered having seen on Lucius's face.

Norma looked away at the wreckage around her. As she steered her way past a large sofa that, for some reason, had ended up in the middle of the street, she saw an elderly lady, who looked lost, wandering up the street towards them carrying a standard lamp, and a frying pan that appeared to be full of stew.

"I know there are things I should have told you," said Alec, "about me and my brother. Things I have never even told Hatchett. You see . . . I was my father's favourite. I was absolutely my father's favourite and . . ." He stopped. "I can't talk about this," he said. "I can't talk about what went on in my childhood. I just can't. What did Lucius say to you?"

"Nothing," said Norma. "He said nothing." Alec looked sideways at her. He seemed nervous about something. Norma did not respond.

"I did things in France I was ashamed of," Alec went on, "and I sort of . . . redeemed myself a bit today. But I don't . . . fight for things somehow. I let Jennifer sort of . . . take me over."

"You shouldn't let people take you over," said Norma. "You have a choice. All of life is about moral choices. There's nothing else." She indicated the desolation round them. "Otherwise," she said, "you end up with this."

"You," said Alec, "are fearfully clever. I am not fearfully clever. But you are. You're almost not like a woman at all sometimes."

Norma threw back her head and laughed. "All men are clever," she said, in a deep voice. "Norma is clever. Therefore Norma is a man!"

Alec leaned into her, suddenly passionate. "But don't you see, now, just now, after this afternoon, after I did the decent thing for once, I can see? I can suddenly see. It's all wrong with Jennifer. I should never have proposed to her. I mean, all you have to do is to . . . you know . . . say if you . . . you know . . ."

Norma stiffened. "Is this another proposal, Alec?" she said. "Because if it is it is a rather incompetent one."

Alec looked as if he was about to curl up into a ball or suck his thumb. "I'll tell her it's all a mistake," he said. "I'll tell her. I mean, I've given her my word and all, and if I have to I'll see it through but she won't . . . you know . . . make me, will she?" Norma, who had a better idea than Alec of how women, and especially women like Jennifer Doran, got what they want, did not answer. She reached out and touched his hand. It was soft and dry and warm. When his eyes turned to hers she remembered how extraordinarily beautiful he was. But, although this wasn't quite what she wanted to feel, she had the impression of being his elder sister, someone protecting him, guiding him. "I can't, Alec," she heard herself say, although she did not want to say it. "I can't marry you. Not now. Oh, if you had put it to me another way perhaps . . . I don't know. I might have said yes. Because that is what part of me wants to say. But I can't say it. It would be like running away somehow. What happens between you and Jennifer is your affair."

"Now is all there is," said Alec. "It isn't running away. It's you I want. It's you."

She moved away from him then because she thought he was going to touch her and his touch, she knew, would be hard to resist. With the heavy feeling that she was making the worst decision of her life but that there was nothing she could do about it, she said, "Everything has changed between us. It just has. You know it has. You have to face that. I don't know why but it has. I'm not the same person I was a year ago. A lot of things have happened. I do wish you the best of luck. In spite of what you may feel I think you're brave and honest and decent and kind and . . ." she couldn't stop herself saying the next thing but hated herself for doing so ". . . frightfully attractive. Goodbye."

"Norma –" said Alec, his mouth opening and closing like a fish's. "Is it Hatchett? Have you decided you love him? Has he been . . . you know . . . has he been . . . talking to you?"

She hated him suddenly. She hated all men, come to that. She hated their self-obsession, their ridiculously misplaced confidence in themselves (and their lack of it), their absurd necks, the way they never knew what to do with their arms. Has Hatchett what? All men care for is each other. I will die a mad old spinster, she thought, like Everett, with her crazy, unhealthy obsessions.

"Norma!" he called, as she walked away. "Norma! Don't go! Stay just a bit longer!" But she knew that if, like Orpheus, she turned, she would be lost. She was so inexperienced in matters of the heart that her feelings might betray her into doing something her intellect knew to be wrong. Love, as much as anything else, was a matter of choice. And she had chosen not to love a man to whom she was still violently attracted. It was that simple. Why then, as she walked, did she so yearn to look behind her? Why did she feel her feet as heavy as those of a convict, newly chained, walking in the grim path of duty and penance?

"In you come!" called his father. "We'll have something to drink before Lucius goes!"

Lucius had been in for thirty overs. There was a rule that you had to retire after thirty overs but Lucius seemed to have forgotten it. What made it worse was that almost all thirty had been bowled by Alec. Hatchett appeared to have given up. He was fielding so far away that, most of the time, Alec had to go and get the ball himself. He was lying on his back now, chewing a blade of grass. He could, thought Alec, be jolly irritating sometimes.

"So," said Alec, as he pulled out the stumps, savagely, "drawn game!"

"Was it?" said Lucius, in the offhand, lordly manner that Alec found so offensive.

"Yes," said Alec. "In case you hadn't noticed I have not even been in to bat."

"No," drawled Lucius. "I think if you had bowled till next September you would not have been in to bat. I was playing really rather well, wasn't I?" Over on the boundary, Hatchett was struggling to his feet. "And you can tell the others what you like, we both know what really happened and we will always know. So you'd better be careful. I'll get the handkerchief back. It's evidence. And if they get evidence they send you to jail. Or hang you."

"They don't hang children!" said Alec.

"Of course they do, stupid!" said Lucius. "They have a special shed. It's like the shed where they hang grown-ups only smaller. And the gallows is smaller. But they hang you all right. And they hang you in plastic pants because you pee yourself just like your friend Hatchett. They string you up by the neck, they do."

There was no arguing with this.

Lucius would be taken out with his hands tied behind his back. They would put a white cap on his head and stand him on a trap-door and pull a lever and he would fall through the floor. There would be a horrible cracking sound. Why was he looking so calm? Oh, the reason he was looking so calm was that he would plead NOT GUILTY. He would tamper with evidence. It would be Alec who would hang.

"I hereby condemn you, Alec Lycett, to swing by the neck until you be thoroughly dead. To be cut down and buried in quicklime or taken in a cart to the woods behind ALBION HOUSE where the terrible murder was committed and there to be buried until your ghost rises to haunt the house where you were born!"

"Is Mummy here?" Hatchett, apparently unaware of how disgracefully he had behaved, had bounded up to them.

"I am sure," said Lucius, "that Mummy won't miss her bit of free food!"

This, Alec knew, was a horrid thing to say because Hatchett's mummy was quite poor, which was why Hatchett liked coming to their nice house and eating their nice food. Hatchett was scowling and going red. Perhaps the two of them should really bash Lucius.

"Shall we go in?"

Alec's daddy had appeared at the back door. He was smiling. It was hard to connect him with the man who had stood in the woods that afternoon, holding his bloodied hands to his face and crying like a baby. He was crying because of the thing Sheila had done. Sheila was Alec's mummy, except he never called her that. It was another Sheila that Daddy had been crying about, who did terrible things that Alec's mummy never would have done.

"With him! With him! With him!" That was what he had said. And Alec and Lucius had heard him.

"Is Mummy here?" said Hatchett to Alec's daddy.

"She is," said Alec's daddy, as if Hatchett had asked a very, very clever question, "and she is staying for a cup of tea." He ruffled Hatchett's hair as he said this. But it looked, thought Alec, as if he wanted someone to come along and pat him on the head because of what he had done for Hatchett.

The four of them went inside to the kitchen. Hatchett's mummy was sitting at the end of the table drinking a cup of tea. Alec's mummy was sitting next to her, drinking a cup of tea. "It is awful for you," she was saying. "No one can imagine how such a thing could have happened. He just disappeared. It is utterly extraordinary. Awful!" She glanced at Alec's daddy as she said this. Alec's daddy looked away. He always looked away.

"The police," he said, finally, in a peculiar voice, "do nothing. The police are useless. The police are worse than useless. Don't you think, Maria?"

Alec could never get used to the fact that Hatchett's mummy had a first name. Or that people used it. Mrs Hatchett, by the same token, did not really become herself until, by calling "Dennis!" and looking, suddenly, like a dog sniffing at some distant prey, she reminded him that she, too, was a mother. But he was aware, as always, of a great hatred in the room, of an anger that he could not place, and yet for which, he knew with the certainty of Bible truth, he was responsible.

"I suppose," said Hatchett's mummy, "they try." Then she gave Hatchett an embarrassed sort of squeeze and said it was getting late.

Alec was glad his friend was staying the night but, more than ever before, he was aware that while Lucius was here it was important not to offend him. After tonight he would be out of the way. If only he could make him disappear, make him no longer part of the equation, neutralize him, then from now on he would be able to be himself.

"Up you go now," said Alec's daddy.

The three boys trooped upstairs.

In Alec and Lucius's bedroom was a large grey trunk. It was open. Inside it were Lucius's books and the smart white shirt he wore when he was in the first eleven cricket team. There were things scattered around the floor – Lucius's cricket bat, Arthur Mee's *Children's Encyclopedia* – but Lucius paid them no attention.

He went to his bed and lay down upon it. "I suppose," he drawled, "that Wetlegs is going to sleep in my bed? When I am away? As I am never coming back?" Nobody said anything. "I forbid it," said Lucius. "For a start I don't like the idea of my sheets getting . . . you know . . . wet!" Still nobody spoke.

"You can't forbid it," said Alec, "because you won't be here."

The hot summer night had made trickles of sweat down Alec's chest. Lucius's face, as always, seemed to mock him. It danced before him like a mask in a pantomime, questioning any easy judgement about who might lie beneath it.

"I'll always be here," said Lucius. "I'll always be beside you. I will never leave you, Alec, however far that pathetic father of ours may try to send me. Remember that." He looked across at Hatchett and, for a moment, there was an expression on his face that was almost like sympathy. "I mean," he said, "you and I know what we know. We know what the truth is. But we're not going to squeal, are we? If you're English you don't squeal. You back up your friends, Alec, and you know that's right. No one will ever know the truth of it because we won't tell. We're English, in case you've forgotten, little brother. We keep ourselves to ourselves in Albion House and don't you forget it, little brother. Don't you forget it!"

Alec didn't say anything.

PART SIX

Dennis Hatchett's Diary

3 September 1940

8 a.m.

Writing this at home. I am sitting at my desk, which looks out over the Downs, and in front of me is an old pair of Mother's glasses. They are smeared with dirt and as I look at them I conjure up the physical fact of her and mourn her absence once again. I never felt I was nice enough to her. I always blamed her for my father's disappearance. I always thought that if she had been nicer to him he might have stayed. What a terrible impact our love-lives have upon our children!

I couldn't cope with the false teeth. They went in the bin the day after we buried her.

The usual bizarre collection turned up at the funeral – though not Norma. Norma – this is strange – has never met my mother. She may have met her casually in the street once or twice, but I think that for all these years I kept them, consciously, apart. Loosebottom, however, as I must stop calling her father, was there. I never realized he knew her but it turned out they had been "quite close" when I was about seven. He looked, as older people always do at funerals, amazingly sprightly and glad it wasn't him in the box. He kept looking at me in an odd way as if he knew something I didn't. He sang all the Latin bits very loud and off key.

As we walked out after the service he pressed my hand and said, "Your mother was a good and patient woman, Dennis. She had a lot to put up with."

"Yes," I said. "Me!"

"I don't mean you," he said, in a significant tone of voice. What was the gossip about my father? I have never bothered to try to find out what it was. Other women, I suppose.

A returning bomber unloaded a few hundredweight of high explosive on the churchyard last week. As well as knocking out a few family tombs it blew a substantial hole in the roof so during the service I was able to look up at the sky. Half-way through, a pigeon got in and, landing in the area behind the altar, waddled around the most sacred places of the church, pecking at things. We all pretended it wasn't there.

It's curious to think we are fighting for our lives. Well – we're not. A few hundred young men in aircraft are fighting for our lives.

It seems that Alec's premonition about Lucius was horribly correct. Twins do seem to know. I think that that was what they both found unbearable about the relationship. Lucius's plane went missing over the Channel on the day they bombed Croydon aerodrome. No record of how it happened. He just disappeared. Anyway, Alec and Jennifer Doran are to get married on the fourteenth. I do not know how I feel about this.

Veitch has been put in charge of the Crotchett Green Home Guard. It turns out he "saw action" in the First War, although he is cagey about what this action was. Perhaps they poked him up over the top of one of the trenches in the hopes that his headmasterly gravitas would cow the Boche into submission. Groenig and I consented to be drilled by him. He has somehow got hold of an old revolver, God knows how, and the day before yesterday he shot Mrs Piddinghoe's dog. The dog, most of us agreed, had had it coming. Ever since it defecated in Mr Piddinghoe's mortarboard (it taught him never to leave it lying around upside down) it had had few supporters but I understand it was not a pleasant death. God knows what will happen if the Germans really do manage to get across the Channel. I am looking round for possible traitors and have selected Alec's mother as the Woman Most Likely to Co-operate with Nazis.

I can't believe it is only a year since this war started. And exactly a year since that day in the church when Lycett first plucked up the courage to propose marriage to Norma. It only took him about ten years, I suppose. Now he is marrying a domestic-science mistress – a woman I once asked whether she liked Baudelaire, to which she replied, "I've never been there." I know I have sometimes tried to make it look as if Alec is a boneheaded hearty. Actually, he isn't that at all. I don't know what to do about his new friendship. It ought to make my approach to Norma easier. Actually, it makes our relationship even more complicated. I don't know what to do about this. Probably, as at the Gare du Nord, I shall say the wrong thing at the wrong time in the wrong way and we will all go our separate ways until the end of time.

Norma and I went to see Jacqueline Rissett the other day. The poor girl seems to be dying of her liver complaint. The house was shrouded in gloom and her devoted mother could scarcely bring herself to speak. We did talk about Breeze's last letter, the contents of which, as far as the police are concerned, seem to have satisfied everyone that he is the murderer. The argument runs that anyone who seduces schoolgirls is probably a killer. Anyway, there are hardly any policemen left on account of the war.

Rumour still trickles through the school. Mayhew still occasionally makes blood-curdling remarks about knowing what she knows and telling what she will tell when the time be right, but no one, as ever, takes her seriously. But I didn't go to see Jacqueline because I was still thinking about the murders. I went because I have got very fond of her, as I have, in a way, of all of Norma's girls, even the appalling Janet and Elinor. Even – although she is the hardest to love – of strict governess Mabel with the quasi-Fascist parents and the distinctly unhealthy feelings she harbours for female staff members. Including, I fear, Norma.

Jacqueline looked terrible. She was sitting up in bed, her face that ghastly yellow colour, and her mother asked us not to stay too long.

"Isn't it exciting," she said, "about Rachel? Her being quite a famous scientist and everything, Miss Lewis."

"It is," said Norma, "but if you hadn't been so brave and clever, Jacqueline, we would never have got her back to England. You were really ingenious with your stories and you helped us save her from those horrible people."

Jacqueline smiled feebly. She was very weak. She moved herself against the pillows and I saw, once again, the fine lines of her face, the uneasy adult nature of her movements. "I did tell Mabel," she said. "Mabel is very helpful. She looks after people. And she was very kind to me. She comes almost every day to see me, you know. She brings me soup and things."

"That," I said, "is very kind of her."

I didn't think it was right to ask her about Breeze and the murders. To be honest, since our last conversation I haven't thought much about them. There may or may not be significance in the fact that Jacqueline and Breeze spent their time poring over Agatha Christie. But I suspect that life does not imitate art (if you can call Miss Christie art) to any real degree.

"You see," said Jacqueline, "I think I may have done wrong by saying what I said about Mr Breeze and Miss Everett. I think it may have turned Alan's head. I think he may have got jealous of her. He always hated her. I think that that was what may have happened. And he killed those other teachers because they suspected." She looked, pathetically, at Norma. "I didn't do wrong, did I, Miss Lewis? Did I do wrong?"

"Of course you didn't, Jacqueline," came a dark brown voice from the door. It was Mabel Hughes. She was loaded with gifts. There was a bowl of soup. There was a bowl of fruit. And, as always at the bedside of the sick, there were games and trifles and books. She had come, Jacqueline told us, every day since she had been seriously ill, and although I personally have always found the girl sinister, I did feel that she was genuinely concerned for her friend.

"Are you feeling better?" she said, setting down the bowl of soup on the bedside table then plumping up Jacqueline's pillows. "I've been worried about you." She turned to me. "I'm sorry if I was a bit funny with you, Mr Hatchett," she said. "Do you remember that day in the hospital? It is just that I'm very fond of Jacqueline. Very, very fond of her."

"I see that!" I said. "You've brought her some books! That was very kind of you!"

Jacqueline's eyes shifted uneasily between the two of us. "She's always bringing me books," she said, "and sometimes we read them together, don't we, Mabel?"

Norma lifted her eyes in my direction and I got to my feet. As we left, Mabel was spooning soup solicitously in the direction of her friend, who was giggling feebly at her bossiness. On the way out, as I always do, I glanced at the books Mabel had brought, and noticed that several of them, unsurprisingly, were by Agatha Christie. I picked up the first four in the pile, and stuffed them in my pockets, perhaps with the vague idea that they might provide some insight into what had been going on at the school, but then didn't think any more about it. Perhaps because Norma, as we got outside the house, said, "I think we should stop seeing each other, Dennis."

"Why?" I said.

"Because," said Norma, slightly peevishly, "people are talking. And there is nothing to talk about. We are just friends. That is all we are. You know we are. But it is becoming embarrassing. Even to be just friends. Embarrassing. It is." There was a silence. Then she said, "And he is getting married to that ridiculous woman."

"Yes," I said, "I'm afraid he is."

12.30 p.m.

Have just got out the books I pinched from Jacqueline Rissett the other day. All intellectuals are book thieves. They are: *The Mysterious Affair at Styles*; *Black Coffee* (a play); *The ABC Murders*; and *Dumb Witness*. All four were inscribed, dated and manically annotated in the way that schoolgirls seem to love. *The Mysterious Affair at Styles* had been lent to Mabel on 7 November of last year, *Black Coffee* lent on 6 June of last year and returned on 30 June, *The ABC Murders* lent on 1 February of this year and returned exactly a week later. *Dumb Witness*, on the other hand, was a slower burn. Mabel seemed to have kept it for months and had only just returned it. Why? I flicked through the book and found it was unmarked, apart from a rather dubious-looking squiggle next to a section dealing with phosphorus poisoning. (What is wrong with Miss Christie? Why is she so unhealthily obsessed with the wrongful use of pharmaceuticals?)

I could not bear to read any of them. Life is too short for Agatha Christie when there are also Montaigne, Goethe and Raymond Chandler.

3 p.m.

Had interview with man from Bletchley. More interested in how I might manage to propose to Norma, this time getting it vaguely right. Wandered around garden practising proposal.

Whatever happens I refuse to get down on one knee, as Lycett is reported to have done. After some reports of wobbling, the Lycett/Doran marriage is on and it appears that Lycett Senior is overjoyed at the prospect of his son marrying the most ignorant, charmless domestic-science mistress ever to crawl out of Croydon. This could be why Alec has not spoken to me for about a fortnight. When your best friend marries a woman you completely despise it does rather hit at the relationship. Still – I thought he might have asked Norma and me to the wedding, although it appears he has not done so.

I passed his father in the street the other day and I could see he was wondering whether to cut me dead. In the end his upper-middle-class English manners prevailed on him to cross over and try to be pleasant, which was, in my view, a less preferable option. We exchanged inane remarks.

4.30 p.m.

Have just read *The Mysterious Affair at Styles* complete with Mabel's annotations. The book is devoid of literary merit. But the method of murder – the precipitation of strychnine in a tonic by the addition of a bromide – is precisely the one used in the despatching of Leafy Green. That is why no one needed to be tipping the poison directly into the old bat's medicine. I am going to have to read more of this rubbish in order to understand more of this rubbish.

5.15 p.m.

Just read *The ABC Murders* (that is how long it takes). The second victim is strangled with her own belt – *vide* Miss Leach. And guess what? It seems that the murder victim in the quite appalling play of Miss Christie's entitled *Black Coffee* is poisoned by the addition of hyoscine hydrobromide to a cup of the eponymous substance.

7.32 p.m.
Just received a call from Norma. Jacqueline Rissett died half an hour ago. She seems to have left a note confessing to all the murders and making much mention of Miss Agatha Christie.

16

14 *September 1940*

"Where is our worse than useless vicar? He is running horribly late," said Hatchett, squinting sideways at his watch. "If he arrives any later than this he will end up burying and marrying two of his parishioners at the same moment. We'll all be chucking earth at Jennifer Doran's head."

"You shouldn't make jokes at a funeral," said Norma, although she herself had heard that Alec's wedding had been booked uncomfortably close to the last farewell for Jacqueline Rissett, since he had been called back to his regiment and was due to leave at eight that very evening.

"Nor," said Hatchett, "should you be gloomy at a wedding." He looked round the church. "But neither occasion is quite what they are supposed to be. Everything's upside down." He bit his nails. "One minute," he went on, "I think I've got to the bottom of these horrible murders. And then it all slips away from me." He looked over his shoulder, and scanned the congregation. He seemed, thought Norma, nervous. He started to mutter to himself. "She's not here! She's not here!" Then he seemed to see what he was looking for. He let out his breath slowly and steadied himself, as if preparing for some terrible struggle.

"What is it?" she said. But he did not answer her.

In his black tie and black suit, thought Norma, as she studied Hatchett, he looked definitely handsome. He had been so different over the last month. There had been a time when she had thought he was playing at Hatchett the Detective. Not now. There was a grim, impressive seriousness about him. There was a rumour he had found a rather secret kind of war work and was to be leaving the school shortly. He had spent hours asking everyone question after question about every single circumstance surrounding every single murder.

She put her ear to one side and listened for the sound of aircraft. Day after day now the huge German bombers swaggered overhead – on their way to the capital in broad daylight. There was an insolence about them that Norma had come to hate.

She shifted edgily in her seat. The heat! How could you even think about the war in this weather? A crazy world. She still could not quite believe that the coffin standing on a trestle in front of the altar contained Jacqueline Rissett. The poor girl had ended up in a casket that was as low-key as her life. Mr Japp and his assistant Frederick were standing over to her right, under a stained-glass window that showed St George and the Dragon. As far as Norma could make out, knight and mythical beast seemed to be bowing to each other – like Japanese wrestlers at the start of a bout. The undertakers, hands crossed reverently over their fly-buttons, cast their eyes down like obedient wives. Norma still could not credit, either, that the girl whose life they were supposed to be celebrating was the one who had killed Alice Everett, Leafy Green and Miss Helena Bonham Leach. Jacqueline, she thought idly, had brought an energy to the business of murder that she had consistently refused to display in her schoolwork.

"Here we go," whispered Hatchett. "Here comes Mary. I do not envy him the task he now faces."

He was clutching a small pile of books, as usual, and his face was tense and concentrated. As Norma watched, he picked one out of the pile and started to flick through it, like a student revising for an examination for which he is not totally prepared. He looked, she thought, like a man about to give some major speech. But this funeral wasn't anything to do with him. Was it?

Some of those in the know said that it was very bad taste to have Jacqueline Rissett buried at all. Shouldn't murderers be thrown into quicklime or, at least, given the kind of muted send-off one might accord a not very popular pet? Was Mary going to give them a few minutes of Jacqueline's good qualities (punctuality, humility, almost excessive politeness) then turn on a sixpence to give them

379

something along the lines of "Then it all went disastrously wrong!" followed by a ten-minute character assassination that let the audience know that this little killer was going to fry for ever? Should he discuss the victims – all of whom he had buried? Or say nothing about any of the circumstances that led to her death?

Norma, suddenly, felt sick. She was sick of trying to rise above the horror of it. There had been something so sad about Jacqueline when alive; it seemed to make her death even more pointless. What was "yellow atrophy of the liver" anyway? She had been ill a long time, they said. And the knowledge that she was going to die was what had made her leave that note. Behind its curt, almost formal nature, Norma read a whole tragic history. She could see how the affair with Breeze had started – some lecherous overture during the school journey, the terrible fear and then the terrible passion. Norma shuddered slightly as she recalled the tragic artlessness of Jacqueline's thoughts on the subject of the chemistry master. "Wonderful love", "real and true passion", "deep feeling" – all these phrases of which Norma felt so suspicious were there, often underlined or bracketed by inverted commas in the traditional manner of those who seek to give a cliché authenticity.

She had read the girl's essays on Ronsard, for God's sake. They were bad enough.

She had been the first to be told. Hatchett had told her to tell no one. He had not told Mrs Rissett. The only other person who had known originally about the note was Mabel. But now, by one of those processes familiar in village life, everyone seemed to know apart from the police. Presumably Mabel had blabbed. It was impossible to get schoolgirls to keep quiet about anything. When Norma asked Hatchett what he was going to do with the note he said, "Keep it."

"Why?" said Norma. "Can't we try to forget the whole thing now?"

Hatchett pursed his lips quizzically. "There are things I don't understand about it," he said.

"What things?"

"It doesn't explain the books."

"What books?" Norma said.

"The Agatha Christie books, of course."

"What on earth," said Norma, "has Agatha Christie got to do with murder? With real murder anyway?"

"What has John Buchan got to do with war?" said Hatchett. "But we are still at war, are we not?" He looked around the congregation with that same, strange, restless energy. Then he leaned over to Norma and grabbed her by the arm. "Why didn't they ask Mayhew?" he said. "Why didn't they ask Mayhew?"

"I don't know," said Norma. "Because she isn't very reliable, I suppose."

The vicar had last been spotted near the rood screen but, as always, he liked to creep up on the congregation from a direction they least expected. Word had got round that he was coming in from the back of the left aisle, so almost all heads were craned in that direction when the vicar of St Mary's and All Angels, Crotchett Green, popped up, as if by magic, in the pulpit.

"Jacqueline Rissett," he said, in sepulchral tones, as his parishioners jerked round to face him, "was too young to die." This obvious truth was too much for Mrs Rissett. She had been amazingly composed up to this moment, thought Norma, but now she buried her head in her best friend's shoulder and began to howl with grief. Mary seemed quietly pleased to have made so much impact so quickly. "She was only seventeen years old," he went on, "which means that she had almost certainly not experienced the things we associate with adult life – married love, for example." He stopped here and flushed a deep scarlet. "I am not referring," he went on, "to sex. Sex is not the only thing that dignifies our adult life. And it is not necessarily a cause for sadness that Jacqueline had not directly encountered it in her life. For the passionate physical feelings that many of us have for other adult people are not the be-all and end-all of our existence. Oh, no. In many ways it is better to die young, a virgin, than racked with torment and guilt about desires we may feel to be base and unclean and perverted. No, she died young but she died, almost certainly, as I say, undefiled by the sickening rapacity of lust. She died pure and she died clean."

So, thought Norma, the news had even got as far as the vicar. Mrs Rissett had stopped crying and was sitting bolt upright. She looked ready to leap out of her pew, make a dash for the pulpit and start clawing out Mr Anstruther's eyes. Hatchett seemed to be muttering to himself. From time to time he would turn round and stare, rudely, at the rest of the congregation. Norma leaned a little way in his direction and heard him say, "She's not here. Why isn't she here? She'd come here, wouldn't she?"

On her other side Rachel was sitting, hands folded neatly in her lap, eyes straight ahead of her. Her beautiful black hair was combed back with puritanical thoroughness and her mind, as so often since Jacqueline's death, seemed to be otherwise occupied than with the present. Hatchett seemed to have caught sight of something. But what was it? Norma tried to follow his gaze but her view was blocked by a woman in a large black hat.

"So many people," boomed Mary, "have died. Have died on the battlefield. And have died here, in peaceful Crotchett Green. If the Germans arrive, make no mistake about it, there will be considerably fewer of us here to resist them. But even before that invasion happens, which it may, of course, not, although it looks increasingly likely, people have been dying anyway. Not of German bullets but of murder. Killing, wilfully and deliberately, which, as far as we know, is not how young Jacqueline died."

Hatchett was still looking behind him. As Mary staggered through to the end of a speech that was closer to mild criticism than eulogy, he raised his left hand aloft, the signal he used when bidding the congregation to prayer. Well drilled in Mr Anstruther's body language, the faithful of Crotchett Green started to pitch forward. Hatchett, as he always did, clambered down on to his knees, while Norma, who didn't like the idea of prostrating herself before anyone, let alone someone as cruel, inefficient and whimsical as God, slumped forward and leaned her forehead on her right hand. She looked back over her shoulder. The big black hat was at half mast and she could see, now, whom Hatchett had been looking for. Mabel Hughes, flanked by both of her parents, was standing against the back wall of St Mary's, the black eyes in her gaunt white face fixed on Jacqueline's coffin.

To Norma's horror, Hatchett started to get to his feet. Mary had just got to the bit about the resurrection and the life, when the senior modern-languages master of Kirkby Grammar School, in a voice long practised at compelling attention in class, said, "This funeral must not be allowed to continue." Most of the Crotchett Green residents were so busy being on their knees and mumbling that at first they paid him absolutely no attention. Hatchett pulled out his spectacles case from his jacket and rapped it on the pew in front of him. "This funeral," he said, once more, in an even louder voice, "must stop at once."

A few at a time, faces turned up towards the sound of his voice, like flowers following the sun. "Why," said Hatchett, who suddenly appeared quite composed and almost alarmingly confident of his audience, "was Miss Everett poisoned with hyoscine hydrobromide? Was it just because it was a drug that had been prescribed for her? I do not think so!" By now, almost no one was bothering to pray. Only Miss Leach's sister, who was ninety and stone deaf, continued to kneel and mutter in the front pew. The light from a stained-glass window caught Hatchett's face as he stepped forward closer to the coffin. "I'll tell you why," he went on, "because hyoscine hydrobromide figures in a play by Miss Agatha Christie called *Black Coffee*."

The mood in the church had altered. No one, judging from the expressions on their faces, could judge where he might be leading them – but they were inclined to follow. And it was certainly much more entertaining than a funeral. Even Mrs Rissett was listening, her jaw wide and her eyes fixed on Hatchett. She clearly found him a lot more use than the Bible in her present predicament. "Miss Green, too," Hatchett continued, "was killed as a kind of homage to the first published work of fiction by Miss Agatha Christie, *The Mysterious Affair at Styles*, in which the victim is killed by the precipitation of strychnine in a bottle of tonic. Miss Leach was strangled with her own belt, which is precisely what happens to the second victim in Miss Christie's almost bearable tale *The ABC*

Murders. Every single one of the Saltdene Girls' School Murders was carried out by a method taken from the work of our most famous detective-story writer."

He waved the books he had brought with him above his head. Hatchett, as usual, was having no problem compelling an audience to listen to him. But Norma, entranced as she was by his theory and his way of propounding it, could not believe something so, so . . . complicated.

"Why, though?" said Hatchett, anticipating her thoughts and answering them in ringing tones. "Why go to such elaborate lengths? Isn't murder usually a question of bashing one's target over the head with a piece of lead piping or whatever comes nearest to hand? To which the answer is, 'Sometimes.' These methods of murder may have been elaborate but they were selected for a very simple reason. To further incriminate Jacqueline Rissett, who, as everyone knew, was the most fervent of Miss Christie's admirers and about the only girl in the class who could ever remember the plots."

Hatchett's theory, thought Norma, was no less absurd than the times that had created it. Who would have thought a year ago that they would be seriously expecting the Germans to arrive in Dorking? It was a mad world – and no one had ever said that methods of murder were supposed to be neat or rational. "But why?" Hatchett was saying in deep, persuasive tones. "Why kill Miss Everett in the first place? And why become so obsessed with laying the blame at Jacqueline's door? What had poor Jacqueline ever done, or Miss Everett for that matter, to offend this compulsive layer of false trails, this hoaxer, this elaborate liar, this drummer-up of false clues, this trickster for the times? The answer is not hard to find. We're at war. Politics is a matter of truth against falsehood, isn't it? And lies are as much to do with these murders as they are to do with what we are fighting against in Europe."

Everyone in the church was now fixed on Dennis Hatchett. He might, thought Norma, who had heard about but never heard or seen his father preach, be the long absent Reverend Arthur Hatchett, compelling them in a way their current vicar would never be able to do.

"I'll tell you," said Hatchett. "Jacqueline had done something unspeakable. Jacqueline had said that Alan Breeze and Alice Everett were having an affair. And that was not allowed. Because our murderer felt she owned Alice Everett. She is here in this church and her name is Mabel Hughes."

Mabel's face did not alter, although she moved, restlessly, like an animal on a leash. But then, thought Norma, the girl never did show much emotion. She looked, as she always did, formal, correct, self-contained. The corners of her mouth were even curved in the beginnings of a smile.

"I would never do anything to hurt Alice or Leafy or dear, dear Miss Leach," she said. "And everyone knows how fond I was of poor Jacqueline."

"Oh, you loved them, all right," Hatchett said. "You loved Alice Everett so much that when you thought she was having an affair with Alan Breeze you were filled with violent rage. You wanted to punish her. And punish Breeze, which was why, when no one believed you, you killed Miss Green and forged a letter from her pointing the finger of suspicion at him. That is why Miss Leach was killed – she knew you well enough to know that letter was a forgery."

A note of tetchiness came into Mabel's voice. "I don't see exactly . . ."

"Just as you forged a confession note from Jacqueline. After all, she was known for being a Christie fan, not you. And Jacqueline didn't die of a liver complaint, she died of phosphorus poisoning, the method used in a book you had from her and kept for as long as it took you to kill her – *Dumb Witness*. You loved her, all right, you loved taking care of her, feeding her –"

"You can't prove any of this," said Mabel. "It's just a stupid story like those books. You can't prove anything!"

"Oh, yes, I can," said Hatchett, "because the witness you discounted, the witness everyone discounted, is here in the church. She saw you in Paris, didn't she? She saw you slip something into Miss Everett's coffee. But no one paid any attention to her. No one would believe such a ridiculous story from such a common little person. She wasn't even attractive enough to merit being killed, was she?"

Mabel's face changed. It bore, now, a look of extraordinary complacency and conceit. "Not necessarily," she said. "I told her that if she did tell anyone she had seen me I would dispose of her. So . . ."

Mabel did not seem to realize what she had just said. Her parents were looking pale with horror.

"Did you see her, Mayhew?" said Hatchett. "Did you see her slip something into Miss Everett's coffee?"

Mayhew's pinched little face screwed itself even tighter. She looked, thought Norma, even more insecure than usual. "I seen what I seen," she said, "and I'm going to tell. I seen some pretty bad things. I seen dreadful things done. And don't you forget it!"

Mary pressed both palms together, lowered his head and closed both eyes very tightly, in the way he always did when seeking an immediate conference with the Almighty. As usual, he seemed to have got through it very quickly for he spread his arms and, with his vestments rising like Dracula's cloak, said, "Dearly beloved, if what we have heard is true then it has very grave implications for our worship this morning. We are gathered here in the presence of Jesus Christ to ask for His guidance on a number of matters and this, obviously, is now one of them, and so that we do not act rashly or hastily or intemperately, but courteously, thoughtfully and elegantly, I suggest we ask Him who –"

"What on earth are you on about?" said a voice from the front row. "What, in God's name, are you drivelling on about this time? Ask Jesus Christ what? We've been asking Him favours for two thousand years and He hasn't yet stopped people killing each other and lying and cheating and doing wicked, shameful things and getting away with them, has He?"

It was Mrs Rissett. Norma had never heard her say more than three words in her life, but her face, as she turned to Mabel Hughes, was full of the passion her only daughter had inspired in her. She must once, thought Norma, have been as pretty as her poor dead daughter.

"We won't do any more praying, thank you," she said. "I don't think I will ever pray again if you want to know. For anything!" Mrs Rissett hardly ever spoke above a whisper but her voice was immediately audible: cracking with the strain of projection and grief, it carried through the church.

"I don't think so. I loved my daughter. I don't know whether anybody else did but I did, all right. She was all I had, if you want to know. She was literally everything to me. I so wanted her to be safe. I got her two of everything to be safe. I got her two scarves for winter and two coats for when it was rainy and two pairs of school shoes and two extra sets of pens and pencils because you're always losing them, aren't you?, and two of each of her school books. Only one grave, though. Only one coffin. I loved Jacqueline so much. I wanted her to have nice friends but she didn't until little Rachel arrived." Here she turned to face Mabel. "And you were never really her friend. You bullied her the way you bully all those girls while pretending to be such a respectable person. You're a right little Hitler, you are, aren't you? You and those stuck-up parents of yours. They're as bad. She hated you, Mabel Hughes. And she was afraid of you. Well, I'm not afraid of you. We'll wait here and send for the police because what Mr Hatchett says is right. And when we get our autopsy and we find there is this stuff inside of her then we will know it was you because the only other person who fed her was me and she was all I had. All I ever had."

She started to cry then, huge, helpless tears, and Norma felt herself close to crying with her for the pity of it. But Mabel, stepping forward, lost, in a moment, all that carefully cultivated poise. White face pulsing with hatred, she shook in the grip of a rage that threatened to stifle her words; but she found them, in a witch-like howl that chilled all those who heard it. "You stupid common little woman!" yelled Mabel. "You can't prove any of this! And neither can that stupid little teacher who loves Jews so much! That – that – Hatchett!"

"I think," said Hatchett, very quietly, "that we just did."

"Dearly beloved," said Mary, badly shaken by the fact that his congregation had started not only to answer back but also to talk among themselves, "I am sure that Mr Smith our churchwarden will . . . er . . . call the police and while we are . . . er . . . waiting for them to arrive I think we should . . . er . . . pray, because prayer, I always find, does help one to . . . pass the time in the sense that . . ."

The vicar was still lost in the middle of this sentence, when the heavy door at the back swung open and Alec Lycett, accompanied by his best man Bob Betterton, the captain of the Croydon Casuals Rugby Team, stepped into the church. "I hope this isn't inconvenient, Vicar," he said, in slightly hesitant tones, "but . . . er . . . is this funeral going to go on much longer? Because I am due to get married. Sort of now-ish. I hope that's OK. There are rather a lot of people out here and they are champing at the bit. Rather. OK?"

17

Norma had never heard Alec talk like this. It was only now that she realized this was probably how he talked to tradesmen. There was a slightly bullying tone about him, a condescension she had never heard before. That was when she started to understand things about Hatchett and Lycett that neither of them really wanted to face. Not that she saw it all yet. But she did see, clearly, that Alec had always been the one with money and power and influence. And that Hatchett, even if he didn't always know it, resented the fact.

She also noticed that the church seemed to have acquired, already, an awful lot of people in grey suits with white carnations, as well as women in distinctly cheerful hats. They must have been trickling in through the side door while Hatchett was speaking. Over in the left-hand corner, a group of children, who looked as if they might well be bridesmaids, were whispering together. A fat girl in a red dress, whom Norma thought she recognized from Three F, was saying, in quite a loud voice, as she pointed at the coffin, "What's that box doing there?"

Mary, who was legendary for double-booking christenings, forgetting confirmations and changing the date of the Harvest Festival without telling anyone, was trying to respond to the new arrivals in an appropriate manner. He was nodding. He was smiling. And then, seconds later, catching sight of someone in a black tie or a face-obliterating veil, his features would collapse into simulated reverence for the brevity of life and the sadness of things in general.

Mabel Hughes showed no sign of wanting to leave. She stood, a little apart from her parents, in what looked like triumph. But the paradox of her behaviour was more than matched by that of those around her. Norma blinked rapidly. She looked round the congregation. More people from Alec and Jennifer's party had trickled into the church so that it was now a weird mixture of mourning and marriage. Over to her left a big, handsome, vacuous-looking man in grey tails (Alec's father, of course, looking oddly sombre) was standing next to an undertaker's assistant, who was carrying a large wreath. The fat bridesmaid was wandering around the front of the church and, as Norma looked at her, she said, in a squeaky voice, "No one will tell me what that box is doing there." Out by the door – which was now open to the light again – a couple of surly-looking gravediggers were asking two wedding guests whether the poor girl was going to be brought out yet and the wedding guests were trying to tell them she would be coming into the church on her father's arm. A distant relative of Jennifer Doran's had just asked a distant relative of Jacqueline Rissett's whether she was bride or groom and, when told she was the deceased's second cousin, had burst into tears and had to be taken into the fresh air.

"Look," Alec was saying, "I have to go back to my regiment and I think we should get on with this, Vicar."

He hadn't even told her he was going back to his regiment, thought Norma, as Mary nodded rhythmically in agreement with his distinguished parishioner.

"This," said the vicar, "is a church. And a church is where we come when we are born, and when we get married and when we . . . er . . . die. There is nothing wrong with any of these things. And there is nothing wrong, either, with celebrating them or, indeed . . . er . . . mourning them at the . . . er . . . same time, and if you would like to come forward, Alec . . ." His voice acquired a liturgical chant. "For matrimony is a holy estate . . . and . . . er . . ." With which he extended one beringed hand in Alec's direction. And Alec, very much the squire's son, stepped up to the front of the church, turned to the congregation and told them all that they were all, yes, all, really most welcome to stay. More and more wedding guests were piling in so that, in a neighbouring pew, Norma saw, or thought she saw, Amanda Fish, who was no better than a prostitute, sitting, in her mauve dress with the plunge neckline, on the knee of a man in full mourning.

The atmosphere veered between carnival and collapse. Some

grieving relatives, on hearing the news that there was a happy couple in the church who were about to get married, found themselves surprised by joy and slapping people on the back, while some wedding guests, on being told the story of how Jacqueline Rissett had died, found they were moved to tears. Mary, who seemed finally to have taken leave of his senses, wandered around near the foot of the pulpit muttering that whom God hath joined no man should cut down like a flower because in the midst of marriage we are in death to whom shall we turn for man and wife?

A vicious row broke out between the ugliest of the bridesmaids and Mr Japp when she accused him of "looking miserable" and asked him to "cheer up for the poor girl's sake", and he replied by saying that he was unable to see what she was supposed to enjoy about being carted out in a shroud and stuck in a hole six feet deep.

It was hard to say when Jacqueline Rissett's funeral turned into Alec Lycett's wedding, but it did. The people who went for the police – in the end Mr Veitch and the churchwarden set off together – announced that the coffin was not to be moved and that no one was to leave the building until Inspector Roach arrived. This was clearly aimed at Mr and Mrs Hughes, who had been edging towards the door but were stopped by Bob Betterton's brother and Mr Groenig. Two more Kirkby teachers were standing on either side of Mabel Hughes. She did not attempt to move. And, as more and more wedding guests crowded into the packed church, the pressure to have some kind of service grew stronger and stronger.

Mary, however, after his bold seven-word venture into the marriage service, seemed to have seriously lost his nerve. Norma watched him scamper back up to the high altar, where he once more bowed his head and tensed his shoulders in preparation for a few really intense words with God. But as far as she could see he wasn't getting through, for after a minute or so he gave up and stared off, hungrily, in the direction of the choirboys.

In spite of his abandon-ship attitude, everyone else seemed determined to make the best of things and to trust that, after a decent pause, the vicar was going to do his duty. A small brass band of male and female pupils from Saltdene and Kirkby played a medley of tunes including "We'll Meet Again" – which had a very bad effect on some of the mourners – and culminating in a double-time version of "The Bridal March".

And here comes the bride, thought Norma, oh, my Lord, here she does come indeed!

The material in her dress could have provided at least three parachutes, and billowed behind her as if Jennifer had just landed with their help. The rear section was held up by at least eight bridesmaids, one of whom looked as if she was pushing thirty, but Jennifer herself was so determinedly radiant that she clearly saw no fault in any aspect of her outfit or companions. Her left brassière strap was partially visible, but, thought Norma, she looked pretty confident that she was . . . well . . . good enough to eat.

"She is not going to like this," Norma muttered to Hatchett. "She will not be amused by the presence at her wedding of large numbers of people in full mourning."

From remarks around her, she could tell that quite a lot of people were worried about the bride, but when Jennifer started down the aisle on her father's arm (he turned out to be a surprisingly elderly man in an ARP outfit), she did not, at first, appear to notice that there was a coffin immediately to the left of her husband-to-be. Her veil, thought Norma, was so closely textured that it was surprising she had managed to locate the church. As she made her way down the aisle, simpering to right and left of her, she did not seem unduly disturbed by the large number of black ties, suits, dresses and hats in the congregation or that at least three people in the front pew were sobbing helplessly.

What a stupid walk she's got, thought Norma. A silly, self-conscious lope, like a dog prospecting for food. And why did a tall, thin girl like her need extra-high heels? Or those stupid leg-o'-mutton sleeves? Who had done her hair? If it was one person, why did it look as if it was the result of a violent dispute between two rival schools of hairdressing? Was it a wig? How had Norma ever imagined that this foolish, self-absorbed, incredibly stupid domestic-science teacher was her best friend?

You wanted feelings to be constant. You wanted to think there was something fixed about a marriage. Or something final. But this ceremony seemed to Norma as provisional as anything else in this war-haunted world. She couldn't take it seriously. And yet there was a small part of her that regretted it bitterly, that couldn't understand why she was allowing it to happen.

She had not fought for Alec. He had asked her to marry him a second time and she had closed herself off from him. Perhaps that was just a matter of hurt pride. Since that day the aerodrome was bombed, she had asked herself, more than once, whether it was Alec that she really wanted.

Perhaps love was simply a question of making up your mind.

Jennifer had reached the altar steps now, although Mary still did not seem to have the courage to face his congregation. She was peering into Alec's face, as if checking she had got the right bridegroom.

All this time Mary had been lurking up by the altar like Thomas à Becket faced by those men in chain-mail who were keen to see the world population reduced by one turbulent priest. But, although obviously uncomfortable and confused, he had been finally prevailed upon to do his stuff. Porteous Minor, of whom he was suspiciously fond, had tempted him out of his hole with a stirring rendition of "Et Exultavit Spiritus Meus!" and he was now, to use his own favourite phrase, "front of house", staring round at his church piled high with wedding guests, mourners and uniformed policemen.

"We are gathered here together in the sight of God," began Mary, with a sudden access of unctuous enthusiasm, "to join . . ." he looked about him wildly and found Alec, at whom he pointed dramatically ". . . this man . . ." another wild stare and a jab at Jennifer ". . . and this woman in holy matrimony." He turned and appeared to see the coffin for the first time. His jaw dropped and for a few moments he was completely silent.

"Which is," hissed somebody in the front row, "a blessed estate."

"Is it?" said Mary, with what sounded like genuine curiosity. He recovered himself enough to focus on his prayer book. But he appeared to be too shocked to open it. "Which is," he repeated, "a

393

blessed estate . . ." For a moment Norma thought he was going to dry again, and then, with the confidence of one who has performed this service hundreds and hundreds of times, he went on, ". . . a blessed estate ordained by God for the procreation of children and not one to be entered into lightly or casually or . . ." another pause here but no attempt to look down at the words ". . . in a sort of 'why don't we try this?' sort of way but reverently and holily and properly in the sight of God!"

His confidence seemed to have increased now that he was off the book and, perhaps anxious to bolster up the source of his new-found self-esteem, he strayed even further from the Authorized Version, his voice gaining in strength and authority as he did so. "Forasmuch," he boomed, "forasmuch as you, Jennifer Doran, for example, a schoolteacher, and you, Alec Lycett, a schoolmaster obviously also of this parish, have chosen to plight your troth in front of these people and in front of . . . er . . ." here he looked left and once more caught sight of Jacqueline Rissett's coffin ". . . in front of . . . that thing over there and say in the eyes of the Lord that you will be together in sickness and in health, well . . ." a look of panic came into his eyes as he studied Jennifer, but her gaze was fixed on his face as if some great truth was hidden there ". . . well, do you, Jennifer Doran, do you promise to have and to hold and love and honour and obey and keep in sickness and in health and so on?"

Jennifer nodded awkwardly. "Speak up, girl!" said the vicar, rather brusquely.

"Yes," said Jennifer Doran. "Yes, I do. All those things. I will obey."

"Good!" said Mary.

There had been a little awkwardness at first, a feeling that this was not quite proper, but once he was up and running, Mary delivered his lines with such passion and force that they seemed quite as, if not more, credible than the prescribed form of the *Book of Common Prayer*. "And you," he said, shifting his gaze to Alec, who was staring straight ahead of him. "You! I'm speaking to you!" Alec re-engaged the vicar's glance. "Do you . . . er . . . Alec . . . Alec

Lycett . . . do you personally feel that you and this woman are ready?"

"Ready for what?" said Alec.

"Marriage," said Mary. "The bringing together of man and woman in holy matrimony, which is a state ordained by God for the procreation of children and not, as I said, one to be entered into lightly or contemptuously or carelessly but carefully and thoughtfully and considerately and sensibly and intelligently and with a bit of common sense, not just dropping into it in a sort of 'oh-why-not?' kind of way."

"No," said Alec. "I mean, yes. Yes, I will. And I do take it pretty seriously."

"Good," said the vicar, "because not everybody does. So you are telling me that you, Alec Lycett, as I said, obviously, will swear to have this woman and cherish her and hold her and honour her and be with her and gratify her every desire within reason and tolerate her little moods and so on and be by her side permanently, as it were, for as long as ye both shall live, amen?"

"I do!" said Alec, in ringing tones.

There was a sigh of satisfaction in the church.

"Because," went on Mary, "it is not easy. Nobody said it was easy because it isn't. It just isn't. Because . . ." His voice died again. He was staring at the coffin once more. "Because it does not last. It is fleeting. It is incredibly fleeting. You have no sooner started it than you realize it is time to finish and you have hardly tasted the intimate joys of married life, the sex-love joys with which we consecrate our bodies to each other, when we . . . er . . . die. I now pronounce you man and wife." The abruptness of this transition seemed to horrify him. "The ring," he murmured to himself. "I forgot the ring."

Bob Betterton took it out of his pocket. "We noticed," he said.

Mary took it from him and reached out for Jennifer Doran's hand. "By the putting on of this ring," he said, jamming it on to her finger, "I thee wed."

"I thee wed!" said Alec.

Mary gave him a puzzled glance, as if the man was trying to

upstage him. "That's what I said," he said. "I thee wed and I thee declare, as I said, man and wife and whom any hath so joined then let no man attempt to put asunder in the sight of Jesus." This line brought him up short again. "Talking of which," he said, "if there is anyone here, and there probably isn't but if there is, if there is anyone who thinks that this man and this woman have an impediment and should not or could not get married then he'd better pipe up now or for ever, you know . . ."

There was profound silence.

"I mean," said Mary, "this is important. If anyone here knows something that we don't then let him come forward. If one of them has a horrible disability that they have not admitted to or is a lunatic of some kind and not responsible for their actions or, as does happen, if one or other or both of them turn out to be married to someone else already then all this is a waste of time and a complete farce and we might as well know now and put an end to it on the spot. Let's face it. Because otherwise this man and this woman are effectively sealed in together like the . . . er . . . poor young girl in that box over there."

The thought of Jacqueline was too much for the vicar. He simply stood there staring at the coffin and, as the silence lengthened, Hatchett stepped out into the aisle.

"Well," he said, "he doesn't love her. Does that count? Is that a just cause or impediment to getting married?" Jennifer Doran's head, still encumbered with her veil, turned, very slowly, in Hatchett's direction. "I mean," said Hatchett, "he quite likes her. He finds her attractive. She has many good qualities. She is kind. She is highly organized. She is not unintelligent." He paused.

Is he going to give her marks out of ten? thought Norma. Does he grade everyone as if they were an examination paper? How would I do, come to that? B?+ for intelligence? A?− in the *poitrine* department?

"Loving someone isn't as simple as catching their eye across the room," continued Hatchett, still in pedagogic mode, "or liking their hair or eyes or smile, although of course all those things are involved in love. But love is horribly simple. And it is about one thing. You know. The way you know when the soul has left the body. So I know. I know with whom Alec Lycett is in love. He is in love with the woman I wish to marry. Norma Lewis."

Although she had not been asked to do so, Jennifer was pushing back her veil. The angle and attitude of her elbow suggested petulance. And when her face emerged, such a little, little face, so charmingly dusted with freckles, it was quivering with anger. "Listen –" she began.

But before she could finish, Alec turned on Hatchett. "What the hell do you think you're playing at?" he said. "Who the hell do you think you are? What right do you have to talk to me like this?" Alec's mother was stony-faced, as always. Alec's father was looking at Hatchett with a kind of horrified pity and fascination.

Something about his expression started Norma asking unspoken questions, once again, about their childhood together, the nature of their friendship and the weird, still mysterious history of Alec's twin.

"I'm your friend, Alec," said Hatchett.

"Once you may have been," said Alec. "Not now."

"Listen," said Hatchett, "when you and I were kids and your father –"

"Will you shut up about my father?" Alec screamed suddenly. "Will you just shut up about all of that?" Now he let go of Jennifer's hand and stepped towards Hatchett.

For a moment Norma thought he was going to hit him but he stopped after only a few paces. His shoulders stooped. He looked beaten. He is beaten, thought Norma, but why?

"Well," Alec said softly, almost to himself, "you know I love her. You know that."

Norma saw his eyes flick over to her.

"Who?" said Jennifer Doran, in the shrill voice that women like her affect when they feel left out of a conversation. "Who do you love?"

Alec looked back at her.

Norma swallowed hard.

"Who?" said Jennifer, her voice rising. "Who do you love?"

He's waiting for me to say something, thought Norma, and he'll wait for ever. Hatchett, she realized, was looking at her as if he, too, expected some declaration. "You look as if you thought that was an unfair question," said Hatchett to Norma.

"You seem to think you know the answer to it," said Norma. "You seem absolutely sure Alec loves me. But it's a matter for him, isn't it?"

There was an animal howl from down near the altar. "What is any of this to do with you?" screeched Jennifer. "This is my wedding, isn't it, not yours? Isn't it supposed to be my day?"

There appeared to be no easy answer to this question. But, as if in response to the profound awkwardness it had generated, Jennifer seemed to notice the coffin for the first time. "What's that doing there?" she squeaked. "That's a coffin. What's it doing there?"

Mary leaned forward. "The coffin," he said, in a low voice, "contains the body of Jacqueline Rissett. I think you may know her." As he said this he did a lot of high-profile eyebrow work in the direction of the congregation, perhaps in an attempt to suggest that there were quite a few other people out there who had known Jacqueline Rissett and perhaps she ought to be given a fair share in these proceedings too.

"I know about Jacqueline Rissett," snorted Jennifer impatiently, "and of course I feel frightfully sorry she's dead, although I think a little more care could have been taken with the timing of the funeral." There were murmurs of assent at this remark. "But I'm not talking about Jacqueline Rissett, I'm talking about me. Because it's my day. I'm the bride, in case you hadn't noticed."

The vicar of St Mary and All Angels, the man who was chiefly responsible for the planning and execution of this disastrous afternoon, tried to regain control of it. "I feel, brethren –" he began.

"And besides," came Jennifer's voice, sounding now ever so slightly proprietorial, "we're married. We're husband and wife in the sight of God." She gave a challenging glance in the direction of the vicar, who looked like a man about to get on the blower to the General Synod to find out whether this was true.

"Actually," said Mary, in a light, tense voice, "I am not absolutely sure that that is the case. I think I got a few things wrong in the service there and I am not sure it actually counts if you get the words wrong." Jennifer's jaw dropped. The vicar, apparently unaware of the impression he was creating, was warming to his theme.

He was a man, thought Norma, who, although he preached the Word of God, was really only interested in the footnotes.

"You see, just because you are on consecrated ground and standing there while some idiot shouts gibberish at you doesn't mean you are actually married because –"

"Shut up!" screeched Jennifer, and then, "Come on, Alec. Stop wandering around like that!"

Alec had, indeed, started to wander up the aisle. The sharpness in her tone brought him up like a dog on a lead. But his eyes, those clear, blue, honest-seeming eyes, were still trying to find Norma's. "You love me, Alec," Jennifer was saying. "That's why you wanted to marry me. That's why you have actually just married me, isn't it?" Alec didn't answer.

"An awful lot of things, Alec," said Hatchett, in the deathly hush of the church, "hang on the answer to that question. Telling the truth is the most important thing there is. You know that, because you never talk about that thing that happened with Lucius –" He stopped himself, as if aware that he had said too much. "Every lie does terrible harm with the passage of time but this . . . this . . . this is the deciding moment of your life, isn't it?"

Alec still didn't answer. He just stood there looking helplessly in Norma's direction. "She hasn't said anything," he said, in a sullen tone.

"No," said Hatchett. And he turned to Norma. "Well?" he said.

"What do you mean 'well'?" said Norma. "Are you asking me to make up my mind? Why is everyone asking me to make up my mind?"

"Alec," said Jennifer sharply, "come here!"

Alec did not move. He looked across at Norma with hang-dog eyes. "A year ago," he said, "I was a different person. I thought I was a terribly simple sort of chap. But it seems I'm a bit more complicated than that." Then he turned to Hatchett. "You think you know me, Dennis," he said, "and you think you know about my family and what went on with them twenty years ago. But you don't. I haven't told you. I haven't told any of you anything, really."

Then he turned, at last, to face Jennifer. "I love you, darling," he said, in tones of quite appalling insincerity. "I love you, and all I want to do is to make you happy. I think you're the most wonderful woman in the world and I'm going to devote myself to you. I'm really glad I found you." Clearly Jennifer thought this was along the right lines. She pushed her veil further back into her hair and shot a vicious glance in Norma's direction. "You see?" she said. Then she put her head to one side, and, with one hand on her hip, addressed her husband. "Go on, Alec!" she said.

Alec, who evidently thought he had said more than enough, went on, "I think you're marvellous," he said. "I think you're . . . radiant. I think you're sweet and kind and clever and funny and . . . er . . . good."

Jennifer nodded implacably. She seemed to think he had not yet finished.

"And . . . decent . . ." went on Alec. This brought a slight furrow to Jennifer's lips. "You are what I want," went on Alec hurriedly, "and I don't want anyone else. I know you'll be true and I will try to be true to you because you're . . ." Jennifer stood very still. She looked at him. "You're incredible. You're amazing. I want you to have my children. And I want to have yours obviously. Let's have three. If you want four, let's have four. If you want fifteen, let's have fifteen, you know? What you want is what I want. If you want anything, I want it, and I am going to go out and get it because I am a pretty determined person and –"

Alec broke off suddenly. He looked across at his father, who had listened to this speech with detached, dispassionate attention, and then Lieutenant Lycett rounded on Hatchett. "And I take a pretty dim view of people who barge into other people's weddings and start throwing their weight about. You don't know me. You've never known me, Hatchett. You don't know about women either. You're still the same grubby little ink-stained boy I took pity on all those years ago. She probably won't even have you, Hatchett, because she's a cold fish like you. And, if you want to know, I never want to see either of you again." He had moved up the aisle as he said this so that he was within a couple of yards of Norma and Hatchett.

Alec Senior's voice, loud, confident, rang out across the crowded church. "I think," said the elder Lycett, "that it is time we brought these ridiculous proceedings to a close and if these young people wish to get married, which I am sure they do, I think they should do it as soon as possible, preferably under the auspices of a vicar who is not a dribbling idiot!"

"I think," said Mary, in soft, fluting tones, "that that is a very good idea. And I am a dribbling idiot. I am. And I wish to apologize for my . . . behaviour here. I wish to apologize to all of you unreservedly and to say how deeply I regret what I have done and I hope you will forgive me as Christians. Let us pray. Let us pray and go! And in the words Our Lord has taught say, Our Father, which art in Heaven, hallowed be thy name, and so on, and Thy Kingdom come on Earth as it is in Heaven. Amen!"

"Amen!" said Hatchett, as the congregation rose *en masse* and headed for the day outside. "A-bloody-men!"

"Why did I do that?" said Hatchett. "What on earth made me do that?"

"I don't know. I suppose he's your friend. You love him, really. He's the person closest to you in all the world."

"Not as of now," said Hatchett, glancing over to where the wedding party were standing disconsolately among the graves in the sunny churchyard. There was a rumour they were to try again in half an hour with another vicar.

Oh, well, thought Norma, an autopsy instead of a funeral, a row instead of a wedding. Perhaps it was all for the best. Hatchett and Lycett, for as long as she had known them, had never made a point of telling each other the truth. Indeed, from what she could see, their friendship, like so many others, depended largely on mutual deceit. In a sense it was a relief that Hatchett had started to say, at last, what he really thought even if he had chosen to share those insights with half the population of Crotchett Green.

He was pacing up and down now, cracking his fingers. He had spoken to the new man from Croydon CID, who was called Rossiter, and a great improvement on Inspector Roach, and Rossiter, after a brief conversation with Mayhew and Mrs Rissett, had driven Mabel and her parents off to the police station. The last glimpse Norma had had of her pupil was a white face looking back from the car. Mabel stared at the mourners and the guests as if they were messy gatecrashers to some social occasion at which she was in charge of catering and entertainment.

Wedding and funeral were still mixed like paint in water. Rachel was talking earnestly to Mrs Rissett. Over in the Lycett camp, Jennifer Doran was crying on the shoulder of Eleanor Furze the gym mistress. She had, in the course of the last half hour, cried on the shoulders of Sandra Beale the Latin mistress, Merridew Fleece the English mistress and Paula Looms the Teacher Who Refused to Retire. From time to time she shot spiteful glances in Norma's direction.

Norma didn't care. If the stupid girl thought that marriage was the end, not the beginning, of a love affair, she was going to have a pretty miserable life, with or without a German invasion, which seemed to be yet another planned feature of life in Croydon, these days. Life was minute to minute, wasn't it? And never more so than now.

For what seemed like hours the big bombers had gone overhead, on their way to London for what Hatchett termed "the biggest daylight raid of the season". Since his announcement that he was about to depart on some kind of war work that was so secret he couldn't even tell her what it was (was it, Norma wondered, something to do with Otto Frisch?), he had become extraordinarily knowledgeable about almost every aspect of the conduct of the conflict.

She looked up at the sky, anxious, if she could help it, not to talk too much about Alec or Jennifer. "What's going to happen?" she said. "Will those planes destroy everything?"

"It's his last throw," said Hatchett, who did not need to refer to Hitler by name. "If he can't make this work then he won't invade. The weather is turning. We have the Channel and he will not invade if he cannot secure victory in the air."

"And will he get it?" said Norma.

"It depends on how our boys have done today," said Hatchett. "Boys like Lucius. Whatever he may or may not have done in the past, I feel so bad about –"

"You were only children," said Norma. "You didn't really know."

"Oh," said Hatchett, "but really-knowing is all that counts with me. Always the teacher, me!"

Norma looked across at Alec. He was talking to Bob Betterton and from time to time, when he thought they wouldn't notice, looking across at the two of them. Norma couldn't work out what he was feeling, he looked both angry and confused, but for one weird moment she thought he might almost be grateful for what Hatchett had said so publicly in the church. He looked at Bob

Betterton, shrugged, and then laughed. Norma hoped he hadn't decided to take Hatchett's advice. In some ways Alec and Jennifer Doran were ideally suited.

To her horror, Alec had broken away from Betterton and was coming over towards them. It was only when he got closer to them that she realized she had misread his mood entirely. Lieutenant Alec Lycett was very, very angry indeed. "What the hell did you think you were playing at back there?" he said.

"Telling the truth," said Hatchett.

"Oh, for God's sake," said Alec, "just because you were hanging around Norma while I was away fighting for my country, and you hoped that she might –"

"Please, Alec," said Hatchett. "Please don't do this."

"Do what?" said Alec. "Tell you the truth the way you are always so keen to tell me? You have, Hatchett! You have spent the whole of this year trying to undermine me with her while I had the guts to join up and go to war for the things I believe in!"

"That simply isn't true, Alec," said Hatchett quietly. "That simply isn't true. Please don't say it. The three of us are far too important to each other for that."

For the first time, Alec looked at Norma. His face was distorted with bitterness. "There is no 'three of us', Hatchett. There never was. And now there are two couples. You and Miss Prism here and me and Jennifer. And I don't imagine either of us is going to be asking the other round for Sunday lunch. You think you know me, Hatchett, but you don't. You never really knew me. You never really knew what went on between me and Lucius."

"Lucius was –" began Hatchett, but Alec shouted over him.

"I loved Lucius," he said, "of course I did. And you came between us. You used your clever talk and your little-boy-lost act the way you used them with Norma. You worked your way into my family, Hatchett, exactly the way you worked yourself in between me and my fiancée!" He was stabbing at Hatchett, now, with his forefinger.

Oh, no, thought Norma, he hates that!

"We were kind to you because we felt sorry for you and in return you stir things up. Why are you doing this to me?"

Hatchett was shaking. He put his hand on his friend's arm and said, "My dear man," he said, "my dear, dear man –"

"Don't you 'dear man' me!" spat Alec. "You are not my dear man!"

Bob Betterton and Jennifer were watching this row with interest. Betterton, like most of the rugby crowd, loathed Hatchett. "You carry on like my brother but you're not," Alec continued. "My brother died fighting for his country, which is more than you ever will do. You're not my brother, Hatchett!" A troubled look came over his face. He lifted his head and, for the first time since the row had started, seemed full of doubt and self-hatred. "Although I suppose, come to think of it, you may be," he said. "I suppose I can tell you now Lucius is dead. Not that we look very alike, do we? Half-brothers, though, is conceivable. Poor Lucius. It wasn't some tramp he killed in the woods behind Albion House. It was your precious father. The Reverend Lustful Hatchett."

Hatchett had gone white. Norma went towards him.

Alec rounded on her. "Lend him your support, Norma old thing, won't you?" he continued. "We kept it from you, Hatchett, and the only reason I am telling you now is because Lucius is dead. Your horrible crazy father was doing it with my mother. But I don't think I can be any son of his because at least I am a decent physical specimen unlike . . ." He was so angry he could hardly speak.

He can't mean this, thought Norma, this isn't him.

And then – but this is him. He does mean it.

"Unlike you! He'd been doing it in the woods with my mother, and my poor sap of a father found them and he knocked Hatchett Senior around and then burst into tears. Lucius and I were hiding in the woods where we used to hide all those years ago and we saw the whole thing. My father knocked him unconscious and off he staggers blubbing like a great baby. But it was Lucius who went to the shed and got the petrol and poured it all over him and set light to him. God, how he screamed, Hatchett! What a noise he made!"

Oh, my God, thought Norma, the body's still there! At the back of the house! Hatchett was swaying like a drunk man. She held on to him, hard.

"Oh, I begged him to stop and called Daddy, but it was too late by then, he was burning, Hatchett, all his clothes were alight, he was burning and screaming and screaming, and we tried to put the fire out but we couldn't. I didn't know what was happening until it was too late but, oh, Jesus, a part of me understood why Lucius had done it, if you want to know. That was why Lucius was sent away. He was even proud of it. He was quite capable of telling someone we had dug a grave and buried your precious father out there in the woods. Yes, that was why he was sent away and I was taught he was a wicked, wicked boy, but I tell you now, Hatchett, I'm proud of him for what he did to your fucking father!"

Alec stood there, his arms swinging loosely at his sides. His eyes were those of an untrustworthy dog. There was spittle at the side of his mouth.

"Now, why don't you bugger off, Hatchett, because I never, never, never want to see you or her ever again. There's nothing you can do about it because whatever you say I shall deny it, and if you want to go sniffing round you can and I don't give a damn. It's our little secret, isn't it? Just between the two of us." Here he looked at Norma. "Sorry. Three of us. There were three of us once upon a time, that's quite right, and we can keep this between us as a memory of all that time we bloody wasted together, can't we?"

Although they had not heard a word of this, Betterton and Jennifer Doran were still watching from a distance. They were smirking at each other as Alec strode back to them in his brilliant blue dress uniform, very much the officer and the gentleman who has just given an oik a dressing-down.

Norma wondered, idly, where they were sending him. Somewhere dangerous, perhaps. Somewhere very, very dangerous. "Are you all right, Hatchett?" she said.

"Stop calling me Hatchett, for God's sake, can't you?" said Hatchett.

"I can't," said Norma. "I have tried but I can't. I've been doing it for too long to stop now. Anyway I prefer Hatchett to Dennis. Dennis is a completely stupid name." This was better. She had made him smile at least. He had stopped shaking. "Is this just some stupid fantasy of his?" she said, eventually.

"I don't think so," said Hatchett. "I found a handkerchief, you see. Oh, all this is years ago and I couldn't think why they . . . My father always had his initials on his handkerchiefs. If I had seen the initials, you see, I would have known. That was why they took it off me, you see. I didn't understand. I didn't know. I had no idea."

None of this made any sense to Norma. He was talking, too, like a crazy man, someone in delirium, more to himself than to anyone else. What, in God's name, do we do now? thought Norma. What, in God's name, do you do with information like that? Try to forget it probably. But you wouldn't be able to forget it. Not ever. Alec had hugged it to himself for all these years and it had poisoned him. He had spoken as if the words were a physical release. And he had left them with the ugliness and the horror of it.

Lucius had made amends in his own way, thought Norma, thinking about him again. In a way his unregenerate honesty was more bearable than the hypocrisy that had bound Alec Junior and Alec Senior so tightly for all these years. She looked across at the wedding party. She had no desire to stay here any longer. Rachel seemed to have finished her talk with Mrs Rissett. Damn these Lycetts! Damn them and their stupid Albion House! Rachel was coming over to them.

"Shall we go?" Norma said to Hatchett when Rachel joined them. He still looked badly shaken. "I must get home to Loose-bottom," she said, because she knew he was amused by stupid things like that.

Hatchett twitched. "I don't know why we called him that," he said feebly.

"I am going to call him that. To his face," said Norma. "And my ghastly stepmother will be Mrs Loosebottom!" Hatchett managed another smile. "Are you all right?" she said to him, as they moved away.

"I don't know," said Hatchett. "I haven't really taken it in. I just don't . . . I mean, I never really knew him, you see. But I want to find out everything now. I want to know. I am determined to know. He can't just tell me that and expect me to . . . I mean, he doesn't know what he's started, Norma. He has no idea what he has started."

"He's jealous of you," said Norma, as he took her arm.

"Why should he be jealous of me?" said Hatchett.

"Because of what I feel about you, I suppose," said Norma.

"Oh," said Hatchett slowly. "Oh! I see!"

The three of them made their way out of the churchyard and on to the lane that led towards the village and, below it, Albion House. She didn't feel like going in that direction, she realized, and so, at the Green, she turned left towards the Downs. Hatchett, who seemed to have no idea of where he was or where they were headed, walked with her, muttering still, more to himself than to her.

"I never knew him, you see," he was saying, "I never really knew my father. Not really. I suppose he went against everything he believed in if he did . . . but that isn't the point, is it? That isn't what you take from your parents. I do remember things he said. I do remember him being very strong and very clear. I do remember him saying that you had to tell the truth and fight for the truth and never cheat or betray those close to you. And even if he said that so often because he was ashamed of what he was, that is still the lesson I learned from him. And, Jesus, Mary and Joseph, he was a hell of a preacher. You saw the fires of hell when he talked."

They were out of the village now. The only sound was the wind in the trees. Somewhere over to their left came the panicked whirring of a woodpecker's wings as it started up from the ground. The sun was lower in the sky, and the clouds over to the west, drifting into the horizon, were as vivid as a Viking funeral. Rachel walked a little apart from them, but it was a companionable group, among the early-evening fields.

"Whatever happens, we have to try to be good, Norma," Hatchett was saying, "and if children do wicked things it isn't something we can condemn as easily as we condemn those who have the knowledge and experience to know better. However, I feel now I have to think that one day Alec and I could . . . could . . ."

"Do you believe him?" she said, as they strolled on. "I am still not sure I do entirely. I certainly don't think you are any kind of brothers. Wouldn't you look more alike?"

Hatchett paused. "Anything is possible," he said. "It would

explain some things about us, I suppose. Lycett's mother never had other children, did she? And as for looking alike . . ."

"It's what Alec chooses to believe, for some reason," said Norma slowly. "However improbable. I suppose that's the most important thing about it. Poor Lucius!"

"The man who murdered my father is dead. Died defending you and me, as Alec said," said Hatchett. "That seems to be certainly true. And whether Alec is or is not my brother isn't really relevant. He has always felt like my brother. I know that when he has stopped being angry with me for telling the truth – which is all I was doing – he will come back and we will talk about it and we will find out exactly what happened."

Norma did not like to say so but she was not at all sure that Alec would ever stop being angry with Hatchett. She liked him the less for it but she was almost sure it was the case. And she liked Hatchett the more for this touch of naïveté about him – this almost childlike concern for the truth or the idea that the whole truth about people could ever be told. She decided to change the subject. "And you're going away. What will you do at wherever it is you're going?"

"Crosswords," said Hatchett.

She snorted irritably. "You don't tell me anything, do you?" she said.

There was a silence. "I tell you what I feel," said Hatchett. "I tell you how much I love you. I have never tired of doing that. However much you are not supposed to do things like that. However much you are supposed to be cool and mysterious and distant to arouse a woman's interest. I have never done that. I say exactly what I feel when I feel it."

With a start Norma realized that that was probably true. And at the same time she saw clearly that, over the last year, she had looked forward to the moments when he let her know that he still cared for her. That his love for her was, unlike so many other things in the world, constant. That when he came round the door of the staffroom or waylaid her in the quad or chaffed her in the street in that gruff, quizzical voice of his, her heart fluttered quite as surely as it did when she saw Alec Lycett stride into vision looking so

409

clear and frank and handsome. She hadn't really done any of the things with Hatchett that you were supposed to do with men. She hadn't been dancing à *deux* or visited his house or shared any kind of a meal with him, apart from school dinners. Why then, with a feeling of breathless excitement, did she hear herself say, "You do! I think that's one of the things I love about you! Your feelings are so clumsy and public!"

Hatchett didn't seem to mind this. "Would you come back to the house?" he said. "Since Mother died it's . . ."

Norma put her hand on his arm. "Lonely?"

"A bit," he said, quite without self-pity.

"I'm sorry I never really knew her," said Norma.

"It seems as if I didn't!" said Hatchett. "How much did the poor old thing know about what was going on? I can't imagine. I feel a terrible sense of guilt about her. We think we understand our parents' lives, Norma, but we do not. Maybe you don't really understand what made your father . . . why your father . . . You know, what I mean."

"Mrs Loosebottom, you mean?" said Norma. This set them both laughing. Norma looked back at Rachel. "We're going to Mr Hatchett's," she said.

Rachel's face lit up. "Goody!" she said.

I couldn't love anyone whom Rachel didn't love, Norma thought, and I couldn't love anyone who didn't love Rachel. Awoken from whatever reverie had detained her, the girl ran towards them along the tree-lined lane.

"Rachel's been there a couple of times after school," said Hatchett. "Mr Groenig gives her lessons there sometimes. Or she gives him lessons, I should say."

"You've been playing with my niece without my permission," said Norma.

"She's my niece as well," said Hatchett.

"I found her first," said Norma.

"I found you, Auntie," said Rachel. "And then I found Mr Hatchett. And now I have papers!" She looked, for a moment, very serious. "I will do important work in physics," she said. "I know I will. And I know that when the war is over I will go home and I will see my father. I know I will. I am sure of this now. I think about him every night before I go to sleep."

"I am sure you will," said Norma.

Rachel looked between the two of them and smiled. She did not often smile but when she did you wanted it to stay on her face for longer than seemed possible. Which, indeed, at the moment, was what the smile seemed to be doing. "I will run along to Mr Hatchett's house," she said. "You two must walk along more slowly." Her eyes sparkled and her smile became roguish. "It is very romantic!" she said.

"Really, Rachel!" said Norma.

"It is," said Hatchett, taking her arm. She clucked slightly to herself as he did this, but she did not resist. Rachel ran on ahead down the lane and the two of them watched her until she rounded the corner at the bottom of the hill. Before she passed out of sight she turned again and smiled and waved, and Norma waved back, the way she had waved to her mother as the car took her away to hospital for the last time.

Then she was alone with Hatchett.

There was a tension between them that she had noticed before. It had been there that day she found the note supposedly written by Miss Green, when she had felt Hatchett's eyes boring into her back. It had been there on the day when they went to Poundsea, when poor Peckerley was killed; she remembered now how when she had finally managed to cry it was Hatchett's arms who had held her. It had been there on the day the bombs fell, although she hadn't really seen it at the time. Well, all of this time, she had been too busy to see what was immediately in front of her.

As they walked on down the road, they seemed to be brushing against each other. Although there was no shortage of room they seemed to be competing, time after time, for the same patch of Tarmac. They came to the bottom of the lane, rounded the corner and, ahead of them, saw Rachel disappearing into the distance. The pressure to resolve the clumsy series of collisions on which they now seemed to be engaged was intense. Norma was wearing a rather formal black skirt and yet, as they walked on, she was aware of, almost embarrassed by, the way it fenced in her legs at each stride. She felt, suddenly, as if she was going to fall. If only he would put his hand on her arm to balance her! Why did he never seem to read the signs she must be clearly displaying?

She heard the aeroplane before he did.

You could hear straight away that there was something wrong with the engines. She had heard enough aircraft now to know. And she knew enough, too, to look for the black cross on the underside of the wing although, even before she looked up, she had registered that it was a Dornier. It had been hit somewhere. There was smoke coming out of the tail on the far side, as it veered drunkenly south, trying and failing to regain height.

There were people in the road. A man in an open-necked shirt and trousers that seemed to be tied up with string was running out of a neighbouring field. He was carrying a pitchfork, which he waved defiantly at the retreating aircraft. "Just you wait!" he yelled. Then he turned to Hatchett. "They lost two hundred!" he said, in authoritative tones. "We only lost fifty!" With which statistics (where had he got them? thought Norma) he set off in pursuit of the tons of metal. He did not seem to be daunted by the fact that they were heading away from him at hundreds of miles an hour and at a height of a few thousand feet. "You swine!" he yelled, shaking his pitchfork as he ran. "Just you wait! You swine!"

Hatchett and Norma watched as the aircraft passed over the top of Crazyman Hill. It wasn't until long after the man had disappeared that they heard the crash. It was a long way away but so surprising and vivid was the noise in the peaceful afternoon that Norma was sure, when she turned to look at Hatchett, that she saw an impossible thing – the flames consuming the enemy craft reflected in his glasses, fire in his eyes as, at last, he reached for her hand.

"My dear," he began, in his most pompous way.

"Oh, don't call me 'my dear' like that!" said Norma. "You make me feel as if I was at a parents' evening."

"You are," said Hatchett. "What are we going to call them? Mary, Anne, Margaret, Susan, John, Hugh, Martin?"

"What are you talking about?" she said.

"Our children, of course," said Hatchett.

"Are we going to have children?" said Norma.

"Oh, yes, we are!" said Hatchett, and with these words he seized her by the waist and began to carry her, kicking and giggling helplessly on down the road.

"Put me down, Mr Hatchett!" she said. "Put me down at once!"

"Not until you call me Dennis!" said Hatchett.

"All right, then, Dennis! Dennis, Dennis, Dennis! Whoever you are, put me down at once!" She was laughing, though, and she was still laughing when he deposited her on the ground.

"Now," he said, "give us a kiss!"

"Don't be so stupid, Mr Hatchett!" said Norma. "I couldn't possibly."

"Oh, no?" said Hatchett.

"No," said Norma. "You kiss at . . . parties . . . or dances . . . or . . . late at night . . . or . . ."

"You," said Hatchett, "are the kind of girl who is in bed by nine. And you don't go to parties. Which is why I love you."

Norma did not like to admit that this was true (although it was) even to herself. And so she said, "I go to lots of parties!"

Hatchett snorted.

They walked on, amicably and calmly now, the physical tension between them somehow resolved for the moment. After a while Hatchett said, in reasonable, conversational tones, "Why won't you give me a kiss?" He hunched his shoulders suddenly, scuttled in front of her like a crab and blocked her path. "Is it that I am only the half-brother of the handsome Lycett?" he said, in a voice that reminded her of Charles Laughton in the film of *The Hunchback of Notre Dame*. "Or is it that you think I look like a frog? I might turn into a prince? Or is that what you're frightened of? Would you rather I looked like a frog? I don't think so. I think you are frightened I won't turn into a prince. That after kissing you I will simply be . . ." here he pursed his lips and thrust them out in front of him ". . . an excited frog."

She was laughing again. "I don't know," she said, "I really

413

don't know." The two of them stopped, as if according to some prearranged signal. "It's funny," said Norma, "I keep thinking about Lucius. I mean, I forget – the way I forget about Peckerley and all of the others and everything that's happened. And then suddenly it comes back to me."

Hatchett nodded. "There will be a lot more things like that," he said, looking up at the sky. "It's not over yet. It really isn't over yet. I don't know who I am exactly or what any of us is. But at least I feel I have started to find out."

Feeling he was about to give one of his schoolmasterly speeches, Norma walked on briskly.

"So," said Hatchett, hunching up his shoulders again and scampering along beside her, swinging his arms loosely, "when do I get a kiss?"

"I don't know," said Norma. "When I feel like it, I suppose." The silence was less amicable than before but still not unfriendly. It was as if, she thought, they had discussed and agreed upon something terribly important, even if neither of them quite knew what it was.

After the lane turned it rose steeply up towards a small horizon dotted with oak trees. There was no sign of Rachel. She must be well on her way to Hatchett's house, one of the small row of cottages on the other side of the skyline. "I would grow on you," said Hatchett suddenly.

"I'm sorry?" said Norma, who had been thinking about Rachel.

"You may not think you love me now," said Hatchett, "but in time you will be unable to do without me. I am an addictive presence."

"Are you?" said Norma, stiffly.

"I am," said Hatchett. Then he said, "About a year ago, I asked you a question. I asked you to marry me."

"I remember," said Norma.

"I'm asking you again," said Hatchett.

"Oh," said Norma. "You're asking a lot this afternoon, aren't you?"

"I know," said Hatchett.

"First it's a kiss," said Norma. "Now you want to marry me. What will it be next?"

There was a long silence. "So," said Hatchett, "will you marry me?" There was an even longer silence.

Norma shrugged. "I suppose I might as well," she said.

"Good," said Hatchett. Neither of them could think what to say after this. Then Hatchett said, "Can I have a kiss?"

Norma looked at him. "At some point you can," she said, "but not now."

Hatchett nodded slowly. "When you say 'at some point'," he said, "do you mean minutes, hours, weeks, years?"

"I don't know," said Norma. "I really can't tell you that. But not now anyway."

"Fair enough," said Hatchett.

Their walk had ground to a halt again. This time it was Hatchett who started to move first. "So . . . when . . ." he said.

"When what?"

"When are we going to get married?"

Norma shrugged. "As soon as possible, I suppose," she said. "We might all be dead by the end of next week. Or in a German prison camp or something."

"That," said Hatchett thoughtfully, "is true. As soon as possible, then."

"Yes," said Norma, "we might as well get it over with."

Hatchett looked at her. "I love you, you know that," he said.

"Yes," said Norma, "I know that." Then she leaned over and, taking him by surprise, she kissed him, warmly, on the cheek. It felt rough but curiously reassuring.

"That's my kiss, then," he said.

"Yes," she said.

She reflected, afterwards, that he had never asked her whether she loved him – which was a relief really because she was so perverse that she might have been unable to say that she did. But the question of whether she did or she didn't didn't seem, for the moment, to arise, because when he had taken her arm, Rachel came running back down the lane, her smile bright and her eyes alive with happiness. It was pretty clear that Hatchett had been about to try to embrace her but immediately the girl appeared there was no need for any of that. The two of them stood watching her as she ran towards them in the English afternoon, her hair streaming behind her, her face like that of one who has never known any troubles and never will.

"I have just asked Miss Lewis to marry me," said Hatchett gravely.

Rachel, too, looked solemn. "What did she say?" she said.

"She said she might as well," said Hatchett.

"Did I say that?" said Norma.

"That," said Hatchett, "is what you said."

"I cannot believe I said that. I did not say that," said Norma, appalled by her own behaviour.

"What did you say, then?" said Hatchett.

"I said, 'Yes'," said Norma, in slightly irritable tones. "I said 'Yes! Yes! Yes! Yes!'"

Rachel continued to look solemn. Then she took Hatchett's right hand and Norma's left and folded them into each other. "I think," she said, "you must kiss each other now."

"We will," said Norma, "but not just yet." She wasn't, she realized, particularly interested in being kissed. His enthusiasm for the activity would probably be enough for both of them. Perhaps when they were married she would be able to discover that side of life. For the moment, she reflected, it was enough that she was able to talk to him. They walked on for a little while, but when Rachel had run on ahead again she found she was more receptive to the idea of his kissing her. So when he took her in his arms and held her very carefully, as if she was breakable, she gave herself up to him and let his lips meet hers. There was a sweetness about this kiss that surprised her. It brought back memories of the only other man who had ever tried to do it. Years ago, she remembered, at some dance at the university. She couldn't even remember the man's name or face. It brought back memories, too, of other dances, when she was an awkward teenager, looking in at couples necking on the edge of the dance-floor and wishing she could be wrapped up in another the way they seemed to be. There was an enormous comfort in it, she thought, as Hatchett's arms dropped and his strong hands gripped her waist. The entirely illogical thought occurred to her that, as long as she was in this position, nothing bad would ever happen.

Harris, that was the man's name. Harris.

The kiss seemed to be over. It had lasted an enormously long time. Where was Rachel? It was only when she had looked off down the lane and seen the girl running ahead of them, absorbed in the beauties of the day, that she said, in quiet, conversational tones, "I love you, I think."

To which Hatchett replied, "I know you do. I've always known that. It was obvious."

Epilogue

20 August 1921

"They're here!"

That was Mummy. In fact, Alec had heard the car draw up about ten minutes ago. Lucius hadn't spoken. He just lay on the bed with his face to the wall. Hatchett was in the corner, playing chess with himself. He was good at doing things by himself. He had already played patience, written a story and drawn a funny picture of him and Alec playing football. He had drawn himself as very small and Alec as a giant, with huge muscles. Alec thought it was a good picture.

"Come on, Lucius! Uncle John's here!"

Uncle John wasn't really an uncle, although he was some sort of relative. He was, thought Alec, quite kind. It wouldn't be so bad for Lucius. He was looking like a cry-baby now.

"Don't care!"

"You have to care, I'm afraid," said Alec. "Daddy says you've got to go and so you've got to go!" It was going to be so good when Lucius was gone. He was like some extra leg that you had to drag round. And because he was always naughty, people noticed him. When he was gone they would start to notice Alec.

Hatchett finished playing with the chess set and stood up, wiping his knees. He was wearing, as usual, ridiculous baggy shorts that ballooned out all round him. They were his only pair. When he came to stay, thought Alec, he would lend him some of his clothes. He would be grateful for that.

"Lucius, they are here!"

Lucius hadn't said any more. Looking at Hatchett, Alec tried to remember once more that it was his daddy who had been burned alive in the woods. It still didn't make sense. Mostly Alec didn't

418

think about it. When you didn't think about it, it was as if it had never happened. It was only since that business with the handkerchief that the image of Hatchett's daddy had come back to him and, as always, once it was before your eyes it would not go away however hard you tried. It was the smell that was so horrible. First the clothes, then the singeing smell of the hair and then that roasting aroma as if it was pork for lunch or something. But it wasn't pork. It was a man and he screamed and he screamed and he screamed.

"I'm coming," called Lucius, in answer to his mummy. "No need to get so ratty!" He went to the window and looked down to where Daddy was talking to Uncle John. "I hate Daddy," said Lucius. "I hate him! I hate him! I hate him! You'll hate him one day! You like him now because he is all nice to you but one day you will hate him like I hate him!"

Hatchett was watching this, in silence, from the other end of the room.

The handkerchief had had his father's initials on it as well as the blood. AffH. Arthur ffrangcon Hatchett. He was Welsh or something. Alec remembered him speaking in a funny sing-song way when he came to Sunday lunch, oh, ages ago. He must have been sweet on Mummy even then. Alec did not want to think about that or any of the things he had heard Daddy and Hatchett's daddy say to each other in the woods when he and Lucius had watched from their hiding-place deep in the bramble bush.

Down below Alec's daddy and Uncle John turned to look up at them and waved. Alec waved back. Lucius just stared. Alec hoped he wasn't going to scream when he got into the car. He did scream sometimes when he didn't get his own way. He screamed on and on and on, and they had to slap him round the face. There was something wrong with him, which was partly why he was going away. He had screamed when they first had to admit to their daddy about Hatchett's daddy. It was better he was going away, Daddy said, because he would make up stories and tell lies and it wasn't safe. When he was gone Hatchett would stay in Lucius's bed and they would talk and Alec wouldn't have nightmares any more.

It was hard not to smile at this thought but Alec made it look as if the smile was for the benefit of Uncle John, as he waved and waved and Lucius stared and stared.

"We'd better go, I suppose," said Hatchett.

"Since when do you tell me what to do?" said Lucius. Hatchett looked a bit scared at this. Lucius could bash him and quite often did. Hatchett's mummy came out to the front of the house and stood in the drive by Uncle John's car. Alec hoped she would go away because, when you saw her, it was hard not to think about what had happened to Hatchett's daddy. His parents just lied and she believed them. People did believe lies.

Hatchett walked ahead of them down the stairs.

It was true, really, thought Alec, that the woods behind Albion House were haunted. The ghost of Hatchett's daddy would walk there because he had been murdered – that was what it was, murder – and he would haunt the woods and the house until someone found out, or he and Lucius told because they just couldn't keep it a secret any more. That was why Lucius had to go away and they had to move because, just as Daddy said, the house had a curse on it.

It was funny. Because of what he had heard and seen and done in the woods, Alec wanted Hatchett even more as his friend. It was a way, of course, of keeping the secret. As the three of them went out into the August half-light, he thought of something his daddy had said: "Keep your friends close but your enemies closer." Hatchett wasn't his enemy, of course, but if he knew, he would be. He must never, ever know. He shouldn't have said that stupid stuff about the tramp.

Although it was probably a good idea to tell a bit of the truth. The best lies had a bit of truth in them. You had to do that sometimes. If you were late for school it was a good idea to tell a story that had actually happened. Once, Alec had seen a man knocked off his bicycle and in one of his stories he pretended it was him. When he took money from Mummy's secret box he was always very, very careful to put it back just as he found it. So if it ever did come out he would be all right because he was a better liar than Lucius. When he had –

"Well done!"

Bella the maid had lugged Lucius's trunk downstairs and Uncle John and Daddy were loading it into Uncle John's car.

"Well, young Lucius! The time hath come!" said Alec's daddy, talking, as usual, to Alec's twin as if he had just met him. Daddy had always hated Lucius. That was why he hadn't believed him about what had happened in the woods. He had hated him from the moment he was born. It was impossible to know why. He just did. Maybe, thought Alec, it was all to do with what he had done in a previous life. He believed we had previous lives and that we were punished for what we had done in them.

It was funny. Now it was almost as if Lucius believed it had happened the way Alec told it. He didn't have any choice, really, did he?

"Into the car we go!"

Alec could tell that his mummy was going to cry. And that probably Hatchett's mummy would cry as well because she always joined in everything Alec's mummy did, although she did not do it so well. But Lucius, who had looked such a cry-baby earlier, was stiff-faced. He wasn't going to let Daddy see. He wasn't going to let him see he had hurt him.

Daddy was actually holding out his hand to shake. This, thought Alec, was about the most stupid thing he had seen him do all day. What on earth was the point of that? Lucius, who was looking at his father's hand in a puzzled sort of way, seemed to feel the same.

"Give me your hand, old chap," said Alec's daddy.

Very, very slowly Lucius looked down at his hand as if it did not really belong to him. Still looking at it, but without offering it to his father, he said, "Well, here it is. Lucius's hand!" And then, very slowly, he lowered it to his side. He turned to Uncle John. "I might as well get into the car now. I don't want to stay with him anyway. I hate him. I hate him. I hate all of them. They're all against me. Nothing I say makes any difference. So I say nothing."

"You see?" said Alec's daddy, in a funny voice to Uncle John. "You see what we're up against?"

"Come on, then!" said Uncle John, in what was really quite a jolly voice. "Come on, Lucius!"

Alec had heard in history about the tumbrils that they used in the French Revolution to carry off the aristocrats before they cut their heads off. The aristocrats, with their hands tied behind their backs and their smart, rather girlish white shirts but with hairy chests, usually climbed up into them in a special sort of way. That was how Lucius got into the car. He did not look back once. He sat next to Uncle John, and though Uncle John and Mummy and Daddy and Alec and Hatchett all waved like crazy, Lucius did not wave once. He just stared straight ahead of him as they drove away, as if none of them had ever existed, as if the last eight years had never happened.

Mummy started crying when the car was out of sight. Lucius was her favourite, of course. She was being punished by him being sent away. Punished for being sweet on Hatchett's daddy. Alec's daddy put his arm round her but she did not stop crying. But Alec, though he looked all serious, was glad. Now Lucius had gone away he would be a good boy and they would all be happy and they would never need to see Lucius again, with his tempers and his cleverness and the things he knew and might tell if they were not careful and all pulling together like a team.

That seemed to be what Alec's daddy was saying as they all went back into the house. And so it was that Hatchett and Lycett, famous for being best friends, went up the stairs together to bed. And washed their faces and cleaned their teeth and said their prayers to God as they always did.

It was not until Hatchett was actually tucked up in Lucius's bed and Mummy had kissed them goodnight that Hatchett started his story. He told different stories but they were the same story, really, and Hatchett and Lycett were always in it. They were often in danger but always rescued, although as soon as they had been rescued they were off again to another remote corner of the globe where they were shot at, ambushed by tribesmen and, finally, rewarded with money and beautiful clothes. As Hatchett started his story, in the dark, Alec closed his eyes tightly.

Hatchett was really Alec's brother. He had heard Hatchett's

daddy say that to Alec's daddy in the woods. Alec thought that was probably true because of the way he said it but, then again, it might just be another story. Everything was a story, really. It was all a matter of which story you decided to tell. You told it and then it was the truth. Hatchett would never know, of course, the truth of who had found the pe ol and poured it on his daddy while he lay on the ground. Lucius was good at lots of things, thought Alec, but he wasn't good at lying. And Alec was. Alec told the story his daddy wanted to hear.

Even so, even now, lying safe under the clean sheets, there were moments when he was sure the lie would surface, like Hatchett's daddy's ghost. It was Hatchett's daddy who had said, in church, that if you told a lie or did a bad deed it might be hidden for years and years but in the end it would come to the surface. And in the meanwhile, while you tried to keep it away from notice, it would make you do even worse things because it was a lie and it would infect you and make you burn in the flames of hell, as Hatchett's daddy had done in the wood behind the house when he had blackened in the fire and screamed and screamed and screamed.

Alec thought about that as Hatchett's voice whispered on in the dark, and, as always at such moments, he was frightened about what he might become and what the future would hold for him.

Note

Otto Frisch and Rudolph Peierls were, of course, real people and the story of their discovery that the building of the atom bomb was a possibility was indeed made in the University of Birmingham Physics Department in the winter of 1939 and the spring of 1940. I have telescoped events for dramatic purposes but the moment of discovery in the novel is very much as described in Richard Rhodes's superb *The Making of the Atomic Bomb* (Penguin, 1988) and Frisch's enchanting autobiography *What Little I Remember* (Cambridge University Press, 1979). Although there was, of course, no one present when they made their extraordinary discovery, Frisch records that he "playfully" plugged Peierls's formula into the figures for the cross-section of U235. Which I thought entitled me to have a fictional character suggest it. Also useful on the background of the German Atomic Fission programme – and the appalling dilemma faced by someone like Rachel's father – was Thomas Powers's *Heisenberg's War* (Penguin, 1994). The description of the bombing of Croydon Aerodrome – the first daylight attack of its kind on the British mainland – is taken from contemporary accounts from the local studies department of Croydon Public Library, to whom my thanks.

I would like to thank my agent Gillon Aitken for his help and support, my editor Tony Lacey for his patience and useful comments over four drafts, and finally my wife, Suzan Harrison, a busy lady, whose work on this book went well beyond the call of duty.

Nigel Williams